Ace Books by Sarah Monette

MÉLUSINE

THE VIRTU

The Vir

The Virtu

Sarah Monette

ACE BOOKS, NEW YORK

THE BERKLEY PUBLISHING GROUP
Published by the Penguin Group
Penguin Group (USA) Inc.
375 Hudson Street, New York, New York 10014, USA
Penguin Group (Canada), 90 Eglinton Avenue East, Suite 700, Toronto, Ontario M4P 2Y3, Canada
(a division of Pearson Penguin Canada Inc.)
Penguin Books Ltd., 80 Strand, London WC2R 0RL, England
Penguin Group Ireland, 25 St. Stephen's Green, Dublin 2, Ireland (a division of Penguin Books Ltd.)
Penguin Group (Australia), 250 Camberwell Road, Camberwell, Victoria 3124, Australia
(a division of Pearson Australia Group Pty. Ltd.)
Penguin Books India Pvt. Ltd., 11 Community Centre, Panchsheel Park, New Delhi—110 017, India
Penguin Group (NZ), Cnr. Airborne and Rosedale Roads, Albany, Auckland 1310, New Zealand
(a division of Pearson New Zealand Ltd.)
Penguin Books (South Africa) (Pty.) Ltd., 24 Sturdee Avenue, Rosebank, Johannesburg 2196,
South Africa

Penguin Books Ltd., Registered Offices: 80 Strand, London WC2R 0RL, England

This book is an original publication of The Berkley Publishing Group.

First edition: July 2006

Library of Congress Cataloging-in-Publication Data

Monette, Sarah.
    The Virtu / Sarah Monette.— 1st ed.
       p. cm.
    ISBN 0-441-01404-6
    1. Wizards—Fiction. I. Title.

    PS3613.O5246V57 2006
    813'.6—dc22
                                        2006001714

PRINTED IN THE UNITED STATES OF AMERICA

10 9 8 7 6 5 4 3 2 1

For A.L.M.

Part One

Chapter 1

Mildmay

When I opened the door, I could tell that Thamuris was dosed to the gills on laudanum.

"You sure about this?" I said.

Thamuris came drifting into the room like a ghost. His feet were bare, and his hair was down, and he was wearing something that looked basically like a bedsheet. I hoped like fuck nobody'd noticed him on his way here. "I have to," he said, and there was something about the way he said it—I can't explain it, but I knew there wasn't a thing in the world I could say that would mean anything to him. He was past the point where anybody could talk him down. I took a deep breath, let it out, admitted to myself that I was going to get in trouble over this and I was okay with it. Then I shut the door and said, "What d'you want me to do?"

Thamuris had asked me for a favor. Maybe that don't sound so weird, but you got to understand. He was a Celebrant Celestial, which meant he outranked everybody for a Great Septad mile around, including the lady who ran the Gardens of Nephele. And me, I was just a lamed-up cat burglar who used to murder people for money, no education, no morals, and the only reason people here put up with me at all was my half brother Felix Harrowgate, who was a hocus and could charm the stars down out of the sky besides. So there was no way somebody like Thamuris should've been asking somebody like me for favors. But he had.

He wanted to perform a divination, he said, but none of the celebrants would help him. Seemed like they all thought it was a really shitty idea. And maybe it was. I'm annemer, no kind of hocus at all, and you could fill books with what I don't know about magic, and, I mean, he was dying of consumption. It only figured that there was a Great Septad and a septad and six things he shouldn't be doing, whether he wanted to on not. But I owed Thamuris. He'd tried to help me when nobody else cared enough to spit on me, when my leg wasn't healing right and they didn't want to hear about it because I was a murderer and they'd got some things back to front about my relationship with Felix besides. Which ain't exactly surprising, seeing as how he was crazy and mixed up in his own head about who I was, and they weren't about to ask *me* what was going on. And I can even sort of see it, since they thought I'd been beating him up and powers know what all else, and if I was what they thought I was, I only would've lied about it anyway.

Only I wasn't and I wouldn't, and even if I didn't blame them exactly, I couldn't really forgive them either.

So even though Thamuris hadn't been able to get none of them stuck-up bastards to listen to him, I still owed him. For *trying*. And this was the only thing he'd ever asked me for—fuck, the only thing he'd ever seemed to *want*—and I knew there wasn't a single fucking other thing in the world I could do for him. That's how consumption is.

It took a second for my question to get through the laudanum to him, but then his whole face lit up, like the big chandelier in the cathedral of Phi-Kethetin that I was probably never going to see again. "I've had to adapt the ritual, so you will have to take two parts. You must be both querent and anchor." He gave me a look like he expected me to know what that meant and to be pissed off about it.

"Spell it out for me, Thamuris. Stupid annemer, remember?"

He sat down on the bed. "As my anchor," he said, "you help me maintain my link to my body, to the tangible world. I will need you to hold onto my hands—that's where the khresmos can take hold."

He wanted me to hold his hands. I could do that. "Okay. What about the other thing? The q-whatsit?"

"Oh, that's easy. You just ask me a question."

"Wait—what?"

"It is dangerous, stupid, and useless to open oneself to the huphantike without a specific question in mind."

"Why can't *you* ask one?"

"It doesn't work. You can't ask questions for yourself."

Mavortian von Heber sure could—him being the only other fortune-teller I'd ever met. But I was willing to bet there was more Mavortian *hadn't* told me than what he had, and besides I wasn't about to try and tell Thamuris he didn't know what he was talking about.

Well, fuck, I thought. I couldn't think of a single thing I wanted to know. The future felt like a herd of buffalo stampeding straight at me, and all I wanted was to get the fuck out of the way.

"Give me a minute," I said.

"As long as you need," Thamuris said, and I knew he'd wait all the way to the end of time and out the other side. I was stuck. This was the thing Thamuris wanted. So I racked my brain for some kind of question I could ask that wouldn't be a cheat or a waste of time, but wouldn't tell me something I couldn't stand to live with.

Thamuris said, very quietly, "What are you afraid of?"

"I ain't afraid," I said, and we both knew I was lying.

"Then ask." He came and knelt in front of me and held out his hands. "Take my hands and ask."

It didn't feel like anything I meant to do, but I found myself holding his hands. They were cold. And I heard myself say in a dry sort of croak, "What's going to happen to me?"

His fingers suddenly clamped down—not quite hard enough to hurt, but hard enough that I really wasn't going nowhere—and his eyes rolled back in his head, which ain't no nice thing to see right up close. I would've thought he'd fainted except he didn't fall down, and he didn't loose his grip on my hands. Which made it most likely that he'd started his divination, and I just hoped he didn't need me to do nothing but sit there.

Whatever was going on with Thamuris, it wasn't nothing I could see or hear or feel. All I could do was sit there with his cold fingers digging into my wrists tighter and tighter, waiting for something to happen and hoping it wouldn't be nothing bad. I had that feeling again, like I was doing something wrong and everybody in the Gardens was going to be pissed at me. But Thamuris trusted me and wanted my help, and so I sat and waited. My new career.

And then, just when I'd pretty much resigned myself to sitting there that way until dawn and Khrysogonos or somebody walked in and found us, and, powers, that was going to be a nasty scene—Thamuris's eyes came rolling back down, although they didn't look like his eyes at all. They looked too old and too far away and too mean. It was somebody else looking at me out of Thamuris's eyes. I don't know who, and I don't want to. I knew whatever this person had to say to me I didn't want to hear it, but I wasn't going to be able to break Thamuris's grip without hurting him, so there was nothing to do but sit there and take it.

Thamuris said, "Love and betrayal, the gorgon and the wheel. The dead tree will not shelter you, and the dead will not stay dead. Though you do not seek revenge, it will seek you all the same."

I know it sounds like complete bullshit, but the voice was cold and kind of bored, and those eyes were watching me like they wanted to see me flinch, and it might be Thamuris's hands, but the power grinding my bones together wasn't nothing to do with him, and I knew those words were the truth. I didn't know what the fuck they meant, but I knew for sure I was going to be sorry when I found out.

I felt it leave Thamuris, because his shudder damn near broke my wrists. His eyes were shut and his face screwed up like something was hurting him, and he fell straight over backwards like he'd been poleaxed.

I stared at him for a moment, and then I realized he wasn't breathing.

Felix

I was woken, from a confused and frightening dream of searching the Mirador for a pocket watch Shannon had given me and I had lost long ago, by the sound of someone knocking on the door. I was on my feet almost before I was awake; my first coherent thought was gratitude that I'd made Astyanax go back to his own room after we'd made love.

I called witchlight, snatched up my robe, shouted at the door, "What?"

Sudden silence.

I tied the robe, ran my hands through my hair, and flung the door open. "What?"

A small acolyte started back, her eyes wide. "Oh! Please, I'm sorry, sir, but I was told . . . the Celebrant Lunar said I ought . . ." I stood and waited, letting my eyebrows rise. She turned scarlet and said in an embarrassed mutter, "Your brother."

"What about my brother?"

"The Celebrant Lunar said you should come."

"Is there time for me to get dressed first?" I said and smiled at her, which caused her to turn an even more alarming color and back up a step, as if she was afraid I might ravish her then and there.

"Thank you," I said, shut the door, and scrambled into yesterday's clothes. If it had been truly urgent, Xanthippe would have told this silly child to tell me so; I knew that, but the residue of my dream, the almost-nightmare of looking for something that could not be found, tainted even that certainty. As I followed the acolyte through the stately maze of the Nephelion, I could feel the truth pounding in my heart: if something has happened to him, it is my fault. He is only here because of me. I know they don't understand him; I know he hates them. I have done nothing to help him.

It had been a month and a half since the wizards and healers of the Gardens of Nephele had cured me of my madness. I no longer saw monsters in every shadow or imagined that those trying to help me were tormentors long dead. I was whole again, clearheaded, vital and focused in a way I hadn't been since I was first learning magic, first learning to be free. On some days, it was almost as if the last year and more had not happened, as if my life before the Virtu of the Mirador had been broken—before Malkar had broken it, using me as his weapon—could truly be stitched together seamlessly with my life here in the Gardens. But on other days, I knew that was not true. And if I needed reminding, there was my half brother, lamed in trying to help me, apparently unwilling to move without me for all that we were nearly strangers to each other.

The door of Mildmay's room was open, lamplight pouring out. At first glance, the room looked as if Troians had descended on it like locusts, but the impression resolved itself into Xanthippe, speaking in a low, venomous voice to a pallid young man I did not recognize; Oribasios, a Celebrant Terrestrial I knew vaguely, standing in the middle of the room performing something easily recognizable as a ritual dispersement; and Khrysogonos, the acolyte assigned to my brother's care, kneeling by the armchair where Mildmay sat. I was peripherally aware of my little acolyte attaching herself to Xanthippe's presence like a limpet.

I looked at Mildmay and was appalled; I had not been spending much time with him, but how had I not noticed how thin he was getting? His cheekbones were stark against his skin; his hands and wrists were nothing but knobs and staring blue veins. He was ashen, colorless except for the poison green of his eyes and his burnished fox-red hair; the scar that disfigured his face was a livid line of despair from his mouth to his left temple.

But his eyes were open, aware; I saw him note my arrival before he looked back at Khrysogonos. A weight of dread and guilt rolled off my shoulders, and I crossed the room to say to him, "You seem to have been busy this evening."

Khrysogonos glared at me, but Mildmay just tilted his head back a little and said, "Yeah. Got bored."

"So what were you doing?"

"Magic."

"Magic?" I said and let my eyebrows go up. "*Really?* What branch did you choose for your maiden voyage? Necromancy? Geomancy?"

"Divination. I think." I saw his gaze flick toward the pallid young man.

"Ah, yes. Your partner in crime. To whom I believe I have *not* been introduced."

"That's Thamuris," Mildmay said.

"He is a Celebrant Celestial of the Euryganeic Covenant," Khrysogonos said aggrievedly, although I wasn't sure if he was mad at me, Mildmay, or Thamuris—or if he even knew himself.

"Which means?" I said.

"He should have known better than to do such an insanely dangerous, stupid, and selfish thing," Xanthippe said behind me. Khrysogonos went nearly as white as Mildmay.

I turned around. The pallid young man was staring down at his hands; Xanthippe was almost crackling with fury.

"What exactly did he do?" I said.

Xanthippe glared at the bowed head of the pallid young man. "He used your brother as an anchor in a pythian casting."

"And that is?"

"Pythian casting is the form of divination preferred by the covenant of Euryganeia. It requires four trained celebrants in addition to the diviner, and even then it is quite dangerous."

"And he just used Mildmay."

"Apparently."

I turned back to Mildmay, "And you *let* him?"

Mildmay gave me a half shrug. "He trusted me."

I bit back the first three responses that came to mind and said, quite levelly, "You could very easily have been killed."

Another half shrug, an impatient jerk of one shoulder, as if he were throwing off an intrusive hand. "No big loss."

"No big *loss*? Are you out of your *mind*?" They were all staring at me, and I realized that my calm, level voice had become a shriek. I turned on the pallid young man, made a conscious effort to modulate my voice, and said, "What did you think you were doing?"

His golden eyes were dreamy with fever and drugs, lambent in his white face. He was consumptive, and that explained a great deal. He said, "I didn't hurt him. I would never have hurt him. I just had to . . ."

"Thamuris," Xanthippe said gently.

He turned to her, wide-eyed, pleading, "Xanthippe, it was perfectly safe. I swear it."

"You'll forgive me," I said, "if I am skeptical."

Xanthippe shot me a *not now* look and sat down next to Thamuris on the bed. "I know you would never do anything intentionally to hurt anyone," she said, taking his hands and making him look at her, "but you don't have the strength you used to. If something had gone wrong, you couldn't have controlled it."

"But I *had* to," he said, and I saw his dream-hazed eyes fill with tears. "Xanthippe, I *had* to."

She sighed, touched his cheek, and said, "Khrysogonos, Oribasios, Hesione, would you see that Thamuris gets safely to bed?"

Acolytes and Celebrant Terrestrial, they helped Thamuris to his feet and half led, half carried him out of the room, leaving Xanthippe and me staring at each other and Mildmay slumped grayly in his chair, staring at nothing.

I pushed my hair off my face. "Xanthippe, what just happened here?"

She sighed, rubbing restlessly at the ache of arthritis in her hands. "Thamuris is dying."

"Yes, I recognize consumption when I see it. That isn't an explanation."

She looked past me at Mildmay. "What did he tell you?"

He didn't move, but he seemed to sink even lower into the chair. "He asked me not to tell anyone. He said it wouldn't be hard. I was gonna be two things for him. Anchor and . . . and some word I didn't know."

"Querent?" Xanthippe said in a tone indicating she knew the answer and didn't want to hear it.

"Yeah. That was it. And he was going to tell the future."

"That's *it*?"

"Um. Yeah."

Xanthippe said some things under her breath that I politely pretended not to hear.

"He didn't hurt me," Mildmay said, and there was perhaps a hint of anxiety in his voice. "I'm really okay."

"Then what happened to your hands?" I said.

"I bruise easy," he said. He met my eyes as he said it and made no effort to hide the rising bruises on his wrists. I wasn't going to be able to stampede him into giving anything away.

Xanthippe said in a slow, measured voice, "The fact that you are neither dead nor insane is a miracle. Thamuris should *never* have performed a pythian casting with an annemer."

"Didn't look like nobody else was helping him," Mildmay said, with the first spark of real feeling I'd heard since I came into the room.

"Not helping him kill himself? No. No, we aren't."

Mildmay's flinch was all in his eyes. He said nothing.

"I'm sorry," Xanthippe said. "That was unkind. You had no way of knowing that the celebrants of Hakko sent Thamuris here precisely to keep him from doing what he has done." Her mouth compressed, bitter, angry, helpless. "What they themselves trained him to do. In Euryganeic thinking, it is what he was *created* to do."

Mildmay muttered something.

"What?" I said.

"Junkie," Mildmay said in Marathine.

"I'm not sure the analogy of addiction is going to be a very popular one here," I said, also in Marathine.

"It's what it was like. Or maybe that was just the laudanum." He sank back down into himself and shut his eyes.

Xanthippe was waiting politely, her eyebrows raised. "So what was this evening's demonstration about?" I said to her.

"I don't know, and it troubles me. Using an annemer as an anchor is not unheard of, but it has not been done since the ascendancy of the House Hippothontis, precisely because it is so dangerous."

"Well, if no one else would help him," I said, "and if he was as desperate as it seems he was—"

"He wanted it," Mildmay said without opening his eyes. "Only thing I've ever seen him want." And that, I thought, was essentially what he'd said to me in Marathine, merely stripped of the ugly metaphor. "He didn't care if it killed him. Almost did, too. I had to—" He broke off with a sharp, painful shake of his head.

Xanthippe went over to Mildmay, touched his hand lightly. When he looked up at her, she said, "I do not know if you did the right thing, but you did the best thing it was in you to do." The silence remaining when she had left, the heels of her shoes beating a slow but impatient rhythm down the corridor, was heavy and cold, like great blocks of ice.

Mildmay said, out of that coldness, "Don't have to stay."

"There's no point in going back to bed," I said. "I'm quite thoroughly awake."

"Sorry," he said, turning his head to look out at the dark-drowned garden.

"Mildmay."

When he tilted his head back, I realized I was about to do something terribly wrong, and knelt quickly down beside him, so that our eyes were level. With the six-inch difference in our heights, it was not a vantage we had on each other very often. His face was expressionless; it was always expressionless, and sometimes it made me want to shake him until his spine rattled.

I said, very carefully, "You do know it would have been a, er, 'big loss' to me if you had died tonight."

He didn't even give me the twitch of an eyebrow, just sat there, watching me, silent.

"I haven't forgotten," I said.

"I know that." Flat, heavy words; I had a momentary, ugly flash of stones falling from Diokletian's mouth, a memory of my madness, and shook it away.

"I am . . . grateful."

He looked away, muttered something I couldn't understand.

"What?"

"Don't want that."

"Don't want what?"

"I don't want you to be grateful."

"Then what *do* you want?"

I watched, fascinated, as a slow tide of crimson washed over his face; he said nothing.

"Tell me," I said, as gently as I could.

He shook his head. "It's stupid."

"If you're feeling suicidal, nothing's—"

"I ain't."

"Then quit acting like it!"

"I don't want to be a crip, okay? And I can't have that and I know it and it's stupid. So fuck off and leave me alone."

The silence in the room felt like a bubble made of crystal, as if the slightest movement, even a breath, would shatter it. I reached out slowly and took his hands. They felt like bunches of sticks, and they were shaking with the fear and unhappiness he would not let anyone see on his face.

I had expected him to jerk away from me, but he did not move.

There were all sorts of things I could have said—*should* have said—but too many of them were things I didn't want to say, or he didn't want to hear. I said, "I think it's about time we went home."

His head came up at that, and I could see the darkness leaving his eyes like shadows fleeing from the sun.

"Okay," he said, and after a moment, struck dumb and breathless by his sudden beauty, I remembered to let go of his hands.

$\backsim$

I spent the next two days in the library, trying to bury that terrible flash of desire.

I had desired him in Kekropia, I remembered; I had been mad then and surely could be forgiven. But this . . .

He is your brother, I said to myself, and even in my own mind, the voice sounded pleading rather than stern. He was my brother, and I knew I should not desire him. But knowing that changed nothing.

And in fleeing from my own monstrosity, I achieved nothing more than confronting myself with another monster I did not want to face: the *De Doctrina Labyrinthorum* of Ephreal Sand.

I had never read Sand's *Doctrine of Labyrinths*; I would not have said I'd even heard of it. But when I had come across it in the Gardens' library, it had been familiar in a nagging, terrible, senseless way. Every effort I made to prove to myself that it was coincidence merely reinforced the knowledge that it was not. It was not quite déjà vu; it was too diffuse, too persistent. I had tried to avoid it, much as I had tried to avoid Mildmay, distracting myself with the search through the Gardens' resources for possible ways to mend the Virtu, to reweave the torn and tangled magic of the Mirador. But Sand's book fretted at me like a headache, so that I hated reading it and yet could not leave it alone.

De Doctrina Labyrinthorum seemed at first a simple catalogue of labyrinths in the Empire, and for a time I had lost sight of my dread in wonder at how many there were—or, at least, how many Ephreal Sand claimed to have found. Until I remembered something else.

He had gone mad.

There was a voice in my ear, a Kekropian-accented tenor with a precise cadence that was achingly familiar: *He began to draw mazes that could not be solved. At first his apprentices thought it was but a new phase of their master's research, some new theoretical bauble. But days became weeks became months, and still Ephreal Sand did nothing but draw these snarls and tangles, and when they asked him why, he would merely point at the maze he was drawing, as if it contained within itself the only possible or necessary answer.*

I shook my head, and the voice was gone. It was not a voice I knew—it was not Thaddeus de Lalage or any of the other Kekropian wizards who lived and worked in the Mirador—and yet it was *familiar*. I could hear the way the aspirants eroded away from "th" and "ph"—the way "Ephreal" was almost but not quite "Epreal"—as clearly as if the man who had spoken those words were standing next to me now in the library's dimness.

Reflexively, I reached for a pocket watch I no longer owned. And stopped, sitting with my hand halfway in my trouser pocket, for a moment unable to breathe. That pain, that sharp, shocking, mortal pain, mocked all my efforts to make of my past a mere nightmare, dismissible, forgettable, all my efforts to pretend it didn't matter.

So *do* something, I said to myself, exasperated. Ask the questions you know how to ask while you still have the opportunity to ask them. I pushed away from the table and went to find the historian who could tell me about the lost city of Nera, the city I knew more about than I should. I had seen it mentioned in the *De Doctrina Labyrinthorum,* and had had a sudden terrible knowledge of Nera's fall, knowledge I could not explain.

Themistokles was a Celebrant Terrestrial, an archivist. His specialty was the Empire of Kekropia and its history as a territory of Troia. Nephelian Celebrants, I had learned, were as likely to be scholars as healers, and many were both. Theirs was the only magic-practicing covenant that prized the past as more than merely the source of tradition and precedent; wizards of a scholarly bent gravitated to the Nephelians, and although the focus of their research remained healing, the scope of their studies had gradually broadened, until there were now a number of archivists, like Themistokles, whose specialties had only the most tenuous connection with their ostensible purpose. No one seemed to mind; I understood that the Gardens' relationship with the university in Haigisikhora was remarkably cordial.

I found Themistokles in his office, a dusty, closet-sized room with parchments and codices overflowing from the shelves, stacked on the desk and the windowsill and the floor, so that only Themistokles himself could move safely through the labyrinth.

And then I wished I hadn't thought that.

"Felix!" Themistokles said, taking off his spectacles and waving them at me in a hospitable fashion. "Come in, have a seat! What can I do for you?"

Since there was nowhere in Themistokles' office to sit, I stayed where I was, leaning against the doorframe.

"I need to ask you about Nera," I said.

"Nera?" he said, putting his spectacles back on to frown at me. There was ink staining his fingers and a long smudge of it down one cheekbone. "Good gracious, what about it?"

"Well," I said, and bit back the insane impulse to say, *I've been having visions in the library*. "Just . . . it was destroyed, wasn't it? By Troians?"

"Oh, yes. Back in the ascendancy of the House Atreis."

"Why?"

"Why?" he echoed, baffled.

"Why was it destroyed? What did they do?"

"They worshipped abominations," Themistokles said, as if surprised I had to ask.

"Did they *practice* abominations?" I said, too sharply.

He blinked at me, taken aback and a little hurt. "Felix, this is ancient history!"

Not for me, I nearly said. "What sort of abominations? Did it involve . . . mazes?"

Themistokles gave me a narrow, searching look. Absentminded he might be, and very little interested in anything outside his research, but he was not obtuse, and I had been too distressed (I realized belatedly) to be subtle.

After an agonizing moment, he decided he would not ask. "The state religion of Lucrèce," he said, "included a number of strange and unsavory deities. I shan't detail them all, if you're interested in mazes . . . ?" He trailed off, eyebrows raised.

"Yes."

"Then you want to know about their death goddess."

"Do I? Grand."

Themistokles leaned back, his expression becoming abstracted and distant. "She was called the White-Eyed Lady. She has no name—or, rather, her name died with her last worshipper. It was anathema to write it down, or to speak it to anyone who was not an initiate in her mysteries."

"It was a mystery cult?"

"Yes. Does it matter?"

"No," I said, remembering the stories of the Obscurantists I had heard as a child. "Please go on."

"She was worshipped in labyrinths. Or *with* labyrinths. The texts are unclear. There's a hymn—unless it's an apotropaic prayer—that begins, 'She is the center of every maze.' Since she is death and despair and mikkary, I for one don't find it a comforting thought."

"Wait. What did you say? Death, despair, and what?"

"Mikkary."

"What's that?"

"A Midlander word, I think. The etymology is singularly obscure. It means . . . well, it means a number of things."

"It sounds like a Marathine word: 'misery.' " I gave the Kekropian. "Is that close?"

Themistokles grimaced. "Well, yes and no. It'll do for a start, but mikkary is more than that. There isn't a word in Troian for it. But it means something like insanity and something like ecstasy—in the theological sense, not as in the throes of delight—and something like terror. And the texts we have always describe it in conjunction with buildings, especially but not exclusively their goddess's labyrinths."

"It sounds lovely," I said and couldn't quite repress a shiver.

"It was her miasma, her perfume if you will. She was a goddess of fear and pain. Her rites were performed in darkness. Her followers drank the blood of their own children."

This goddess was sounding more and more like the God of the Obscured Sun. "And the Troians eradicated her worship?"

"Three thousand years ago, give or take."

"Do you know, was there anything special about the labyrinth in Nera?"

He frowned thoughtfully. "Well, Nera was the Lucrètian capital, so I imagine the labyrinth of Nera would have been notably opulent. But I've never heard anything about it particularly. Why?"

"Just something I came across in the archives. I'm working my way through your Midlander books, you know. I found de Kalends's treatise on linguistic borrowings quite fascinating."

"Oh, yes," Themistokles said, his vague eyes lighting. Here, as in the Mirador, it was not difficult to decoy academic wizards onto their specialties; I escaped a half hour later without having to answer any more questions about my interest in Nera's labyrinth.

Mildmay

Felix showed up in the evening and dragged me to the Gardens' refectory for dinner. I wanted not to like it—and it sure did piss me off the way everybody stared, like I had three heads and a couple extra arms or something. But there was a stupid little kid inside me, and that stupid little kid was so fucking happy to be getting attention from Felix that I couldn't hate eating dinner with him the way I thought I should. It was purely embarrassing. About the only good thing I could see in it was I didn't have to talk to Felix about it.

Mostly, I didn't have to talk at all with Felix. Mostly, Felix was happy as a drunk saint doing all the talking himself, and powers and saints, the way he talked I could listen for hours and not get bored. He talked about everything—the plants in the gardens, the books he was reading, gossip about the celebrants. I could just sit and listen and not have to try and be smart and not have to worry about how I sounded or nothing. And that was good.

That night I could tell he was on edge about something. It didn't show exactly, but he was talking just a little too fast and gesturing with his hands a little too much. And his spooky mismatched eyes were too bright.

But he let me eat in peace—aside from talking my ear off, I mean—and it wasn't until I was done and he was sitting there with his brandy that he said, "Do you know anything about Nera?"

"Nera? You mean the place where . . ." And then my mind caught up with my mouth.

"Where what?" Felix said after a moment.

"I dunno," I said. "I mean, you're the one knew what it was."

"Knew what *what* was?"

"Don't you remember?" He didn't really flinch, but his face tightened up for a second, and I said, "Oh shit you *don't* remember."

"Don't be absurd," he said, which ain't even remotely the same thing as, *Yes, I do, and I can prove it.*

"You wouldn't be asking if you did."

There was a minute there when he thought he was just going to bull through on brass alone, but then he sighed and said, "All right. I *don't* remember. I remember almost nothing from the entire time I was . . . was not myself."

"So you don't remember what happened in Hermione or with Mavortian or Gideon or anything?"

"Gideon?" His eyes went sharp suddenly. "That's a Kekropian name."

"Um, yeah. He's a Kekropian. Little guy, looks sort of like a choirboy, sort of like a clerk. Really smart. A hocus."

"Ah," he said. "I think I do remember Gideon. Slightly."

It occurred to me to be damn fucking glad that he'd remembered me at all. "I'm sorry." Kethe, Milly-Fox, do you think you could say anything *stupider?*

He waved it off. "Tell me about Nera."

So I told him. I told him about the crossroads and the dragoons and him hearing crying people and how we'd walked for two days. I left out the part about me getting locked in a farmhouse cellar, because it didn't seem like it mattered. But I told him about the valley and how he'd told me it was the ruins of a city called Nera and how the people that had died there wanted a maze so they could get shut of the world and rest. And about us making the maze, and how it had seemed like all them ghosts had used it the way they wanted.

By that time he was white as a sheet, and I could see his jaw muscles all tensed up, so I left out the part about how I'd had to beat him up to keep him from following the ghosts through the maze. I didn't feel like that would help the situation none, and Kethe it wasn't nothing I wanted to talk about anyway.

"So we made a maze," he said finally.

"Yeah."

"So the ghosts could reach Hell?"

"I guess." It hadn't been that long ago, but, well, he'd been crazy and I hadn't been crippled and there was a whole ocean we'd crossed between here and there. So it took me a moment to remember what he'd said. "You said their goddess liked mazes or something."

"Oh," he said, and if he'd been anybody else, it would have been a swearword.

"What?"

"Nothing. Something I read today. It doesn't matter."

"And that's why you look like you been served up a dish of eyeballs?"

He actually laughed a little. "Thank you for *that* vivid piece of imagery. I can't explain it. I don't know what's going on. But that book I've been reading . . . ?"

He raised his eyebrows at me, like he thought I should remember this book of his *and* know why it mattered.

"Yeah?"

Like a quarter sigh, just enough to let me know he'd expected better. *"De Doctrina Labyrinthorum. Of the Doctrine of Labyrinths."*

"Oh. That." And now I remembered him talking about it, because I hadn't known what a labyrinth was. A maze. Like the curtain-mazes. Like that maze we'd made in Nera. Oh fuck.

"It mentions Nera," he said.

Well, I mean, what the fuck do you say to that? I couldn't think of nothing, so I just sat there, staring at him like a half-wit dog—which I was compared to him, no question, but it still ain't no nice feeling. And after a bit, he kind of shook himself and said, "Would you . . . I was wondering if . . . ?"

"What?"

"Would you do something for me?"

I probably looked even stupider then, because I couldn't fucking believe my ears. I pulled myself together and said, "Um, sure. What?"

He was frowning now, just a little, and staring off into space. "Do you . . . I remember, I think. I remember that you are good with maps."

"I guess. Why?"

"Because we have an empire between us and Mélusine." He looked at me and said, "What?"

"Nothing."

He raised one eyebrow. Powers, I hated that look. And that's probably what made me tell him the truth. "I just ain't used to you doing the thinking."

He went red, which was kind of satisfying in a nasty, mean-hearted way. For a second, we both thought he was going to chew me out up one side and down the other, but then he stopped and shut his eyes and made a kind of little pushing-away gesture, like he was just shoving it to the side. Then he looked at me and said, "Will you look at maps for me?"

"Sure. I mean, I got nothing better to do."

He kind of flicked a frown at me, like I wasn't supposed to be, you know, honest about it. "I'll have the archivists send their maps of Kekropia to your room tomorrow. I know . . . that is, I didn't think you'd want to come to the library."

"Not 'specially. What d'you want me to be looking for?"

"How to stay as far away from the Bastion as possible."

My belly went cold clear back to my spine at the thought of what the Bastion would do to him if they caught him. "I hear you," I said.

Chapter 2

Felix

I dream of the Omphalos.

In the waking world it is a small and dingy structure, a pinched dome supported on weathered columns, the entire thing made dark and dank by the suffocating embrace of clematis vines. Many celebrants like to spend time there, but I don't understand the attraction.

In my dream, the Omphalos is beautiful. The dome is vast, airy, the color of the sky; the columns are tall and straight and blindingly white. I feel drenched in peace, as golden and slow as sunlight. I step out onto the peripeteia and see the gardens spreading out around me, tapestries of green. There are no people anywhere in view, just these soft myriad greens shading in and out of each other in an endless dance whose steps I almost know.

I come down the steps of the Omphalos. The paths which spiderweb away in all directions are paved with white marble, the pieces fitting together as neatly and randomly as the scraps of fabric in a crazy quilt. I pick a path vaulted by the intertwining branches of the perseïd trees, begin walking.

There is no sense of urgency, no purpose, merely the pleasure of the smooth marble beneath my bare feet and the heady scent of the white perseïd flowers.

The first two or three times I pass a ghost, I don't recognize them for what they are, dismissing them vaguely as heat haze, the mirages of my weak eye, even some strange property of the dream itself. But finally, I happen to see one head-on, come face-to-face with a red-haired, yellow-eyed, transparent woman, and as she walks indifferently through me, I realize the truth. The gardens are not deserted, but their paths are walked only by those who cannot see or hear or feel me.

I did not regard my isolation when I believed myself to be alone, but now I am crushed beneath a weight of loneliness so heavy that I wake.

☙

I lay sprawled across my bed, chest heaving, staring at the ceiling without seeing it. Part of my mind was screaming at me to get up and go find another human being—Mildmay, Astyanax, Diokletian . . . anyone. But my body seemed too heavy to move, and there was a strange, chafing feeling of recognition.

I've dreamed about that garden before.

The thought seemed nonsensical, but I could not rid myself of it. I'd dreamed about the gardens several times since waking up here, but that wasn't the source of this nagging, frustrating sense of déjà vu. I'd dreamed about *that* garden before, with its white marble paths and the Omphalos like the vault of the heavens. I could not remember that earlier dream; I could not remember *having* the dream. But I knew that I had dreamed it before, that radiant garden I had never seen.

I let my head roll to the side, and the window showed me the sky, awash in the luminous gray that was the precursor of dawn. I couldn't quite stifle a groan. My fatigue crushed me to the bed like the peine forte et dure, but sleep was a dream as distant as the ghost-haunted garden, and it was no more than an hour or two before I would have to get up anyway.

I groaned again and dragged myself upright.

I bathed and dressed and wandered to the refectory, still puzzling over the strange familiarity of the dream. I made a detour to request that the acolyte who was opening the library have all available maps of Kekropia delivered to my brother's room. The sun was up now, bathing everything in early-morning clarity. And there was something else nagging at me, as I became more alert, something Diokletian had said . . .

When I went into the refectory, the only person there, aside from the cheerfully yawning staff, was Diokletian himself. It felt like a sign. A portent, an omen, an augury. I exchanged good mornings with the shy child who brought me tea, yogurt, honey, and a half cantaloupe, and carried my breakfast to the table where Diokletian sat pretending he was so absorbed in his book that he had not noticed me.

I contemplated him as I stirred honey into the yogurt. He was in his early fifties, slightly less than twice my age. He was one of the many men who might have been my father; my mother, Xanthippe had told me, had always refused to say. I was conscious of an unworthy hope that it was not Diokletian. He was kind enough, but he was so stiff, so repressed. And it was clear—despite the fact that he was married, with two daughters—that he had never gotten over my mother. I had come to hate the way his eyes searched my face for signs of her.

I ate most of my breakfast with only a view of his hair and forehead as he stared at his book. At last, he could stand it no longer and looked up, meeting my eyes. I smiled at him and said, "You said something about oneiromancy."

"I beg your pardon?"

"Oneiromancy." I said it slower, dragging out the syllables as if I believed he hadn't understood me or didn't know the word. His face twitched with irritation. "When I woke up here, you said you'd been experimenting with oneiromancy."

"Yes." Cautious now, not trusting where I might be going.

"Tell me about it."

"What?"

"Tell me about Troian oneiromancy."

"Why?"

"I hunger for knowledge."

He reddened, scowled. "You're mocking me."

"No, I'm perfectly serious. I want to know about the Troian magic of dreams. Tell me."

"I don't understand what you want to know."

"Did I not make it plain enough? Oneiromancy. The theory and understanding thereof as practiced in Troia."

"It isn't."

"I beg your pardon?"

"Oneiromancy is not practiced in Troia."

"But you said . . . I didn't imagine it!"

I winced at my own vehemence, and Diokletian said, "No, no, it's quite true. *I* was practicing oneiromancy. But that was . . . Let's talk about this somewhere else."

"As you wish," I said and followed him back to his room.

We did not speak on the way there, and he must have used the time to collect and order his thoughts, for as soon as he had closed the door behind us, he said, "The practice of oneiromancy was discontinued in Troia one hundred and thirty-nine years ago."

We sat down. "Forbidden?" I said.

"No. Not exactly. It was deemed . . . ineffective, unnecessary." One corner of his mouth quirked up bitterly. "A waste of time."

"And you disagree?"

"I believe that the great past practitioners—oneiromancers like Tigranes and Galinthias—could work with dreams in ways that no other kind of magic can copy. The whole of the Euryganeic covenant followed Hakko and abandoned dream-casting in favor of pythian casting almost three hundred years ago, and I think knowledge was lost that we cannot even begin to imagine."

"Why did they abandon dream-casting?" I said, thinking of that white-faced Euryganeic, those bruises on Mildmay's hands. "Pythian casting seems unacceptably dangerous."

"It's reliable. The Euryganeics were losing favor with the Aisxime—the Parliament and the court. They believed, whether rightly or wrongly I do not know, that their covenant would not survive if the Aisxime turned away from them. They sacrificed much to keep the approbation of fools."

"You sound bitter."

His face was set, grim. "I was an acolyte of the Euryganeic Covenant, but I did not have the strength for pythian casting. I endured convulsion after convulsion, splitting headaches, nosebleeds, until the celebrants finally admitted that it was not laziness or malingering. And then they told me that I could stay, swear the covenant of Euryganeia, be raised to celebrant—as a bookkeeper, a caretaker, a servant to those of my peers who could withstand what I could not. I asked about other methods of divination and was laughed at."

"So that's why you came here."

"Yes. I have some talent for healing—and I have come to see, with age and distance, that I am better here than I would ever have been as a Euryganeic."

"Indeed," I murmured.

"But my dreams . . . my dreams have always been prescient. I know there's something there, if I could just learn to wield it. I believe I have read every text the library has that mentions oneiromancy, interpretation of dreams, anything of the sort. There is frustratingly little, but I found references over and over again to something called the Khloïdanikos, the Dream of the Garden. Later books describe it merely as a mental construct, such as clerks use . . . ?"

"I am familiar with the idea."

"But the earlier texts talk about it in very different terms. A construct, yes, but an *oneiromantic* construct."

"For what purpose?"

"I don't know. That was one of the things I wanted to discover." He sighed, the fierce energy seeming to drain out of him. "But all I ever discovered was you."

"Me?"

He continued as if I had not spoken. "I found the Dream of the Garden easily enough, but I could do nothing with it. It was merely . . ." He waved a hand. "The Gardens. As they were hundreds of years ago, when the Dream was created by the oneiromancers. I walked in the Dream, I don't know, twenty times? Twenty-five? It remained unchanging—unapproachable, for all that I stood within it. When I saw you, I thought at first . . ." But he did not tell me what he had thought, and I found that I did not want to know.

After a time, he seemed to shake himself out of his dismal reverie and said, "So if you want to know about oneiromancy, I am afraid you will have to ask someone else."

"But it seems, from what you have said, that there is no one else to ask."

"True."

I took a deep breath, gathered my resolve, and said, "Let me tell you about my dream."

Once he had absorbed the implications of what I had dreamed, it took very little time for Diokletian to tell me everything he knew about the Dream of the Garden. It wasn't very much. It took more time for him to describe the mental exercises he used to send his sleeping or entranced mind into the Dream of the Garden. They sounded insanely complicated, and I said so.

"Oh, I can bring you in."

"No," I said. "You can't."

"I did before," he said, offended.

The thought made me ill. "That was . . . different. I assure you, whatever techniques you used before will prove ineffectual now."

He bridled, but I went on before he could speak: "I can find my own way in."

"But you haven't been trained to—"

"Neither have you."

I had spoken more sharply than I had intended to; his silence was both hurt and reproachful.

"Trust me," I said. "I'll get in. Shall we try it now?"

"Now?"

"Why not?"

"I scarcely think you know the meditation techniques necessary to reach the Khloïdanikos without being in deep natural sleep."

"You have no idea of what I do or don't know," I said, catching his gaze and holding it. After a moment, he looked away uncomfortably.

"If you insist," he said, trying to sound as if he was merely humoring my delusion.

I made myself comfortable in the chair. "I do. I'll see you there," I said and shut my eyes.

Malkar had trained me in certain kinds of meditation, but most of what I knew I had learned from Iosephinus Pompey, a tremendously ancient wizard who had himself been taught by wizards who remembered what magic had been like in the Mirador before the Wizards' Coup. He had been taught principles of oneiromancy, although it was heresy, and he had taught them to me because I confessed my nightmares to him. He told me that his own teacher, Rosindy Clerk, had believed that the magic of wizards with great natural talent—like me—often bled into their dreams, whether they had training in oneiromancy or not.

Iosephinus had taught me well, after swearing me to secrecy with a barrage of frightening oaths, and the steps of the ritual felt as comfortable and familiar as an old, much-washed shirt, even though I could not remember the last time I had performed it.

I called up my mental construct of Mélusine, and then imagined myself opening my eyes. Iosephinus called it "opening the third eye," but I had always shied away from such blatantly mystical language; Malkar would have laughed himself sick if he'd ever heard me talking about third eyes.

I was fully in trance; when I opened my eyes, my schematic of Mélusine lay spread around me, as if I stood on the Crown of Nails. It had been so long since I had done this that for a moment I couldn't identify what was wrong, although my nerves were screaming with it. And then I saw: the river.

I had never loved the Sim, although my childhood fear of it had waned once I was safely established in the Mirador. My mental representation of it had always been as a thin, sinuous blue line, like a river on a map. But now it was wide, black, a trail of ichor left by some unimaginable wounded beast. Although I knew I could not, I seemed to smell it, the Sim's own bitter metallic reek mixed with a scent of rot and corruption and death.

Perplexed and beginning to be frightened, I traced the vile river's course from its entry into the city from the northwest, southeast to the Mirador, where I myself stood, and then south from the Mirador through the Lower City and . . .

I stared, aghast. In the real Mélusine, the Sim flowed out of the city beneath a tremendous arch, which the denizens of the Lower City called the Septad Gate, and into the St. Grandin Swamp. In this construct-Mélusine, the river had torn a horrid, jagged, weeping hole in the city wall; beyond it I could see a festering, noxious darkness, and whether I could smell it or not, I knew the stench was there. Swamp, graveyard, abattoir: it was all those things, and still nothing that I had created—at least, not on purpose.

If it had not been for Diokletian, I would have broken my trance. But I had told him I would find my own way into the Dream of the Garden, and I was not willing to prove myself a liar merely for some unexpected garbage in a mental construct. Iosephinus had told me that properly constructed oneiromantic portals were in a sense alive—that they would change to reflect everything along their borders, the dreaming self as much as the waking. If I did not fully understand the demonstration, I was entirely cognizant of the theory. There was nothing here at which to take alarm.

Or so I told myself.

I knew which gate I wanted; Horn Gate was the gate of true dreams, oneiromantically charged dreams. I wrenched myself away from my horrified contemplation of the Septad Gate and turned to the northeast. There was Horn Gate and there was the Dream of the Garden. I could see the perseïdes, and the memory of their smell helped to counteract the imagined stench of the Sim. Without hesitation, I left the Crown of Nails and walked through Horn Gate into the Dream of the Garden.

It was as it had been in my dream: verdant, idyllic, deserted except for the Troian ghosts who roamed its paths. I wondered, now that I knew what this garden was, what *they* were. Were they true ghosts, or traces of the oneiromancers who had once used this construct? Or, speculating more wildly as my search for Diokletian ranged farther and farther, were they those oneiromancers themselves, coming to the Khloïdanikos from their own time? Did I appear a ghost to them, as they did to me? That thought became more unsettling the longer I contemplated it. I was glad, when I came in sight of the Omphalos, for the notion to search for Diokletian there.

I made my way to the Omphalos; sure enough, he was standing beneath the center of the dome. He turned to face me as I came between the columns, and I stopped short. We stood, staring at each other.

"Oh," he said, sounding vaguely surprised. "You look like yourself now."

"I . . . *what?*"

"Well, you didn't. Before."

"Before what?"

"When I first found you, before we healed you. You looked quite different." He tilted his head, appraising me. "It must have been what you thought you looked like."

I decided I didn't want a description. "Many things were different then." And, because a jibe was the best distraction: "I told you I could manage for myself."

"Yes," he said, although he scarcely seemed to hear me. Then he shook his head and said more vigorously, "Yes, and now that you are here, what do you propose to do?"

"I don't know," I said, annoyed. "I suppose I'd like to find out why I was dreaming in your construct."

"It isn't *my* construct—"

"You're the one who was experimenting with it."

He glared at me.

"Look," I said. "What is the Khloïdanikos *for?*"

"I told you. The oneiromancers—"

"No. Not who built it or what they thought their reasons were. What is it *for?*"

"I don't understand you," he said stiffly.

"No, probably not." I felt more cheerful with a thaumaturgic riddle to solve. "The man who taught me what I know of oneiromancy told me that all good constructs have a life of their own. *That*'s what I'm after: what is the life of the Khloïdanikos?"

"I have no idea."

Somehow we were at cross-purposes. Diokletian seemed to be having a different conversation, in which all the words meant something else and every word I spoke was an insult.

I tried again. "Why was I drawn here when I was mad?"

"Why are you asking me?"

"Oh, I don't know—because there's no one else to ask?" I waved an arm furiously at the empty, ghost-ridden Khloïdanikos. "Because I thought, silly me, that you were interested? Because if we put the little bits of oneiromancy each of us knows together we might *learn* something?" He was staring at me wide-eyed, as if I'd thrown my head back and howled at the moon; he looked uncommonly half-witted. "*What?*"

He said in a vague, dazed voice, "She would never care so much about . . ."

I resisted, with difficulty, the urge to employ some of Mildmay's more colorful vocabulary. I closed the distance between us, took him by the shoulders with a slight shake, and said distinctly and emphatically, staring him in the eyes, "*I am not Methony.*"

He looked back at me, his gaze more unguarded than it had ever been in the waking world, and I found myself backing away from him before I'd even fully identified what I saw in his face.

"No," I said. "Oh, no. You *can't*."

"Why not?" said Diokletian, not moving but still watching me hungrily. "Isn't it what you want, to have every man who sees you desire you?"

"Me! Not my mother's ghost! You don't want me—you can barely tolerate me. You want *her*, and I am not flattered at being deemed an acceptable stand-in."

"You are so like her," he said dreamily, "your looks . . . your voice . . ."

"My career as a prostitute," I said, desperate to shake him out of his strange, abstracted absorption. I wasn't frightened of him physically, but the way he looked at me made me feel insubstantial, as if I were merely a veil between him and the woman he had desired for nearly thirty years.

His head jerked back as if I had threatened to slap him.

"Besides," I said, letting my voice become throatier, a parody of seduction, "I understand you could be my father. I wouldn't mind, but I think you might."

He backed up a pace, raising his hands as if to ward me off. I saw horror, revulsion, self-loathing on his face, and then all at once, like a soap bubble, he vanished. He had broken his trance, and I wondered if it had been intentional.

I did not care to remain in the Khloïdanikos alone, and with my body unprotected from whatever Diokletian might choose to do. I took a deep breath and started back toward the ungainly bulk of Horn Gate, alien among the perseïd trees.

Mildmay

Whatever else you could say about him, it did seem like Felix kept his promises. I was up and dressed and peeling an orange when there was a tap at the door. Khrysogonos still didn't knock, and Felix always banged on the door like he was ready to break it down if I didn't answer fast enough. My mouth dried up, along of suddenly being afraid it was Astyanax. Astyanax who hated me and was fucking Felix—or being fucked by him, and that was just one of those questions I was never going to ask. He'd looked through me good and hard the first time we came up against each other when Felix was around, and I'd gotten the message. And that was fine with me. Wasn't like I wanted to talk about it or anything. All I wanted was to keep the fuck away from him.

But even if it was Astyanax, I couldn't hide in here all day. So I said, "Come in."

And it wasn't Astyanax, just a skinny little acolyte with braids most of the way to her knees, carrying a big clumsy stack of parchments.

She dropped me a kind of curtsy—best she could do with all that parchment—and said, "Your brother said that I should bring these to you."

"Maps?" I said, and she nodded.

"Grand. Put 'em here," and I cleared off a space on the table. She put 'em down and skittered away before I could even say thank you.

I finished the orange—love 'em—got my hands cleaned off and started in with the maps.

A bunch of 'em were written in Troian, which made them not much good to me. I can limp along in Marathine, 'bout as fast as a slow turtle, and I can recognize names in Midlander, but Kekropian and Troian have this whole different alphabet, and I can't tell a gorgon from a wheel. But one of those had the best drawing on it, and I put it on one side while I looked through the ones with the Midlander writing.

I'd had a map myself when me and Felix had been going across Kekropia. It'd been lost with everything else when the *Morskaiakrov* sank. But I remembered it well enough to sort of hold it up against these maps and see the places where there were some serious differences of opinion. Mostly, these Troian maps didn't make Kekropia look anywhere near wide enough, and only one or two of 'em had even a feeble guess on where Mélusine and the Mirador was at. That didn't matter so much though as where they thought the Bastion was, it being the place where all the Kekropian hocuses hung out and the thing we principally wanted to avoid. I figured if we got that far, we could find Mélusine on our own.

If we got that far.

The maps all put the Bastion around about the middle of Kekropia, but you could tell the mapmakers were basically just guessing. They knew it was out there somewhere, and I don't suppose anybody but the Eusebians themselves can actually pinpoint it any better than that. So exactly how far north it was from anything, or how far west . . . well, I couldn't tell, and I stared at those damn maps until I swear I could feel my eyes crossing.

When we'd been going east, it hadn't mattered so much, because, for one thing, we'd been following the route Mavortian von Heber had chosen, and for another, Felix had been crazy, and Gideon had thought that would keep the Bastion from noticing him. Which looked like it had worked, because, I mean, they hadn't. But Felix wasn't crazy now, and if he was where the Eusebians could feel him with their spells—however the fuck *that* worked, and I didn't know and didn't want to—my understanding was they'd know right off he was a Cabaline, and then we might as well kiss our asses good-bye.

So there wasn't no point in trying to finesse it. We wanted to circle either way to the north or way to the south. I couldn't see that there was much to recommend either direction—going south we ended up in the duchies that were sort of a part of the empire and sort of their own thing, and I'd heard enough gossip going east to know we didn't particularly want to fuck with them, but going north took us up into Norvena Magna, and all I knew about that was it was likely to be extremely fucking cold. And then when we wanted to swing south again, there were all kinds of little countries that had hacked themselves out a space where none of the big players cared enough to come and get them, and I'd learned when I was doing smuggling runs for Keeper that who was friends with who changed pretty much by the hour, and none of 'em had much use for Marathat to begin with. At least going south we wouldn't have to wonder.

I didn't particularly like either plan, but then I remembered something that made the decision easier. We were pretty far south on Troia's coastline—I'd found a little square labeled GARDENS OF NEPHELE on one of the Midlander maps—and so going north would take longer, take us farther out of our way, and moreover would mean, almost as sure as eggs are eggs, that we'd have to go through Aigisthos, the capital of the Empire of Kekropia. And I remembered just how much Gideon had said we didn't want to go there.

We'd have to go around to the south.

I looked at all them little duchies, like a particularly crazy kind of crazy quilt, and thought, Kethe, I hope we can pull this off.

Felix

When I opened my eyes to Diokletian's bedroom, I was relieved to discover myself still in the chair, exactly as I had been when I went into my trance. Diokletian was sitting on the floor, his back against the wall, knees pulled up and his face buried in his hands.

I stood up, deliberately noisy. Diokletian did not move. I wanted simply to leave, wanted it in the same way one wants water to quench a thirst, but I knew that would give this silly, rather tawdry contretemps a kind of weight and meaning that it did not deserve. So I said, lightly, "Are you all right?"

"Fine," he said, still without moving. "Please, just go."

"This isn't the end of the world, you know."

That got his head up; his face was ashen and his yellow eyes staring. "What, to discover that I'm lusting after a man? And that man quite possibly my own son?"

"You aren't lusting after me. You're remembering her. And I may very well *not* be your son."

He shook his head. "That's not the point." He stood up, staring at me now with pain in his eyes. "I love my wife, my daughters. I never felt for my wife what I did for Methony, and I have never, thank the Tetrarchs," the hint of a wry smile crooking the corners of his mouth, "felt anything for my daughters that even remotely resembles what I feel for you."

"Which is?"

"Oh, you were right. I don't like you. This is something else. This is some madness in my blood. I would never . . . I don't know what happened there, in that . . ."

"Nothing to worry about," I said. "Neither of us is going to act on it—"

"And if we shut our eyes and put our fingers in our ears, it'll just go away? I had expected better of you."

"Well, Mildmay and I will be leaving the Gardens soon, so it's not as if—"

"Soon? How soon?"

"A few days."

"You're *leaving*?"

"Of course I'm leaving. You didn't think I was going to settle down here for the rest of my life, did you?"

His gaze shifted away from my face.

"Well, I'm not," I said.

"Because your brother doesn't want to."

"I beg your pardon?"

"It's true, is it not? You are leaving because your brother does not want to stay."

"Diokletian, I thought we—"

"Just answer the question."

"Mildmay doesn't want to stay, that's true, but neither do I."

"You've seemed very happy here."

"Of course I'm *happy*, you nitwit. That's not the point."

"Then what is the point?"

"There's something I have to do. In the Mirador."

"The *Mirador*?"

"It is my home," I said, treading carefully now among the truth, the lies, the omissions and evasions. "I . . . I am needed there." To repair the damage I did. Yes, indeed, the Mirador needed me, although there was a good chance I'd be tied to a stake with the flames licking my ankles before any of them calmed down enough to realize it. But that, too, didn't matter.

Diokletian snorted. "After the abysmal job they did taking care of you, I don't think—"

"You don't understand the circumstances."

"Then explain them."

And that was the last thing on earth I was likely to do. "It doesn't matter," I said. "I'm not accountable to you."

"I had thought your gratitude might run a little deeper," he said bitterly.

"Gratitude? What does that have to do with anything?"

"We saved your life—you and your trained bear—"

"*Don't* talk about him that way."

He gave an impatient jerky half shrug. He hadn't been trying to bait me; that was genuinely how he thought about Mildmay. "We saved your life, your sanity. We've fed, sheltered, and clothed you for the past three months . . ."

"I didn't realize I was running up a tab," I said, in Marathine because I didn't know the word in Troian.

"What?"

Back into Troian: I wasn't about to let him condescend to me about my language skills. "I didn't know anyone was keeping score."

"What? Of course not!"

"Then why are you trying to make me feel guilty about it?"

"We have done a great deal for you, and although we did not do it with thoughts of recompense, I *did* think—"

"That I'd—what? Join your covenant? Be your acolyte?"

"You're being unfair."

I couldn't help it; I laughed. "*Unfair?* And trying to talk me out of leaving by reminding me how much I owe you—*we did not do it with thoughts of recompense.*" I mimicked him savagely and was pleased to see him flinch. "That's the epitome of impartial fair dealing?"

"You're twisting my words."

"No," I said. "I'm not. And I *am* grateful, but it has no bearing on the matter. I have to go back."

"Xanthippe will not be pleased."

"And I will be sorry for it, but I am still leaving. As soon as Mildmay and I can be ready."

It was an exit line, and I took it.

☙

Having been through one unpleasant scene, I decided there was no sense in wasting the aggrieved feeling of martyrdom and set out to find what I fully expected to be another, possibly even more unpleasant.

Astyanax was where he always was at this time of day, holding court in the atrium of the Nephelion, his crowd of sycophants around him. He smiled when he caught sight of me, and it was a good effort, but I had been Lord Shannon Teverius's lover for five years, and it took more than this boy could muster to turn my knees to water.

I made my way to him through his resentful clique and said, "We need to talk."

He caught the seriousness. "Talk? What? Is it—"

"Not here," I said, because I owed him that much. "Come on."

He came, and I was glad of his docility, although I knew it would have bored me senseless if our affair had been protracted. For the first time I thought clearly, It is good to be leaving.

I made for a particular bench in the middle of the formal part of the gardens, where no one could approach us without being observed and where, from the main thoroughfares, we would be merely another pair of red-haired men.

Astyanax sat down beside me, his face worried. "Felix, what is it? What's going on?"

"I thought I should tell you privately," I said, keeping my voice light and unconcerned, as if I did not think this situation was about to explode in my face. "Mildmay and I will be leaving in a couple of days."

"*Leaving?* You mean, for good?"

"We're going home," I said simply, as if every word in that sentence did not carry its own fraught burden along with it.

"Is it . . . is it because of me?"

I bit down hard on the inside of my lower lip and did not laugh. "No, it's nothing to do with you. It's just time for us to leave."

"Is that what I am to you? Nothing?"

"No, not nothing. But this isn't true love, if that's what you were thinking."

I had meant it as a joke, but the deepening crimson of his face and the there-and-gone flash of a snarl told me that that was *exactly* what he had been thinking. And not in regard to his own feelings, either.

I burst out laughing. I knew it was the worst possible reaction, but I could not help it. I wasn't sure I would have been able to keep from laughing even if there had been a knife at my throat.

He shot to his feet and started away, as stiff and bristling as an offended cat.

I choked down my laughter. "Astyanax, wait!"

He stopped and turned. There was a strange mixture of affront and hope on his face, as if he thought I might yet change my mind, declare my true feelings for him. I said, "We don't have to part like this. Our . . . liaison was mutually satisfactory, and—"

"If you dare to say, 'I hope we shall always be friends,' I will hit you," he said, his voice high and trembling. Indignation, not heartbreak: he was wounded in nothing but his vanity.

I raised my eyebrows. "No, frankly, my hope is that we never see each other again—a hope which is growing stronger and more heartfelt with each passing moment. But I would prefer us to part amiably."

"Ha!" he said. I could tell that he was longing for a more stinging retort, but could not find one. He turned on his heel and stomped off. This time I let him go.

When I was sure he was well away, I got up and started for Mildmay's room, to tell him that unless some catastrophe intervened, we would be leaving the Gardens the day after tomorrow.

It was time to go home.

Mildmay

I had to ask how to find Thamuris's room.

We'd be leaving in the morning, and there was some kind of party tonight that Felix said I had to go to. So this was my last chance to talk to Thamuris. And I didn't have nothing to say to Thamuris, but it seemed like the least I could do was go and say nothing to his face.

I stood for a moment outside his door because this was going to be a bitch, no two ways about it. Then I took a deep breath and knocked.

Nothing happened for a while, but about the time I was wondering if I should knock again or try the doorknob or just go the fuck away, Thamuris called, "Come in!"

He was laying in bed, propped up on enough pillows to stock a small hotel. "Mildmay." He didn't sound much of anything, and I just hoped he wasn't pissed off under all that laudanum. After a moment, he went on, "Sit down. I'm sure there's a chair somewhere." One hand twitched in a feeble sort of wave.

There was a chair, right beside the bed. I sat down, said, "Thamuris," and waited until he turned his head. His pupils were down to almost noth-ing. It was like he had a pair of gorgons in his head instead of eyes.

"Me and Felix, we're leaving tomorrow."

"Going back to your blind city?" There still wasn't much of anything in his voice, but he gave me a smile.

"Um. Yeah."

"Good." He let out a breath like he wanted to let out a bunch of other stuff along with it. Like his life. "You weren't happy here."

"No," I said, because there wasn't no point denying it. "I'm just sorry . . . I mean, I know you ain't happy here, either."

"No," he said, "but . . ." And then he lost track of whatever he'd been going to say. Powers and saints, I hate laudanum. But it was better than where he'd be at without it, even so.

We sat for a while, and then he said, "I'm sorry."

"Sorry?"

"For . . . using you. Xanthippe was right. It was abominable of me." His breath shortened up, and I guess there for a moment we were both praying for him not to start coughing.

This time it went on by him, so I could say, "It's okay, really. I let you. I mean . . ." It wasn't like what that fucker Astyanax had done, laying a compulsion on me to make me answer his questions. And I couldn't even care that he'd done it to help cure Felix. All there was for me was how much it'd hurt and how much he'd liked hurting me.

"You trusted me, and you should not have," Thamuris said, with a break in the middle where the cough almost got away from him. I was go-ing to have to go soon, because however much time he had left, I didn't want him to have less of it—or spend more of it coughing—just on account of me. But he caught his breath and said, sounding almost like he had the first time I'd met him, "Do you know why I'm here?"

"Sorry. What?"

"Here. In the Gardens. This isn't my covenant, you know."

"Yeah, I got that. But, I mean, I thought—"

"I am dying of consumption. Yes. But I could do that anywhere."

"Oh." I wasn't sure I should admit that the Arkhon had told me and Felix about him. "I, um—"

"I am here so that I would not do exactly what I did. The celebrants of Hakko decided I was not trustworthy, and I have proved them right."

"Thamuris, it don't—"

"Yes, it does." But he'd worn himself out. His head fell back against the pillows, and there was sweat on his forehead.

"I should go," I said and got up.

"Yes," he said. "But, please . . ."

I looked at him a moment, and then said, carefully, "If you need to know that I forgive you, then, yeah, I do. It's good between us. Right?"

"Yes," he said, in a voice like a half-dead cat. "Good."

"Okay," I said. And there was no wish I could make for him, "be well," or "think of me," or nothing, because all there was ahead of him was him dying, and it would be stupid and mean to say anything pretending otherwise. So I just touched his hand and said, "Good-bye."

"Good-bye, Mildmay," he said.

I turned and limped out of the room without looking back. I kept on not looking back, all the way to my room, and then I shut the door behind me and sat down on the bed, and then I rubbed the water out of my eyes and tried real hard to think about something else. And I don't suppose I need to tell you how well *that* worked.

෫෬

If there'd been any way in this world, Hell, or anywhere else, I could've got out of going to that fucking party, I would've taken it. But Felix wanted me there, and I was finding out real fast that I sucked at saying no to anything Felix wanted. Besides which, Khrysogonos was all over me about would I go, and it would be good for me, and on and on, all that fucking bullshit pretending like he cared.

So I went.

And I hated it.

They had the common decency to leave me alone, which meant I could stand in a corner by myself with my ugly cane in case I fell down or something, and watch all these red-haired people laughing and talking and drinking, and Felix in the middle of it. I could see Khrysogonos somewhere near him, staring at him like—well, let's be honest, Milly-Fox, like you do when you're sure nobody's looking, like he hung the fucking stars. So I was hating Felix for being the way he was, and hating Khrysogonos for being able to look at him like that and not fucking *worry* about it or be afraid that Felix would use it like leverage in a wrestling match, and especially hating everybody else who could look at Felix any damn way they pleased. I was watching for Astyanax—the way sometimes you'll pick at a scab, you know, because you *want* it to hurt—but I didn't see him. Which was probably a good thing because the way I was feeling I would've done something stupid.

So I stood there and kept my face blank and wondered how long I'd have to stay to make Felix happy. Wondered if he'd even notice if I left. Nobody else would, that was for sure.

Then all at once, everybody was getting quiet, and the Arkhon was standing next to Felix, smiling and saying shit about colleagues and friends and blood ties and success and on and on, and Felix was watching her with an expression on his face I couldn't quite make out, and then she took a box out of her coat pocket, a jewelry box, long and narrow, and handed it to him.

He looked like he thought it might bite him, but he opened it. And Kethe, the thing that happened to his face then—I felt sick for a second, just knowing that no matter what I did, I'd never be able to get that look from him, that wonder and happiness and just . . . I don't know.

And he turned to the Arkhon and said, stammering a little which wasn't like him, "I—I can't."

"Of course you can," she said. "We are all in agreement."

And he looked around at all them red-haired people, all of them just grinning like fools, and I ducked sideways a little to be sure I wasn't in his line of sight, although he wasn't looking for me and I knew it. Then he said, "I shouldn't . . . I know I should give them back . . . but I can't!" And he laughed, purely with delight, and I felt even worse.

I edged back to where I could see him, and watched him take rings out of that box, ten rings, one at a time, and slide them on his fingers. They were gold and garnet, each the length of the first-finger joint, sized exactly, and I wondered if they'd taken his measurements when he was crazy or if it was some kind of spell. And when he was wearing them all and tucked the box into his own pocket, he held up his hands so everybody could see, and they laughed and cheered and clapped, and I was glad I had a wall to lean against because otherwise I would have ended up on the floor. Because the rings and the tattoos, and oh Kethe he was a Cabaline and for the first time since I'd known him, he *looked* it. And I realized I could never tell him that I looked at him like that and all I thought of was my friend Zephyr being burned because the Cabalines had decided to believe he was a heretic.

Nobody was going to notice if I left. This little gift-giving was all about him, like everything else here—and what would they have given me anyway, a new knife to replace the one I'd lost when the *Morskaiakrov* went down?—and nobody was watching me. Even if they did notice, I wasn't stupid enough to think even Felix would care.

I slipped out and went back to my room. We'd be leaving tomorrow, and I held on to that thought like grim spooked-out death.

Felix

It was strange to have rings again, strange and wonderful, and these heavy, archaic, beautiful rings were like something out of a fairy tale. I knew I should have refused them, and I had not been able to.

It was not that I did not need new rings, now that I was sane and free and had my power again. My own rings, silver set with moonstones, had most likely been melted down after I was convicted of breaking the Virtu. Even if they hadn't been, I could never wear them again, not after what Malkar had done. And it was not that I did not want these, beautiful thorny serpents that they were. But I knew full well I did not deserve rings like these. Xanthippe had told me they were patterned after the rings of Idomeneos, the Celebrant Celestial who had founded the Gardens unimaginable centuries before, and they did not belong on the hands of a badly trained, heretical prostitute whose greatest magical ability had proved to be as a pawn in betraying everything in which his school of magic believed. Everyone was smiling, though, delighted to have surprised me, to have found something that they were sure I would want, and in the end my desire was stronger than my scruples, as indeed it ever had been. I kept catching myself glancing, faux-casually, at my hands, and being shocked and thrilled all over again at their barbaric splendor.

I felt as if I was standing at the center of a blood-red and gold kaleidoscope; although I'd had only a single glass of wine, I felt dizzy, light-headed, almost effervescent. I lost track of the people I talked to, could no longer tell whose names I knew and whose I didn't. And then, all at once, there was a hand gripping my upper arm, dragging me, not gently, out of the kaleidoscope and into a narrow, dark hallway.

"I want you to see this," Diokletian said.

I freed my arm from his grip. "See what?"

"Your mother."

I was following him reflexively while my brain struggled to make sense of his words. "*What* did you say?"

"Just for once in your life hold your tongue and come with me."

The rawness in his voice silenced me more than the command. I followed him into a part of the Nephelion I had never seen: narrow back corridors, cramped, twisting staircases. It looked more like the Mirador than anything I had seen in Troia, and I was conscious of my pulse accelerating, my mouth going dry.

"Where are we?" I said and hoped Diokletian would believe I had intended the words to come out in a whisper.

"These are the acolytes' quarters," he said. "What? Did you think they slept out on the grass?"

"No, of course not," I said, annoyed to feel my face heating. "I just hadn't . . ."

"Furnished with castoffs, memories, the history that no one wants to speak of. I've often thought it a mercy that the acolytes are too preoccupied with becoming celebrants to stop and look around themselves. Here."

He halted in the middle of a corridor, no different to my eyes from any other, and called witchlight, sending it to illuminate one of the pictures on the wall. "This is your mother, painted the year before you were born."

Whoever the portraitist had been, they had had a gift. The young woman in the portrait, eighteen or nineteen at a guess, seemed so vividly alive that I almost expected her to step out of the frame, or at least to push back the strands of hair falling in her eyes.

She looked almost exactly like me—or, rather, I looked almost exactly like her. Save for my slightly heavier bone structure, save for my one blue eye, I could have been looking at a mirror instead of a picture. My resemblance to Mildmay was close enough to be startling, but this . . . this was uncanny.

"Are you sure I had any father at all?" I murmured. "Are you sure she did not create me entirely from herself?" Cheekbones, nose, that slight sardonic hitch in one eyebrow that said louder than words how little value she placed in having her features recorded for posterity.

"Only the laws of nature stand against your theory," Diokletian said. His voice sounded easier, as if seeing me here, seeing me with the portrait, had purged something that had been festering in him. "And if anyone could find a way around that, it would be she."

"Tell me about her," I said.

He glowered at me. "You talked to Xanthippe, you said. So you already know."

"That in my mother's case, it was not a matter of *sinking* to prostitution?"

"It wasn't like that."

"Then what *was* it like? This is your chance. Tell me who she was. Make me believe she was something better than a whore."

"You have no idea what you're talking about," he said, almost growled.

"No," I said in exasperation. "I don't. That's the problem I'm inviting you to rectify. I'm told she slept with so many men that no one knows who my father is, and yet you say she wasn't a whore. You do see the paradox, don't you?"

His expression was mistrustful, and suddenly I understood. He had been defending Methony for twenty-seven years, defending her to people who would not listen to what he tried to say, who took his words and twisted them—as he undoubtedly felt I had been doing—so that they came around again to *slut, harlot, whore.*

"I was a prostitute," I said, still calm. "I know it isn't the worst thing one can be." No, because I'd found that worst thing for myself. But Diokletian didn't know about that, and he wasn't going to. "Tell me."

He must have wanted to, must have put the words together over and over, in different ways, with different inflections, because this time, when he started to talk, it all came spilling out.

Methony had been the daughter of a Celebrant Major of little power but tremendous organizational skill: Periander of the House Demetrias. Her mother, Theseia, a daughter of the House Leontis, had died when Methony was barely five, leaving Periander to raise his daughter alone.

"He did a bad job of it," Diokletian said. "He couldn't control her."

My eyebrows went up, and he smiled, very slightly. "I know, I know. Certainly it's not the verb I'd want to use with *my* daughters. But it was how he thought, and it was the worst way he could have chosen. She was . . . if I say willful, it gives entirely the wrong impression. She was the most obstinate woman I have ever known. And it was more than that. She would not *let* him control her."

"I think I understand. It seems to be a familial trait."

He could not understand the source of the bitterness in my voice as I remembered the things Malkar had done to make me obey him, how I had fought against him and been defeated. But after a moment's puzzled look, he went on. "Her . . . wantonness was, I think, aimed partly at her father, in defiance of his ideals, his plans for her. But it was also a way—maybe the only way, I have thought since—that she could reach the celebrants as an equal."

"You'll have to say that again."

He grimaced, but now it was only because he could not find the words he wanted. "She had power, but only a tiny amount, even less than her father. And I do not truthfully know whether she was interested in entering a covenant, ours or one of the others. But it drove her mad, to be surrounded by wizards who talked to her as if she were annemer. And so she seduced them. I don't know when she started, or who her first target was, but by the time I came here as a Celebrant Minor, she was already . . ." He stopped, started again. "I don't think the Celebrants Terrestrial knew, or any of the wizards her father's age. But we younger ones . . . she could have any one of us she wanted, with nothing more than a raised eyebrow. Men, women, the Tetrarchs know *she* didn't care. Never the same lover two nights in a row. And so when she announced she was pregnant . . . everyone asked, of course— everyone who *could* have been the father—and she just smiled and said, 'If you needed to know that, I would have told you.' That's what she said to Periander, too."

"I see," I said. I wasn't quite sure how I felt now; it wasn't as if I had any warm, glowing memories of my mother to be trampled into the mud by these revelations. And certainly this story was no worse than what I had believed to be the truth. But it was still strange, unsettling, like looking at myself in a distorting mirror—or perhaps a mirror that did not distort at all.

I glanced at him. He was staring at the portrait with a rueful smile; he seemed almost to have forgotten about me. After a moment, he said, still not looking at me, "How did she die?"

"I don't know exactly," I said. "I was . . . not living with her. But there was a fire."

"A fire."

"Oh, that doesn't even begin to convey it. It was . . ." I made a frustrated gesture with my hands, and then had to laugh at myself. I could taste ashes and smoke again, as I had for weeks when I was eleven. "Almost everyone I knew died. The . . . the place where she worked," the brothel, but we both knew that and I did not need to hurt him by saying it again, "it burned to the ground. No one got out."

"An ugly death," he said softly, flatly.

"Most deaths are. But yes." I remembered Joline, dying of smoke inhalation and burns in the middle of the Rue Orphée while I held her and wept and all around us the city burned and raved, writhing in agonies that were still not enough to kill it. I remembered that for a long time afterward I had wished I had died with Joline.

Diokletian heaved a sigh that seemed as if it came from the bottom of his soul. "We should go back," he said. I wondered if he would lie awake tonight, tormented by images of my mother choking, screaming, the flesh burning off her exquisite bones.

"Yes." I checked the instinctive reach for my pocket watch. "It's getting late."

"Yes," he said, answering many things neither of us had said aloud, and silently started back the way we had come.

🜍

When we returned to the party, I looked for Mildmay and did not find him. I tried to remember the last time I'd seen him and couldn't. It was clear without necessity of experiment that there was no point in asking any of the celebrants. But I caught Khrysogonos and said in his ear, "When did Mildmay leave?"

"He's gone?" Khrysogonos frowned. "I know I saw him just before the Celebrant Lunar started speaking, but I'm not sure . . ."

That was Mildmay; one moment he was there, and the next moment he had simply evaporated. "You know where he'd be likely to go in the gardens. Will you check? I'll look in his room."

"Of course, but . . . is there something wrong? Do you think he—"

"I don't know. It's probably nothing." But I didn't like the fact that he'd left without telling me. It wasn't *unlike* him, exactly, but there was just something . . .

"Nothing," Khrysogonos agreed, smiled at me, and hastened toward the garden door.

I said good night to Xanthippe—remembering to be gracious, charming, serene—and left. I walked through the dark, silent halls of the Nephelion without noticing anything beyond the swiftest route to Mildmay's room. I wanted to find him and assure myself that he was all right. I knew that the most likely explanation was that he'd gotten tired and gone to bed, but some part of me simply refused to believe it. I was a wizard; I had been trained to listen to my instincts, and they said something was wrong.

I let myself through the door of Mildmay's corridor and was instantly aware of raised voices. I recognized Mildmay's deep curt tone without thought, but my relief was tempered by the other voice, shriller, aggressive. Who was that?

Mildmay's door was open. The shriller voice overrode Mildmay's, too quick for my comprehension of spoken Troian, although I could hear the ugliness and anger in every syllable and the words I could catch, I did not like: *murderer* was one, *parasite* another. I stopped in the doorway, staring. Mildmay sat in his favorite armchair by the window, expressionlessly watching Astyanax, who stood in the middle of the room, holding Mildmay's cane as if he intended to use it as a weapon.

Mildmay's eyes flicked past Astyanax to me, and I saw his shoulders relax infinitesimally. Relieved that he was counting me as an ally, I pitched my voice to carry and said, "What, exactly, is going on here?"

Astyanax whipped around, dropping the cane with a clatter. For a long, horrid moment, we stared at each other, and then he looked away, making a show of straightening his cuffs.

Mildmay said, his voice level and uninterested, but I could see the pinscratch frown between his eyebrows, "He thinks it's my fault you're leaving."

I resisted my first impulse, which was to throttle Astyanax on the spot, and merely raised an eyebrow at him.

"He has been poisoning your mind," Astyanax said.

"I *beg* your pardon?"

"He is a liar," Astyanax said, with a depth of unexpected venom; I hadn't thought he'd noticed Mildmay any more than anyone else here ever did.

I looked past him at Mildmay. "Are you?"

He shrugged a little. "Sometimes, I guess."

"He doesn't want to stay here," Astyanax said, his voice sharp and jealous, demanding my attention. "You could be happy here, Felix, you know you could, if you just didn't have *him* to worry about."

I could feel Mildmay's gaze like hot coals. "No."

Astyanax's eyes were eating up his face. "What has he told you about me? What lies has he infected your mind with?"

"Gracious, what rhetoric. Mildmay hasn't said anything about you to me. Should he have?" I looked back at Mildmay. "Anything you want to tell me about Astyanax?"

I said it only to bait Astyanax, but the way the color drained from Mildmay's face, the way that pin-scratch frown deepened for a moment before he smoothed it away completely, indicated that I might have hit on the head a nail I hadn't even known was there.

"Nothing," Mildmay said.

"By the Tetrarchs, you are a hypocrite! You've told him already. I can see it in your face."

Then I should be taking lessons from you, I thought, because all I can see in Mildmay's face is that he really doesn't want to talk about this. "Shut up, Astyanax," I said out loud. "Mildmay, what is he talking about? There's got to be a fire somewhere under all this smoke."

He shook his head; I couldn't tell if he meant that he wouldn't tell me, or that there was nothing to tell, or perhaps something else entirely.

"I can tell you," said a voice from the door.

We all three jerked around.

"*You*," Astyanax said, with loathing.

It was Khrysogonos; not finding Mildmay in the gardens, he must have come here to check with me. He ignored Astyanax, looking from me to Mildmay with his eyebrows raised.

"Go ahead," I said; Mildmay sank back in his chair as if at news of some terrible defeat or betrayal.

Khrysogonos sighed a little, as if he didn't want to say any of this, either, and then said, "Astyanax laid a compulsion on your brother to gain information to help with your cure."

And here I had thought Mildmay vanished whenever Astyanax was around because he was repulsed by my sexual preferences. I could feel something inside myself freezing, hardening, could feel darkness rising like a tide. "I see," I said, my voice remote and uninvolved. "Is this true?"

Astyanax said, "Felix, you can't—"

"I wasn't asking you. Mildmay? Is this true?"

Mildmay's face was ashen, but he nodded, a tiny jerk of his head.

"Thank you. Would you excuse us just one moment?" I grabbed Astyanax by the arm and dragged him out into the corridor, kicking the door shut as we passed. I slammed him up against the wall, watched with satisfaction as his eyes widened in a mixture of surprise, pain, and fear. I waited until I was quite sure his entire attention was focused on me, and then said in a pleasant, conversational voice, "Where I come from, you would be burned at the stake for doing something like that."

He wanted to justify himself, to explain, to excuse; I saw it in his face, just as I saw his resolve crumbling away when he met my eyes. When the silence had held long enough that I knew he was not going to speak, I said, "Fortunately for you, it isn't heresy here. And fortunately for you, we're leaving tomorrow morning. Because if you *ever* came near him again, I wouldn't bother with the stake."

His face worked, crumpled. "It was for you!"

"You think that makes a difference?" I released my hold on him, stepped back. "Go on. Clear out."

He stared at me for a moment, vanity and rage and wounded, throbbing, screaming self-love contorting his face. Then he said, feigning disdain, "I hope for your sake he's as good in bed as I am."

I let myself smile, sharp, wicked. "Darling, that wouldn't be hard."

He was frozen for a moment, not believing I could say such a thing, then turned and bolted, the thump of his running feet, the slam of the corridor door, like the curse he hadn't spoken. I let him go. He would find one of his clique, and they would tell him lies until it sounded like truth again.

I leaned against the wall for a moment, staring at nothing, trying to rein my temper in, trying above all not to admit how much of myself I had seen and recognized in Astyanax's eyes. Then, because I could do nothing else, I opened the door to Mildmay's room and went back in.

Khrysogonos and Mildmay had clearly been frozen in silence, like an unlikely pair of waxworks; Khrysogonos said gratefully, "I'll just be going then," and whisked away.

I shut the door and turned to look at Mildmay. He was still sitting, unmoving, staring out the window at the night. I wondered if he was really seeing anything, or if it was just an excuse to avoid looking at me.

"Why didn't you say anything?"

His reply was unintelligible.

"What?"

He raised his voice, spoke slower, but did not turn his head. "I said I didn't think you'd care. If you believed me."

"You didn't think I'd *care*? What kind of monster do you think I am?"

"Not like that. Just . . . you seemed happy, and there wasn't no harm done—"

"The fuck there wasn't."

His head turned then, an unguarded jerk. I had to shut my eyes for a moment, swallow hard. We'd both heard Simside in my voice, and although I could pretend I'd done it on purpose, done it to make him look at me, it would be a lie. It had just happened, and that told me how precariously we were balanced. Mildmay did not deserve my rage, my darkness, the lust for pain surging in my blood. I opened my eyes again, said slowly, distinctly, every consonant and vowel a separate brick placed in the wall between me and the thing I had been, "He hurt you. I don't know of a single compulsion spell that doesn't hurt more than all the beatings in the world. I don't agree with the Mirador on everything, but there is a reason those spells were pronounced anathema. You should have *said*."

"It ain't heresy here. It wouldn't've—"

"If I'd known he'd done that to you, I would never have slept with him."

I hadn't intended to mention that, hadn't intended to bring sex into this discussion at all. My nerves still raw from the confrontation with Astyanax, I was burningly aware of Mildmay's beauty, his bones, his grace, the walls and shadows in his eyes. Burningly aware that he was my brother and, more than that, he did not want me.

"Oh," Mildmay said, a beat too late to pretend it didn't bother him.

"I told Astyanax that if he came near you again, I would kill him, and I meant it."

He looked away, down at his scarred, lumpy-knuckled hands.

"Mildmay."

He raised his head reluctantly, but his green eyes met mine steadily. And the words died on my tongue, the easy glib words to charm and manipulate, to make him give without giving anything of myself in return. I knew, all at once, what he'd meant when he said he didn't want my gratitude, knew what it was he wanted instead, but could never ask for.

I said, "I do care."

He blushed brilliant scarlet, and I knew I was right. He might not desire me, but that did not mean he did not love me in his own way, although the realization made me as uncomfortable as it clearly made him. After a moment, he managed to mumble, "Thanks."

It was late; we were both tired, and it was a miracle I'd made it this far without yelling at him. Or kissing him. I shoved that thought away. "Do you need . . . anything? Your cane?"

"Nah. I'm good." He stood up, limped across to the bed. "I ain't taking that thing tomorrow."

"You aren't? Are you sure?"

"Don't need it," he said, starting to undo his shirt buttons, and if I didn't get out of the room soon, I was going to do something unforgivable. "Hate it."

"It's your leg." I was already halfway to the door. I wasn't sure he was making the right decision, but staying to argue tonight would not help anything. We could buy him a cane in Kekropia if we had to—and I didn't like that cane either. "Good night," I said, and barely waited for his answering " 'Night," before I fled.

Chapter 3

Felix

The nearest port was a little town called Endumion. We rode there with one of the Gardens' cooks, who was on his way to buy fresh fish.

Only Xanthippe had seen us off, very formal and gracious, with no opportunities for any unfortunate displays of personality. She had unexpectedly presented me with another gift, enough money (she said) to buy our passage to Kekropia and, if we were thrifty, engage a hotel room for a day or two until we could make unspecified "other arrangements."

I tried to refuse, but she would have none of it, and I would have admitted, if asked, that I did not try very hard. Neither Mildmay nor I had been particularly sanguine about what we might end up doing if we had to work our passage, and it was a tremendous relief to have that weight lifted from my shoulders.

So now we stood on the docks of Endumion and surveyed our options. They were two: the *Penelope* and the *Asprophellos*, or the *White Otter*. Mildmay and I agreed with a glance that we did not want to buy passage on the *Penelope* if we could help it. Penelope was a name of ill omen in Mélusine, and the ship herself looked unclean, ill cared for.

The *White Otter* appeared more promising. Mildmay called out a greeting, a slangy-sounding phrase of Troian he must have picked up on the *Morskaiakrov*. In response, a woman appeared at the top of the gangplank. She wore trousers and a halter top, and her red hair hung down her back in a multitude of narrow braids. She and Mildmay plunged into an elliptical, intricate exchange, out of which I understood maybe one word in five. I stood and tried to look pleasantly nonthreatening, marveling inwardly at Mildmay's effortless grasp of gutter Troian. I was phenomenally stupid at languages and knew it, but I had somehow never expected my pathologically taciturn brother to be so comfortable in *any* language, much less a foreign one.

He turned to me and said in Marathine, "She wants to know if you're a hocus. And she's looking at your hands."

I looked at them myself, the garish tattoos, the gaudy rings. "Tell her the truth. It's not something I had any hope or intention of hiding."

"You'll be singing a different song once we get to Kekropia," he said. He and the sailor woman exchanged another burst of Troian.

There was an intermission as she vanished to fetch someone—"the captain," Mildmay told me—and then an even more vigorous exchange between Mildmay and the captain, a weather-beaten man of about Diokletian's age.

When he turned back to me, Mildmay said, "They're going to Klepsydra, and they got room for two more passengers."

Even for Mildmay, he looked notably less than thrilled. I said, "I can feel the 'but' coming. What is it?"

"They got whatchamacallit—things they want."

"Conditions?"

"Yeah. Them."

"Well?"

"Half the money up front."

"That's reasonable."

"We sleep in separate cabins."

"Lest we plot a coup? How cautious of them. But if they *have* separate cabins, I don't object."

I could see him bracing himself. "You give your rings to the captain 'til we dock in Klepsydra and at the first sign of witchery they'll throw you overboard."

I swallowed the first several replies that came to mind.

"They seem honest," he said, watching my face sidelong. "The gal said as how the *Penelope*'d take us if you were a fire-breathing dragon, but she wouldn't lay odds on us reaching Kekropia alive. 'Sides, *Penelope*'s heading for Aigisthos. Which we don't want."

"We don't?" I rather thought we would survive a journey in the *Penelope*, regardless of her crew's intentions.

"No. Gideon said—" He caught himself sharply, as if he was afraid that mention of the mysterious Gideon would offend or wound me.

"Go on," I said. "What did *Gideon* say?"

"There's Eusebians in Aigisthos. At the court. They'd recognize the tattoos."

"I wasn't planning on seeking an audience with the emperor."

"We can't risk it. And it ain't the way we want to go."

It took a moment for me to decipher that. "You want to go *south*? Are you mad or just suicidally stupid? We won't survive a week in the duchies!"

"We did fine on the way out," he said, and I hated the mulish set to his chin.

"This is neither the time nor the place to argue about it," I said through my teeth. "And I am *not* giving up my rings."

"It's not like they can steal 'em. Nowhere to fence 'em in the middle of the ocean."

I couldn't choke back a bark of laughter at this relentlessly pragmatic view of the problem. But still, "Do you understand what they're asking?"

He met my eyes. "Some guarantee that you won't hex them all into being your slaves."

"I would *never*—!"

"No, 'course not. But it's the kind of thing gets said about hocuses." He eyed me a moment. "They ain't being unreasonable, Felix."

"*Aren't*," I said like a curse.

He made no response, simply stood and waited, as patient as stone. As opaque as stone, too: I couldn't tell if he was *expecting* me to give in, or what he would do if I did not. I looked back at the *Penelope* and could not entirely repress a shiver at how low she rode in the water, how unsavory she looked. I thought about the weeks—four at least, Mildmay said and Xanthippe confirmed—we would be at sea. I thought about spending those weeks on a vessel that looked untrustworthy in the bright sunshine and innocuous surroundings of the Endumion docks. I did not remember the sinking of the

Morskaiakrov as anything more than a few flashes of pain and fear, but I knew that to avoid that nightmare, that death, was worth even the price the *White Otter* demanded.

"We will talk about crossing Kekropia later," I said, trying not to snarl, and waved Mildmay ahead of me up the plank.

At the top, the captain stood waiting. He was more than a little alarming at close range; his eyes, marked by crow's-feet, were a strange, dark, smoky yellow, and the grim lines of his face suggested that he was no happier about having me on board than I was about being there.

"Rings," he said, his voice as dark and smoky as his eyes, and held out his hand.

I would not let him rush me. I set down my valise, opened it, and found the case that went with the rings. I took them off one by one, setting each in its precisely fitted velvet hollow. I closed the case and cast a small locking spell on it—nothing that would even inconvenience a wizard, but it would keep the annemer out—my words deliberately audible and clear. Then I handed the case to the captain, with a glare to match his own.

He put the case in his coat pocket and said, dour but not hostile, "Welcome aboard. I am Elektros Yarth."

"Felix Harrowgate," I said. "And my brother Mildmay . . . Mildmay Foxe." Mildmay had told me of his soubriquet, Mildmay the Fox, which suited him so well it had proved useless for me even to attempt to disassociate my brother from the animal. It made an unexceptionable Marathine surname, a marker of respectability that I had a lowering presentiment we were going to need.

"The money?" said Elektros Yarth, disdaining to waste time on social niceties. I left him and Mildmay to their haggling and made my way to the far side of the boat to look at the sea. There was no sense in hiding from it, and I hoped that if I faced it now, perhaps my fear would not be so great, perhaps I would not become paralyzed by the sea as I had been paralyzed by the Sim as a child.

But a moment later, I had turned away, my heart pounding and my mouth gone dry, my body suddenly clammy with sweat. It was . . . it was too much, that was all. Any attempt to stare down the Kelephanian Ocean was only going to result in an extremely public display of hysterics. I felt naked without my rings, and cold.

I did not know how long I stood there, staring desperately at the ship's rigging, tracing the ropes in their struggle for the sky, before Mildmay said, "You okay?" He was standing to my left, careful—as he was always careful—not to come up on my bad side. How exactly he had learned my blue eye was close to blind, I did not know; doubtless it was one of the many things I had betrayed of myself in my madness. He never mentioned it, never seemed to notice. Except that he always, *always*, approached me from the left.

I turned my head, as slow and stiff as a rusted clockwork gear. "Fine," I said.

"You look like shit."

"Thank you. I am fine. What word from our worthy captain?"

His eyes met mine a moment longer, absinthe-green and cold as jade; then he let it go and said, "Ship sails tomorrow at the septad-day. Captain says we can sleep on board tonight. I said yes."

"Did you now?"

He gave a half shrug, barely enough to acknowledge the venom in my tone. "Money's tight." His eyes met mine again, and he said, "I ain't going back to the Gardens."

He meant it. I would have had to use magic on him to move him off the ship. "Am not," I said, "not ain't."

He continued to stare at me, levelly, not angry or upset, simply waiting for me either to capitulate or issue an ultimatum of my own.

"All right," I said. "Fine." Think of it as practice, I said to myself. I couldn't deny I was going to need it.

Mildmay

I could tell Felix was scared half out of his mind, but he seemed like he'd sooner kill himself than admit it, and I figured it'd be better all around if I just kept my mouth shut. 'Cause, I mean, there wasn't nothing we could do about it. If we wanted to get back to Mélusine—which we both did—we had to get on the other side of all this water somehow.

So I just said, like I couldn't see his face was the color of bone or nothing, "Captain says come meet the others."

"A delightful treat, to be sure," he said, mostly under his breath, and walked with me down to where the captain was standing with the rest of the passengers.

There were five of them. A middle-aged Kekropian couple and their kid, who was a couple indictions short of finishing his second septad. Another kid, a Troian, somewhere in the middle of his third septad, with a look on his face like he'd been born biting into a lemon. And another guy, a couple years older than Felix, Norvenan—you could tell by the blond— tall and heavyset. He had sharp blue eyes and big, soft, ink-stained hands, so I wasn't surprised when he got introduced as the secretary of the middle-aged guy with the kid.

The middle-aged guy was named Leontes Gauthy. He was a merchant of some kind, trading between Troia and Kekropia, which looked like it was a pretty good gig from the way him and his wife and the kid were dressed—and from the fact that apparently most of the *White Otter*'s cargo belonged to him. The wife's name was Theokrita, and the kid was Florian. The secretary was named Ingvard Vilker, and he stood there with a super-polite look on his face while Mr. Gauthy was pronouncing it. Kekropian don't got the "v" and it was mostly coming out "w."

The Troian kid said his name was Phaëthon, and then he shut his mouth and looked even more lemony. I'd've laid odds he was running away from something, but it wasn't none of my business, and I figured anything I said to him, he'd just look all lemony at me, and I didn't need the grief.

The captain divvied up the cabins, glaring at me and Felix like he thought we were going to make a scene. Felix caught it and stood there looking as sweet and harmless and innocent as a kitten. The *White Otter* had three passenger cabins, one largish and two smallish. The largish one was going to the Gauthys, and the captain put me and the Troian kid in one of the littler ones and Felix and Mr. Vilker in the other. The kid gave me a look like he could smell the dirt from where he was standing, but he swallowed whatever complaint he would've made. Felix and Mr. Vilker shook hands, and there was a kind of twinkle in Mr. Vilker's eyes that said he'd picked up on the joke, even if he didn't know what it was about Felix that had the captain's drawers in a knot. I breathed a little easier seeing that, because it meant maybe him and Felix wouldn't kill each other somewhere out in the middle of the ocean.

And right about then, I was figuring that was the best I could hope for.

𝟛𝕽

I'd been worried about what might happen with a whole day to wait before we left. I kept having these like, I don't know, nightmares or something— except for being wide-awake—of the celebrants all showing up on the dock and convincing Felix he really wanted to stay at the Gardens after all. Or, what was more likely, Felix having too long to think about all that damn water and running back to the Gardens like a dog on the losing end of a nasty fight. And if that happened, I was fucked. So you can understand me being a little nervous, but Ingvard Vilker turned out to be the answer to my prayers. Him and Felix hadn't been talking but a couple minutes before they got on to the subject of Troian history, and a septad-minute after that Mr. Vilker had whipped out this book that was all dog-eared and scuffed and looked like it'd maybe fallen in the ocean a time or two, and it turned out to be a guidebook to Troia to tell you what all the places were you were supposed to see because something important had happened there or somebody important had been born there or died there or what have you. They had 'em for Mélusine, but the way I heard it, no two books ever agreed on what the important things were. And if they did, they'd have two completely different stories about why you were supposed to give a rat's ass. Which I wasn't going to. Not about anything in Troia.

But Felix and Mr. Vilker, they put their heads together and figured out there was some kind of ruined temple or something about an hour from Endumion. And then Mr. Vilker turned and did some smooth talking at Mr. Gauthy and convinced him it was educational, and so him and Felix should take Florian Gauthy to see it, and Mr. Gauthy should pay for the hired horses. Mrs. Gauthy was standing there giving Mr. Vilker the hairy eyeball, but Mr. Gauthy didn't notice her, and anyway Florian Gauthy looked like he was about to die of joy on the spot, so off they went.

They were at the top of the gangplank when Felix turned back and asked me, "Do you want to come?"

"Nope."

He raised his eyebrows, grinning a little. I didn't want to get into how I felt about Troia, so I said, "Don't need to see old rocks, thanks. Got those at home."

"Barbarian," he said cheerfully, and not mean at all, and followed Mr. Vilker and the kid back onto dry land. And I had to admire him. I mean, I knew how he felt about deep water, and I was watching him pretty close, and I still couldn't hardly tell how much of a relief it was to him to have solid ground under his feet.

Mr. Gauthy'd already gone off to do some more trading, being the kind of guy who breathed, slept, and ate his business. And the captain'd cleared out as soon as he'd done what he was obliged to and given our names to the

other passengers. So that left me and Mrs. Gauthy and the Troian kid standing there giving each other nasty looks.

It took me a second to see the funny side of it, which I did at the same
time I realized I didn't want to talk to either of them anyway, so I didn't
need to stand here until they'd thought up a really good insult to be sure I
didn't.

"See y'all 'round," I said and went back to where I'd found Felix all
spooked out earlier. I hadn't been meaning to do much but look at the water for a while and see if it could clear out some of the pricker-bushes I was
feeling about this whole damn thing—the day and the ship and the journey
and what we were going to have to deal with once we made it to Kekropia
and all the fucking rest of it. But there were a couple of sailors there, a guy
about my age and a gal a little older, doing something with the ropes—
which, from the two decades I'd spent on the *Morskaiakrov* I knew was
pretty much a given—and after a little while I couldn't stand it no more and
said, "Hey, can I ask y'all a question?"

The look they gave me said they'd been told not to sass the passengers,
but that was all the slack I got.

You can't back down now, Milly-Fox. Cough it up. "I been wanting
news about a ship called *Morskaiakrov*. Y'all know anything?"

The look they were giving me now was like I'd smacked 'em upside the
head with a dead flounder apiece. After a moment, the gal got her shit together and said, "You ask after the *Morskaiakrov*?"

"Yeah."

"You know Dmitri?"

"A little. Look, I just want to know if everybody got off okay."

The captain said behind me, "The crew of the *Morskaiakrov* came safe
to land near Ikaros. They lost one man, I think, but the rest suffered no
more than the broken limbs and coughs and chills that are to be expected.
And, of course, it will be many years before Dmitri will be able to afford
another ship."

I turned around careful, 'cause he wasn't sneaking up on me to kill me
and I didn't want to do nothing embarrassing before we'd even left the
dock. So I looked up at Captain Yarth and said, "Who died?"

He said, "I believe the name was Piotr."

"Oh." Not Ilia, then, or Vasili or Dmitri or even Yevgeni who'd been an
asshole but who I'd kind of liked for it. No, just Piotr, who'd been quiet
and kept to himself and told a story I'd never heard before, about a witch

named Lisaveta and why the combs she wore in her hair were made of human bone. Shit.

"Thanks," I said to the captain and "thanks" kind of more generally to the sailors, who were still staring at me like I'd fallen out of the sky and set the ship on fire. And then, 'cause I needed all at once to get away from people who were alive and hadn't died in that storm—or almost died, and I wasn't kidding myself about how close I'd come—I went back down to the main part of the ship and kept going, down the gangplank, back along the dock, and into the nearest alleyway, just to get out of sight of the *White Otter*. And then I leaned against the wall and stared at the bricks of the wall opposite for a while.

Piotr was dead. Well, I could add him to the list. Zephyr and Ginevra and Margot's little Badgers and Griselda Kilkenny and Lucastus the Weaver and Bartimus Cawley and Cornell Teverius and Cerberus Cresset . . . And Thamuris, because he'd probably be dead before we reached Klepsydra. And—fuck, there was no sense telling myself fairy tales—Gideon and Mavortian and Bernard. All those dead people and what the fuck was I doing still alive?

I didn't have an answer, and no matter how long I stared at them, the bricks couldn't give me one.

Felix

Ingvard hired a buggy and pair, and we rattled out of Endumion in fine style. I sat beside Ingvard, and the boy took the rumble seat, leaning eagerly over our shoulders to ask question after question. It was a beautiful day, bright and clear. The Troian countryside was ripe with summer, and peaceful; the bad blood between the local houses of Attalis and Erekhthais, which I had heard about at exhaustive length from half the celebrants in the Gardens, had not extended its reach into the lives of the farmers and shepherds whom we spotted from time to time. Florian asked questions about crops and wool—a merchant's son to be sure, but one with a good head on his shoulders. Ingvard answered those questions easily; clearly he had his employer's business at his fingertips. I sat and looked at the bountiful drowsiness and felt myself expanding with delight. It was as if some dark weight had been lifted from my shoulders, leaden shackles struck off my wrists. We were halfway to Huakinthe before I put my finger on why, and then I wished I hadn't.

For an afternoon, I was free of Mildmay. Ingvard and Florian were cheerful, normal people, who did not know I had been mad, who had not been lamed and nearly killed on my account, who did not represent, simply by the way they talked, everything about my childhood I most desperately wished to forget. They were not silent, opaque, resentful, unhappy. They did not suffer from wounds I did not know how to heal. They did not set a fire raging in my blood that I could not acknowledge, much less surrender to. And I was so glad to be away from him, away from those cold absinthe eyes, that scarred stone face, that I felt like singing.

"Ker Harrowgate? Are you all right?" Ingvard Vilker's voice jerked me out of my reverie.

"Fine, thanks." I smiled at him. "And, please, call me Felix."

"Ingvard," he said in return, stressing the "v" with a quick mock-glare over his shoulder at Florian. "Not 'Ingward.'"

"I don't say it like that!" Florian protested.

"Not anymore."

"You can't blame me for being stupid when I was six. Besides, Father still says it wrong, and you don't nag *him* about it."

"That, dear boy, is because he pays me."

"Are you Norvenan by birth, or were you born in the empire?" I asked.

"Born and bred in Karolinsberg," Ingvard said. "I came south when I reached my majority to seek my fortune. And found it, I think."

"As my father's secretary?" Florian demanded.

"A fortune is what you make of it," Ingvard said. "Here, Florian. Read to us about Huakinthe."

"But—"

"I promised your father this would be educational."

"Oh, all right," Florian said, not nearly as sulkily as he might have.

He read well for a boy his age, stumbling occasionally over unfamiliar words, but managing the sense of the passage as well as the sounds. Huakinthe, he told us, was a ruin from Troia's imperial past. It had been a major port in the trade between the empire and its daughter-colony. With the fall of the empire, Huakinthe itself had been abandoned, and when trade between Troia and Kekropia was reestablished, the more northerly port of Erigone had taken Huakinthe's place.

Florian broke off and said, "Why'd they abandon the city?"

"No trade means no jobs," Ingvard said.

"Oh. But . . ."

"The fall of the Troian empire was . . . ugly," I said, having to pause a moment to find an accurate but decorously inexpressive word. "The city itself may have developed unpleasant associations or a reputation for bad luck."

"Oh," Florian said again, and I caught a glance of lively interest from Ingvard.

"I didn't know you were so interested in Troian history. He should talk to Ker Tantony, shouldn't he, Florian?"

"Ker Tantony?" I said.

"Florian's tutor. Jeremias Tantony. He's quite the amateur historian."

"Oh, Ker Tantony's all right," Florian said. "Ker Harrowgate, what did you mean, the fall of the empire was ugly?"

"Civil war is always ugly," I said. "If your tutor's a historian, he must have taught you that much. Towns were burned, innocent people killed. There were two years of famine and an outbreak of some sort of plague. I understand that the Euryganeics called it the end of the world. They might not have been far wrong."

There was an uncomfortable silence, and I realized I had let my fragmentary, nightmarish memories of Nera, another city lost in another empire's fall, color my tone too vividly. I was about to apologize when Ingvard said, mock-sternly, "Florian, you aren't done reading."

"Oh! Right." And Florian continued reading, tripping over his words at first, but gradually regaining his equilibrium.

The sights of interest in Huakinthe included the city wall, the palace of the Anthemais, the family who had ruled the city, and a temple. "It says it's the oldest known temple of . . . I don't know this goddess's name."

"Let me see," I said, and Florian handed the book forward. I found the place at which he had stopped. ". . . the goddess Graia, an ancient and primitive goddess whose worship died out in most of Troia nearly five thousand years ago. Cities such as Huakinthe and Prokne, which felt themselves to be under her especial protection, continued to honor her, although the public rites had become solely symbolic by the time the city was abandoned."

"What sort of rites do you suppose they're talking about?" Ingvard said.

"Fertility, most likely," I said without thinking.

Florian said, puzzled, "But how can you have nonsymbolic . . . oh. Oh, *disgusting.*"

Ingvard and I burst out laughing, and Ingvard turned the conversation to other matters until we reached Huakinthe. I had been skeptical of the guidebook's claim that the city wall of Huakinthe would be of interest. As a child in Simside, I had had my world bounded by the city wall of Mélusine to the south, just as it was bounded by the Sim to the west. During my tenure at the Mirador, I had frequently climbed to the highest ring of battlements, the Crown of Nails, and looked at the city, and from that vantage point I had come to have a more rational—though no less awed—understanding of the city walls. They were a mere seven hundred years old, but their height and mathematically exact lines and the beauty of the way the six gates and the river were accommodated . . . I understood entirely the Ophidian king who had decreed that the boundary marked by those walls should be honored in perpetuity and that anyone caught damaging the walls would be found guilty of treason to the city of Mélusine—making it a crime in a class by itself. Despite the changes of dynasty and government in the intervening centuries, no one had ever rescinded or repudiated that particular law. Her walls were Mélusine's pride.

I expected to be entirely unimpressed by Huakinthe's walls, and indeed it was true that they did not even compare to Mélusine's. But then, Mélusine's walls did not compare to Huakinthe's, either.

There were only two isolated stretches of Huakinthe's walls still standing, one maybe twenty-five feet long and the other twice that, out in the middle of the pastureland like two monumental foreigners who had gotten lost on their way to the sea. Ingvard hobbled the horses, and he and Florian and I walked to the nearer and shorter of the two stretches of wall. The cows watched us go by with placid disinterest.

It was clear that the city wall had once been higher than these remnants, impossible to tell by how much. But the ragged progress of the top of the wall showed where stones had been taken away, or had fallen. It was still twenty feet tall at its highest point, a looming sadness. The most remarkable thing, though, was the size of the individual blocks. Ingvard made Florian lie down beside the wall because not one of the three of us could believe the evidence of our own eyes that the stones were longer than he was tall.

He scrambled up again, already asking, "How did they move the stones? Do you think they used magic?"

"Probably," Ingvard said as I hastily pretended to be too interested in the ferns growing from the cracks between the stones to have heard the question. I didn't know if Captain Yarth had told the other passengers I was a wizard, and I wasn't sure how they'd feel about it if they knew. I realized I'd been extraordinarily lucky thus far that Florian's roving curiosity had not prompted him to ask about my tattoos. Of course, by the same token, no one had recognized the tattoos for what they were—markers of my status as a sworn Cabaline, an enemy of the Bastion and the Empire—and I went cold as I realized that I was going to have to come up with some explanation for why I was neither Eusebian nor covenanted. I couldn't expect the captain and his crew to keep the matter a secret—at least, not without explaining to them *why* I wanted it kept secret, and no matter how stupidly blind I'd been, I wasn't stupid enough to think that that particular explanation wouldn't make everything several times worse.

I knelt down to hide my face as the answer occurred to me, because the grimace would certainly have alarmed Florian and Ingvard if they had seen it. Malkar had solved this problem for me almost fifteen years ago, when he invented a tale to confound the Mirador's curiosity. No one on the *White Otter* would know anything more about Caloxan wizards than I did. I bit the inside of my lower lip savagely to keep from erupting in hysterical giggles and stood up again. Ingvard and Florian had moved a little way farther along the wall and were arguing about how heavy the stones might be. I joined them, and presently suggested that we continue on to the palace of the Anthemais. They concurred amiably, and we returned to the buggy.

Ingvard's guidebook provided directions for finding the palace, which proved to be fortunate as the ruins were not visible from the road. The palace was nothing more than paving stones. I left Ingvard and Florian in earnest speculation about its original dimensions and layout, and made my way toward the stumps of columns like half-rotted teeth that marked the temple.

As the other ruins had been, this, too, was silent and deserted, just the double row of eroded columns and the moss-grown paving stones in between. And, I discovered by painful experience, a thriving population of briar bushes. I disentangled myself from them at the cost of several raking scratches on my hands and wrists, and found myself standing in what was nearly the geometric center of the colonnade.

My heartbeat pounded in my ears; the air was heavy with smoke, with the stench of blood. Blackness, the lurid light of fire, voices screaming, sobbing, cursing.

The temple is Nera.

Before the thought was even clear in my head, I had bolted back out of the ruins, acquiring several more scratches and a torn trouser leg. And then I stood, my chest heaving like a bellows and my whole body damp and prickling with sweat, and thought, The temple is *Nera*? What in the world is *that* supposed to mean?

But there was no explanation, the panic gone as suddenly as it had come, taking the hallucinations with it—if "hallucinations" was the correct word. I had gathered from what Mildmay had said that there wasn't even as much left of Nera as there was of Huakinthe, so surely I could not have been *reminded* of Nera. But I could think of no theory that was not even less plausible.

Somehow, I was certain that the goddess worshipped here had not been interested in fertility.

I saw Ingvard and Florian approaching and called out to warn them of the briars before I started slowly and abstractedly back toward the buggy. The shadows were lengthening; we would need to leave soon, and besides, I did not want to be anywhere near the temple of Graia as it welcomed in the night.

Mildmay

Felix was in a mood by the time he got back to the *White Otter*. Florian Gauthy and Mr. Vilker were giving him these weird looks, like they couldn't tell if it was their fault or not, but he didn't even seem to notice. I kept my mouth shut and went to bed early.

Only, of course, that didn't get me out of trouble, because the Troian kid was already in the cabin we were sharing, and he looked mightily put out to see me.

I got as much right to be here as him, I told myself and said, "You okay with the top bunk?"

"I *beg* your pardon?"

"You planning on keeping that stick up your ass all the way to Klepsydra?"

He went first white, then bright, blotchy red. Powers, Milly-Fox, why did anybody bother with teaching you to talk? "I'm sorry," I said. "I shouldn't've said that."

Phaëthon had turned away, and for a minute I thought I wasn't going to get no answer at all and wasn't *that* going to be a fun way to spend a month? Then he said, without turning around, "I will take the top bunk."

"Thanks." I sat down on the lower bunk and couldn't quite keep back a sigh of relief at getting my weight off my leg. But it was okay. I mean, it was sore, but nothing out of the ordinary. You're gonna be okay, I said to myself and almost believed it.

The kid didn't say nothing and I didn't say nothing, and after a while he climbed up to the top bunk, still wearing his shirt and trousers. Well, I'd pegged him for a flash kid, and if he was that kind of prude, I was probably right.

The lamp was up at his level, wired to the wall in this sort of cage arrangement. After he'd been up there a little while, he said, "Are you . . . I should like to go to sleep now."

"Sure. I can take my shoes off in the dark just fine." There was stuff for my leg, stuff to keep the scarring from binding in like creepers smothering a tree, but I could do that some other time, sometime when I could get the cabin to myself for a septad-minute.

"Oh. Oh, yes, of course." And out went the light.

He didn't so much as move a muscle while I was unlacing my shoes and taking my trousers off—I mean, just because he was a prude didn't mean I had to be uncomfortable. I lay down. The bunk was narrow and hard, but at least it wasn't too short for me the way it would be for Felix. And better this than that nice soft bed in the Gardens, regardless.

And then Phaëthon said, "Mildmay?"

"Yeah?"

"Nothing. I was just . . . it's an odd name."

And Phaëthon ain't? I thought, but the kid hadn't meant anything nasty by it. It was even sort of, in a funny way, an apology, like Felix's apologies that weren't, and I figured whatever this kid's story was, he'd probably been having one fuck of a bad day, if not a whole bad decad. So I said, "Yeah. My mother had some weird ideas."

"Oh. Well, good night then, Mildmay."

"G'night," I said back, and if the kid said anything else, I was asleep before I heard it.

🙰

I dreamed about fucking.

Keeper first, the woman who'd raised me from my third indiction and started fucking me before I'd quite finished my second septad, and you'd think after three indictions, some of it would start to fade, but everything was clear and sharp, like it had only been this morning that I'd gotten up out of that bed for the last time. Her long white body, her little tits and narrow hips. Once when I'd had two septads and two, she'd waited until I was all the way inside her, then locked her legs around the backs of my thighs and said, "Imagine I'm a boy. Imagine you're fucking a *boy*, Milly-Fox," and then laughed when I tried to pull back and couldn't. Whenever I couldn't get hard, she'd tell me I was going molly, that pretty soon there wouldn't be nothing left for her to do but send me to one of the boy brothels in Pharaohlight. I never quite believed her—I mean, no madam in their right mind would take me, for one thing—but I knew she could do it if she wanted. I knew Keeper could do anything.

Keeper liked a lot of light when she fucked, so there were candles everywhere. I didn't dare close my eyes, even though I didn't want to look at her, because she was watching my face and I had to keep my guard up. She didn't like me to kiss her, because of the scar, and she wouldn't let me hide my face in her shoulder. "I want to *see*, Milly-Fox," she'd said once, yanking my head back by the hair hard enough to make my eyes water. So I had to keep my face from giving anything away, giving her anything she could use.

Her long fingernails were digging into my shoulders. Sometimes she left welts, and if the other kids saw them, they didn't say nothing. Her thighs were like a vise against my hips, and she was hot and tight, and I knew she'd be pissed if I came too soon. If you were one of Keeper's kids, you learned to do things her way, and that didn't change just because she decided to fuck you.

"Talk to me, Milly-Fox," she said, one hand tracing up the back of my neck and grabbing my hair.

"What?"

"Talk to me. Tell me how it feels."

"You know I don't—"

The hand in my hair tugged hard, just once, and then slid around to my face, running along the scar where I couldn't really feel it.

"You used to be such a chatterbox. I miss it. So talk to me."

"Keeper, please . . ."

"Mildmay." She almost never used my real name, and it was always a bad sign when she did. She was watching my face now, greedy like a kid at a pantomime. I wanted this to stop. I wanted not to be touching her, not to be fucking her, not to be trapped in this thing with her like a fly in a spiderweb. But, you know, my hips were still moving, and my cock didn't care about my pride.

"I'm waiting," said Keeper.

I said, hoping she'd think I was gasping because of the sex, "Hot . . . smooth . . . tight . . ."

"You can do better than that, darling." And she sounded so cool and amused, like she didn't even care about what we were doing.

I shut my eyes, because it didn't matter now anyway. And somewhere in my head, I was shouting at myself, This is a dream! You don't have to do this, you stupid fuck! You're dreaming, and it don't have to be Keeper!

I thought of Ginevra. Remembered her eyes and hair and skin, how different her body was from Keeper's, how it had felt fucking her on that old swaybacked bed in Midwinter—back before she'd dumped me, before she'd been murdered on the say-so of Vey Coruscant, the blood-witch who ran Mélusine's Dassament district—and the dream stretched and pulled like taffy, and I was still in Keeper's bed with all them stupid candles, but it was Ginevra under me making those amazing throaty little noises, and the scent of her was like honey, and I could rest my head against the pillow and not think about nothing except her, about the softness of her skin and the pressure of her tits against my chest, how easy it was to fuck her and not worry about . . . wetness and heat against my shoulder.

I jerked up. It was blood. Ginevra's throat was cut, and there was blood everywhere—blood in her hair, spreading across the sheets, blood running down her stomach and between her legs, oiling our fucking like some kind of terrible clockwork. And suddenly Ginevra's legs were clamped around mine, and when her eyes opened, they were full of blood, and she said, laughing, "Fuck me harder, Mildmay. I'm dead now, so I can't feel it unless you fuck . . . me . . . *harder*."

I wanted to scream, but I couldn't. And the blood made it so smooth, like flying, but there was no heat except the blood, because she was dead and I could smell the rot starting. I wanted to get away from her even more than I'd wanted to get away from Keeper, but I couldn't stop, slamming into her harder and harder and I could feel her body starting to fall apart under me, and she started laughing, and I still couldn't stop, and she brought her hands up and touched her cheeks, and then reached out with her bloody hands toward my face.

And I woke up. With everything throbbing. Cock, balls, head, every separate muscle in my back and neck. I was facedown on the mattress, and I knew if I moved, I'd either come or puke. Maybe both.

I didn't want to come from having a dream like that. Stupid, I know, but there it was. Plus there was the whole embarrassment part, and what kind of disgusting freak would Phaëthon think I was—

Oh, shit. Phaëthon. I kept perfectly still, praying I hadn't made enough noise to wake him up. I was dripping with sweat. The cabin felt like a potter's kiln, and the darkness was like this hot, wet blanket pressing me down.

I stayed like that for I don't know how long, my heart hammering in my chest like I'd run from Chalcedony Gate up to the Plaza del'Archimago. No sign that Phaëthon was awake and wondering what the fuck was wrong with me. And the crazy pain in my balls and cock settled back to just, you know, *pain*, and I could roll over and lay there and feel stupid and dirty and disgusting.

And there I lay 'til morning.

Felix

The *White Otter* sailed out of Endumion at noon. Ingvard, like the other passengers, was on deck, watching raptly as the distance widened between Troia and this, our small, floating world. He had not pressed me when I had said I preferred to stay in our cabin, but I knew he thought it odd.

He could think me as odd as he liked; he would think me odder still if I lost my self-control on the main deck of the *White Otter*. Better to stay below and pretend it was not happening, that safety was still almost within my reach. I lay on the top bunk and stared at the ceiling—if that was what one called it on a ship—trying very hard not to think of anything and succeeding only in thinking about the temple of Graia and the dim horror of Nera, which I could not see clearly but which thronged my mind with shadows.

Mildmay had not, I suspected, told me quite everything about Nera. He had been nervous, disquieted, uncomfortable, and I knew him well enough to understand that those feelings would make him try to close down the discussion as quickly as he could. I did not think he had lied to me, but I thought he had probably edited the story considerably. It infuriated me that I could not draw on my own memories for corroboration, but all I could consciously remember of Nera was blood and smoke and the thick taste of terror.

The ship lurched beneath me; after a moment of incandescent panic, during which the ship lurched again in the identical fashion, I reasoned out that it was not a sign that we were sinking, merely that we had come out past the breakwater and were starting into the open sea. I had never heard a phrase in my life that I detested as much as I detested "the open sea" at that moment. Would it have been so bad, a voice whispered treacherously in my mind, to have stayed in the Gardens? Astyanax was right, you know, you could have been perfectly happy there.

Mildmay, I thought, a little desperately. I couldn't have asked Mildmay to stay there. It would have killed him.

And, as if on cue, Mildmay said from the doorway, "Felix?"

Without the cane, he moved as silently as a cat—perhaps another reason he was determined to do without it—and he made me jump so that I nearly brained myself. "What?" I said, and my voice was sharp with startlement and guilt.

"Are you okay? Mr. Vilker said you—"

"And you were worried. How touching."

"I know you don't like deep water."

I wanted to scream at him, howl and curse and gibber. I said, "I'm *fine*. You don't need to worry about me."

"I won't then." And he left. I could have called him back, but I didn't. I did not want to.

Mildmay

Well, look, Milly-Fox, you did *another* stupid thing. Big fucking surprise.

I shouldn't've got mad at Felix, and I knew it before I'd gone a septad-foot. I knew what he was like. I knew how much he hated anybody knowing he wasn't perfect. I mean, I'd known he'd most likely be snippy when I'd gone down there. But it still pissed me off, and I thought as I was going back up on deck, Fuck him if he thinks I'm going to apologize for not doing nothing wrong. He wants to make up, he can come to me. And that was stupid, too.

'Cause Felix wasn't crazy now, and he didn't need me. I saw that as soon as he came up on deck, and there was Mr. Vilker and Mrs. Gauthy and Mr. Gauthy and Florian and Phaëthon all over him. His laugh carried across to where I was standing, and I thought, Fuck me sideways 'til I cry, and pretended I was staring at the ocean.

And I couldn't swallow my pride. I don't know if it was the dream or the news about the *Morskaiakrov* or what, but I'd think about crawling to Felix, begging him to be friends again, and then I'd remember to unclench my hands. I couldn't do it, no matter how miserable I got.

It probably would've looked funny to anybody who wasn't a part of it, 'cause day after day, there was that group of six people in their one particular place where Felix liked to hold court, and then there was me at the other end of the ship, staring out at the water. I was especially careful not to ask the sailors what they thought was going on, although I caught the way some of them looked at me, and I think they had a pretty good idea.

Meals were the worst. Meals were pure uncut Hell, and I was probably dropping weight again, and I didn't care. I hate having people look at me when I eat anyway, and then the conversation—powers and fucking saints. Felix and the Gauthys and Mr. Vilker and Captain Yarth would just go off on history and literature and all that other stuff, and Phaëthon and Florian would listen, and sometimes ask questions. And you could feel everybody focused on Felix, like they were all sunflowers and he was the sun. I swear it was like a cult, because I watched the captain, that first decad, go from giving Felix the seriously hairy eyeball to talking and laughing with him like he'd completely forgotten Felix was a hocus.

I tried a couple times to join in, when they were talking about stuff I knew, but nobody but Felix could understand what I said to start with, and then either Mr. Vilker proved me wrong or Felix made an answer that took me so far out of my depth I might as well have just jumped overboard and drowned for real. So I kept my mouth shut and tried not to care.

In our cabin, Phaëthon wasn't mean or nothing, but we didn't have a thing in the world to say to each other besides "good morning" and "good night." And although I didn't have no more dreams as bad as the one I'd had the first night on the *White Otter*, I wasn't sleeping well, and I kept dreaming about Ginevra. I felt like shit, and if Felix had been talking to me at all—besides correcting my grammar every fucking time I opened my mouth—I would have asked him to ward my dreams again, like he had back in the Gardens when he'd still liked me. But I couldn't ask that, either.

So that's how things stood. We were twelve days out, and I was standing at the stern, watching our wake, when Florian Gauthy came up beside me and said, "Why do you spend so much time looking at the ocean?"

I couldn't help my reflexive glance back, but his parents were laughing at something Felix had said and hadn't noticed Florian had gone. But that gave me time to kill my first answer, which was, *'Cause it beats the shit out of my other options.* I just shrugged and said, "I like it."

"Oh," he said, like that wasn't the answer he wanted.

We stood there a while, me looking at the water and him looking at me, the water, then back at me again. I kept expecting one of his parents to come drag him away, but they didn't.

And finally Florian couldn't stand it no more and said, "How'd you get that scar on your face?"

Powers and saints, I thought. "A knife fight."

"Like a duel?" And he was all wide-eyed, like a little kid listening to a story.

"No, like a knife fight. I was about your age."

"Oh," he said, disappointed again. "Were your parents terribly cross?"

I really didn't mean to laugh, no matter what Felix said later. But I couldn't help it, and of course Florian wanted to know what was so funny, and I'm a shitty liar, so I told him the truth.

And then he wanted to know, if my parents weren't around, who looked after me, and I tried to explain about Keeper without actually explaining, if you follow me, but I'm no good at shit like that, and nobody, not even a kid like Florian, was going to believe I'd been to a flash boarding school like they got in Ferrau, and so somehow I ended up telling him all about being trained as a pickpocket. I didn't tell him none of the other things I'd been trained to do—I hadn't gone *completely* batfuck—but I told him way more than I should've. I don't know what the fuck got into me— maybe it was just that Florian was listening and interested and didn't mind at all that sometimes he had to ask me to repeat things—but I stood there on the deck of the *White Otter* and spilled my guts to Florian Gauthy the way I'd never done with anybody in my life.

And Florian drank it all in and wanted to know more about the Cheaps and the cade-skiffs and the Trials. I don't think he really believed most of the things I told him about the Arcane, but that was okay. Some of it I wouldn't have believed myself if I hadn't been there.

We were sitting, leaning against the side of the ship, and I was telling him some of the tamer stories about Vey Coruscant, when Felix came up looking like the end of the world and said, all polite and smooth and horrible, "Mildmay, could I talk to you for a moment, please?"

I think Florian caught the danger signals, because he stood up in a hurry and said, "I'd better be going. Thanks, Ker Foxe!"

He bounded down the companionway, and I stood up. And when I was up, I looked at Felix, and he said in this low, controlled, fucking *petrifying* voice, "What were you telling him?"

"Dunno," I said. "Stories."

"You were telling him about Mélusine. *Weren't* you?"

"Um, yeah. So?"

"So?" He was still keeping his voice down, but I almost wished he'd shout. Because he was reminding me of a steam boiler about to bust. I'd seen people after that happened once, down in Lyonesse, and I think that was the first time I'd really understood that things could have been a lot fucking worse than my stupid scar.

"Yeah. Why's it matter?"

"Why does it matter? We've been going around admitting we're brothers all over the place and now you're telling them you're from Mélusine and you want to know why it *matters?*"

"Yeah. More and more, actually."

He stared at me for a moment, then made a sort of growling noise and clenched his hands in his hair like he wanted to start ripping it out in handfuls. If there'd been anywhere I could've gone to get away from him, believe me, I'd already have been there. But, you know, I figured nothing he could pull could actually be worse than some of the stuff he'd done when he was crazy, and I'd come out the other side of that. And if he thought I was afraid of him, I'd *really* be fucked. So I just waited, and after a minute he fetched a deep breath and brought his hands down. And when he opened his eyes, I could see he was still royally pissed, but he didn't look like he was fixing to explode. At least not right away.

He said, real careful, like he thought if he went any faster I wouldn't understand him, "The people on this ship know I'm a wizard, right?"

He stopped and raised his eyebrows at me, so I said, "Yeah."

"Eusebians don't have tattoos, right?"

"Yeah."

"Nor do Troian wizards. *Right?*"

"Okay."

"So how am I supposed to explain being a wizard and yet not being of any of the . . . acceptable schools?"

"Dunno."

"No, I didn't think you did," he said, mean as a snake. "They may not recognize the tattoos, but they'll recognize the name of the Mirador. I have to be from somewhere else."

And he had lost me. "Huh?"

He rolled his eyes. "If they ask where I'm from or what school I practice, I can't tell them the truth, or they'll hand us straight over to the dragoons when we dock in Klepsydra."

"Yeah, I told you as much back in Endumion."

Me and my fucking mouth. You'd think me of all people could learn when to keep it shut, but I never do. I saw Felix's jaw clench and thought for a second he was going to turn me into a frog or hit me with a lightning bolt or something. He said through his teeth, *"They already knew."*

'Cause you were wearing them fucking rings, I thought, but this time I managed not to say it.

He gave me this look like somehow he'd heard me anyway and said, "Since I can't lie about being a wizard, I have to lie about where I'm from. And I can't do that if you're telling everybody on the ship heartwarming stories about growing up a gutter rat in Mélusine."

"Well, if you'd *told* me—"

"I didn't imagine I needed to. Clearly, I radically overestimated your intelligence—a mistake I won't be making again."

Septad and six nasty things I could've said, and I didn't say 'em. Didn't say nothing, actually, because I *still* wasn't going to crawl to Felix, and I figured that was about all he was going to want to hear from me. So I didn't say nothing, and he didn't say nothing, and there were a couple sailors down on the main deck pretending like they weren't trying to get close enough to eavesdrop.

Felix looked away first, muttering, "I suppose it is unlikely that Florian will repeat your stories to his parents."

"Pretty safe bet he won't," I said, and it came out sharper than was maybe a good idea.

"So you're entrusting our safety to the discretion of a twelve-year-old boy? Brilliant."

"I'm just saying Florian ain't gonna do nothing to get himself in trouble. Which he would do."

He looked at me. I saw the spark in his eye and I knew what was coming. *"Is not going to do anything,* not *ain't gonna do nothing."* And, Kethe, his imitation of me was spot-fucking-on.

"Fuck you," I said and turned back to the sea. Yeah, since you ask, I'd rather've left, but for all that my leg was better, those damn stairs were still an ugly scene, and it would just give Felix a whole new crop of nasty things to say. Turned out to work the same anyway, because after a moment *Felix* left.

I stood there 'til the sun was almost down, saying a bunch of things to the water that I'd wanted to say to Felix. Ocean didn't care.

Felix

That I had not murdered my brother by the end of the second week of our voyage was something of a miracle. I could feel his sullen, silent presence everywhere I went, and the ostentatious way he refused to join the social circle of the passengers irritated me nearly to screaming point. And then from playing the solitary, brooding misanthrope to turn around and tell Florian Gauthy the one thing we most desperately needed our traveling companions not to know . . . if I *had* murdered him, he would have deserved it.

I cursed Mildmay for being an idiot. I cursed Captain Yarth for separating Mildmay and me. Sometimes, for variety, I cursed the Mirador instead. Mercifully, Ingvard Vilker did not ask about the tattoos, any more than he seemed to notice that he never saw me without my shirt. He displayed, in fact, a remarkable lack of curiosity, which I was both grateful for and a little unnerved by. Good manners, I said to myself. Just because *yours* are atrocious . . . I relaxed and talked history and literature with Ingvard and listened to his stories of working in the Gauthy household.

Theokrita Gauthy, it seemed, was a domestic despot, ruling children and servants alike with an iron fist. The housemaids were apparently sacked on a regular basis and for the most minor transgressions. Ingvard and the other higher-class employees, the boys' tutor and the girls' governess, had at least a modicum of autonomy, though the tutor and governess were required to sleep in the house, within earshot of the children. "They never have a breath to call their own," Ingvard said.

"But your situation is different?" We were indulging in slow preparations for bed, dragging out the opportunity to talk without one or the other of the Gauthys hanging over our shoulders.

"I sleep out, thank you very much. And I have as little to do with the children as I can arrange."

"Wise," I said, laughing. "So you have lodgings of your own?"

"A very nice private flat. My salary is generous, and Keria Gauthy is not so concerned about my morals as long as I do not debauch anyone under her roof."

"Do you make a practice of debauchery?"

He gave me a sly, sidelong look and said, "I wouldn't call it 'debauchery,' no matter what Keria Gauthy thinks."

"Is she very straightlaced then?"

"She is not a tolerant woman. She believes piety lies in rectitude."

"Oh. One of those."

"Yes, exactly," Ingvard said with a grimace. "Fortunately, she is not observant."

"What about her husband?"

He snorted. "Ker Gauthy's energies belong to his business. In other matters, he lets his wife do his thinking."

"A bad habit," I said, moving past him toward the bunks.

At that moment, the *White Otter* pitched into a wave with unaccustomed vigor. I stumbled against Ingvard. He caught my upper arms—to steady me, I thought, but then he kissed me hard, almost violently, and I staggered back against the bunks. He followed eagerly, and I had to hold him off with both hands.

"Ingvard, what—"

He caught my face between his palms and kissed me again, ruthlessly. I was taller, but he was heavier. "We both know what we want," he murmured as I half sat, half fell on the lower bunk, hitting my head painfully in the process. Ingvard was right there with me, still kissing my face and throat, his hands cradling my skull.

"Ingvard, wait!" I said, as breathless as a virgin. The scars on my back seemed to be burning; I could not bear the shame of having him discover them. And I did not like this feeling of being assaulted, overpowered. "Stop!"

He did, sat back, frowning. "What's wrong?"

"I didn't expect . . ." I said feebly, and he hooted with laughter.

"Didn't *expect*? Are you asking me to believe you *haven't* been flirting outrageously for the past fortnight?"

I could feel myself blushing; worse, I could feel myself shaking. "No," I said, almost whispering. "But . . ."

"But what? I'm sorry if I rushed you, but you also can't expect me to believe you're a virgin." He was leaning closer, and one hand was now on my thigh, hot as a branding iron through my trousers.

"No. I . . ." I couldn't breathe, couldn't find my self-possession, my strength. "I can't do this," I said, the words coming out in a strangled whisper. I lurched to my feet, knocking his hands away, and fled from the cabin out into the moonless night.

I hid like a child, and when Ingvard opened the door and stood peering out, he could not see me. He called my name in a low voice, but was clearly loath to come after me, for which I did not blame him. Quite the contrary, I was grateful. I was shaking, my body awash with nauseating heat, and any attempt on my part to speak or move—*anything*—would result only in hysterical weeping. I stayed where I was, crouched in the shelter of a rain barrel, and presently Ingvard retreated and closed the door.

I knew there would be sailors about—one could not leave a sailing vessel unattended while all on board got a good night's sleep—but they did not seem to have noticed the melodrama being acted on their stage, and I hoped I had found a sufficiently out-of-the-way niche that I would not be discovered at least until I had myself under somewhat better control.

To say that I did not understand what had happened would have been the grossest of understatements. I had never cared to be dominated—six years with Malkar would be enough to give anyone a distaste for that role—but I had never found it frightening, *never* been reduced to a state of panic merely by being kissed. I was still frightened now, but not by Ingvard; I was frightened by my reaction to him.

There had not been even a hint of this trouble with Astyanax. We had done a great deal more than merely kiss, and I had felt nothing but lazy pleasure. Of course, he had made no attempt to dominate me, or even take the initiative. But still, if I were going to be traumatized in the aftermath of what Malkar had done to me, I would have expected it to be triggered by nakedness, or the sight of another man's arousal. Not by something as trivial as a kiss.

Something must have happened to me. Something else. Something that caused this incalculable reaction to a man using his strength against me. I clenched my hands on my shins, pressing my forehead against my knees. Something had happened to me that I did not remember. The mere idea made me feel ill, furious . . . helpless. I was shivering, but I could not go back to the cabin and could not think of anywhere else to go. The ship was too small a world; it was a miracle that I had found an unoccupied and unobserved corner to begin with. But I could not stay out here all night.

It took me some time to admit to myself that there was one place I could go that would be safe.

Mildmay

It was almost the septad-night. Me and Phaëthon were both laying in our bunks. I was awake, and I knew he was, too, because I could hear him turning over and thrashing around, trying to find some way to lay that was comfortable. My leg was aching—the weather'd been sharp today, and there was rain coming, and powers and saints but I hated the fact I could tell that. So he was restless and I was achy, and neither one of us looked like we were getting to sleep anytime soon.

The knock on the door made us both start up like we'd been stabbed. I heard Phaëthon kind of squeak, and I was cursing myself for not having got a knife. But I went to the door—cabin that size, you don't need lights—and said, "Who's there?"

"It's me." Felix's voice. "I need to talk to you."

So I'm a dog, to be whistled up when you want me? But I didn't say it, no matter how loud I was thinking it, because he wouldn't be wandering around at this hour of the night just to yank my chain. And, even allowing for the whispering, his voice sounded funny—and not funny in a good way, neither.

"Gimme a second," I said.

He said something, but it wasn't loud enough to make out. Might've been "please," or "need," and I could feel the gooseflesh rising on my arms and bunching my shoulders up. Because it wasn't like him, and this was seeming worse and worse.

"What is it?" Phaëthon hissed while I was dragging on my trousers. "What's going on?"

"M'brother," I said. "It'll just take a minute. You okay?"

"Of course. Go ahead. Do you want the light?" He sounded worried, too. Of course, he liked Felix. They all did.

"Nah. It's okay. But thanks."

I opened the door and slipped out.

It took a minute for my eyes to adjust, and I still couldn't see much of Felix. But I could see how wide his eyes were, and when he touched my arm, like he had to prove to himself I was really there, I could feel how cold his fingers were and how he was shaking. And I think it was right then that I forgot to be mad.

"Are you okay?" I said, even though I knew he wasn't. I'd learned all about giving Felix space, and besides I was trying hard to pretend that he didn't look like he'd spooked right the fuck out, gone back down that well where his crazies were.

"I'm all right," he said, but it was a creaky little whisper and he *sounded* like his head had gone bad again, like we were still in Kekropia, all alone out in the grass.

"What happened?" I said.

"N-nothing. It was nothing. But I need a . . . a favor."

Oh fuck, sacred bleeding fuck, this was bad. For him to admit that he needed anything, especially that he needed anything from me—this was worse than bad. "Anything," I said, although that wasn't a smart thing to say to Felix, and I knew it. "Just tell me what."

He made some movement—nothing I could make out clearly—and it was a moment before he said, in that same creaky little voice, "Trade cabins with me. Please."

"Sure. But why? Did Mr. Vilker do something to you?"

"No!" he said, so quick and panicky that I knew the answer was "yes." "It wasn't his fault."

"What wasn't his fault?"

"Mildmay, *please*. Just . . . please."

"Okay," I said. Whatever Mr. Vilker had or hadn't done, it didn't matter nearly as much as getting Felix calmed down and to where he was himself again. He might drive me absolutely screaming batfuck nuts, but I didn't want him back the way he was before. "We trade cabins, and you get some sleep, right?"

"I'll try. And—you mustn't say anything to him. You *mustn't*."

"I won't pick no fights," I said. Which wasn't what he'd said, but he didn't call me on it, just sort of nodded and said, "Thank you," and went into the cabin where Phaëthon was for sure wondering what the fuck was going on.

I wished I could have told him. But I didn't know either. I didn't think either me or Phaëthon was going to get answers from Felix, but I did wonder if maybe Mr. Vilker might cough up the problem. If it really wasn't his fault, he was probably about as confused as I was.

So I wasn't quite as slow getting over to the other cabin as I might have been. I mean, it wasn't nothing I was exactly looking forward to—I already knew Mr. Vilker didn't care for me, and whatever had gone down between him and Felix, it couldn't've been much fun. But I sincerely did want to find out what the fuck had happened, partly out of my own fucking curiosity but more because I wanted in the worst way to know if this was going to be a one-time thing, or if the celebrants hadn't done quite as good a job on Felix as they all said they had. Because if this sort of thing was going to start happening regularly . . . well, it was going to make getting back across Kekropia even more interesting, and I'd already thought it was looking way more interesting than it needed to be.

I knocked on the cabin door and heard Mr. Vilker say, "Felix? Is that you?" He sounded half-hopeful and half-worried, and I figured that at least Felix hadn't been lying when he'd said it hadn't been Mr. Vilker's fault. Because he sounded like somebody who'd bitten into a pear and found out it was a lemon and was now trying to figure out where the fuck he'd gone wrong, and that wasn't what he'd've sounded like if he'd meant any harm.

I opened the door and went in. "Nope," I said. "Me."

He was sitting on the bottom bunk, and he didn't look pleased to see me. "Where's Felix?" he said.

"In the other cabin. He asked me to swap."

"Did he? Sent you with his apologies?"

"Um, no. He just asked me to swap." Mr. Vilker was looking pretty much like a thundercloud, so I added cautiously, "He didn't tell me what happened."

"A gentleman," Mr. Vilker said like it was an insult.

"He seemed pretty shook up," I said, still cautious.

There was this pause where both of us were waiting for the other guy to say something. And then Mr. Vilker kind of laughed, and shook his head, and said, "Well, it's hardly the first time I've made a fool of myself. But I really did think . . ." He looked at me, and I could see he was worried as well as pissed. "He wouldn't tell Ker Gauthy, would he?"

"No," I said, because no matter what had happened, of all the things Felix might do, telling *anybody* was about as likely as him sprouting wings and flying home. Less likely, even, because if he *could* sprout wings, I'd back him to do it.

"Oh! Then he is . . ."

"Yeah?"

"Nothing." And I would've bet all the money me and Felix had that he'd been within an inch of asking me if Felix was molly.

I said, 'cause I figured Mr. Vilker deserved something, "He's got a thing about deep water. It makes him twitchy. And don't tell him I told you, or he'd most likely drop me over the side."

His laugh sounded better this time. "My mother was terrified of spiders. And she handled it not half so well as Ker Harrowgate."

"Yeah. It's rough on him."

"I can imagine."

Another gap, and I said, "I'm sorry, but I ain't gonna be able to reach the top bunk."

"What? Oh! Oh, of course. I beg your pardon. Did he roust you out of your own bed?"

"Pretty much."

He got up, eyeing me like now he was wondering if I was molly and likely to make a pass at him. Which even if I had been, I wasn't.

Mr. Vilker crawled up into the top bunk, and I laid down with a sigh. "You can put out the light whenever," I said.

"All right," he said, like it wasn't what he'd been expecting me to say. But fucked if I was going to give him anything more. Him and Felix could just work it the fuck out on their own.

He snuffed the lamp, and I laid there and prayed I didn't dream about Ginevra again.

Felix

Phaëthon kindled the light as I closed the door behind me.

"Mildmay, what—oh."

"I'm sorry to disturb you," I said.

"Where's Mildmay?" the boy said, his eyes wide, as if I might have murdered my brother and thrown the body over the side. "Are you . . . is he all right?"

And of course, being an idiot, I had not had sufficient foresight to think of a plausible story. Mildmay would not press me, but I could not expect such tact and gentleness from anyone else on the *White Otter*.

"Nightmare," I said. "Old superstition—if you change beds, the nightmare won't follow you. *You* know." That wasn't *exactly* how I'd been taught to banish nightmares as a child, but Phaëthon was looking skeptical enough without the more esoteric details.

"And you couldn't just change bunks with Vilker?"

Damn the boy for applying logic. "No," I said, now inventing frantically. "You have to change rooms. Crossing a boundary, closing gates, that sort of thing."

Phaëthon now looked merely as if he thought I was crazy, which was unpleasant but better than concerned curiosity.

I sat down on the lower bunk. I was still too jittery to sleep, but sitting or lying quietly in the dark sounded like gift enough.

"Well, since you've disturbed my sleep *anyway*," Phaëthon said, "I'm going to the latrine."

Prudish child, I thought, but I had no objection to his leaving the cabin. As far as I was concerned, the longer he was gone the better.

He climbed slowly down; as he put his hand on the door latch, I saw the stain on the seat of his trousers and said before I thought, "You're bleeding."

He whipped around, eyes wide and jaw slack with fear.

"Are you hurt?" I said. "Did someone . . ." And then it occurred to me that one might have reasons other than prudery to eschew the use of a chamber pot. I looked again at the bone structure of the face, the delicacy of wrists and hands.

"What is your real name?" I said softly.

She raised her chin defiantly and said, "Arakhne of the House Attalis."

Chapter 4

Felix

I got no sleep that night. Accepting that her secret had been discovered, Arakhne seemed almost frantic for a confidant, and although it was a role I knew myself to be temperamentally unsuited for, it was beyond the bounds of even my selfishness to refuse her.

She got herself cleaned up and then came and sat on one end of the lower bunk, while I sat on the other and her trousers were spread across the top bunk to dry, and told me her story.

Her house and the House Erekhthais had been at feud for fifty years. She was the last heir of the major line of the House Attalis, and therefore the last major impediment between the House Erekhthais and their goals: an end to the endless series of suit and countersuit before the Aisxime—and the attendant, though disavowed, raids and assassinations—and the absorption of the House Attalis holdings into their assets. The claims of Arakhne's more distant cousins were in fact no better than the claim of Hesukhios of the House Erekhthais, whose grandmother had been a daughter of the House Attalis.

"But first," she said, "they need me either dead or married to an Erekhthaid. The Emperor and the Parliament cannot ignore *my* right."

Unfortunately, not yet being of age, she had no recourse to either action or protection in Troia without making herself dependent on one of the other houses, which would merely be trading one greedy predator for another and would not improve either her situation or her chances of living to reach her majority. She was fleeing to Kekropia to claim sanctuary of the Emperor Dionusios Griphos—here there was a long, involved digression about the role of Kekropia in Troian politics, from which I gathered mostly that the Kekropians were as much inclined to meddle in the affairs of their neighbors to the east as they were in those of their neighbors to the west. Arakhne had not liked the looks of the *Penelope* any better than Mildmay and I had; she had therefore decided to take passage on the *White Otter* and find some way north once she was on Kekropian soil.

"And, er, the disguise?" I asked.

"The House Attalis has no sons of my age remaining," she said with gruesome matter-of-factness. "And a boy traveling alone is much less likely to be bothered—or even noticed—than a girl. Assuming one's disguise holds." She glowered disgustedly into the middle distance.

"I won't betray your secret," I said, although I felt like the howlingest of hypocrites, considering how many secrets of my own I was so desperately concealing.

"Thank you," she said. "I confess, I have been growing increasingly nervous. I do not think your brother suspects, but it's hard to be sure without asking outright."

"Mildmay wouldn't betray you."

Her look was frankly skeptical.

"He wouldn't."

"Then he *isn't* the hired thug he looks, acts, and sounds like?" she said acidly.

"No. He is not."

"Well, you would know," she said, dismissing Mildmay completely, and went on to tell me in great detail about all the stratagems by which she had eluded her Erekhthaid pursuers.

I barely heard her. I had been viciously skewered, again, by the apparently irreconcilable difference between my perception of Mildmay and that of everyone else. In the Gardens, I had assumed the disjunct came from the celebrants' gross initial misapprehension that Mildmay had terrorized and brutalized me from one end of Kekropia to the other. But Arakhne had no such false information; she knew nothing of us except what she had seen over the past two and a half weeks.

Certainly it was evident from Mildmay's speech that he was uneducated; certainly the scar on his face gave him a forbidding aspect. But was it truly so difficult to look beyond that?

I thought of Mildmay standing alone and watching the waves, thought of him sitting silent and ignored at meals. Realized, my face heating even as I maintained the appearance of rapt interest in Arakhne's convoluted and breathless narrative, that my treatment of Mildmay since we had come on board the *White Otter* would not have given any observer the impression that I regarded him as *other* than a hired thug.

Malkar had placed stringent restrictions on my behavior, lest I disgrace him, but it was a new and appalling idea that my attitude toward another person could cause other people to disdain him.

My memory promptly offered up my own cruel laughter, making mock of one or another unfortunate who had incurred my displeasure. And the laughter of my friends, my coterie . . . my clique.

I thought again, as I had thought before, that the world might well have been a better place if my mother had drowned me at birth.

"Felix?" said Arakhne. "Are you all right?"

"Just tired," I said. "It hasn't exactly been a restful night, you know."

She checked her pocket watch and had the grace to look guilty. "It's almost dawn. I didn't mean . . ."

"It's no matter. But I think I'll go out and watch the sunrise if you want the lower bunk for a while."

"You're *very* kind."

I smiled back at her and made my escape. It wasn't kindness; I just wanted to get away from her.

Outside the cabin, the world disappeared into fog, which was much more soothing than a clear view of the sea would have been. I went up on the cabin deck, where I would not be in the sailors' way, and stared at the beautiful blank grayness and wondered what to do now.

I did not delude myself. I was not a kind person, and my instincts were always to wound. And the combination of Mildmay's stone face and the vulnerability he hid behind it would bring out—had already brought out—the worst in my nature.

Someday he will murder you, I said to myself, and you will deserve it.

Mildmay

Florian Gauthy wouldn't fucking leave me alone.

Now, you'd think seeing Felix just about blow a gasket would be enough to warn a kid off—and if not, then for sure the chewing out I heard him getting from his mother. But Florian Gauthy was as stubborn as they come, and he kept on trotting along after me like a puppy dog. The crew thought it was the best joke they'd ever seen.

And I guess I can see how it would be funny if it didn't happen to be you. I mean, Florian was about as bourgeois as you can get, and I can't even *pass* for bourgeois. And I don't suppose I looked like I wanted him around. Which I didn't, but he didn't care about that neither.

And I couldn't seem to bring myself to tell him to go away. For one thing, I figured the only thing likely to piss Mrs. Gauthy off worse than having Florian hang around with me would be if I didn't let him. And aside from that, I was lonely. I couldn't really make friends with the crew—Felix had given me this snotty little speech a couple days out about "low company," and while I itched to ask him what he thought I was, that looked like being a pretty surefire way to get him to never talk to me again. And none of the passengers except Florian wanted to give me the time of day. Mr. Vilker wasn't mean about sharing the cabin or nothing, but we both knew I wasn't the guy he wanted in there. And Phaëthon had turned out to be Felix's new best friend. I couldn't keep myself from wondering if they were fucking.

Felix still wasn't talking to me, although in a different way now. Seemed like every time I turned around he was staring at me with this weird little frown on his face. I couldn't figure out what I'd done, or if he was really even still mad at me, and since he wouldn't come near me, I couldn't ask.

And there was Florian Gauthy, asking questions, telling me about Klepsydra, looking for whales and seals and mermaids and Kethe knows what all, and after a couple days it just felt natural to talk to him, and a couple days after that I started telling him stories. Because it was better than answering questions about me.

Florian ate my stories up like they were candy. He didn't seem to know none of 'em, and when I asked, he said he'd read plenty of stories in books, but he'd never heard anybody *tell* a story before. I think it was about then that I quit caring what Mrs. Gauthy thought and just started telling Florian every story I could think of. 'Cause, I mean, I'm sure stories in books are okay, but they ain't real. Stories ain't real unless you hear 'em.

And Florian listened with his ears flapping. He always wanted to know where the stories were from and where I'd heard them and if I was telling 'em exactly like they'd been told to me. Which, of course, no, I wasn't, because you don't. I tried to explain it to him, how the story is what happens when you tell it for yourself, but I didn't say it very well, and I don't think he really understood me. But I told him stories I'd heard as a kid, stories I'd heard in the Arcane, in the Cheaps, stories Cardenio had told me that he'd heard from other cade-skiffs—and I hoped Cardenio was okay, and someday I'd be able to go and tell him that I'd told the story of Elisabeth Raphenia's wedding night on a ship on the far side of Kekropia and be able to see his eyes get big as bell wheels. I told Florian stories I'd heard in Kekropia, traveling east with my crazy brother—although I didn't tell him that part—and I told him stories I'd heard on the *Morskaiakrov*, because they were the ones that weren't mine yet.

I didn't particularly want to talk about the *Morskaiakrov*, but when Florian learned me and Felix had gotten to Troia on a Merrow ship, that turned into something else he wouldn't fucking leave alone.

"Were they *pirates*?" he said.

"Well, they were smugglers," I said doubtfully, because I wasn't quite sure what he meant—or thought he meant—by "pirates."

"Did the Imperial Armada chase you? Did you have to fight them off?"

"Fuck, no." He looked disappointed. "What, you think having these Armada guys show up would've been fun?"

His eyes brightened, and he started telling me about this book he'd read, where the hero was accused of something he hadn't done and had to run off with a pirate ship and have the sort of adventures that the smugglers I'd met would have gone clear to St. Millefleur out of their way so as not to get involved in. I didn't quite have the heart to say that to Florian, though—and even if I had, I don't think I could've fit it in, because he went straight from that into complaining about how boring living in Klepsydra was and how nothing ever happened and even if it did, his mother would make sure he never knew about it until it had been over for a month.

I guess people have to be stupid when they're his age. Kethe knows I was. So I didn't tell him I'd trade my life for his in a heartbeat, just listened, and when he'd worked some of the boil off, it turned out that what was really getting up his nose wasn't so much the not being a pirate as it was the fact that he was the youngest of six, and only the second boy, and his mother seemed to want to keep him in cotton wool until he was old and gray and toothless. Which I could at least see as being something you'd get sick of in a hurry. And what really pissed him off, as far as I could tell, was the way his brother and sisters got in on the act. His oldest sisters treated him like they were his mother, too, and the younger girls and his brother, Kechever, used him like a kind of screen. "They could get away with murder while Mother was scolding me," Florian said bitterly. "And the servants are just as bad as Mother. Even Ker Tantony won't let me—"

He stopped, gulped, and turned bright brick red. I remembered Tantony was the name of his tutor, and although this wasn't anything I 'specially wanted to get into, I said, "Even Mr. Tantony won't let you what?" because . . . well, I guess, really, because it's what my friend Margot would have said.

"Nothing," Florian said. "He treats me like I'm an idiot, too."

Which I'd've bet my eyeballs wasn't what he'd been going to say. But it wasn't like I could say so or nothing, and it really wasn't like it was any of my business. So I kind of waited, long enough that he knew I hadn't quite bought it, then said "Uh-huh," and asked some stupid, easy question that would get us both off the hook. And Florian answered it, and then asked me to tell another story I'd heard on the *Morskaiakrov*, and it was like we'd just thrown the whole thing overboard and let it sink.

Except of course for the part where I couldn't quite forget about it. I wondered if I should tell somebody, but figured that Mrs. Gauthy wouldn't believe me, and she wouldn't be grateful anyway, and if what Florian hated most in the world was people treating him like he was too little and too stupid to be trusted not to eat the soap, then he wasn't going to love me at all, neither, for pulling a stunt like that. And I didn't even pretend to myself that Felix would care.

So I put it out of my mind as best I could, and mostly just worried about Felix and Mr. Vilker and what I was going to do with myself now. My leg was better, but I still limped, and that wasn't ever going to go all the way away. 'Cause it hadn't healed straight. I'd been trying and trying to pretend to myself that that wasn't what it was, that it was just the muscles weren't strong enough yet, but somewhere out in the middle of the ocean between Endumion and Klepsydra, I just gave up on lying about it. I could see it myself if I watched my feet, and I could feel it clearer and clearer because my leg muscles *were* getting stronger and so the thing that was fundamentally wrong was showing up better. It was like . . . Kethe, I don't know what it was like, not so as to be able to describe it. But it was like at the midpoint of my thigh, someone had taken the bone and turned it like a fraction of a circle, barely even enough to notice, you'd think, to the left. And then strapped an iron bar or something along from my thigh to my heel, so it couldn't turn back the way it was supposed to and so that knee had to fight the rod to bend. It wasn't so much that it hurt as that it just wouldn't *go*.

So it worked okay for getting around on, but I couldn't trust it no more. I had to face it. I was a crip now, and crip cat burglars—well, let's just say there's a reason you ain't never heard of one. But I didn't have the first fucking clue what I was going to do instead.

It got into my dreams, worse even than it had that first couple of decads in the Gardens. Keeper'd send me out after something, and I'd fall out a window or something stupid like that, and there I'd be in Ginevra's grave with her cold, rotting arms around me and her voice in my ear all thick and slow, "Love me, Milly-Fox. Make me warm," and then I'd jolt awake and laid there, panting and sweating and scared to move, and listen to Mr. Vilker snore until dawn.

I was starting to almost look forward to us getting to Klepsydra, because probably nothing good was going to happen there—I mean, odds were seriously against it—but at least I could get off the *White Otter* and maybe leave these fucking dreams behind.

Felix

The *White Otter* danced with the Kelephanian, making her way toward Klepsydra, and I caught myself again and again watching Mildmay, trying to make sense of who he was, trying to sort my idea of him out into order and coherence. Trying to find an understanding that would help me not to hurt him again.

I was hampered in my progress by two things. One was my own, irrational, insuperable desire for him, a lust like a slow-burning fuse that paid no attention to details such as our blood kinship or the fact that he was not inclined toward men or that I now apparently panicked at the approach of sexual intimacy. I wanted him—wanted the coarse fox-red hair he braided back and tied with a scrap of indigo ribbon, wanted his body, his broad shoulders and stocky frame, lithe and muscular as an acrobat's. I wanted his deep, slurred, Lower City voice, wanted the growl that threaded through his words. I wanted his eyes, cold absinthe-green jade, wanted his face, those feral bones, that stone scar. I wanted to watch passion transform him from stone and jade to flesh and blood, wanted to know if he cried out when he came, and what he sounded like when he did.

But I could not have him, and the tension between that knowledge and the unabated *wanting* made it difficult to think, even more so as it intertwined with that ugly, failed encounter with Ingvard and made me uncertain of myself, of my own desires and longings, in a way that I had not been since I was eleven.

And as if that were not enough, I further found that my idea of Mildmay, my understanding of him, was at once as clear and sharp as a chirurgeon's knives, and clouded, obscure, impenetrable. I knew that I trusted him, but I did not know why. When I tried to understand it, my memory gave me only senseless flashes: him handing me a turnip that I did not want, him sitting under a streetlamp in a strange city, putting laces in a pair of shoes . . . memories of Joline, who had died when I was eleven and whom I had loved like a sister—like this brother whom I had not then known I had.

It made no *sense*, and it frustrated me. I could deduce that these strange snippets of memory were from the year and more that I had lost to madness, and even that they were moments at which Mildmay had been kind, protective, loving. But I could not know that that was true. They might have been things I had imagined, or dreamed. They might have been things that in my madness I had completely misinterpreted.

I became irritable, snapped at Arakhne, argued with Leontes, avoided Ingvard's increasingly blatant attempts to get me alone. I knew that I needed to talk to Mildmay, and I could not bring myself to do it. It seemed as if we had had this conversation too many times already. It would change nothing; it would not make me other than I was; it would not resolve this discord between us.

And then, five days from Klepsydra (or so said Captain Yarth), I thought, Maybe I should tell him *that*. It was such a stupidly obvious idea that I burst out laughing even as I turned to look for Mildmay—and found myself face-to-face with Ingvard.

I fell back a pace, narrowly suppressing a yelp. But my alarm must have shown on my face, for he stepped back as well, raising his hands palms out; his smile was more than slightly sardonic, and it annoyed me.

"Ingvard," I said.

"You've been avoiding me."

"Gracious. I wonder why." I was as cold and supercilious as I could be and had the satisfaction of seeing Ingvard's face go blotchy red with annoyance.

"Felix, what happened?"

"Your advances were unwelcome," I said coldly. "I am surprised you need to ask."

His manner had lost its last trace of amusement, and I was savagely pleased. Whatever else he might do, he would not sneer at me.

He took a deep breath and said with obvious care, "You frightened me. I've been worried."

"That's very sweet of you, Ingvard." I smiled. "But unnecessary."

For a moment, it seemed as if he would make some rejoinder, then he let the breath out wordlessly. He gave me a long, searching look, but I was proof against it.

"All right," he said. "I don't . . . but it is no business of mine. I'm sorry to have bothered you." He turned and crossed the deck to where his employer was standing, trying to instruct Florian in the rudiments of navigation. I watched him until I was sure he was not going to change his mind and return, and then I started, again, to look for Mildmay. I needed to explain.

Mildmay

So Florian's father had come and dragged him off, and I was just sitting in the sun, kind of half-dozing, when I heard somebody coming up the ladder. I opened my eyes, figuring that Florian must have got loose somehow, and found myself staring at Felix's trousers, with the tear in the leg I'd mended myself.

I kind of lurched, starting to get up, figuring he was pissed at me again, but he said, "No, don't," and sat down beside me.

I looked at him sideways, trying to figure out what was going on and if I was in trouble, and he was sitting, knees up and his arms resting on them, with his hands hanging down, right in the sun so the tattoos showed up like they were on fire. He wasn't looking at me. He was staring straight ahead, with this weird kind of little frown, not like he was angry, but like he was trying to remember something, or was thinking about something he didn't much like. I couldn't tell. So I sat and waited for him to cough it up.

And after a while he took a deep breath, still not looking at me, and said, "I need to explain something."

He stopped, like when a hand-wagon hits a step. I said, "Okay."

Another deep breath, and he was frowning off into space now, but if he was mad at me, he would've been looking at me, so I figured I was still okay. "I am not a nice person."

I could've said some seriously snarky things back to that, but I didn't. For one, I didn't want him pissed at me if he wasn't already, and besides, he was struggling with something, and he didn't need me getting in the way.

"These fights we have," he said, and stopped again.

"Yeah," I said. "I remember." Which was nastier maybe than it needed to be, but he was still fighting with whatever it was in his head and didn't pay no mind.

And then he just blurted it out. "They aren't going to stop. The fights. And they're going to be my fault. It's . . . it's what I am."

He didn't say he was sorry, but Felix *didn't* say that and the fact that he'd said anything at all was pretty much an apology on its own. I didn't know what to say, though, because *it's okay* would have been a big fat hairy lie. Likewise *I understand* and everything else I could think of. And I didn't feel like lying was going to make this thing between us any better.

And he'd only stopped because he'd hit another step, not because he was waiting for me. "I've always been like this. It's not you." He turned then, and I couldn't help a tiny bit of a flinch, because his eyes were so spooky, and it was the first time in a couple decads that he'd looked at me straight on and like both of us were really there. "That's the important thing. It's not your fault. It's me. And I'd promise to change, except that it would be a lie."

"And that wouldn't help," I said, because it was what I'd just been thinking.

"No. It wouldn't. And I don't know that telling you this will help, either. But . . . I had to try."

This time, he stopped because he was done. And I sat and thought it over, and for once he didn't try to rush me or get impatient or nothing. He just sat and watched me, his spooky skew eyes burning out of his face, like we had all the time there ever was and this was the only thing that was ever going to matter.

And you know, I hated him for that. Just a little. I hated him for being able to turn that feeling on and off like a cistern tap. Because he was making me feel like I really mattered to him, but I knew he was right. A couple days, a couple hours, a septad-minute, and he'd be walking over me like I wasn't there again, or making some nasty, catty little joke about the way I talked. Like he'd said, it was what he was.

I was afraid to say any of that, though. Because I didn't think it would come out the way I wanted, and by the time I'd figured out how to say it, he'd most likely be bored. Or somebody would've come up to talk to him. Or something. So I just said, "It does help. A little."

He smiled. Not one of the dazzlers he used to get his own way. Just a smile, a little one, kind of crooked. And Kethe, it was like I'd never been mad at him at all.

෫෬

Mr. Vilker was in a stew that night. I laid on my bunk and watched him pace around our tiny cabin. He had about two steps each way, and I thought of telling him to open the door, so he could at least get himself a sort of half-assed triangle, but I still didn't think he liked me much, and he probably wouldn't appreciate lip from me.

But it was seriously getting to the point where I wanted to hit him over the head just to get him to fucking stop, when he did stop, right in front of the bunk and staring at me, and said, "Is he really your brother?"

"Sorry?" I said.

"Is Felix Harrowgate really your brother?" he said, sort of through his teeth.

"Half brother. Yeah."

And damned if he didn't start pacing again. But in about half a minute he stopped, dead center and square on to me again and said, "Were you raised together?"

"What?"

"Were you raised in the same household?"

"No."

He snorted, like I'd disappointed him somehow, and said, "Do you think he's mentally stable?"

"Do I what?"

"Your half brother. Do you think he's sane?"

"Um. Dunno," I said. "D'you think he's crazy?"

"I don't know *what* to think." I remembered Felix saying this afternoon, *It's what I am*. Mr. Vilker took another two steps up, two steps back. "You know what he is, don't you?"

I could think of a bunch of things he might mean by that, most of them somewhere between lousy and the end of the world. "Um," I said.

"That he . . . that his tastes aren't . . ." Mr. Vilker was going a nice sort of cherry color.

"Oh. You mean he's a moll. Yeah, I know that."

"A what?"

Well, I didn't know no nice Kekropian words for it. "He fucks guys."

Mr. Vilker's eyes got big and round, and he went even redder. Nice manners, Milly-Fox. Very smooth. "Um," said Mr. Vilker, "yes." Another quick up and back, and he said, "Do you think he's sleeping with Phaëthon?"

Well, since I'd been wondering the same thing, it wasn't like I could say no, and have it sound like I meant it. "Dunno," is what I actually came up with. But that explained what Mr. Vilker was fretting about. Jealousy's jealousy, and if him and Felix had had some kind of scene, you couldn't really blame the guy—what with Felix latching on to Phaëthon all of two minutes later—not for the wondering and not for the part where he felt kind of shitty about it.

He was pacing again. I said, 'cause I couldn't quite tell, "D'you even *like* him?"

"I don't know. How can I, when every time I talk to him, it's as if I'm talking to a different person?"

"He don't like people knowing too much about his business," I said, which I figured was about as far as I could go without Felix hunting me down and skinning me with a dull knife. And then I said, "He ain't worth driving yourself nuts over."

Which Felix really would have skinned me if he'd heard me say it, but, I mean, it was the truth. It wasn't worth Mr. Vilker's time to get dragged into this.

"Is that your considered opinion?" he said, nasty and sharp.

"I'm just saying. It ain't worth it to you."

"You can't know that."

And, powers, I felt like I was the oldest thing in the world, like I'd been the first thing to come up out of the rocks and mud when Phi-Kethetin started singing fire. "You ain't gonna get what you want from him. Whatever it is." Because as far as I could tell, nobody got what they wanted from Felix unless it was exactly what he happened to want to give.

He gave me an ugly look. "What has he told you?"

"Fuck all. But I know him. You don't."

The look got uglier for a moment, and then he said, "I'm going to bed."

"Don't let me keep you up," I said, and we kind of snarled at each other, and then he climbed into the top bunk and snuffed the light.

Damn you, Felix, I said, but only to myself.

Felix

In the dream, I am in a place I don't know—a cellar, a basement, something like that. Somewhere dark and dank and reeking of the Sim.

It is a maze as well as a basement, and I am lost in it. There's a staircase somewhere—there has to be—but I can't find it, can't find my way up out of the dark and the cold. I go on searching, hopelessly, because I know that no one will come to help me, that no one would care if I died down here, left my skeleton in the corner of one of the odd-shaped little rooms that smell so sweetly and foully of death.

And then, after a bitter eternity of groping in the dark, I see light ahead, the warm flickering of torchlight. I feel sure that it must be the staircase and run toward it.

But it is not the way out. It is the heart of the maze, the place where the monster lives. The monster is not there, but its scent is harsh in my nostrils, and I know it is nearby. It has left its own heart behind it, and I stand in the doorway, unable to move, staring at the monster's heart, which is a table. A wooden table. Fitted with straps, and I cannot keep myself from mapping where each one would go on my own body. Those around the ankles, that one across the hips, those at the wrists, that pinning the shoulders flat. The last strap, narrow and very short, would grip my neck tight enough to choke me. Standing there, my breath coming in harsh labored sounds like the cries of a hurt animal, I can feel it pressing against my jawbone, constricting my throat so that I can barely swallow.

I cannot look away. I want to turn, plunge back into the darkness, lose myself again. But I am rooted to the earth, turned to stone within my own skin. The monster will return soon and find me, strap me to the table that is its heart. It will not kill me. I know that. It will do something even more terrible.

Something touches my shoulder. I jerk around, making a strangled noise, one arm going up to ward the monster off—

3

And Arakhne's voice said in the darkness, "Felix? Are you all right?"

A dream, I thought, knotting my fingers in the coarse fabric of the mattress cover. It was a dream. I could hear myself breathing, feel my chest heaving, as if I had been running for miles, as if I had been battling dragons and ogres. It was just a dream.

"I'm fine," I said. "Just a . . . a bad dream."

"I thought you were dying."

I remembered that last moment of the dream, my arm going up, remembered a distinctly undreamlike sensation of it colliding with something. "Did I hurt you?"

"No. Just scared me. A little."

"For future reference, it's probably better *not* to wake people up by shaking them."

"Oh," she said, sullenly. I wasn't appreciating her selfless concern, and it irritated her.

Fortunately, I was still breathing so heavily that she couldn't have detected my sigh. I was looking forward with intense anticipation to docking in Klepsydra and being free of the galling necessity of sharing a tiny room with a spoiled and frightened teenage girl. I said, "You should probably try to get back to sleep."

"You're not going to have another fit, are you?"

She was angry still, but I detected real fear in her voice. I wondered, my skin prickling with humiliation, just what kind of noises I had been making. "No," I said. "I think I'll go out on deck for a while, clear my head."

"All right," she said, and I heard her climb back into her bunk.

We both slept fully clothed and did not discuss the reasons why. I got up, opened the door.

Arakhne said, "Felix?"

"Yes?"

"What were you dreaming about? It sounded terrible. And I thought switching cabins was going to help."

"Well, nothing helps with nightmares for long. Go to sleep."

I went out, gratefully closing the door behind me. I did not blame Arakhne for her limpetlike tendencies, but I found them profoundly wearying and even more profoundly aggravating. I couldn't turn around without falling over the silly child, and she stood too close to me, monopolized too much of the conversation, as if she were the one who knew my secrets instead of the other way around. I was not about to give her so much as an inch more leverage. I most certainly was not going to discuss my dreams with her.

I wished I could discuss the dream with someone, though. Other than Mildmay, that was, who would listen and then say, at most, *Dunno what it means, but it sounds fucked up.*

I was accustomed to nightmares, but I had never been so upset by one that had no people in it. Dreams about Malkar, Keeper, long dead though he was, Lorenzo, even Shannon: those I was accustomed to, if not inured to. When I woke in limp misery from one of those dreams, I knew what had happened. But this—the narrow subterranean passages, the torches, the table that was at once perfectly innocuous and entirely terrifying—I did not hold the key to this dream, and I did not know why it had such power over me.

And that frightened me more than anything else.

☾☽

We docked in Klepsydra on a beautiful, shining morning. All of us were up on deck, staring eagerly at the fast-approaching city. There would be a slight delay, Captain Yarth had told us, before we would be allowed to disembark, a matter of tariffs and inspections, agreements between the empires of Troia and Kekropia that I did not perfectly understand, nor cared to. It seemed to matter a great deal to Leontes Gauthy, though; he and Ingvard stood a little to one side, muttering together over inventories and invoices.

Theokrita and Florian and Arakhne and I stood together, Arakhne too close as usual. I was aware of Mildmay, standing alone, just within earshot. I admitted to myself with some surprise that I would rather have been standing with him, but Arakhne was so tense I could almost feel her vibrating, and I wanted at all costs and above all other desires to avoid giving her any opportunity to create a scene. She had told me the night before, in the tones of one trying hard to convince herself, that it was highly unlikely the House Erekhthais would have been able to notify their agents in Klepsydra to be on the watch for her.

"I thought you said you'd shaken them off," I'd said—unwisely, for I had noticed the way in which Arakhne's stories changed as she told them.

"Well, of course they'd know it would be very likely I'd make for Aigisthos," she said, and I made no rejoinder. But I wondered now just how much the House Erekhthais might know and just what kind of resources it had at its command.

The *White Otter* came gliding gracefully into the harbor of Klepsydra, which Florian informed me—loudly, and pointedly not looking at Mildmay—was named the Elphenore. Glancing past him to Theokrita's glowering face, I gathered that she had again forbidden him to "bother" my brother. This time, seeing how near our journey was to completion, her edict might hold. I considered telling her that if either of us were to corrupt Florian, it was much more likely to be me than Mildmay, but that was an idle fancy born of anger on Mildmay's behalf—anger and a reprehensibly wicked desire to see the look on Theokrita's face. I said nothing.

The ship docked; the captain sent a sailor trotting to the Customs office. We waited. Leontes and Ingvard continued to pore over their lists and ledgers. Florian pestered his mother and me indiscriminately with questions and speculations about the other ships in the harbor. Theokrita could have done herself a tremendous favor by letting Florian stand with Mildmay this last morning. But I didn't say that, either. Beside me, Arakhne scanned the wharves obsessively, but I doubted if she knew what she was looking for.

Captain Yarth paced the deck behind us, growling under his breath with increasing vehemence as half an hour became an hour became an hour and a quarter. Finally, the sailor reappeared; Captain Yarth strode to meet her as she came up the gangplank, and they plunged into a heated discussion, the sailor looking no less annoyed with the delay than the captain. Mildmay was standing near enough to hear them, and after a couple of minutes, he came limping along the deck and said, "Felix?"

I raised my eyebrows at him, and he jerked his head at the opposite railing. Both Theokrita and Arakhne looked as if they wanted to protest, and that was annoying enough that I didn't argue with Mildmay but followed him across to the other side of the ship.

"Well?" I said.

"Most of what held Vera up ain't no business of ours, but a guy stopped her on the way back wanting to know about all the Troian passengers."

I looked across at Arakhne before I could stop myself. She was watching me anxiously.

Mildmay said, "Oh. D'you think it's him they're after? I was figuring . . ."

He had been exercising the caution of the fox he resembled, who walked into nothing without checking first to see if it was a trap. I said, "No. We may be pursued across Kekropia, but I hardly think our enemies would be waiting for us on the docks."

"Mostly, I just thought it was weird and you should know."

"Yes," I said. "Excuse me one moment." I crossed back to Arakhne and said, "We need to talk."

Spoiled she might be, but she wasn't stupid. There was no color in her face as she followed me into the cabin we had shared.

I told her what Mildmay had told me. Her yellow eyes were huge pale disks in her bone-white face. She whispered, "What shall I do?"

I did not know if it was cruelty or optimism that made me say, "You escaped them before."

"Not like this. Not . . ." She caught at my sleeve; I held myself in and did not strike at her hand or shake her off. "Felix, help me, please. They'll kill me. It's not worth their while to take me back to Troia now. They'll kill me, and that will be the end of the House Attalis as well as me. Please."

I cared not a scrap for the House Attalis, but if I had not been able to repulse Arakhne before this, I could not abandon her now, knowing that it would be to her death.

"Do they know you're disguised as a boy?"

"Yes," she said miserably. She had told me previously that they did not.

"Then I think I have an idea. But it will require telling my brother the truth."

"Him? Why?"

"Because there are three 'Troian' passengers," I said, "and I'm much too tall."

The idea had come into my head even as I was telling Mildmay that our enemies would not be waiting for us on the docks. It was a primitive ruse, but I could see no reason why it would not work.

"Oh," said Arakhne; it was almost a gasp. "Would he?"

"Let me get him in here. Unless you have a better idea?"

She hesitated a moment, clearly wishing she did, then said, "No. If you think he'll do it."

"He'll do it," I said.

I went back out and waved at Mildmay. He followed me into the cabin, where Arakhne was sitting on the bunk, twisting her fingers together nervously in her lap.

"Shall I tell him or will you?" I asked her.

She did not answer me immediately, and Mildmay said, "Tell me what?"

A nasty, fraught little silence. Arakhne opened her mouth, hesitated, and said, "I am Arakhne of the House Attalis."

"Not Phaëthon?"

"No. I was . . . I was traveling disguised as a boy to escape my House's enemies. But their agents are—"

"Uh-huh." He turned to me. "And you knew about this?"

"Yes."

"How long?"

"Mildmay, it doesn't—"

"How fucking long?"

"A week and a half. About."

"And you're telling me now. Why?"

"You know why," I said, annoyed; it had, after all, been he who had told me about the man asking questions.

"Not what I meant." He shut his mouth like a trap and stared at me.

"What *did* you mean?"

The look he gave me was scathing. "What d'you want, Felix?"

It rattled me. Not just the look or the question—although those were bad enough—but the realization that he'd simply taken a shortcut through the conversation I'd anticipated having and reached the finish line ahead of me. I'd known he was much smarter than he seemed, but I hadn't appreciated before how quick he was, that his mind was not in any way hobbled by the scar that slowed and distorted his speech. It was so terribly easy to forget that.

I said, after a taken-aback pause, "We need to get Arakhne safely off this ship. A decoy."

"A decoy." He looked at Arakhne and back at me. "You want me to pretend to be her."

"Yes."

"So the goons after her will bash my head in instead?"

I flinched and despised myself for it. "They'll have no reason to harm you when they realize they've made a mistake."

"Uh-huh." But he looked at Arakhne again, and I supposed he could see as plainly as I could how frightened she was, for he said, "Okay. Assuming I can ditch the goons, where do I find you?"

Something in his voice, some note of weary familiarity, told me that he had done things like this before, that his career as a kept-thief had been more varied and dangerous than mine.

"We'll have to find a hotel," I said.

"Yeah. Bet Klepsydra's got a lot of 'em."

"Shut up," I said. I recognized that particular form of being absolutely unhelpful without actually starting an argument. Cabaline wizards excelled at its more subtle and sophisticated variants. "Both of you, stay here."

Theokrita was more than happy to recommend hotels, even after I curbed her enthusiasm by mentioning that distasteful word, "budget." Glancing over her shoulder, I noticed a man in Imperial uniform deep in discussion with Leontes and Ingvard, and surmised that that must be the Customs officer. His presence meant it probably would not be much longer before we were expected to disembark.

I extracted myself from what was promising to be an exhaustive review of every hotel in Klepsydra and returned to the cabin, where the silence was thick enough to cut.

"The Pig-whistle on Blue Lantern Street," I said to Mildmay, and repeated the directions Theokrita had given me. "Does that satisfy your lordship?"

"Okay," he said. "Let's get this the fuck over with."

Mildmay

Powers, I was so fucking mad I could hardly see straight. I could have garotted Felix and never thought about it twice. I *would* have told him to go fuck himself, except that the person who'd really get fucked over if I did was the girl. And I hadn't liked her much when she was a guy, and I didn't like her no better now—her making sheep's eyes at Felix and him acting like he didn't notice—but it wasn't the sort of thing she ought to end up dead over, any more than Felix being a complete fucking prick was.

So I let her braid my hair the way she did hers, and we swapped coats, which wasn't comfortable for neither of us, but we could get by, and her and Felix went out so they could be sure they got off the ship as soon as they could. The goons might not be completely fooled, but they'd be inclined to wait instead of follow. And then I could make like I was sneaking off, and they'd be sure to come after me, and wouldn't that be fucking grand? Felix was awfully flip about it, but I was betting he didn't know hired goons the way I did. And if everything went right, he wouldn't have to.

You know, that made me mad, too, the way I'd catch myself trying to protect him, like he was still crazy and not to blame for the fucked-up situation he'd landed us in. Well, landed me in.

"Fuck it," I said under my breath and tried to stop thinking.

After a while, I heard everybody clomping down the gangplank. I hoped Felix had got his damn rings back, because I had a feeling I knew who'd be sent after 'em if he'd forgot.

Climb the wall in front of you, Milly-Fox, I said to myself. I judged time the way I always had on a job, doing "Jeniard's Lover" in my head. Last time I'd done that, I'd been in Mélusine on a hotel roof in the rain, coming down with the Winter Fever, fixing to meet Mavortian von Heber for the first time. All I'd known about Felix Harrowgate was that he was the hocus who'd broken the Virtu. That life had sucked, but I wished I could get back to it and tell myself to tell Mavortian to fuck off. Because both my legs had worked right then, and I didn't have a prick of a hocus ordering me around like his own personal dog.

I finished up with "Jeniard's Lover" and went out on deck. There was nobody around—I mean, nobody I knew—and one look was enough to spot the fat Kekropian leaning against a warehouse and pretending like he wasn't watching the *White Otter*. At worst, if there'd been two guys set to watch, we'd split them up. But I was betting this guy was it for lookout, and Felix and Arakhne had got past him. There's a reason smart people don't hire goons.

If I'd actually wanted to get off the ship without being seen, I'd've gone over the side and swum for it. So I was just as glad that wasn't the point here, because I was *pretty* sure I'd be able to make it, but not, you know, completely convinced. Small favors—all I had to do was act like I thought

I was being all sneaky, which was mostly wearing this big hat that Arakhne'd pulled out of her luggage. Stupid thing, and if that was the best she could do, it was no wonder there were goons waiting for her, but it was doing what I wanted just fine. Which was mainly getting in the way of the goon getting a good look at my face.

I saw the goon see me and pretended like I didn't. Felix and Arakhne were heading north for the Pig-whistle, so I headed straight west, inland, and the goon fell in behind me. My limp was little enough now that it didn't matter so much—and when I thought of all the work I'd put in, it made me want to sit down and laugh until I puked, that *this* was the good I got out of it. First major street I crossed, I looked around, and sure enough the goon had picked up some friends. Three or four of them, although it was hard to tell without turning around to count.

That was probably the lot, then, and now I had to figure out how I was going to get *them* to figure out I wasn't a stupid little Troian girl. What they did then was anybody's guess, but as long as they didn't catch on to the truth, it didn't much matter.

I wished—a lot—that I could have picked this whole stupid game up and dropped it down in Mélusine. Didn't even have to be the Lower City, although that would've been best. 'Cause I could guess about which way to go and which not in this city, but that's all I was doing. Guessing.

And, wouldn't you know it, I guessed wrong.

One of Keeper's friends used to say, *If you're gonna fuck up, go ahead and fuck up big.* Now Keeper didn't like that, along of how she thought you shouldn't be fucking up in the first place, but I'd always kind of liked it. So I guess I should've been glad to see myself taking Cleophée's advice, only of course there was the part where I ended up in deep shit.

I'd turned left down a perfectly ordinary-looking street, aiming to work a little farther from Felix and Arakhne before I did anything about making the goons lose interest. It was getting on toward the septad-day, and the crowd had been thinning out, so I didn't pay quite enough attention quite soon enough to the way there wasn't nobody on this piece of road except the goons and me.

And then I turned a corner and found out why. Fucking dead end was why, and the goons must've been laughing their asses off, 'cause I went to head back quick the other way, and there they were. All six of them.

I said, "Do y'all want something?"

The looks on their faces were almost worth it. They'd been following the red braids and the way I'd been acting like I thought I might be followed.

"You ain't a girl," one of them said, like I'd done it on purpose to insult him.

"Never said I was." I figured I'd better keep on like a cit. "Y'all looking for somebody?"

"Yeah," said the guy at the back. "Maybe you've seen her. Red-haired girl, about your height. Named Arakhne, although of course she might be calling herself something else."

He wasn't no dummy. He'd smelled the rat.

"Nope," I said. "Sorry. Stranger in town."

"Oh this girl ain't a local," the guy in the back said. The six of them were spreading out, boxing me in, and a good look at that guy, the one with the brains, sent my heart down into my stomach. He was broad as a fucking church door, and wasn't none of it fat. Fuck, I thought and took a careful step back.

"Fact is," Church Door went on, "we'd heard pretty reliable that she was on that ship you came off of, so I'm thinking maybe you can tell us where she is."

"Nope."

"Now is that 'cause you *can't* or 'cause you *won't*?"

"No girls on board. Nice middle-aged society lady, but I don't figure it's her you're after."

The goons were still closing in.

"How about boys?" said Church Door, and I wasn't fooling him one little bit.

"Fuck it," I said and got rid of that fucking hat.

Now six on one ain't good odds. Wouldn't've been good odds even if I hadn't been a crip, although at least then I'd've had the option to try and outrun them. Things were messy for a little while, but they ended up about like we'd all expected, with me on the ground and Church Door's boot on my neck. Now most of his goons were cussing and bleeding, and one of 'em was just starting to come 'round, but the meat of the situation was my neck and his boot, which was what my friend Zephyr would have called unambiguous.

"Let's take this somewhere private," Church Door said. "'Less you feel like just answering the question."

I didn't waste my breath on saying nothing. Church Door kicked me twice in the head and once more for luck, and while I didn't exactly miss nothing, it all got real uninteresting for a while. The goons hauled me up and dragged me after Church Door. I don't know quite where we went or how we got there, along of, like I said, being not interested at the time. When things cleared up, we were in a big, echoey, empty building, an abandoned warehouse or something. I was lucky—small fucking favors—that they hadn't really been ready for catching somebody other than that damn stupid girl. They didn't even have a chair to tie me to or anything, just dumped me on the floor. Not that it looked like Church Door needed a chair—or anything else. He looked like maybe he didn't need nothing more than his fingers to cause all the pain he wanted.

"It's a simple question, friend," he said. "Tell us where the girl is, and we'll let you go."

I kept my mouth shut and watched him circling in on me.

"You ain't Troian, no matter what color your hair is. She don't mean nothing to you."

Which was true, but also not the point. I kept on saying nothing, and he kept on circling. He was enjoying himself, and that was bad bad news. And I was still kind of a little off, so when he came in, I wasn't fast enough, and he got his hand knotted in my hair, right at the base of my skull. I wondered when the braids had come undone, and then Church Door got my attention by jerking my head back almost hard enough to break my neck.

"Whereas me," he said, "I could come to mean quite a lot to you." And he grinned.

I'd seen worse than him. I'd been in the Boneprince at night with Vey Coruscant. I'd done things myself—things I wasn't proud of, but they'd make this two-centime goon piss himself if he knew about them. Which, of course, he didn't, so they didn't hardly matter. It wasn't like he was going to sit still for me to tell him.

I kept my mouth shut and let him hit me. But he must have figured out somehow—felt it, smelled it, I don't know—that wasn't going to get him nowhere, because after he hit me once, he let go of me and stepped back.

"We could kill you, you know," he said.

I just watched him.

"You don't mean any more to us than that girl does to you." He stared at me a moment longer, then said, "Griff, hand me your knife."

Fuck him, he'd found my weak point. I could hear it in his voice. It's 'cause of the scar—I know it is and it don't help none. It's the thing I can't stand, the idea of somebody making my face worse. I was on my feet without even meaning to be, and Church Door was grinning again.

If I'd been tied up, I don't know what he might have got me to say. But he was a cocky bastard, and I was a crip about half his size, and I hadn't put on no particularly exciting show in the first go-round. And he didn't know how I'd got that fucking scar in the first place. He waved his goons back.

Now, my leg was singing Ervenzian opera, and my head felt like somebody'd replaced the bones with iron, and there were all kinds of bruises I was only starting to feel. But my body still remembered how knife fights worked, and Church Door didn't look like he was planning so much on fighting as just cutting. His fucking mistake.

I dodged his first swing at me, and that made the bastard laugh. Be laughing out the other side of your face in a minute, I thought, but I knew I had to end this quick, before he either got bored or realized he was outclassed and called his goons in again to hold me down.

So the next swing I dodged inside instead of out, jammed his wrist, got the knife, and drove it back between my own elbow and side and into his gut. I rolled myself clear because jumping would have been just begging for my leg to take me down. Up on my feet again, turned around, and Church Door was staring at me with this look on his face that said plain as daylight how that wasn't what was supposed to happen. Then his knees buckled and he pitched forward, driving the knife farther into his belly with his own weight. If he wasn't dead now, he would be soon.

I looked around at the five goons. They were staring at me like a bunch of cows, but at least it didn't look like none of them were getting any bright ideas.

I said, slow and careful, "I ain't got no fight with the rest of y'all. 'Less you make me."

After a second, the one called Griff, the one who'd given Church Door his knife, shook his head.

"Good. And the law don't hear about the body, right?"

One of the others spat. "Law don't give a shit."

"Okay. Then I'm gonna leave and you ain't gonna follow me and we ain't ever gonna see each other again. Okay?"

This time they all nodded. I backed to the door, slow and careful, and they stood there and watched me go. Like cows.

I slammed the door shut behind me and set off north, wishing like fuck that I could run.

Felix

The Pig-whistle had seen better days, but the rooms were large, clean, and comfortable. Their rates were reasonable, though sadly not reasonable enough that Mildmay and I could afford separate rooms. Arakhne's funds seemed to be plentiful; she bespoke a room for herself under the name Phaëthon Yarth and then followed me up to the room Mildmay and I would share.

I longed with all my heart to tell her to go away, longed to have the chance to do more than merely check that my rings were all in their case, all unharmed, but she was still wide-eyed and skittish, and it was clear I would have had to use force to get her on the other side of the door.

I took my shoes off and lay down. She perched on the chair by the window and kept an anxious watch on the street. She tried once or twice to engage me in conversation, but I pretended to be sleepy, and she gave up, only sighing deeply from time to time to remind me of the burdens under which she labored.

Time crawled past. After an hour I couldn't maintain my pretense of sleepiness any longer and joined Arakhne at the window. She had the wit not to say anything, and we stared out at Blue Lantern Street in silence, watching for her hat or his red hair or just a man with Mildmay's slight awkwardness in his walk.

I wasn't sure exactly how long it was—eternities, eons, maybe half an hour—before he appeared, a slow, stumbling figure at the foot of the hill.

"Stay here," I snarled at Arakhne, cramming my shoes on, and bolted out of the room.

Up close, he looked dreadfully white. His eyes were strange, blurred, and the awkward, hobbled way he was moving, as if his torso were a solid block of wood without joints or hinges, suggested he was in a good deal of pain—more pain than I could expect him to admit to me.

"What happened?" I said, wanting to offer help but knowing I would be rebuffed.

He stopped, tilted his head back to look at me. "They thought they had a reason," he said and continued on his dogged way up the hill.

I simply stared after him for a moment, baffled, before I remembered saying, earlier in the day, *They'll have no reason to harm you when they realize they've made a mistake.*

"But *what*?" I said, catching up to him. "What reason could they have?"

The look he gave me was withering in its contempt, but he said only, "You better get that damn girl out of town tonight."

"You don't mean you—"

"I didn't tell 'em shit," he said, his voice flat with anger. "But they knew enough already that they'll find her. And they ain't gonna be happy when they do."

"Mildmay, what—"

We had reached the entryway of the Pig-whistle. He stopped and said in Marathine, fast and low and hard, "I just killed a guy, okay? And they ain't gonna give us trouble with the law, but we ain't friends, neither. That enough for you?"

I managed to keep from shrinking back from him or letting my shock show on my face, but I found myself entirely bereft of words.

He looked away first, rubbing one hand over his face. "Sorry," he said. "I just . . . if they catch up to her, they *will* kill her."

It took me two tries to get my voice to work. "Then I guess . . . I guess I'd better get her out of town."

✥

I made Mildmay stay behind, made him lie down on the bed and promise to rest. I knew by the way his gaze followed me coldly around the room that this was not over, but he did not say anything in front of Arakhne, and I was grateful for that.

Arakhne herself mercifully showed no disposition to argue. She was not thrown into any greater state of panic by the news Mildmay brought and did not evince any surprise. It did not make me like her better that, along with surprise, she also failed to show remorse or any particular concern for Mildmay's injuries—which he would not discuss and refused to let me examine. She still thought of him as a hired thug, and this was neither the time nor the place to make her see her error. I hoped someone else would teach her before that way of thinking got her killed.

I spun a quick story for the hotel clerk about messages waiting for my young friend upon his arrival in Klepsydra; the clerk was sympathetic and obliging and lavish with advice. I argued with Arakhne all the way to the stage post at the northern edge of the city whether she would do better to hire a horse and start for Aigisthos on her own, or to wait for the first stagecoach, which left at dawn. She had taken Mildmay's story to heart; she refused to wait. I could have stopped her only by traveling with her. She was not a lost kitten, and my responsibility to Mildmay far outweighed my ridiculous and unfounded sense of responsibility to her.

She came out again. "Half an hour, they say."

"Good. Then I'd best be getting back."

"Felix . . ."

I raised one eyebrow at her. She said, "You could come with me."

Perhaps if I hadn't just had that same discussion with myself, I might not have answered so quickly or with such finality. "No."

"No?" It was half a squawk, indignation and incredulity combined.

"No, I can't. I need to get back to my brother."

"Surely you needn't—"

"Yes, I *do* need. You judge too much by surfaces."

"Felix, please," and somehow she had caught hold of my lapels and was pressed up against me, staring imploringly into my face. "I can't live with the thought of never seeing you again."

"I *beg* your pardon?" I removed my coat from her clutch and stepped back. She followed, although she did not grab me again.

"I never imagined this is what love would feel like. I never knew . . . I wasn't going to say anything, but I can't just walk away from you."

"Yes, you can," I said, wondering what it was that I was doing wrong that I kept attracting passion from persons I did not want, while the one person I did want was never going to look at me twice. "Surfaces, Arakhne. I'm ganumedes and not interested."

The Troian word was better than the ugly Marathine "molly," and there was no doubt she understood me. Her face went blank, and she—finally, blessedly—took a step back. I was bitterly reminded of myself and Mildmay in the doorway of the Pig-whistle.

"Good-bye, Arakhne," I said. "Good luck." It seemed all too probable that she would need it.

༃

Mildmay was waiting for me, sitting propped up against the headboard.

"Well?" he said.

"She's off. Not our concern."

"Good."

I sat down on the edge of the bed and took off my shoes. While I was safely not looking at him, I said, "How are you?"

I could hear the half shrug in the way he said, "I'm okay."

"Really?"

"Yeah. Ain't like I never killed a guy before."

"How many—" I brought myself up short.

"Dunno, exactly." He knew what I'd been going to ask. He'd probably been waiting for me to ask that question for months. His voice was hard, careless. "First guy I killed for money, I had two septads and one."

I looked around; he was staring at the window curtains, but I thought they weren't what he was seeing. He said, "I was good at it."

There was silence for a moment, all sharp edges and hard enough to splinter bone. Then he said, "You want me to kill anybody for you again, you pay me first."

"I didn't *want* you to kill anybody."

"Yeah? And that's why you sent me out there like a Trials lamb?"

"I didn't know—"

"Would it've mattered if you had?" I wasn't sure which was more painful, the contempt in his voice or the resignation.

"I don't know," I said after a moment, and was terrified by my own honesty. "I don't . . . I've never . . ."

"We don't all got to be murderers," he said, and if I'd hated his contempt, I hated his gentleness more.

"How badly are you hurt?" I said, forcing my voice to be cold and disinterested, like a stranger's.

"I'll live," he said, his voice flat again. It occurred to me that it said something very unpleasant about both of us that we saw concern and kindness as attacks.

I got up, paced over to the window, stood and looked out at the late-afternoon traffic.

He burst out, "Why didn't you tell me?"

"What?" I turned back. His face was white and set.

"You knew she was a girl. Why didn't you tell me?"

"It needed to be kept secret."

"And you didn't trust me not to roll over on her?"

"That's not it at all. But Arakhne—"

"Did she ask you not to tell me?"

"Not in so many words, but—"

"You didn't trust me," he said, bleak as winter.

"That has nothing to do with it."

"Then what does? Why the fuck didn't you tell me?"

Because I was trying to avoid talking to you at all. "It just seemed simpler—"

"Simpler!"

"Look, this is no big deal."

"Easy for you to say. You got them all falling over each other to make you happy anyways."

Arakhne's pleading face was suddenly in front of me again, with Ingvard and Astyanax swiftly following. "Jealous, little brother?"

"You'd like it if I was."

"What's that supposed to mean?" I said, half-angry, half-afraid he'd realized the truth, realized that I desired him.

"You like jealousy. You like knowing people want you."

He wasn't talking about sex, and my heart slowed a little. "Is it not natural to want to be liked?"

"That ain't what you want. It's like you got to have everybody's heart, and if they don't give it, you rip it out and watch it bleed."

I flinched from his acuity, and made a desperate stab to regain the offensive: "Maybe I wouldn't have to *take*, if you'd *give* a little more. Give me some trust. It isn't as if—" I could not keep going against the look on his face. It was as if he had died and been petrified into marble.

There was a terrible, frozen silence. He grated out, more like a dog's snarl than a human voice, "Like you gave me the truth?" He stood up, found his shoes, put them on, and tied them, all in perfect, brutal silence. He started for the door.

"Where are you going?" I said, more shrilly than I would have liked.

He opened the door, stepped through, and only then glanced back at me. His eyes were green and cold and brilliant with murder. "Find a whore," he said and slammed the door shut.

Mildmay

I didn't have no trouble at all finding a brothel. The night clerk was more than happy to point the way. He had a couple recommendations, too, but those I didn't pay no mind to. The sort of brothel he'd say was a "nice time" was really just not what I was looking for. Also not the sort of place that'd take me.

But I guess every city has its Pharaohlight. Klepsydra's was a long, snaky street near the docks called Eleusis Row. The nice places were on the city side, while the closer you got to the water, the lower and skankier the dives got. I wanted clean, cheap, and not too fussy, and I'd done enough work in Pharaohlight, both for Keeper and on my own, that I knew what to look for. I picked a house that had its front steps brick-batted and real curtains in the window, but hadn't seen a new coat of paint probably since I'd been born. The sign'd been touched up recently, though. It showed a smiling dog fucking a lady chimera, and I decided to take that as a good omen. They had a bouncer—another good sign—and he didn't like my face, but he let me by when I flashed a Kekropian imperial at him. Which was just as well, 'cause it was the only one I had.

Inside was about the same: old and shabby, but well cared for. The madam reminded me of Elvire, who ran the Goosegirl's Palace in the Arcane, or what Elvire would have been if she hadn't had the brains she did. She was put a little off her stride by her first good look at my face, but she got herself back together like a champ and asked me my pleasure. Exactly like that, too: "What is your pleasure, sir?"

And that put me a little off, so I guess we were even. I said, "Um."

She gestured with her fan at the door on one side of the hall. "Ladies?" And at the other. "Or gentlemen?"

"Oh. Um. Ladies."

"After you, sir," she said.

There were four girls in the parlor—if that's the right word. Anyway, in the room. Two of 'em were septad-to-the-centime brunettes, one was a Norvenan-type blonde, and the fourth was a Troian gal looked more than a little like Felix. They sat up and acted interested when I came in, but it was a professional thing, and I didn't care.

The madam was looking kind of sideways at my face, and she said, "No bloodletting and no bruising."

"I ain't aiming to hurt nobody," I said. And I wasn't. I just wanted to get rid of it, the guy I'd killed, and the dreams I'd been having about Ginevra and Keeper, and the way I felt about Felix, where I just wanted to slam his head against the wall until it crunched.

The blonde had blue eyes, like Ginevra'd had. I said, "Her."

"Anna Sylvia," the madam said, like I cared what the whore's name was. The blonde stood up. She was a skinny little thing, not like Ginevra at all except in the eyes. That was okay. Her and the madam gave each other a look, and then the whore said, "Sir? Will you come with me?"

"I hope so, darlin'," I said. She looked at me blankly, like she didn't get the joke—which was lame, I admit it. A crip joke. Like me. Or maybe she just didn't know what to do with it.

"Okay, then," I said. "Let's go."

She led me back into the hall and then up the stairs. The third door on the left was open, and we went in. Green wallpaper with an ivy pattern. Nice little oil lamp in brass filigree. Thing that wasn't a bed so much as a big sofa—daybeds, they call 'em. More flash-looking than a sagging old mattress, and don't encourage the tricks to stick around.

The blonde shut the door and said, not seductively or anything, just asking, "Tell me what you want."

I didn't laugh out loud, but it was a pretty near thing. What I *wanted*? I wasn't going to find that here, or anywhere I knew of to go looking. Death's one of them things where, once it's happened, you can't take it back or fix it. Less you're into necromancy, and even then I been told it ain't the same. Ain't nothing ever the same, after death's had a go at it.

So I told her what I'd come there for, which was what she was asking: "A hard fuck."

She nodded. Most whores I've known have been pretty much okay with the idea of just doing business like it's business. Saves them the bother of pretending it ain't. "How hard?"

"Your madam said no bruises."

"I don't bruise easy," she said and smiled at me.

Kethe, that just about undid me then and there. Little blonde whore smiles at me, and suddenly I felt like a vase somebody was trying to glue together, only I was more cracks than vase. And I think some of the pieces were just gone.

But I took a deep breath, let it out, said, "You don't have to kiss me."

"Okay," she said. "You don't have to say anything." And she came in close—first time she'd got herself within arm's reach of me—and started working on my shirt buttons. I don't know how she knew to say that, except that she was good at her job, and I figure she wasn't in that shabby, second-rate brothel for long after that. 'Least I hope she moved herself up the scale, because she was wasted where she was. She didn't even blink at the bruises.

Sex don't have to be about love. Most times in my experience it ain't. But it can be about all different kinds of need, and that little blonde girl knew that, and knew what I needed, and she let me slam her into that daybed until we were both panting like dogs and dripping with sweat. And things weren't no better, but at least I wasn't itching to get my fingers round Felix's throat no more. I don't know if she came or not. She didn't fake it for me, and I was glad of that.

And then we got up and put ourselves back together and I paid her and left. And things weren't better. Not one fucking bit.

Chapter 5

Mildmay

If there's anything worse than being stuck in a strange town where anybody who notices you might go trotting off to the dragoons to turn you in for murder or heresy, it's being stuck in a strange town and sharing a room with somebody you ain't on speaking terms with.

I mean, it wasn't that me and Felix weren't talking to each other at all. But I'd pissed him off so bad that he'd walked himself back behind this wall—I swear by all the powers sometimes I could practically fucking see it—and all I got was this kind of hard, bright version of him. He'd flirt with me, but he wouldn't *talk* to me. And I didn't know what to do with the flirting or how to deal with it or nothing. And he started riding me harder and harder about my grammar—and sounding more and more like Keeper the whole time. Keeper'd never got off my case about *isn't* instead of *ain't*, and *doesn't* instead of *don't*, and now here was Felix nagging at me every time I opened my mouth. He didn't say outright that I should stop talking like street trash because it made him look bad, but he didn't have to. And the worst part was, as we got into the tail end of a decad since we'd come off the *White Otter* and still no sign that we were going to stir out of Klepsydra before we got old and died, I couldn't tell if it was because he was really still mad at me or because it was a game to pass the time. The one was as likely as the other.

And as to why we were still in Klepsydra—well, fucked if I know. With Felix not talking to me, I couldn't get real answers from him when I asked, and after a couple days I just quit asking. I think what he was trying to do was find some way to not have to go through the southern duchies. Which I don't blame him for, except for the part where we didn't have a choice. At least he'd decided to believe me about how we didn't want to go anywhere near Aigisthos, but he kept trying to finesse a way of not going as far south as we both knew we had to. He used the last of our money to buy two maps and a guidebook, and then he drew these spiderweb things on the maps and covered every blank bit of paper in the guidebook with diagrams and bits of what looked like poetry and all kinds of weird shit. Hocus stuff was my best guess.

If I'd thought I'd get any kind of an answer, I'd've asked him why he was so set against the southern duchies. I mean, sure, they ain't no nice place, and they believe some really fucked-up things, if the people in the Lower City who hail from there are anything to go by, but it wasn't like we were planning to *live* there or something. But if I'd asked, he wouldn't've told me, so I didn't ask.

So there we were, a decad since we'd come into Klepsydra, still up in that room in the Pig-whistle that we could only maybe pay for, and that was if my luck with the cards was in the night before we had to settle. Or if we—meaning me—did some quick and dirty work among the local populace. And it might come to that, but I wasn't going to do it until Felix actually came out and said that was what he wanted. He was the one had spent our money. He could fucking well be the one to figure out what to do about it.

Felix and his maps and his guidebook and the pen and ink he'd charmed out of the night clerk were all sprawled across the bed. I was in the chair by the window, looking out at the sky, which was hazy with heat. The humidity was like this giant hand, pushing me down in the chair. It made Felix's hair even curlier. I knew that annoyed him, and I was glad of it, in this little spiteful petty sort of way, because short of going out and finding another whore, and maybe bringing her back and fucking her on top of his fucking maps, I wasn't going to make a dent in him this side of doomsday.

And even if I'd had the money—and I could've got it quick enough if it'd really been what I wanted, I guess—another whore wasn't what I needed. The first one hadn't helped with nothing. I was still dreaming about Ginevra, and she was still dead.

So Felix was scratching away at his new idea, whatever the fuck it was, and I was sitting and trying not to think about dead people, and that's when somebody started hammering on the door like they were trying to bust it down.

Felix looked over at me and raised one eyebrow, and he didn't need to say, *Aren't you going to deal with that?* Because somehow it was all my job—the chambermaids, the laundry maids, the clerks and the hotel manager and the hotel manager's fat little dog—just like if the Empire came knocking, it was going to be my job to sweet-talk the dragoons while Felix went out the window. I knew it, and I didn't quite know how he'd done it, and yeah, since you ask, it pissed me off.

But I got up and limped over and opened the door.

Theokrita Gauthy, looking like a buffalo on the rampage, said, *"Where is he?"*

"Felix?" I said. "He's right—"

"Not Felix! Florian! What have you done with my Florian?"

I just kind of gaped at her, and that was when Felix got up and came over. "What's the matter, Theokrita?" he said, calm and nice and all flash with the vowels, like she'd just dropped by for tea or something.

But Mrs. Gauthy wasn't having none of it. "Florian's gone, that's what's the *matter*, and I want to know where he is."

"I'm sure you do," said Felix, "but we haven't seen him."

"Ha!"

"Theokrita, we—"

She turned on me, and I backed right the fuck out of her way. "You've had him twisted around your little finger since the moment he laid eyes on you. Don't tell me you haven't been encouraging him in his silly ideas and egging him on to run away from home and do something stupid and throw away all his chances." She'd got me pinned in the corner, and I didn't know what to do. I mean, if she'd had a knife or something, I knew what to do about that, but this was something else again.

"Theokrita," Felix said, a lot less nice. "As I told you, we have not seen Florian. I take it from your somewhat incoherent remarks that he is missing?"

"He wasn't in his room this morning, and Hetty said his bed hadn't been slept in."

"And you came to us?"

"Where else would he have gone?"

"I haven't the faintest idea, but since he *didn't* come here, it seems a question worth exploring, don't you think?"

She looked at him suspiciously, and then back at me.

"Mrs. Gauthy, I swear by all the powers, I don't know. I ain't seen Florian since we left the *White Otter*."

She looked at Felix, her eyebrows up. I realized after a second she hadn't caught but maybe two words out of everything I'd said.

"He doesn't know," Felix said. "Any more than I do."

"He wouldn't have just run off," Mrs. Gauthy said.

"Kids do," I said, and Felix shot me a *shut up* look.

He said, "Theokrita, whatever has happened to Florian, it is not of our doing, and I am afraid we cannot help you find him. Surely your energies would be better spent elsewhere."

At that—and any half-wit dog could've seen it coming, although apparently Felix didn't—Mrs. Gauthy started crying.

She didn't cry pretty, and I would've laid odds she was faking. And if it'd just been me, I would've let her cry, 'cause if she was faking, she'd quit, and if she wasn't, there wasn't nothing I could do anyway. But Felix looked like somebody'd handed him a pissed-off baby gator, and he kind of fluttered at her, getting her to sit down and sending me off to fetch a cup of water. I wasn't real happy about going, because I could see he'd say anything if it would just get her to stop fucking crying, and I mean, it wasn't that I disagreed with him or nothing, but you don't want to go letting people like that name their own terms. Gets you into more trouble than it gets you out of.

But I went and got the water, and by the time I got back, Felix had got Mrs. Gauthy calmed down, so she was sort of gulping instead of sobbing, and she drank the water—although she didn't say thank you—and that was when Mr. Gauthy showed up to see if we'd kidnapped his wife along with his son. Seems Mrs. Gauthy had left him with the carriage while she came up to rescue Florian or whatever the fuck it was she'd had in mind.

Mr. Gauthy didn't look much calmer than Mrs. Gauthy. Now, he at least believed Felix that we hadn't snatched Florian—which I wasn't sure Mrs. Gauthy did. But what Mr. Gauthy wanted was to put the whole problem in Felix's lap, which I guess is one of them nasty side effects of getting people to practically worship you. Felix was looking pretty sour about it, but then Mr. Gauthy said "anything we can do in return," and Felix lit up like a beacon and said, "We can discuss payment once Florian is safely restored to you."

The Gauthys both looked like people going downstairs in the dark who'd just found out the hard way there was one more step than they'd thought. Me, I was fighting the urge to just strangle him then and there and have done with it. And the look he gave me said he knew it.

But he had some sort of plan, something in view that I couldn't see, and there wasn't nothing I could do—nothing useful anyway—but go along with it. So I got out of the way and let him ask questions.

He started with the simple stuff—when had they last laid eyes on Florian, would he have talked to his sisters, were there friends' houses he might have gone to, shit like that. But Felix didn't come up with nothing the Gauthys hadn't already thought of for themselves. So he started asking about what Florian had done the day before—I think just to buy himself time—and Mr. Gauthy was telling him all about Florian's mathematics and history lessons, when I remembered the thing Florian had started to say on the *White Otter* and stopped. And I hadn't pinned him down 'cause I hadn't figured it was any of my business. Nice going, Milly-Fox.

I said, "Where's his teacher? Mr. Tantony?"

They all three looked at me like I'd started barking. Fuck, I thought, but I said it again, slower, and right then I forgave Felix a whole bunch of things, because he didn't know what I was talking about, but he said without batting an eye, "An excellent question. Where *is* Ker Tantony?"

Mrs. Gauthy said, "But it can't have any bearing on—" At the same time Mr. Gauthy said, "But Jeremias would never—"

Felix was trying hard not to look like a cat given cream, but it was all in his voice when he said, "I beg your pardon. I didn't quite catch that."

"Ker Tantony left the house very early this morning, before anyone else was up."

"Thank you, Theokrita," Felix said. "And what evidence do you have that he didn't take Florian with him?"

Mr. Gauthy said, "Well, he didn't exactly *leave*, so much as that just at the moment he can't be found. But he would never hurt Florian. He's been with us five years, and his references were excellent."

Powers and saints, the things people can talk themselves into believing when they want. And the bourgeoisie more than most. Felix snorted, and

I knew he was thinking the same thing. He said, "So if Ker Tantony didn't leave, but yet can't be found—and somehow this story is sounding awfully familiar—what has become of him?"

A pause. Mr. Gauthy went scarlet. Mrs. Gauthy said, "Witchcraft." And suddenly I thought the whole nasty thing made sense. They'd found out somehow that Felix was a hocus—gossip from the captain, would be my guess—and probably they hadn't thought much more about it 'til Florian and his teacher went missing, and then they drew the obvious conclusion, same as I would've done in their place, except for how this time I knew it was wrong. Felix hadn't been witching nobody.

Thank the powers they ain't realized he's molly, I thought, and then saw Felix had gone white as a sheet and needed me to buy him some time.

"What're you saying exactly?" I said and had to repeat it twice. But Mr. Gauthy was perfectly polite about answering.

He said, "We thought if someone had spirited Florian away by magic, you would be able to tell us." He split a glance between us.

Felix said in kind of a croak, "Why not just go to the authorities?"

Mr. Gauthy made a face, like it was rude to even mention the idea. "Most undesirable publicity. And while the Imperial officers are most excellent fellows, they are common."

"Vulgar," said Mrs. Gauthy.

Felix turned to look out the window like he'd just spotted a dragon or something. I said, "Why didn't you just say so in the first place?"

"I thought Theokrita had," Mr. Gauthy said, puzzled as puzzled could be.

She didn't even blush, the bitch. "I wanted to be sure *he* didn't know anything first." I'd got my story turned around. They knew Felix was a hocus, but they didn't believe he'd ever do anything wrong. I was the one they thought—well, Mrs. Gauthy thought, anyway—would go snatching people, but if it wasn't me, then it was some random hocus come walking out of one of Florian's storybooks or something. Not *Felix Harrowgate,* good gracious no.

Fuck me sideways 'til I cry.

Felix, on the other hand, had swung round and got his bounce back. "Well, I can't do anything from here. If there's any thaumaturgic residue at all, it will be in the subject's room."

Blank little silence.

Felix rolled his eyes. "If I'm going to find any traces of magic, it will be in Florian's bedroom."

"Oh," Mr. Gauthy said. "All right. Now?"

"No, Leontes, let him consult his appointment book," Mrs. Gauthy said—well, basically snarled. "Honestly, sometimes I wonder whether you have an ounce of paternal feeling in your entire body."

Felix said in a hurry, "I am at your disposal," and gave me a look that said I was coming whether I wanted to or not. Which I didn't really, but I also couldn't help thinking maybe I could do something useful about finding Florian. And that mattered more than whether the Gauthys wanted me along or not. Or whether I wanted to go.

Felix

The Gauthys' house was built in what I'd been given to understand was the common eastern Kekropian fashion: a three-story rectangle around a central courtyard, with the public rooms on the side facing the street and the kitchens and servants' quarters at the back. The family's rooms were along the inner sides, each with a window overlooking the courtyard. There were a number of entrances from the house to the courtyard, but only two from the house to the outside world: the massive, formal front door and the kitchen door debouching onto the alley behind the house. Both doors were bolted at night; both had been bolted before Florian said good night to his parents and (presumably) went up to his bedroom. The kitchen door had been unbolted by the cook when she came into the kitchen shortly before dawn, and between then and the discovery that Florian was missing, there had been at least one person in the kitchen at all times, and frequently more like four or five. The front door hadn't been unbolted until after the housemaid Hetty had found Florian's room empty and his bed unslept in. All the exterior windows were barred.

Mildmay and I stood in Florian's bedroom. We had been permitted to inspect Jeremias Tantony's closetlike room with its pristinely unrumpled bed, but it had told us nothing, and I had convinced the Gauthys that I needed privacy and time to detect the residue of any spells that might have been worked in Florian's room, when the truth—as I could have told them in five seconds—was that there was no residue to detect. No one had enchanted Florian Gauthy out of his bedroom.

It was very much the room of a child of the prosperous bourgeoisie, the furniture sturdy and functional, the contents of the wardrobe showing some wear, but all made of the best materials and none of them hand-me-downs. The housemaid said one pair of shoes was missing, plus the clothes Florian had been wearing yesterday and the coat that needed the left elbow darned; all of which suggested strongly, as Mildmay pointed out, that Florian had left of his own volition.

The wallpaper in Florian's room had clearly been of his mother's choosing; no child would want that rather oversophisticated green print, and I was not sure I would have either. Florian's personality was imprinted on the room by the model ship on the bookcase and the collection of rocks, bird feathers, some small animal's jawbone, coins from Norvena Magna, Norvena Parva, Ervenzia, Troia, Skaar—all rather oddly piled in one corner.

Mildmay was inspecting the contents of the bookcase in a fashion both bemused and wondering. He was only barely literate, but he seemed fascinated by the mere existence of these books, his fingers running along their spines as if to prove their reality. I wondered if he'd ever seen that many books in one place before and thought that I should have taken him into the Nephelion's library, whether he would have admitted to wanting to go or not.

I said, "Why has he left his things in the corner like this?"

Mildmay abandoned the bookcase and came over to see what I was talking about. He picked up one of the rocks, a water-polished piece of quartz. "You'd want this where it'd catch the light," he said thoughtfully, turning it over in his fingers. "Wouldn't you?"

"As for example on the windowsill," I said.

The window was large, double-sashed, and wide-open. Not surprising at the sweltering end of summer, but also, in this instance, suggestive. I was just about to propose that we see what reason Florian might have had for opening the window and clearing off the sill when there was a knock on the door.

Mildmay and I looked at each other. He shrugged. I said, "Come in."

A woman stepped into the room and closed the door behind her, then stood regarding us calmly. She was my age or a little older, an inch or two taller than Mildmay, brown-sugar-colored hair scraped back in a knot; her small mouth, slightly receding chin, and snub nose gave her a childish air entirely contradicted by the intelligence of her gaze. She wore round-lensed spectacles, and her dull brown dress muffled her figure almost completely.

"I beg your pardon, Keria . . . ?"

"Mehitabel Parr. I'm the governess."

She certainly looked the part. I said, "And you're here because?"

Her gaze moved deliberately from me to Mildmay and back again. "I thought you might need some help."

"Help? Of what sort?"

"I know more about Jeremias Tantony than either of our employers does."

"And you think Ker Tantony is central to this enigma?"

"He *is* missing."

"Yes."

"And I can assure you that Jeremias Tantony would *not* simply vanish. He would have a plan."

"Then you do not subscribe to the evil wizard theory?"

She snorted, for a moment not like a governess at all. "I subscribe to the my-employers-are-at-their-wits'-end theory, with the addendum that it isn't much of a journey."

I couldn't quite choke back a laugh, and she smiled at me before sobering to add, "I want Florian to be found, and since Ker Gauthy refuses to speak to the civil guard, you look like the best hope of that happening."

"Florian? Not Ker Tantony?"

"Jeremias is an adult, and I feel no responsibility for him. But I think he talked to me more than anyone else in the household, and I am willing to put that knowledge at your disposal."

"Thank you," I said. "We were just about to see why Florian left his window open, if you would care to join the investigation."

"Gladly," she said.

Mildmay gave me an indecipherable look; he went to the window and leaned out.

"Nice strong ivy," he said. "Somebody's been climbing it."

"Keria Gauthy would have five fits," Mehitabel Parr said, forestalling my mostly ironic question as to whether this was a habitual pastime of the household.

"One person," Mildmay continued, leaning even farther. "Climbing down."

"But why would you climb down—or up, for that matter—when there's a perfectly good staircase?"

"Which creaks," said the governess, "like Hell's own hand organ."

"Ah," I said. "So entirely useless for clandestine purposes."

"You might even call it counterproductive."

"But where does climbing down the ivy *get* you?"

Mildmay said, "One way to find out," and swung out the window.

I leaned out after him. "Are you *mad*?"

He didn't even look up at me, just said, "Meet me in the courtyard," and kept climbing down.

I watched for a moment, but he seemed to know what he was about, and if he did fall, there was nothing I could do. I pulled my head back in and said to Mehitabel Parr, "We are to meet him in the courtyard."

Her eyebrows went up. After more than a week with only Mildmay and his stone face for company, I was so grateful for her ordinary human reaction I could almost have kissed her. She said, "Does he often do things like that?"

"I don't—" I bit back the word *know*. "Will you lead the way, keria?"

"Of course, Ker Harrowgate."

I had not been paying attention to the stairs on the way up, being more concerned with convincing the Gauthys to leave me alone, but following Miss Parr down, I observed that she was right; they did creak abominably, and if I had been Leontes Gauthy, I would have had strong words with my carpenters about it. Certainly, this would not be the route one would choose if one wished to go unnoticed.

At the bottom of the stairs, we turned right, and a short passageway brought us to a door opening onto the courtyard. Mildmay was kneeling awkwardly under Florian's window. He glanced around as we came out and said, "Two people in this flower bed. Kid-sized feet'd be Florian, and the other guy in the flashy pointy-toed boots—"

"Jeremias," Mehitabel Parr said and sighed.

"Thanks," Mildmay said, but not quite as if he meant it.

I said, "So they were both here in the courtyard. But why? And where did they go?"

"Since it looks as if they did not obligingly stay in the decorative borders," the governess said, "they must have gone into the center."

"And what? Vanished?" I raised an eyebrow at her. "Are we back to the evil wizard theory?"

"*I* don't know," she said, glaring at me.

I bowed her extravagantly toward the center of the courtyard. "Shall we look?"

The courtyard was far from vast, but it was large enough to have a paved quadrangle with a very small fountain. There were no footprints anywhere;

the stones, of course, would not record them, and the borders on the other three sides were undisturbed. The fountain was *not* deep enough to drown in.

"Would they have come out here only to go back inside?" I asked the governess. "It seems awfully elaborate—"

"Maybe they opened the hollow stone," a voice said above us.

All three of us jumped like startled cats. The speaker was a girl, four or five years older than Florian and much like him to look at, sitting in an open second-story window.

"Delila," said Mehitabel Parr, "what are you doing?"

"Helping. Keria Parr, you *can't* tell us to go back to our rooms because you're going to help the foreign gentlemen find Florian, and then not expect us to help, too."

"Yes, of course. And Angora is with you on this?"

"Yes," the girl said, perfectly cheerfully.

"Kerina Gauthy," I said, "what did you mean by the 'hollow stone'?"

Delila Gauthy turned an alarming shade of pink, and I could hear giggling from the room behind her. But she remained steadfast. "Kechever always said he was going to figure out how to open it, but he never did. But that means Florian *would*."

Miss Parr said, a *sotto voce* aside, "There is a certain matter of fraternal rivalry."

"I don't think Mother and Father know about it," Delila continued, "but Florian will tell Ker Tantony *anything*." She sniffed hard. "Idiot."

"And Ker Tantony would be fascinated," the governess said. "He loves secrets and finding out things he isn't supposed to know."

"Kerina Gauthy, thank you," I said, causing her to become even pinker. "One more thing: where is this hollow stone?"

"Just to the right of where the other gentleman is standing. It sounds different when you stomp on it." With that, her composure expended, she retreated, closing the window behind her.

"The young ladies aren't supposed to talk to strange men," Mehitabel Parr remarked.

"Then it was very good of her to help," I said. I found the stone Delila had indicated, which did in fact sound distinctly hollow when thumped.

"Did Ker Gauthy build this house?" I asked.

Mehitabel Parr said, "My understanding is that he *re*built it. The original house burned down in Empress Eunike's Drought forty years ago. But

I think the courtyard is original, and goodness knows how old that might make it."

"Interesting," I said. The hollow-sounding stone was absolutely flush with its neighbors, and there was no sign of any handhold or a place where a crow might be wedged. "Then if it's operated by a spring, the mechanism is most likely in the fountain."

"Keria Gauthy's been wanting to have it taken out for years, but Ker Gauthy won't agree. He says it has historic significance, and Jeremias agrees with him."

"I imagine he does," I said. "Mildmay, would you . . . ?"

"Sure," he said, and I wondered why he was angry at me now.

The fountain was extremely simple, a basin on a plinth with an odd and very weather-beaten statue in the middle. The water appeared to be pouring from its hands. While Mildmay made his investigations, I said to Miss Parr, "What *is* that?"

"The statue? Very old is all I can tell you for sure. Jeremias has all sorts of elaborate theories—and I believe has been attracting very favorable attention at the Antiquarian Society in Aigisthos with them."

"Indeed. And what is Ker Tantony's theory?"

"Jeremias believes that Klepsydra was the center of a proscribed cult in the early days of the Empire. He says this statue is an archaic Troian deity, who was no longer worshipped in Troia at the time it was carved, and whose name means something like He Who Guards The Threshold."

"And this god was the center of a proscribed Kekropian cult?"

"That was my question. And Jeremias said, 'Not exactly,' and became extremely evasive. And now I see why." Her mouth compressed in a bitter line. "He has been preparing his coup."

Mildmay muttered something under his breath that was almost certainly obscene and probably blasphemous. He took his coat off, rolled up his sleeves, and returned to the fray.

"Keria Parr," I said, "forgive me, but are you fond of Ker Tantony?"

Her eyes met mine steadily, unabashed. "You mean, are we lovers?"

"Yes."

"Yes, we are, but I am not fond of him."

"An honest answer to an impertinent question. Thank you." I smiled at her. She gave me a rather suspicious look and then smiled back.

"So," I said, "the Gauthys have a statue of an ancient Troian god in their courtyard."

"That's Jeremias's theory," she said, and I saw her gratitude that I was not going to pursue the question of why she had taken as her lover a man whom she did not like.

"And if he's a threshold guardian . . ."

"Then what threshold is he guarding? I annoyed Jeremias very much by asking that question. At the time I assumed it was because he didn't know the answer, but now I think it was because he did."

Mildmay let out a choked exclamation of triumph, and the side of the hollow stone nearest the fountain juddered up just far enough that I could wedge my fingers under it and lift. After a second, Mildmay was there to help, and together we swung it up on its concealed hinge.

"Keria Parr," I said, "something to prop it open?"

"Of course," she said. She was gone barely two minutes, returning with a stout length of firewood that did the job handily.

We stood and looked at the dark hole we had discovered.

"There's stairs," Mildmay said, shrugging back into his coat.

"And I suppose we ought to go down them," I said. I could not muster any great enthusiasm for the prospect.

The governess said, "Shouldn't you tell Keria Gauthy first?"

I found that I had even less enthusiasm for *that* prospect.

"Wasting time," Mildmay said. "They might be hurt."

Miss Parr looked at me inquiringly. I said, "He says it's a waste of time. And Florian and Ker Tantony might very well be hurt."

"Oh," she said. "Yes. But . . . wait a moment."

She picked a pebble out of the fountain's basin to toss against Delila Gauthy's window. On the instant, the window went up, and Delila leaned out.

"Delila," said Miss Parr, "Ker Harrowgate and Ker Foxe have found a staircase under the hollow stone. They think it likely that that is where Ker Tantony and Florian have gone. We are going to go after them. Tell your parents, but no one should come after us. We don't know what we may find. Understand?"

"Yes, Keria Parr."

"And give us a quarter hour's head start."

"Yes, Keria Parr." Delila withdrew and shut the window again.

" 'We'?" I said. "You intend to come with us?"

"I'm not going to stand and flutter my handkerchief after you like the heroine of a Tibernian romance, if that's what you mean."

Mildmay opened his mouth and closed it again.

"What?" I said.

"Nothing."

"If you have an objection, you'd do better to make it now."

"Ain't she gonna get in trouble?"

I wasn't entirely convinced that was what he had intended to say, but it was a good question, and I put it to Mehitabel Parr.

"Perhaps," she said, as one to whom the matter was of supreme indifference.

"Keria Parr—"

"No! Ker Harrowgate, I have sufficient reasons, and I beg that you will leave me to deal with the consequences."

Mildmay said something I didn't fully catch; the word "trap," however, came through clear as a bell, and Miss Parr flushed a dull, ugly red.

"I assure you, I would not stoop so low," she said, "nor do I need to."

I wondered why Mildmay had taken such a dislike to Mehitabel Parr, but I said, "Keria Parr, he meant no offense. We are strangers here and unfamiliar with local customs." I glared at Mildmay; he glared back at me, but at least had the sense to hold his tongue.

Miss Parr and I both knew I was lying, but she nodded stiffly and said, "In any event, I assure you I would certainly not be such an imbecile as to try a trick like that on a wizard or anyone under his protection."

"I ain't—"

"Mildmay." I cut him off coldly. "I believe you said something about not wasting time."

The only hint I had that the blow had landed was the hesitation before he said, "Yeah. I'll go first then," and turned to squeeze under the raised stone.

I called witchlights and sent them after him, tiny offerings of peace. Then Mehitabel Parr and I followed him down into the darkness under the Gauthys' respectable house.

Mildmay

Them stairs were a bitch, I'm here to tell you—and I very nearly wasn't a time or two. They were steep and narrow and even with Felix's little green chrysanthemums that spooked me out although I wasn't going to say so, it was hard to see what you were doing. Also, the stairs were all uneven and swaybacked, the way the stairs were in some of the really old parts of the Arcane. I didn't much care for touching the walls, along of the cobwebs and the damp and just generally not liking the looks of things, but there wasn't nothing else to brace yourself on, and I figured I'd like things even less with my neck broke. Oh, and before you ask, my leg fucking *hated* it.

I could hear Felix and the teacher-lady talking behind me. I wished they'd shut the fuck up, but I knew better than to say it. Felix had already showed me perfectly clear where I got off. And if he wanted to buddy up with some strange Kekropian woman we knew purely fuck-all about, that was his problem. I just wished I didn't have the feeling that sooner or later it was going to turn out to be *my* problem.

The stairs weren't in a spiral, but they weren't exactly straight, either. They kept kind of turning, just a little bit at a time, and it really fucked up my sense of direction, which normally nothing can mess with. And, I mean, it wasn't like I was *lost,* really, but just . . . I don't know. Just like nothing was quite where it was supposed to be. Even more than I wanted to tell Felix and Miss Parr to shut up, I wanted to tell them to turn around and go back up these fucking stairs and back out into the daylight. But I didn't, because Florian Gauthy had been nice to me and listened to my stories. And Felix could get lost in a teacup. He wouldn't get what I was trying to say. And I was afraid he'd make fun of me.

So we went down and around in this kind of half-assed circle, and things got damper and damper, and after a while I started thinking I smelled the Sim.

Now, that was all kinds of bad news, and not just on account of a big fucking river being the last thing we needed right now. Felix was scared to death of the Sim, even worse than he was of the ocean, and I really didn't want to deal with him having a fit about it down here in the dark.

He ain't crazy now, I said to myself. He'll be fine. But I remembered his face after he took his first good, long look at the ocean, and I wasn't buying, even before he said, out of the dark behind me, "Mildmay?"

"Yeah, Felix?" I said, like I didn't already know.

"Is that . . . do you smell . . ."

"I think it's the Sim," I said, trying to keep my voice as dull and bored as I could.

There was this horrible kind of gap where Felix should have been saying something to prove he wasn't losing his shit, and then Miss Parr said, "The river, do you mean?"

"Yes," Felix said.

"It's how the city got its name. Klepsydra. Thief of Water. About a mile west of the old city walls, the Phaidris dives underground and never resurfaces. Everyone assumes it empties into the ocean somewhere, but no one really knows. Just as if someone had stolen the river away."

"How quaint," Felix said, and I heard the shake in his voice.

We went down about another ten steps, and then Felix said, trying so hard to sound casual it damn near broke my heart, "Do you suppose this proscribed cult Ker Tantony is on the track of has anything to do with the river?"

"I don't know," Miss Parr said. She sounded kind of cautious, like she'd figured out there was something fucked up but didn't know what. She was smart, all right. "Perhaps."

"Lovely," Felix said, and now I was praying for him to shut up because he was doing a shitty job of hiding how nervous he was, and, I mean, he drove me up the wall, but I didn't want to watch him embarrass himself in front of this strange woman.

So I figured I'd better ask some question to get Miss Parr talking, and I'd better do it before Felix tried to be all casual again. I racked my brain and managed, "What kind of thing would Mr. Tantony be looking for down here? What's he wanting to find?"

Powers, it was a lame question, and Felix had to repeat it for her, but it did the trick. I admit, I didn't pay much attention to what she was saying, along of really not giving a rat's ass, but I noticed when Felix started asking questions, and that he sounded more or less okay again. Then I just completely shut them both out and concentrated on, you know, not falling down them fucking stairs.

And, Kethe, it seemed like they were going to go on forever, and we'd come out on the other side of the world, where the people have heads like dogs and vultures. We went down and down, and I tried not to wonder what kind of nastiness a cult would be into that it needed all these stairs between it and daylight. I could think of some things, along of having heard way too many stories about the Obscurantists, and I know it was just my imagination, but the darkness seemed like it was getting heavier, and I don't know, kind of like it was breathing. And I was starting to hear things, just little funny things I couldn't quite place, and all of a sudden I realized Felix and Miss Parr had quit talking. And you know, as much as I'd been wishing they'd shut up, now I was wishing they'd start yapping again, so I could have something to listen to that I knew was really there. Which just shows you how spooked I was getting.

When the stairs stopped—well, that's pretty much it. The stairs stopped. And so did the rest of the floor. Even with Felix's little chrysanthemums skittering out ahead and back, I only just barely caught myself in time, and there was this long long second where I wondered whether my leg was going to hold or not, and then it was okay, and I was leaning against the wall and could find my voice to say, "Hold up."

"What is it?" Felix said behind me, and I don't suppose he'd've sounded nervous to anybody who didn't know what to listen for.

"Could use some more light," I said, and his chrysanthemums got brighter and found some friends.

"Oh," said Miss Parr, real small.

"Rather," said Felix. "That's quite an exciting new development."

"Yeah," I said. "Exciting."

We were standing at the edge of a pit. I don't think pit's even the right word, 'cause it sounds like something somebody could dig, but I don't know a better one. So, like a pit dug by giants or something. Even with Felix's witchlights, I couldn't really see across to the other side, and I couldn't see the bottom at all. And if I'd gone one step farther, I'd've found the bottom for myself, though I don't reckon I'd've seen much of it even then.

It took me a moment to look away from the pit, because a thing like that can get kind of hypnotizing, but I wasn't going to believe Florian was laying down there somewhere with his neck broke, and that meant there had to be some other way to go aside from the long way down. So I cast around, and sure enough, there in the wall of the stairway, about five steps up, was a square sort of hole, about waist high on me. I'd gone right past it.

"Felix?" I said.

"What?" He sounded like he'd gotten a little distracted by the pit, too.

"Send your lights over this way?"

"Oh. Right. Yes, of course." The little green lights went tumbling into the hole, and we saw, sure enough, more fucking stairs.

"Fuck," I said.

"I beg your pardon," said Miss Parr. Figured.

I said to Felix, "I ain't sure I can do this."

"What do you mean?" he said.

"Claustrophobia?" said Miss Parr, and I wasn't about to give her the joy of asking what the fuck that was.

I said to Felix, although for preference I'd've ripped my own tongue out first, "My leg. I ain't sure it can take no more of this." Because there was something about the stairs, the height or the unevenness or *something*, that just got right into the damaged part of my leg and gnawed away like rats. It was hurting worse than it had for two months.

A silence. He said, "It's either go down or go back up. And surely it can't keep going down *that* much longer."

Wanna bet? But I didn't say it, because he was right. If I didn't go down, I'd have to go back up, and the mere idea was enough to make me sit down and cry.

"Would it be better if I went first?" he said, which was the nicest thing he'd offered to do for me in decades.

"Nah," I said. "If I'm gonna fall, prob'ly better if there ain't nobody to go with me."

"How charmingly you put it," he said, but more just teasing than being mean. "Do you want to rest a minute, though, before we go on?"

"Yeah," I said. "Yeah, that'd be good." I went back up a couple of steps before I sat down, but then I sat down hard.

Felix and Miss Parr sat down, too, and we were all quiet for a while. The red-hot wire running through my leg had plenty to say, but I didn't figure I'd share. Didn't figure they'd want me to.

But Felix hated silence, and after a little bit he said, "The river's louder. Do you suppose it's . . . down there?"

"No way to tell without jumping," I said.

"*Thank* you," he said, and this time he was being nasty, but only just a little.

Some more silence, and then I thought of something. "D'you s'pose these folks went in for booby traps much?"

"For what?" said Miss Parr.

"What do you mean?" said Felix.

"Booby traps," I said. "You know. Things that drop on your head if you step in the wrong spot. Trip wires."

"Yes, yes," Felix said, "I know what booby traps are. What I *don't* know is what you *mean*."

"Well, that's kind of a booby trap, ain't it?" I said and waved at the end of the stairs and the great big nothing after 'em.

"Oh," said Felix.

"And what if it is?" said Miss Parr. "So what?"

I was liking her less and less all the damn time. "So what if that ain't their best effort?"

"I see your point," she said after a moment.

"Do you have any experience with this sort of thing?" Felix asked me.

"Nothing 'specially creative. There's a couple flash houses in Nill got themselves some clever ideas, and I seen the ones in the Arcane that don't work no more. But . . ."

"There can't be anything too dreadful," Miss Parr said, "or Jeremias and Florian would have been caught by it."

"Maybe they were," Felix said.

"No, they must have been coming down here for some time. It explains too many things that were puzzling me about Jeremias's behavior, and you know the Gauthys took Florian to Haigisikhora with them because he was looking 'peaky.' "

"Too much late-night adventuring?"

"Exactly."

"Yeah," I said. "Him and Mr. Tantony, they had a thing before. 'Cause he almost told me about it one time."

"I see," said Miss Parr, and I didn't want to know what she meant by that, so I didn't ask.

"In that case," Felix said, "I suppose we may indeed assume that whatever traps there may be will not be too terribly subtle . . . at least not at first."

"Just be careful, is all," I said and dragged myself back up to my feet.

"Are you ready?" Felix said.

"No, but I ain't gonna be. Let's just do it."

"All right." His witchlights clumped themselves just inside the entrance to the new staircase. I bent myself over double and started down.

After two steps, I hated them stairs. After four steps, I hated the people who'd built 'em. Six steps and I hated Florian for being dumb enough to get lost down here so I had to follow him. I lost count somewhere around the first decad because by then I was hating the whole fucking world.

So I don't know for sure how long that staircase went on. Not as long as the first one, and probably not more than a Great Septad stairs, but Kethe it felt like being crucified upside down with dowel rods. I was seriously considering just getting down and crawling, or sliding down on my ass or something, and never mind the snarky comments Felix and Miss Parr would make, when Kethe took mercy on me in his own particular way, and the stairs ended.

Now, the thing about Kethe's mercy is that when you get it, you mostly wish you hadn't. So there weren't no more stairs, but instead we were in this little room, just barely big enough for me to stand up straight in, and there were three different ways we could go. Which was two too many for what we needed.

Felix and Miss Parr came into the room behind me, and I said to Felix, "Well, now what?" And yeah, it was a snarl, and I didn't care. Let him get mad at me. 'Cause as far as I was concerned it was either snarl at somebody or sit down and start cussing and just not ever stop.

Felix

"Well," Mildmay said, "now what?"

I was taken aback by the hostility in his voice. I hovered for a moment on the verge of answering in kind, but remembered Mehitabel behind me. Whatever this was about, I felt sure we did not want to discuss it in front of her.

To give myself time to think, I looked around. The room was a small one; I had to bend my head to keep from braining myself on the solid rock of the ceiling. The staircase took up one wall, and each of the other three was centered by a square hole big enough for a man of my size to climb through, but not very much bigger. There was a pattern on the floor; I directed my witchlights down, and they illuminated an elaborate twining knot, the sort of design that is impossible to trace with the naked eye for more than an inch or two.

"How likely is it, do you suppose," said Mehitabel, "that that mosaic is merely decorative?"

I looked at those three square holes. "Not very."

"It certainly opens up a whole new realm of possibilities as to why Jeremias and Florian have not returned."

"Yes, but does it help us figure out which way they've gone? Did they have enough sense to mark their path?"

"Don't see no marks," Mildmay said. I sent my witchlights to aid him in his search, but to no better result.

"Jeremias has the common sense of an exceptionally stupid peacock," Mehitabel said, sitting down on the bottom step.

"D'you s'pose if we shouted for 'em . . . ?" But Mildmay sounded unhappy with his own suggestion, and my nerves shrieked in protest against the idea of making any noise loud enough to penetrate beyond the room in which we stood.

"There are three of us," Mehitabel said after a moment. "If we split up—"

"No," Mildmay said.

"No?" she said.

"Felix ain't got no sense of direction."

"*Doesn't have any,*" I said irritably, because I could not deny the truth of what he said.

"Yeah," Mildmay said, shrugging away the finer points of grammar as he always did. "And I dunno about you, keria. So maybe y'all'd better sit tight here, and I'll go look."

"Won't *you* get lost?" Mehitabel said.

"Nope." He ducked into the hole directly across from the stairs. I hurriedly sent half my witchlights after him, and then sat down on the step next to Mehitabel.

We listened as Mildmay's limping footsteps echoed and died away, and Mehitabel said, "Your brother—he *is* your brother, is he not?—doesn't seem to like me very much."

"Half brother," I said. "And I'm the one he's angry at."

"What have you done to make him angry?"

"I don't know," I said, and wondered if I was lying.

"Ah. He's not very communicative, is he?"

"No, he isn't," I said, trying hard not to imagine the weeks it would take to cross Kekropia, with only Mildmay for company.

"And the two of you are a very long way from home," she said. In Marathine.

She couldn't have horrified me more if she had turned and bitten me. I gasped, floundered, and failed utterly to say in my best Troian, *I beg your pardon. What did you say?*

She let me flop on the end of her line a moment longer and then added, still in Marathine, "I recognized the tattoos."

"*How?*"

"I worked in the Bastion for a time," she said, with enough chilly distaste to indicate that, whatever she had done there, she had not enjoyed it.

"Oh," I said feebly and cursed myself for an idiot. I had let myself blindly believe that I would be safe until we left Klepsydra and started traveling west, like a child hiding under the bedclothes—not from monsters, but from a drunken, belligerent adult. And I had been well paid for my willful naïveté.

I pushed my hair away from my face, feeling tired, defeated. "What is it that you want?"

"I beg your pardon?"

"Miss Parr, please. You have picked your moment with considerable care, and you can't really think I'm too stupid to understand the implications. I congratulate you."

"On what, exactly?"

"You were right to say that you did not need to stoop to entrapment. You are holding a much better card."

"Are you accusing me of blackmail?"

"Is that not your purpose?"

"No!" She sounded genuinely indignant, although my witchlights were not strong enough to show her face clearly.

"Then what *do* you want?"

"Are you returning to Marathat?"

"Yes," I said, and added to myself, I hope.

"I want to go with you."

"You want *what*?"

She looked down at her hands and said, "I want to go with you."

"*Why?*"

"My reasons are my own," she said, much as she had said in the Gauthys' courtyard.

"You're going to have to do better than that this time."

"I wish to leave Kekropia."

"By going west? Isn't that a trifle unintuitive?"

"I have not been to Marathat since I was a small child, and I have never seen Mélusine. I wish to broaden my horizons."

"Your mendacity is shocking."

"It's perfectly true."

"Yes, but that's not why you want to travel with us."

"A young woman traveling alone across the Grasslands will be assumed to be . . . available. And I am not."

"Our route is through the duchies." It was the first time I had admitted that, to myself or anyone else, and my hands were suddenly as cold as ice.

"Through the duchies?" she said, her voice rich with polite skepticism. "You know what they'll do to you if they realize you're a wizard?"

"Yes, and I also know what the Bastion will do to me if they catch me. And in any event, you haven't answered my question."

"Which question was that?"

"Why do you want to go to Marathat, and why do you want to travel with us?"

"I told you, I cannot comfortably travel across the Empire on my own."

"Which does not answer either half of the question I asked."

"Why does it matter?" she said in frustration; she took off her spectacles to pinch the bridge of her nose.

"Aside from the inherent folly of taking as a traveling companion someone whose motives and agenda one does not know?"

She was silent.

"Mildmay will never agree to it unless you give us some kind of answer."

"Mildmay? But surely you—"

She stopped, with a noise that was almost a gasp, realizing her mistake. I let the silence hang a moment and then said, "He is my brother, not my servant. And I would trust his good sense over my own any day of the week."

There was a long silence before she said, in a small, desolate voice, "I thought perhaps I could trust you *not* to ask questions." She turned to me, and even my dim witchlights were enough to show her wide eyes, the soft and desperate vulnerability of her mouth. "Mr. Harrowgate, please. I promise, I have not done anything criminal, and you will suffer neither harm nor inconvenience by helping me."

"It isn't exactly illegality I'm worried about," I said, leaning slightly away from her. "But you could make yourself a very wealthy woman by betraying me to the Bastion."

"I would rather die," she said, with such flat, venomous vehemence that I actually flinched.

"It sounds as if you speak from personal experience," I said.

"I do. I want to leave the Empire, and I do not want to go north, where

I run a substantially greater risk of being discovered by my family. I have been racking my brains for months to think of some way I could cross the Grasslands, and you and your brother seem like the answer to my prayers. Truly, that's all."

I was relatively sure that was *not* all—her explanation raised more questions than it answered—but I did not care for playing interrogator down here in the dark, when we were both tired and anxious and her expression and body language were half-hidden by the darkness. "I will talk to Mildmay," I said. "I can promise nothing."

"I understand. Thank you."

We sat in mutually gloomy silence for a few minutes, and then she said, "He's taking an awfully long time. Do you think he could be . . . ?"

"He hasn't been gone as long as it feels like," I said. "And his sense of direction is as good as he says it is. He doesn't brag."

"Yes, but this . . ." She waved one hand in a gesture that was as graceful as it was vague.

"We can't do anything, even if he is lost."

"Just sit here? That's the plan?"

"Until Mildmay comes back, or we're forced to think of a better one. At worst, one of us goes back up to get help, and the other stays here to wait. There is no sense in going after him. The fact that he hasn't returned is enough to tell us that this *is* a labyrinth."

"Yes. I'm sorry. It's just—I hate waiting."

"I understand." And I did. There was something particularly hateful about the situation, sitting in the dark with nothing that we could do, nothing except wait.

Because anything was better than listening to the muffled but still audible noise of the Sim, I said, "Tell me about Jeremias Tantony."

"What do you want to know?"

"Anything. Is he a good tutor?"

"Competent at best. He is very learned, but he is not noticeably interested in imparting that knowledge to others. Especially others he considers not as bright as himself."

"And yet Florian came down here with him."

"Florian . . ." Her sigh was more exasperation than anything else. "Florian is easily led and easily flattered. As Jeremias knows very well."

"So you think he—"

The scream was bone-chilling, a banshee howl of anguish, the like of

which I had not heard since the great Fire that ravaged half the Lower City
when I was eleven. I could remember women keening over the charred bodies of their children, a man who had roamed Simside for days, calling his
wife's name until his voice was nothing but an ashy whisper.

Mehitabel and I looked at each other, both of us wide-eyed. Her face
was ghastly in the green witchlight, and I was sure mine was no better.

She said, "Was that—"

Another scream; this time, ready for it, I could make out the word:
"Ginevra!" And, of course, the voice, but that I'd already known, even
though I'd been wishing desperately to be wrong.

"It's Mildmay," I said, as calmly as if I were speaking of a stranger, of
a character in a romance. "Come on."

She followed me without demur into the labyrinth.

It was not a pleasant place, that labyrinth, and it had not been designed
by nice people. There were no booby traps such as Mildmay had been worried about, but I kept having the uneasy feeling that the labyrinth itself
was a snare, and we were the foolish rabbits who had hopped right into it.
The rooms were cramped, low-ceilinged squares distinguishable only by the
number of egresses in each. Without anything to guide us, Mehitabel and I
would have been hopelessly lost within minutes. As it was, we followed first
those terrible, heartbreaking howls, and later, when he stopped screaming,
we were close enough to follow the sound of his sobbing. The entire time,
we did not speak.

We found Mildmay in a dead end, huddled against one of the blank
walls, both hands pressed flat against the stone. No, not quite flat: the tips
of his fingers were tensed as though he was trying to dig them into the solid
rock. His head was down, and I was glad of it; I did not want to see his face.

"Mildmay?" I said hesitantly. I was afraid to approach him, afraid that
his pain would rip me to shreds.

He made no response.

Mehitabel said in an undertone, "Do you want me to leave? I could
wait in the next room."

"No," I said, more harshly than I had meant to. "No splitting up. Just
wait. Please."

"All right." There was no space for retreat in this cramped room, but
she did the best she could, backing into the corner farthest from Mildmay
and sitting down with her legs curled under her. I wished I could have acceded

to her idea and let her leave, but living in the Mirador had taught me to trust my instincts about the edifices built by dark-purposed men, and I knew that separating was the worst thing we could possibly do.

He's never going to forgive me for seeing him like this, I thought. But that was past remedy.

I took a deep breath, let it out, and stepped forward. "Mildmay?" I said again. "What happened?"

Still no response, but I saw the muscles of his shoulders tighten defensively.

I took another step. "Are you hurt?"

He shook his head, but did not look up.

Another step, and I was standing beside him. I hesitated, excruciatingly aware of Mehitabel witnessing all this, then knelt down. "Please," I said, "just tell me what happened. Did you see something? Hear something?"

"Heard," he said. "Heard her voice. Calling me. From *here.*" He beat the flat of one hand against the wall, still not looking up.

I went cold all through with a sudden horrible suspicion about what had happened. "Mildmay. Look at me."

He turned his head away, his left shoulder rising as if to ward me off.

"It was a spell, all right? Just a spell. But I need to know if it was cast on you, or if it resides in the walls of the labyrinth. I need to see your eyes."

I hated myself for saying it, for bullying him, but it was absolutely true. If the spell had been cast on him, that would be one thing—a more sophisticated definition of "booby trap" than I had been prepared for, for one— but if it was part of the fabric of the walls . . . I thought of Nera, of the temple of Graia, and could not quite repress a shiver. Architectural thaumaturgy was all very well, but not even the specialists in the Mirador could predict with any certainty what would happen when it had been abandoned for several hundred years.

"Okay," Mildmay said, his voice thick, wavering, and somehow terribly empty. He brought his hands down and rubbed his face, then straightened his shoulders and turned to look at me.

I was grateful that the light was bad; it let me pretend that the twisted, ravaged mask of his face was the effect of the unnatural witchlights and the shadows they cast. And what I needed to see had very little to do with light anyway.

The spell hadn't been cast on him.

"Oh damn," I said.

"What?" Mehitabel said; she sounded nervous.

Mildmay lowered his head again, and I wished I could tell him not to be ashamed, either of his grief or of his face. But this was not a good place for truth, and anything I said to him in front of Mehitabel Parr, he would not hear.

"It's a property of the labyrinth. Mildmay, what did you hear?"

"Told you," he said, not looking up. "A voice." I knew he was deliberately letting his words slur; I'd noticed before that he did that when he wanted people to leave him alone and that frequently it worked.

"Yes, but *whose*? Who is Ginevra?"

His head came up, eyes flaring to life with anger and hurt. "Say her name again, and I'll break your fucking nose."

I flinched back, more from his intensity than from the threat. He glared at me a moment longer, then dropped his gaze again. "Sorry. She was my girlfriend couple indictions back. We split up and . . . and she got killed."

And that wasn't the whole story, not by any stretch of the imagination. But prying it out of him would have to wait.

"So you heard her voice? Calling you?"

"Yeah." He met my eyes again, although it was clearly nothing he wanted to be doing. "And it was *her*. I mean, it wasn't, I know that, but it *was*."

I nodded, although it felt very far away. I had been right to think of Nera. "I think I know whose cult this was. And I know why it was proscribed."

"Please don't be gnomic and portentous," Mehitabel said. "Which god was it?"

"I don't know her name," I said. "No one does. A Troian archivist told me her worship had been eradicated three thousand years ago. She was the goddess of Nera."

Mildmay's eyes were wide, and I saw him make the sign to avert hexes.

"So what kind of goddess was she?" Mehitabel demanded.

"She was the goddess of labyrinths," I said. "The goddess of death. Do you know the word *mikkary*?"

"Yes," said Mehitabel. "Why . . . oh."

"Mikkary?" Mildmay said.

"Madness, corruption, and despair," Mehitabel said. "I felt it once, when I was a little girl—the starving wells. Do you know about those?"

Mildmay shook his head; I said, "No."

"They're old," she said. "Not as old as this, but my great-grandfather could remember his father telling him about the last time they'd been used. One of the petty dukes—one of the northern ones, and the duchy doesn't exist any longer—had these holes dug, thirty, maybe forty feet deep. And he had them lined with stone. And if you crossed the duke, they'd lower you into the well with a machine the duke had had made specially, and then you stayed there until you died, or until the duke decided to have you lifted out. They *stank* of mikkary. Two of my cousins tried to dare each other to look into one, but they couldn't do it. Not even on a dare."

There was a small, cold silence. I said, "We'd better keep moving."

"That would be easier if we knew where we were going," Mehitabel said.

We looked at Mildmay, who was rubbing his face with both hands, as if he was trying to restore feeling to something numb. I wondered how much feeling he had on the scarred side of his face. After a moment, he looked up.

"Oh. Forward or back?"

Mehitabel said, "The more I learn about this labyrinth, the less I like the idea of Florian's being trapped down here. And if we go back without him, Keria Gauthy will most likely have all three of us arrested."

"Good point," I said, realizing belatedly with her use of the word *keria* that we were still speaking Marathine. I had not thought about switching back, and apparently she had decided not to try to put that particular cat back in its bag.

"Go on, then?" Mildmay said to me. I contemplated without any anticipatory pleasure the moment when I would have to tell him Mehitabel Parr wanted to travel with us.

"Yes," I said. "If you can."

"Oh sure," he said, as if it wasn't even worth asking about.

Mehitabel and I stood up. Mildmay remained where he was, in that awkward huddle like a broken-stringed marionette. I extended a hand to help him up. He growled, "No thanks," under his breath and stood up on his own, only using the wall for balance.

Mule-headed idiot, I thought, but I knew I was no better.

"Okay," he said and limped across to the room's single egress. His limp was getting worse, I noticed, and I wondered how long he'd be able to keep going, mule-headed or not.

He glanced over his shoulder at me and said, "Guess we'd better keep together."

"Yes," I said, "I think that would be wise." And one by one we left that dead-end room and the mikkary that hung like dust in the air.

Chapter 6

Mildmay

There's two kinds of mazes. There's one where you want to find your way from one door to another—that's the way the curtain-mazes at the Trials are. But there's the other kind, where the maze has a heart, and getting out the other side—or out back the way you came, if that's the kind of maze it is—won't do you a centime's worth of good if you ain't got to the heart first. I was betting this maze was that kind.

I was also trying real hard not to think about the maze me and Felix had made in Nera for the dead people. 'Cause, I mean, I ain't all that bright, but I could do the math. And dead people had talked to him there, the same way Ginevra had talked to me.

Don't *think* about it, I told myself, but it was like telling myself not to blink. Because hearing her had woken up all these things I'd thought I'd been done with, and if it hadn't been for Felix and Miss Parr, I suppose I would've sat there in that ugly little room 'til I died. And I figured that was what Felix meant by mikkary, but that didn't make it no easier to deal with.

It was a pretty nasty maze, even without the voices, twisting around like a poisoned snake, and with dead ends that you didn't find out were dead ends until five rooms later when there was a wall in the way of where you needed to go. I had to backtrack a couple times, and the second time, when we got back to where I'd gone wrong, I said, "Gotta rest," and sat down only just slow enough that it wasn't a fall. Felix and Miss Parr sat down, too, so I guessed I wasn't the only one needing a break.

We were quiet for a while, but the silence was spooking Felix—and, I got to admit, it was pretty bad sitting there and trying not to listen for Ginevra or Zephyr or any of the other dead people whose voices I'd recognize. So I didn't want to talk to him, but I was almost glad when he said, "How do you do it?"

"Do what?"

"This." He waved an arm at the darkness around us. "You could find your way back to the stairs from here, couldn't you?"

"Yeah."

"*How?*"

"Dunno."

"Somehow I knew you were going to say that. But, were you trained to do it?"

"Nope. Just can." Miss Parr didn't say nothing, but she was watching us with her big round dark eyes, and I wished Felix hadn't used that word, "trained." Because I didn't want that teacher-lady knowing all about my past, and "trained" was more than halfway to being a clue if she knew anything about Mélusine. Which since she spoke Marathine, she probably did. So I said, before Felix could ask more questions, "How long we been down here?"

His hand started for his pocket, then stopped. "I don't have a watch."

"I do," Miss Parr said. She pulled a chain out of the neckline of her dress, giving me a flash of Ginevra I really didn't need just then. The chain had a watch strung on it, about the size and shape of a hazelnut. Valuable trinket for a lady in her line of work, and I wondered if Mehitabel Parr might have stuff in her past she didn't want to talk about either.

"About three and a half hours," she said.

"And how long before the Gauthys panic, do you suppose?" Felix asked.

Miss Parr tucked her watch back into her dress and said, "They have great faith in you, Ker Harrowgate."

"Thank you," Felix said, with some sting in it, "but that isn't exactly what I meant."

"I don't believe you need to worry about any of them following us down here, if that's your concern. And Ker Gauthy will be even more resistant now to the idea of notifying anyone in a position of authority."

"Because of the unexpected contents of the cellar, so to speak?"

"Precisely. He will worry—and with some justification—that this will lead the Imperial Assessors to wonder what else the house might be concealing."

"A devoted father."

"That's why he and Keria Gauthy agreed to consult *you*."

"Marvelous," Felix said and pushed his hair out of his eyes. "I suppose we'd best not die down here, then."

I said, "Yeah, let's not," and got up. It wasn't fun, but I could do it, and that was enough to get by on. "Y'all ready?"

"There's no reason to stay in this room when the next one will be just the same," Felix said. He and Miss Parr stood up, and I ducked through the opening I should have taken in the first place.

We were getting closer. I could feel it, although I couldn't explain that any more than I could explain how I knew where I was. It was like a dance—not that I could dance no more, and there's another thing to add to the fucking list—where when you know the steps, you don't have to think about them. You just feel where your feet need to go. That's what it was like.

I knew better than to let it rush me, though. I mean, I couldn't have moved faster if I'd wanted to, but this would be a stupid time to get sloppy. 'Cause the maze didn't want us in its heart. I know it sounds crazy, but I could feel that, too.

And I would've thought it was just me getting spooked out, except Miss Parr said, "God, it's like *breathing* mikkary."

"It is an old place," Felix said, sounding like he was half-asleep. "Like the lowest levels of the Mirador, it has been long undisturbed, long abandoned, left to wait and brood and darken."

I nearly brained myself on the top edge of the hole I was crawling through. Because I remembered plain as day him chewing me out for telling Florian Gauthy about Mélusine, and here he was, telling a teacher-lady—who was *way* more likely than Florian to recognize what he was talking about—that he'd been in the Mirador. I stopped and waited, and when Felix ducked through, I said, "Felix? You okay?"

"Of course," he said, and he had the brass to sound surprised. "Why wouldn't I be?"

"Did you mean to say that?"

"Say what?"

"You know. About the—" Miss Parr came through the hole, and I cut my eyes sideways at her as meaningfully as I could.

"Oh, that," Felix said. "Mehitabel already knows."

"Knows what?" Miss Parr said.

"That I'm a Cabaline," Felix said, cheerful as a gambler raking in the pot, like it was no big deal and never had been.

"Oh," I said. "Okay." I turned and crawled through the next hole. I didn't let my face twist until I was sure neither him nor Miss Parr could see it.

What did you expect, Milly-Fox? I said to myself. She's smart enough he can trust her with a secret, even if you ain't. He told you how it was going to be—ain't his fault if you're too fucking dumb to learn.

I kept moving, because it was either that or try and look Felix in the face, and I kept myself as tight focused as I could on the maze and the holes and the stones. It beat the fuck out of thinking. Behind me, Felix and Miss Parr were talking about something, but I didn't care and I wasn't listening.

And then all at once I wasn't listening for real. "Shut up," I said, and it was probably some kind of miracle, but they did, and I heard the thing I'd thought I'd heard, a voice calling in Kekropian.

"Hello? Is someone there? Really there?"

And that wasn't no ghost voice. That was Florian Gauthy, sounding scared and miserable as a half-drowned cat.

I shouted back, "Florian! It's me! Mildmay! Are you okay?"

There was this sort of breathless little pause, and then Florian shouted, sounding way more like himself, "Mildmay? Where are you? What are you doing down here?"

Trust a bourgeois kid to go straight for the stuff that don't matter. "Are you okay? Are you hurt?"

"No, I'm not hurt. I'm just . . ." And then, a lot quieter, "Lost."

"*Stay put!*" I shouted. "We'll find you."

"All right," Florian called back, although he didn't sound too sure about it.

But it didn't take long—he was only a few rooms farther in, sitting in the corner of the first room we'd come to that didn't look exactly like all the others.

It was more than twice the size, for one thing, and the floor was paved in squares of some stone that didn't look like the rest of the maze at all. It was black, and shiny where Florian had scuffed away the dust. And not a nice kind of shiny, neither.

Florian came bolting to his feet as I dragged myself into the room, and the next thing I knew he had his arms wrapped around me and his face buried in my shoulder, and he was gulping for breath like somebody who'd just run a septad-minute mile.

"Hey, steady on," I said, about as useful as ballet shoes to a duck. "It's okay." I hugged him back, because he needed it.

Then Felix said, "Gracious," and Florian jumped back and made a big business out of straightening his coat. But Felix wasn't paying no mind to him, or me. He was standing just inside the room, staring up at the ceiling like a farmboy seeing Ver-Istenna's dome for the first time and all his little chrysanthemums gone up there like hot-air balloons, too.

Miss Parr had just finished getting herself through the hole. Her and me and Florian looked up, and then for a while there were four farmboy impressions in that one room.

I don't know how to describe that ceiling or what looking at it was like. It was like I was falling down—I mean, up, only it felt like down, into this sort of pit, only worse than the pit I'd almost fallen into on the stairs, because it wasn't just a pit, it was a maze, and if I thought the maze we were in was bad . . . well, all I know is I would've gone stark raving batfuck nuts before I'd've found my way out of the maze carved on that ceiling.

I finally had to look away, and found myself looking straight at Felix. "Somehow 'vertigo' doesn't seem quite strong enough," he said.

"Um," I said, 'cause I wasn't quite sure what 'vertigo' was.

Miss Parr said, "It must have taken *years*."

"Oh, at least," Felix said, and his lights came dropping back down. "Let us, I pray you, speak of something else. Florian!"

Florian kind of jumped, and jerked his head around to look at Felix instead of the ceiling, and said, "Yes, Ker Harrowgate?"

"We were under the impression that you had come down here with Ker Tantony. Is that correct?"

It was hard to tell with only the witchlights, but I thought Florian's face went red. "Yes, sir."

"Then where is he?"

"Didn't he send you after me?"

Florian and Felix stared at each other like a pair of frogs. It was Miss Parr who said, "We haven't seen Ker Tantony. Was he down here with you?"

"Yes, but he went, and he had the map, and—"

"Wait," Felix said, holding up his hands. His rings caught the witchlight in a way I got to say I didn't care for. "Let's start at the beginning. When did you and Ker Tantony start making these expeditions?"

"About a year ago. After Kechever went off to school. I told him about the hollow stone and how Kechever had always said it had to be a secret door, and he found out how it worked. It only took him a week."

"Mildmay found it in under ten minutes," Felix said.

"I knew it was there," I said in a hurry. "That makes a difference."

Florian was staring at me with his mouth hanging open. Then he shook his head and went on. "Anyway, he got it open and he said it was a tremendously important find and I mustn't tell anyone until we knew just what it was. And he said we'd have to take it very slow and careful."

"Thank God he had that much sense," Miss Parr said, not quite under her breath, and made Florian jump again.

"He knew just what to do," he said. "He had a lantern and he drew a map and . . . and *everything*!"

"Yes, quite," Felix said. "But what happened this time?"

"Ker Tantony said we were getting close to the center. He'd thought we were getting close even before Father took me to Troia, but he promised he wouldn't come down here without me. He said he couldn't manage on his own."

"True," Miss Parr said, but this time Florian ignored her.

"We've been coming down here almost every night since I got back, and last night Ker Tantony said that we *had* to be almost there. Here, I mean."

"So this is the center of the labyrinth?" Felix said.

"Yes."

"Then why isn't Ker Tantony here?"

"He's after the heart," I said, and they all three of them looked at me like I was a carny freak with two heads.

"*What* did you say?" Felix said.

I could feel my face turning red as a brick. "Center ain't the heart."

Florian and Miss Parr just looked confused, but Felix was giving me the hairy eyeball with mustard. "How do you know that?" he said, like it was some kind of secret only he was supposed to know.

"Trials teachings. Didn't you ever go?"

"*Trials* teachings?" he said, and I might have been talking about the cities on the moon for all the good it was doing him. "No. Never mind. Later." He turned back to Florian. "So this is the center of the labyrinth and Ker Tantony wasn't satisfied."

"Yes," Florian said, "although he didn't tell me why. He told me to stay here so we could be sure we didn't get lost, and then he took the map and the lantern and went. And he hasn't come back. But he said to stay here, and anyway I don't think I could find my way out without the map and . . . are Mother and Father very angry?"

"They're very worried," Miss Parr said.

Felix said, like a terrier after a rat, "Which door did he take?"

"That one," Florian said and pointed at the hole to the left of the one we'd come in by.

"And you haven't seen him since?"

"No."

"How long has it been?"

"I don't know. A while. The candle's almost burnt out."

"Blow it out," I said. "We got lights."

"Yes, Mildmay," Florian said, and did.

Felix gave that left-hand hole a thoughtful look. "I find myself remarkably unenthused at the prospect of going after Ker Tantony."

"We can't just leave him down here!" Florian and Miss Parr said, on top of one another. It made a weird, ugly sort of echo, and we all froze right where we were until it had died away.

Then Felix said—and I give him credit for managing to sound almost normal—"I wasn't suggesting we abandon him. I was merely remarking that I do not feel sanguine about what we may discover." He looked at me. "Do you think you can find the heart of the labyrinth? Or, failing that, Jeremias Tantony?"

"Yeah," I said. There were a bunch of other things I wanted to say, but I settled for, "Be careful."

"You need have no fear on that score," Miss Parr said, and the three of them followed me out of the center of the maze.

Felix

It unnerved me, the way Mildmay moved through the labyrinth as if it were a house he knew well. We followed him closely, silently, each of us peering into the shadows as if we feared monsters were waiting for us. Considering the nature of the labyrinth, monsters seemed less implausible than I would have liked.

I was trying to remember, through my nerves, everything I had once known about Heth-Eskaladen and his Trials, Mélusine's major religious festival. Keeper had seen religion and festivals merely as another opportunity to fleece the bourgeoisie; Lorenzo, although devout enough in his own grubby, primitive way, had been even less interested in the festivals, except that the Shining Tiger's profits tended to be hefty on festival eves and much less so on the days of celebration themselves. Malkar had taken me out of Mélusine when I was fourteen, and he had sneered openly at all religion. By the time we had returned to Mélusine, to the Mirador, I had learned to ape him in that way as in so many others, and in any event a discreet agnosticism was *de rigueur* at court, no matter what worships and devotions the noble families might perform privately.

I knew a fair amount of theology, as all wizards had to, and even more about obscure Cymellunar gods and obsolete rituals. But the religion of the bourgeoisie and the Lower City was considered vulgar and naïve by even the most orthodox and devout Cabaline, and I had been all too eager to let the sleeping dogs of my childhood lie. And so I had forgotten that Heth-Eskaladen was associated with labyrinths.

Heth-Eskaladen was a librarian-god, an archivist-god. I remembered that he had descended into death and returned—that was what the five days of the Trials commemorated—but I could not remember why, nor what exact part labyrinths had played in his agon. It was infuriating and demeaning to be forced to turn to my semiliterate younger brother for information, but he had come out with one of Ephreal Sand's major tenets as if it was as natural to him as breathing. It did not seem as though I had much choice.

Ahead of me, just on the other side of yet another doorway, Mildmay said, "Oh fuck," and stopped dead.

"Yes?" I said, and he answered in Marathine, "I think I found the guy."

"You *think*?"

"Well, I *think* it's a guy."

"Oh dear," I said as I realized why he had switched into Marathine. "Let me see."

"Be my fucking guest." He moved to one side, and I crawled through the doorway to stand beside him.

This was the heart of the labyrinth, a long, vaulted room with a double row of dark columns making an aisle down the middle, and at last we had found one of the booby traps Mildmay had been worried about.

Jeremias Tantony had found it before us.

It was easy to reconstruct in its brutal simplicity. Jeremias Tantony, who had not had my nightmarish experience in the temple of Graia, had started toward the end of the vault walking between the pillars. He had stepped on a stone that looked just like all the other squares that paved the room, and it had sunk beneath his foot. Somewhere beneath the floor, that weight had pressed down one end of a fulcrum; the other end, rising, had caught a narrow wedge carved out of the left-hand column—again, probably invisible before the trap was triggered. That wedge rose and displaced a wedge that was not stone, but iron. It, falling forward, had caught Jeremias Tantony squarely on the top of the head and split his skull like an egg, lodging itself in his brain. He would have been dead before he even could have realized he'd doomed himself.

Mildmay said in a low, shaky voice, "These people did *not* fuck around."

"No," I said, not much steadier. No wonder Mildmay had been sullen and snappish, knowing all the time that because he was leading the way, he was the one most likely to walk into something like this.

"What is it?" Mehitabel called. "What have you found?"

"Sacred bleeding *fuck*," Mildmay said, and when I looked sideways at him, said in explanation, "Florian."

"Oh," I said and rubbed nervously at my mouth. "Yes. We can't . . . ?"

"Can't go around. Wanna get out, you gotta go through the heart."

"Is Ker Tantony there?" Florian said.

"Um," said Mildmay.

I said, as calmly and slowly as I could, "Florian, there's been an accident." It was the absolute and literal truth as far as Jeremias Tantony was concerned, although from the perspective of the makers of the labyrinth there was nothing accidental in the slightest about what had happened.

"An accident?"

"It's . . . not pretty."

"Is he . . ." Florian stopped, and then said in a much smaller voice, "Is he dead?"

"Um," said Mildmay. "Yeah."

I heard Mehitabel's sharp intake of breath and remembered belatedly that she and Jeremias Tantony had been lovers. I turned; she was already ducking through the hole. Mildmay and I both instinctively backed out of her way. She looked at the body for a moment, expressionlessly. "Yes. That's Jeremias," she said. "Florian, be as brave as you can."

"Yes, Keria Parr," Florian said. He climbed through the hole; Mehitabel held her hand out to him, and he took it before he looked at the body. He stared, then turned away and was violently and comprehensively sick.

Cravenly, Mildmay and I let Mehitabel deal with him, which she did briskly but not unkindly. Or, at least, I was craven. Mildmay, I realized after a moment, was examining the hall we stood in, his sharp gaze quartering the space methodically. He said, in a low voice, "I don't think we want to get between them columns at all."

I decided not to ask what he saw. "But how can we . . . that is, where are we trying to go?"

"There." He pointed, and I sent my witchlights down to the end of the hall, where what I had taken for a deeper well of shadows in the corner proved to be a doorway.

"Is it the way out, do you think?"

"We don't want to go back the way we came."

"Why not?"

" 'Cause it ain't that kind of maze."

His voice was patient, but flat. It was another of his fiats I was becoming so exceedingly tired of. But this was neither the time nor place to argue about it. I was too aware of Mehitabel and Florian, too aware of the crushing darkness around us, far too aware of the stench of the Sim.

And he said, "But we got to get there."

"Right," I said. "Oh dear."

"Yeah. I can see some of what we got to get around, but I'm betting there's stuff I *don't* see."

"I imagine you can count on it."

He pressed the heels of his hands against his eyes for a moment. Mehitabel said, "Are we going to have to stay here much longer?"

"Until we can find a way out that will not involve any of us imitating Ker Tantony," I said waspishly; Mildmay was under enough strain already.

"But can't we—"

"It ain't that kind of maze," Mildmay said without looking up.

Mehitabel's silence was distinctly offended; I wondered wearily whether traveling across the Grasslands with the two of them would actually be any better than traveling with only Mildmay. And then I wondered, stiffening my neck against the impulse to glance at Ker Tantony's corpse, whether that question might not prove to be quite remarkably moot.

I heard him take a deep breath. "Okay," he said. "I think I know how to do it, but y'all *got* to do what I say."

"We will," I said.

He gave me a look narrow with suspicion, as if he thought I was making fun of him.

"I trust you," I growled under my breath, too soft for Mehitabel or Florian to hear.

For a moment I thought he hadn't heard me either, then he turned away as suddenly as if I'd thrown water in his face—or as if I had offended him.

Mehitabel, who now had her arm around Florian, said, "We believe you, Ker Foxe. We will follow where you lead."

"Okay," Mildmay said, still not looking at me. "Then what we want to do is, go along *that* wall. See where there's that worn-down strip?"

We looked in the direction he pointed, and I sent my witchlights across.

"I figure," Mildmay said, "that's where the, you know, the worshippers must've walked. 'Cause you got to have a pretty easy way through here—"

"Or your numbers begin to fall off dramatically, yes, I see," I said.

He said, "If I'm wrong . . . I mean, if I go and something gets me . . . well, I don't know what y'all do then. But I think I'm right."

"As inspirational speeches go, that leaves something to be desired," I said, and he gave me an irritated half shrug, still looking past me at Mehitabel and Florian.

"Y'all got that?"

"Yes, Ker Foxe," Mehitabel said, and Florian echoed her.

"Okay." He limped across to the side of the hall, stopping by the body to pick up the lantern, and I noticed how careful he was about where he put his feet. We followed him, a nervous flock of sheep.

He said to me, "Wait 'til I get to the other end safe, okay?"

"Yes," I said. We stood and watched his progress; I did not know about Mehitabel and Florian, but my pulse was hammering with how fragile he looked, and how brave, perfectly straight except for the slight off-kilter twist of his limp.

The darkness around us, especially the darkness above us, seemed to be drawing closer, getting heavier. I had a momentary, disconcerting feeling of being in the Mirador, and then it was gone, leaving me bewildered.

Halfway along, Mildmay stopped suddenly, almost overbalancing. I heard Mehitabel's breath catch, and was perversely relieved to discover I was not the only one in an advanced state of nerves. But he stayed upright; I noticed how careful he was not to use the wall for balance, and my mind was instantly thronged with disquieting reasons why that might be.

There was a pause, almost like a hitch in the labyrinth's breathing, and I thought idiotically, After all, we are in its heart. Then Mildmay said, "There's a . . . there's a thing here where you don't want to step."

"How will we recognize it?" Mehitabel asked.

" 'Cause when you're close enough," he said, "you can see as how ain't nobody *ever* stepped on it. I'm figuring they got good reason."

Florian said, "You're right across from the fourth column down. So we can tell that way."

"Yeah. That's good." There was something that was almost a waver in his voice. With infinite, excruciating caution, he stepped forward; nothing happened, and after a moment like a prolonged flinch, he kept going.

It seemed very close to a miracle that he reached the other end of the hall safely. He turned and waved at us, almost a salute, and called, "Florian first. Then Keria Parr. Felix, you go last, okay?"

"All right," I called back.

"And don't touch the wall!"

"Wouldn't dream of it," I called, with completely unwarranted cheerfulness, and couldn't help grinning when his response was an obscene gesture I remembered from my childhood.

One by one, we made our way through the heart of the labyrinth beneath Klepsydra. When my own turn came, it felt as if with every step I sank deeper and deeper into a pool of water, invisible, inaudible, but crushing the breath out of me. Without wanting to, I remembered the temple of Graia, remembered through it the choking madness of Nera. Those were the White-Eyed Lady's places, just as this was, as the starving wells were. They were places sacred to her by reason of horror and cruelty and death; she was both torturer and protector. She dwelt in, around, through blood and pain and mikkary.

And finally, I understood mikkary. "Misery" *was* close, but mikkary was more than that. Mikkary was despair and malice, madness and regret— all the festering emotions that drove a man to suicide were mikkary, and a hundred other things besides. Mikkary was arrogance and spite and things less nameable than that. It collected like dust in unused rooms.

And mikkary was my madness. I stopped at the midpoint, just before the stone on which Mildmay had said not to step, and for a moment, I did not think I was going to be able to continue. There seemed to be no reason in the world not to let my foot come down on that one unworn patch in the floor. I belonged in this place more surely than I had ever belonged any-where in my life, and I knew that its bride-price was death. At that moment, it did not seem too high a price to pay.

Then Mildmay said, "Felix? You okay?"

"I . . ." The words would not come; language would not come. Mikkary flowed in my veins like blood. I was more truly the White-Eyed Lady's child than the child of Methony Feucoronne who had died by fire as she had lived. And then I managed somehow to draw a breath, although it felt like swallowing knives, and said, "I'm all right."

"You sure? I can—"

"No! Stay there. I'm . . . just give me a minute."

"Okay," he said, but very doubtfully. I knew that if I did not move soon, he would come after me, and it was that more than anything else that broke my stasis. I could not drag Mildmay down into this pool of mikkary after me.

I stepped over that strange place in the floor, unpolished by any per-son's foot, continued to move, slow, methodical, step after step, and all the while the mikkary throbbing in my temples, running like iron rods down my back.

I could not have told anyone how long it took me to cross the heart of the labyrinth; a second or a century, and it would have felt the same. At the far end, where the others were clumped together, wide-eyed and waiting, I avoided their gazes, avoided Mildmay's half-outstretched hand.

"What now?" I said, and my voice was shrill and thin in my own ears.

"Um," said Mildmay, and I felt the mikkary tightening like a vise around my neck.

"What 'um'?"

"There's, um. A bridge."

"A bridge?"

"Over the . . . over the river." Any other man would have been visibly braced; with Mildmay the only sign that he knew the import of his news was that he was even more inarticulate than usual.

"Over the Sim."

"Yeah."

"And—let me guess—a *narrow* bridge."

"Yeah."

"Balustrade?" And when he only looked blank, "Handrails?"

"Oh. Yeah, I think there was, once. But . . ." He shrugged. "Rope."

Which, of course, would have rotted away in the intervening centuries.

"This just gets better and better," I said. "What else? Fire-breathing dragons? Spectral guardians?"

"Didn't see none," and it took me a moment to decide that he meant it as a very small joke. I couldn't manage to smile at him, but I nodded my appreciation.

He said, "It don't look like . . . I mean, I don't think there's traps or nothing."

"Just the bridge," I said.

"Yeah."

Mehitabel said, "Must we stand here and *discuss* it to death? Ker Foxe assures us that we cannot go back, so I do not see that it matters whether the way forward lies over a bridge or across a field of flowers."

"*Thank* you, Mehitabel," I said. "But, yes, there is no reason to tarry."

Mildmay gave me his irritating you're-the-boss nod and turned to lead the way.

There was only one chamber between the heart of the labyrinth and the bridge, so we reached the edge of the Sim's gorge all too soon. I realized, dizzyingly, that we were standing in the same spatial orientation in which we had found ourselves when we first encountered this abyss, only a distance down that I could not even begin to estimate. The Sim was visible in my witchlights, a rushing, howling death of water.

And the bridge was narrow enough that I was almost tempted to see if I could spot the spider who had spun it. Single file was the only option, and with the Sim close enough beneath to cast its spray up onto the bridge, the footing was self-evidently, murderously slick.

Mildmay glanced at me, then at Florian and Mehitabel, and said something under his breath that I did not ask him to repeat. "Let's do it same as before," he said. "Me first, then Florian, then Keria Parr. You okay with going last?"

"It makes no difference," I said. "Let's just get this over with."

If I had been anxious before, watching Mildmay cross that bridge made my heartbeat so rapid I was almost sick with it. He did not hurry, nor show any sign that he knew how agonizingly slow his progress was. But he did not slip, nor falter, and he was not reduced, as I had thought he might be, to crawling. He made it to the other side and stepped carefully away from the edge before he turned around.

He called across, "It ain't so bad, Florian! Just take your time."

I wondered, distantly, if that had been why he had been so appallingly slow, to encourage Florian Gauthy not to rush himself.

"All right," Florian called back, his voice only slightly shaky. He had a harder time of the crossing than Mildmay—of course, he had not been trained as a cat burglar since he was old enough to walk—but he made it safely. As Mildmay was steadying him off the bridge on the far side, Mehitabel said very softly to me, "Are you all right?"

"I'm fine."

"You look a little green."

"Witchlights," I said. "Everyone looks ill by witchlight."

She did not believe me; the cool, cynical skepticism in her eyes jarred against her childlike face. But she said nothing, and when Mildmay called, "You ready, Keria Parr?" she turned away from me as if I had ceased entirely to interest her.

She crossed the bridge as calmly and steadily as a woman promenading along the harborfront. I told myself firmly that she was *not* doing it on purpose to annoy me, but I could not help the bitter smolder of resentment all the same.

My hands were shaking. I watched Mehitabel join Florian and Mildmay in safety and cast my witchlights as strongly as I could on their side of the river, as much to give myself something to focus on as to give them light. I stepped out onto the bridge.

"Murderously slick" had been an understatement. And the smell of the Sim was everywhere, like the reek of a charnel house. Somewhere in the back of my mind, I could hear the thundering cadences of Keeper's voice. The Sim had been his favored punishment, holding us under like kittens; I couldn't even begin to guess how many children he had drowned before the

Fire had killed him, as it had killed Joline and my mother and everyone else I knew. The smell of the Sim was in my nose and mouth, harsh in the back of my throat. I was choking, and the green lights were getting dimmer. Someone was shouting my name, but it wasn't Joline, and I couldn't . . . couldn't . . .

My knees buckled, and I fell.

Mildmay

Pitch-black.

And, I mean, not just no-lights kind of black. This was like the great-grandmama blackness of the world. And Felix was out in it somewhere, drowning.

"Fuck me sideways." I barely recognized my own voice, and I didn't sound like anybody I wanted to know, neither. I found my lucifers, dropped down beside the lantern where I'd set it on the floor, and lit it. "You two stay here."

"But what—"

"I ain't got time. Just *stay*." I was dragging my boots off, shrugging out of my coat. Before the bitch had time to say some other fool thing, with Felix more likely to be dead with every single second, I went forward and off the bridge. 'Bout as graceful as a dancing bear, since you ask, but this wasn't about grace.

I ain't never been a graceful swimmer, not even when both legs worked right. But I *can* swim, as most folks in the Lower City can't, and I'm strong. Strong enough to have my own way against what the current wanted, strong enough to outswim it, strong enough, even though my leg was howling like a pack of hounds, that when I saw a white blotch, just at the edge of where there was any light from the lantern, I could thrash forward and grab it.

And that's when things went completely fucked. I'd been expecting Felix to be passed out, but he wasn't. He was awake and in a five-alarm panic. It was like the sinking of the *Morskaiakrov* all over again, only worse because it was the Sim and the current was fighting me along with him, and it was like trying to wrestle two gators at once. When I finally managed to thrash us both out of the main current, it felt like both arms were half-wrenched out of their sockets, I had a shiner started where he'd got me in the eye with his elbow, and I was lost.

Now I'm sure that don't sound like nothing, but, see, I don't *get* lost. Never have done. But here I was in the middle of a river in the blackest fucking blackness I'd ever encountered, and I didn't know where the bank was or where I was or where Florian and Miss Parr were, and I could have sat down and cried for the shame of it.

Small favors. The river was shallow enough here that we could stand up. I stood and panted like a dog with sunstroke. Felix was clinging to me like a child, his face pressed into my shoulder and his fingers clawed into my back, his breath coming in sobs. I kind of patted his back, best I could, but he hated to be touched, and I didn't know whether he was crazy or sane or what, and so mostly I just stood there and let him hang on to me as much as he needed.

I don't know how long we stood like that, neither. But after a while we were both breathing better, and Felix had let up a little on the holes he was digging in my shoulder blades. So I took a deep breath and said, "I'm lost." Blackness or no blackness, I could feel myself blushing.

"You're *what*?"

"Lost. You know. I don't know where we are."

"And?" he said after a moment.

"I need a light."

He made a noise that could've been a laugh, a scream, or a sob. Or all three. "I don't know if I can," he said. "You don't . . . you don't know what you're asking."

"Nope. But if I don't get a light, so as I can see where the fuck we're at, we ain't moving. How much longer you wanna stand out here?"

"Damn you," he said. "*Damn* you." I heard and felt him take a deep, shuddery breath. "All right. I'll try."

And then there was a long time where nothing happened. He hadn't let go of me, and I didn't like to say anything about it, because I needed a light a fuck of a lot more than I needed my own personal space back. But we were standing there, dripping wet, pressed up against each other, and I felt . . . Kethe, I felt his cock hardening against me.

There was this scrambling sort of moment, where we both tried to back away from each other and realized we didn't dare, because in all this darkness and water most likely we'd never find each other again. And then his hands were clamped on my upper arms, and he was saying, "I'm sorry. Truly, I'm sorry. I swear I didn't . . ."

He was apologizing, which was as hard to believe as any of the rest of it. He *never* apologized. I said, my voice cracking like I had two septads and one again, "You got the hots for *me?*"

And, you know, I would've believed him if he'd lied, said it was just one of those stupid things that happens when you've almost got killed. I understand how that goes. But there was this silence, and he said, very small, "Yes."

"Kethe," I said, because I couldn't think of nothing else to say. "You . . . Kethe!"

"Please," he said, his voice still barely more than a whisper. "Please don't . . . I know it must disgust you, but *please* . . ."

He sounded like he'd sounded when we were crossing Kekropia and he'd been crazy and sick-scared with it. I said, purely by reflex, "I won't leave." And then, because I didn't know how I felt, and this wasn't even close to the right place to try and work it out, I said, "Light. And we'll worry about it later."

"Yes, of course." A laugh, shaky and not very convincing. "Light."

But it happened easier than I'd expected. Easier than I think he'd expected. One minute there was nothing. The next there were his little green chrysanthemums again, showing us like a pair of drowned rats, and Felix looking everywhere except at my face.

The bank was close, and it was the same sort of jagged stair step deal it was back by the bridge. We dragged each other out of the river and sorted ourselves out as best we could, and Felix still wasn't looking at me, but I wasn't ready to talk about it, either. So I wrung the water out of my hair and said, "Okay. Let's find the others and get the fuck out of here."

We could deal with it later.

෨෬

We came back up out of that labyrinth into what Miss Parr said was an abandoned sewer tunnel. Once, there'd been a spring to shut the door after you came through it, and I could see how it must have been completely flush with the wall, so you wouldn't even be able to tell it was there. It was broken now, and it took me and Felix and Miss Parr all shoving as hard as we could to get the door shut again.

Nobody asked how come we had to shut it, and that was a small favor I was grateful for. My leg was screaming like a butchered pig, and I was so tired from dragging it what felt like halfway to Mélusine and back that I was having trouble keeping my eyes focused. Didn't need no arguments.

Florian didn't look no better off than I was, and Felix had his head down and his shoulders hunched, like he was trying to make himself disappear. Miss Parr still looked fresh as a daisy. Which, you know, nobody's going to send you to the sanguette for, but it sure did make me want to smack her.

After everything else, getting out of the sewer was no big deal, even if Felix and Miss Parr did have to pull me up by main force. Powers, I hated being a crip. We came up in a courtyard like something you'd find in Pennycup and for a moment it was the homesickness that hurt. It was just past sundown, and Felix's witchlights suddenly showed up way too well.

"Put them things out!" I said. Felix jumped like I'd pinched him, and his lights went out. It wasn't quite too dark to see, but it was close.

"Satisfied?" he said nastily.

"You want to talk to anybody about what kind of hocus you ain't?" I said in Marathine. He didn't answer, and I said, "Didn't think so." Then back into Kekropian: "Keria Parr? Florian? Any idea where we are?"

"It's an air shaft," Miss Parr said. "We'll have to go through the building to get out to the street."

"It looks like apartments," Florian said. "There's laundry."

And there was, strung from the balconies, and this was looking more like Pennycup or Lyonesse all the time, and the homesickness was crawling up into my throat and making it hard to breathe.

"Let's go," I said, and my voice came out harsh and mean, which wasn't what I'd wanted at all. But there wasn't no way to explain, so I just started for the courtyard door.

Which was locked. Figured.

"Keria Parr," I said, "a hairpin?"

"A what?"

"Hairpin," I said as clear as I could manage, but I was tired and kind of choked up and the word for hairpin in Kekropian had too many of the wrong kind of consonants.

"Did you understand that?" she said to Felix.

Fuck you, bitch, I'm right here and I ain't no performing dog. But I didn't say that, and I straightened out my hands where they'd clenched into fists.

Felix said in Marathine, "What is it you want?"

"A fucking hairpin, so I can get us through this fucking door. If it ain't too fucking much to ask."

I was glad of the dark, because he couldn't see me, and right then I was glad of how uncomfortable he'd been with me since we'd got ourselves out of the Sim, because he didn't push. He just said to Miss Parr, "I think he wants to pick the lock. A hairpin, keria, please?"

"Oh, yes, of course."

She handed me a hairpin.

"Do you need a light?" Felix said, and I thought he wasn't trying to be snarky, but it was hard to tell. I was pleased in a mean sort of way to be able to tell him, no, I didn't need a light. Because I didn't. Lockpicking is all ears and fingers, and Keeper'd used to make us practice blindfolded anyway.

The hairpin made a lousy lock pick, but then, it was a lousy lock. If I'd been a tenant in that building, I would have had something to say about that to the landlord. I got the door open, got the others through it, locked it again—because we didn't need to be getting nobody in trouble—and then we were in a sort of storage room, and it was just a matter of finding the front door, and we were out on the street, with the lamplighters doing their job, and people walking way wide around us as they went by.

"Oh!" Florian said, at about the same time Miss Parr said, "This is Knot Garden Street." And Florian said, "We're only two blocks from home!"

"Fucking marvelous," I said under my breath in Marathine.

Florian led the way, with Miss Parr hurrying to keep up with him. Felix dropped back to walk beside me.

"Are you all right?" he said.

"I'm fine."

"There's something I need to tell you, before we . . . I need to tell you now."

"I'm listening."

He said in Marathine, "Mehitabel Parr wants to come back to Mélusine with us."

"She wants *what*?" I did remember to keep my voice down, but only just.

"She wishes to travel with us to Mélusine," Felix said, like if he got his grammar all flash, it wouldn't mean the same thing.

"You gonna let her?" Let her come all the way across the Grasslands with us, where you can play her and me against each other and sit back and laugh? Because he was already doing it, the same way he'd done in the

Gardens, the same way he'd done on the *White Otter*. If you didn't give him your heart, he found a way to rip it out.

"It's not that simple."

"Looks like a pretty basic yes or no type thing to me. You gonna let her, or not?"

"It's not that simple."

"Then tell me what's complicated."

"I know you've taken a dislike to her."

"Then you want to invite her along?"

"I didn't say that."

"If *you* didn't want her to come, you wouldn't care."

He wanted to tell me that wasn't true, but he couldn't quite do it. He said, "She could cause a great deal of trouble with the authorities."

"Will she?"

"Mildmay." He shoved his hair off his face in exasperation. And then ahead of us, Florian broke into a run, and Felix said, *"Damn,"* between his teeth. "There's no time. I just . . . I wanted you to know, that's all."

And then he lengthened his stride to catch up with Miss Parr and left me behind without even looking back. I guess he trusted me to follow him wherever he went, and I guess he was right about it, too.

$$\sim$$

About a half hour later, I was sitting outside Mr. Gauthy's study like some pusher's hired goon, while him and Felix thrashed out some kind of a deal. Felix had a plan. I knew that, even if I didn't know what it was, and I figured all I could do was hang on and try to enjoy the ride.

Somewhere else in the house, Mrs. Gauthy was crying her ugly fake tears over Florian, and that was a scene I was just as glad to miss out on. So I sat there with my leg hurting, so tired I would've liked to just lay down right there on the bench I was sitting on, and tried not to think about Ginevra and tried not to think about Felix. Which was one of those things where I could manage one or the other, but not both.

Grief is like getting stuck in the same cyclone over and over and over again. And every time, you think, Man, I have got to get out of the way of this fucker, and then the next time you find you haven't budged a fucking inch. So, yeah, Ginevra was still dead and it still hurt like having iron skewers shoved through my heart, but, I mean, there wasn't nothing to *do* about it. Except try not to think about her.

Felix was different. Because Felix was there, and we weren't getting shut of each other this side of the Grasslands, that was for sure. And I was so tired that if I let my guard down, or let my eyes close, I'd be back there in the dark in the river, feeling him against me.

It didn't make no sense. If it hadn't been for him apologizing and for the fact that he was so mortified I could see it, I would've thought he was just fucking with my head, like he'd been doing flirting with me for a month or more. But it'd been real. He'd meant it. And powers, I mean, he'd had Astyanax and a shot at Mr. Vilker and just about anybody he'd wanted in the Gardens. What the fuck did he want with me?

The part where it was incest—well, it sure wasn't stopping him, and, I mean, maybe it was just me not being raised right or something, but that part didn't bother me. Okay, that's a lie. It *bothered* me, but it would have been way worse to find out somebody I'd grown up with, somebody like Margot, had the hots for me, if you see what I mean. Because me and Margot—even if she still hated me for what'd happened to her little Badgers, she felt like my sister. Felix only felt like somebody I *wanted* to be my brother. It wasn't the same.

And then there was the whole thing where I wasn't molly. But that was at least a little simpler, because he knew I wasn't molly. I figured if he'd had any doubts, he would've gone ahead and made a pass at me and found out that way. But he hadn't, so he knew, and it was pretty clear he hadn't meant me to know about him. Not like that. And if he asked now—which seemed pretty unlikely—all I had to do was say, no thanks. And if I had to . . . well, I'd hit him before, and for worse reasons. That I felt like I could handle.

But it was harder to get rid of the memory of it, and harder to get it to make any kind of sense. I kept telling myself to quit already, I was too tired to think straight and I knew it. But I couldn't seem to let go of it, no matter how much I wanted to.

So I was almost glad when Miss Parr showed up, even though she was mad as a hornet and looking to spread it around, if the glare she gave me was anything to go by.

Felix hadn't told me why he wanted her to come, but I could guess. He'd looked at the maps and he'd looked at me and he'd figured he didn't want to be stuck with just me for company all the way across Kekropia. I couldn't blame him for that. But it didn't make me like her better, and I hadn't liked her much to start with. I know I ain't all that bright, but I don't like people who rub it in.

She said in a high, hard voice, "You may be interested to learn I've just been dismissed from my position, with neither a character nor severance pay."

Oh fuck me sideways, I thought, because there went my last hope of not having to cross the Grasslands with this bitch. But I couldn't help asking, "What *for*?"

"Immorality," she said in a growl.

"What? I mean . . ."

"She found out about Jeremias," Miss Parr said with a toss of her head. "We were sleeping together. And now Keria Gauthy thinks I'm a 'corrupting influence,' and that it's somehow my doing that Florian went off with Jeremias in the first place." She snorted. "I'm sure she'd rather fire Jeremias, but since he had the gross impertinence to die down there, she can't."

"Oh," I said. She didn't look like a lady who was much upset about losing her lover, and I wished I didn't have to sit there and wonder what she'd made of me going to pieces over Ginevra. Powers, I felt like curdled milk.

She was looking at me kind of sideways. I said, "What?"

"Has Felix . . . has your brother told you?"

" 'Bout you wanting to go to Mélusine with us? Yeah."

"I, um, I know we haven't gotten off on the best possible foot, and I know you have no reason to do me any favors, but, Ker Foxe, *please*. He said he wouldn't let me come if you didn't approve."

She knew how pretty her big, dark eyes were, no doubt about that. "I don't got nothing against you," I said. Well, I mumbled it, and she made me repeat it.

"That's good," she said, although she didn't sound very sure about it. "I won't be a burden to you, I promise. I grew up traveling across the Grasslands. I can pull my weight."

"I ain't said you couldn't."

"Ker Foxe . . ."

"Look. If he wants you to come, you can come. I don't care."

"Thank you," she said, like what she really meant was *Fuck you*, but she was too much of a lady to say it. She sat down on the bench across from mine—perfect posture, folded hands, the whole fucking ball of wax. Ginevra'd wanted to have manners like that, but she'd never quite been able to pull it off.

Kethe, you fuckhead, stop thinking about her.

But I couldn't. It hadn't been her, down there in the dark. I knew that.

But at the same time, there was still this sick feeling in my chest, like it *had* been her, and I'd gone and left her, left her down there alone and dead and cold. I could almost hear her, still calling for me, her voice thick and wavery and a little hoarse, like she'd been crying and she was scared.

"Ker Foxe?" said Miss Parr. "Are you all right?"

"Fine," I said.

"You're awfully white. Is it your leg?"

"Yeah," I said. Anything to get the bitch to shut up. "It just needs rest, and it'll be okay."

"Are you sure? Keria Dossia, the cook, is a midwife, and I'd be glad to ask if she has a tisane that would help."

"No," I said carefully. "Thank you." Leave me alone, you fucking bitch.

She looked for a second like she was going to push it, but she must've thought better of it because she sat back and closed her mouth. And I thanked the powers and the saints because I wasn't sure I'd've been able to keep from saying something really nasty, and Felix wanted to let the gal come all the way across the fucking Grasslands with us.

And then the door of Mr. Gauthy's study opened, and him and Felix came out. Felix was looking smug as a cat with the key to the dairy. Whatever it was he wanted, seemed like he'd got it.

They shook hands, and Mr. Gauthy said something about letters and credentials and arrangements and scooted off.

Felix turned to Miss Parr and me, and his eyebrows went up. "You look like the last two mourners at a funeral."

"She got fired," I said.

"Really?" he said, turning to her like he thought I'd got hold of the wrong end of the stick.

"Oh, yes," she said, and I could see that it was eating at her, even while she was trying to pretend she didn't give a rat's ass. And you know, I didn't like her, but I knew what that felt like, and I couldn't help kind of, I don't know, sympathizing with her. There ain't nothing worse than getting fired by somebody you hate, because it means they win and you don't get no rematch.

"My condolences," Felix said. "What will you do now?"

Miss Parr hesitated, looking from him to me, and I wished I could call him a prick right out in the open like this. Because there was only one way to go, and he'd walked me into it as neat as you please.

"I don't mind," I said to her. "If you want to come."

She looked kind of taken aback, but Felix said, "Splendid! That's set-tled then. If you'll come with us, keria, I'll give you the particulars of our traveling arrangements."

There might've been things she wouldn't've done to get out of that house just then, but I had the feeling that the wall Mehitabel Parr would balk at was a lot higher than that one. I was beginning to wonder, even with her manners, whether she was really a lady at all.

Part Two

Chapter 7

Felix

We were a week out of Klepsydra before I realized what was wrong with Mildmay.

At first, I wasn't even sure there was anything wrong at all. I had not expected him to be speaking to me, and thus the fact that he wasn't did not seem to be cause for alarm. And I would have been shocked to see him in the hotel bars in the evenings, especially considering that he would have been sharing a table with Mehitabel.

Mehitabel was becoming a different person as the distance increased between us and Klepsydra. Her manners and appearance were still impeccable; she still had that beautifully erect carriage that must have made Theokrita Gauthy gnash her teeth with envy. But it was as if she had been cut loose from a stiff iron armature. With vitality, her face became beautiful, and her purring laugh was like a gift. Despite Mildmay's sullen rejection of her, I found that I liked her a great deal.

We sat together in the evenings, in hotel bar after hotel bar, and talked.

The farther we traveled into the duchies, the more likely it was that one or both of us would be drinking. It was not wise, for either of us, but it seemed the best of a bad lot of options. If I was drinking with Mehitabel, I wasn't doing anything that might cause me to be suspected of being ganumedes or a wizard.

For her part, Mehitabel drank with me to avoid drinking with our other traveling companions: a succession of acting troupes. She was related, directly or indirectly, to many of the actors. That evening, in the bar of a hotel called The Maid's Morion, in a town whose name I had already forgotten, she had positioned herself with particular care so that the actors at their table across the room could not catch her eye.

After her second glass of gin, I raised my eyebrows inquiringly, and she laughed, a husky, bitter sound.

"They're Zamyatins," she said, signaling the bartender for another drink.

"Is that a Merrovin name?"

"Well back in the family tree now, but yes."

"And you don't want to talk to them because you find their antecedents unsavory?"

She snorted. "Not hardly. My grandfather married Louise Zamyatin. She brought her name and two of her brothers, and that is why my family troupe is the Parr-Zamyatin Players."

"And these?"

"Are the side of the family that didn't want a close alliance with Gran'père Mato."

"They seem friendly enough."

"Family," she said with an expressive sigh. "I don't want to talk to them because they will inevitably want to know why I left my family's troupe."

"And your reason was . . . ?"

"Neither your business nor anyone else's," she said, but smiled to soften it.

"Well, that puts me properly in my place," I said and smiled back.

"Oh come," she said, halfway down her third gin and the alcohol starting to make her reckless. "It's not like you don't have things you won't tell me. Like what Ingvard Vilker's business was with you the morning we left town."

The light in her eyes was a dare. I said, "He'd brought a letter for Mildmay."

"Which he gave to you."

"Mildmay and Ingvard did not take to each other."

"Sir, you shock me. But that's not what you were talking about, so seriously and at such length."

"You sound as if you already know."

"I'm well aware of Ingvard's inclinations," she said, her voice mercifully too low to be heard by anyone but me. "And I recognize a spurned suitor when I see one."

"I didn't spurn him," I protested. "We simply . . . there was a misunderstanding. He wanted us to part friends."

"And did you?"

"I think so. The problem was not entirely his fault, and I told him so."

"Good," she said, and I caught her wrist as she started to wave for a fourth gin.

"Why don't you go upstairs instead? I am. We've got an early start tomorrow, you know."

"We always do," she said, mock-mournfully. "But you're right. Finish your bourbon and let's go."

I glanced from her to the table of actors—two of whom looked away quickly—and back to her. "You want your cousins to think we're sleeping together?"

Sudden anxiety in her dark eyes. "Do you mind?"

"Not at all. Just don't expect any follow-through."

She laughed. I knocked back the last of my bourbon; we settled our tab and left the bar.

We climbed the stairs together without talking; I could not tell if she was preoccupied or merely tired, but the silence suited me well enough. She said good night at the door of her room, and I continued down the hallway to ours.

It was dark and so perfectly still I honestly believed that Mildmay must have gone out—though I could not imagine where he would have gone or why he wouldn't have told me—and conjured a flame to the wick of the candle I knew was by the bed.

The light caught him before he was ready for me to see him.

He was sitting on the side of the bed, his head sunk in his hands. I knew, without the slightest taint of doubt, that he had been sitting in exactly that position for hours, since I had told him I was going down to the bar and left the room. His head came up as I shut the door, and his face was as impassive as ever, but the wretched, defensive hunch of his shoulders told me everything his face did not.

I did not speak for a moment, stripping my gloves off and setting them on top of the carpet bag that contained, now, all my worldly possessions. Mildmay watched me, unspeaking and almost uncaring, except for the caution that did not let him leave anyone unmonitored. I remembered that caution from my childhood.

I went around the foot of the bed and sat down on the edge of the mattress, trying to keep distance between us, to be as unthreatening as I could. I had also thought it possible that his shut-off silence was the result of my inadvertent, shameful confession of lust for him. But now I wondered if perhaps the problem was something quite else, something I had not thought to watch for.

Another moment's silence—and I was now watching him as carefully as he was watching me—and I said, "What's the matter?" I was pleased with myself for making the question sound nonjudgmental, more curious than worried. Clearly, if he'd wanted concern, he would have told me days ago.

"Nothing," he said—unsurprising, but at least it was not an obscenity.

I considered my next move carefully. He watched me, twisted around but still hunched together as if he expected a blow. I did not have to worry that he would become impatient, and with a spark of humor it occurred to me to be grateful that I didn't have to have this conversation with myself. I said, still careful, still light, "Is there anything I can do?"

"No, it's nothing," he said, shaking his head as if the movement pained him. And then added, "Nothing anybody can help with."

It took all my control not to pounce on that hint, which would only frighten him into withdrawal, raising his quills like a porcupine. I said, taking a calculated risk, "Is it me? Is it . . . ?"

"No! Kethe, Felix, no, it ain't you at all. It's . . ." He trailed off again, but that flash of urgency and anxiety reassured me, both that this truly wasn't about me and my idiocy, and that he could still be reached.

"Can it make things any worse to tell me?"

"You'll laugh," he said, and the way his gaze cut away from me reminded me suddenly of how young he was.

"I won't. I promise. I couldn't. Not at something that's upset you this badly."

Too intense: I could feel him shrinking away, like some night-loving creature caught in the sunlight. "It's stupid," he said, mumbling down at his hands as he did when he particularly wanted to be left alone.

But I could not leave him alone with this. I reined in my own concern, my hurt at seeing him in so much pain, and said, "No matter how stupid it is, I'll bet I can top it."

That brought his head up, and I smiled at him, with all the warmth and force I had. His eyes widened a little, and I saw his teeth catch his lower lip, a gesture of nervousness made grotesque by the scar that twisted his upper lip. But although I did not have his stone face, I could control my expression when I had to; I held his gaze and waited.

He did not want to tell me, but I could see how tired he was, worn ragged with carrying this thing, whatever it was, by himself. If he had not been lamed, he might have fled the room, but instead his hands clenched in the bedcovers, and he said, "It's Ginevra."

"Then it's not stupid."

However he had expected me to react—and I suspected that despite my promise, he had expected jeers and mockery—he had not been prepared for acceptance. He went white, then red, and turned quickly away. I said, as gently as I could, "Tell me."

"It's her voice," he said. My hands felt suddenly as if I'd pressed them against a block of ice.

"Her voice?" I said. "You mean . . ."

"Like in the maze, yeah. Calling. And I want to go find her, and I *can't*." His breath hitched, and he lowered his face into his hands again. And said, in the smallest, most timid voice I had ever heard from him, "Is this what going crazy's like?"

"You're not going crazy," I said, having had a little time to think things through. And, really, it only took a moment, and I could have kicked myself for my stupidity in not realizing earlier that the possibility existed. "It's most likely a residue of the spell that made you hear her voice in the first place. Like the way the smell of smoke lingers in your hair or clothes."

"Oh," he said. "Oh, powers, how fucking *stupid*," and his fingers tensed into his hair, disarraying it from its neat queue.

"Think of it as an illness," I offered, trying not to heed the impulse to lean across the bed and unbraid his hair for him. "It's not your fault if you're feverish."

"Not the way Keeper told it." And although I thought he meant it as a little bit of a joke, I was struck by empathy as if by a sword. No wonder he will not tell anyone when he suffers.

It was a moment before I could trust my voice again. I said, "I can disperse it for you."

A quick, worried sideways glance. "Won't that bring the Bastion down on you?"

And a cogent question. "No," I said. "It's too small. And it's not a Cabaline spell. Even the Bastion doesn't police every hedge witch and half-centime wizard in the Empire. Will you let me?"

"What d'you gotta do?"

My mind was immediately flocked with unworthy suggestions, of which the tamest was, Kiss you. I fought them all back and said, as I had said in the labyrinth, "I need to see your eyes."

"Powers and saints," he said, but without any force. He rubbed both palms up his face, then raised his head and turned to look at me. Now that I knew it was there, I could see it: a faint, cruel darkness like a hairline crack in fine porcelain. I reached out and placed my palm against his unscarred cheek. His eyes were very wide, but he held perfectly still, so still that I could feel him trembling.

It was like snapping a taut thread: that quick, that brutal, and that simple. His breath hitched. I said, neutrally, "Did you feel it?"

"Dunno. Felt something. It was . . . weird."

"You felt it." I moved my hand away from his face, not allowing the gesture to be a caress. "Do you still hear her voice?"

His head tilted a little to one side, and his eyes became distant. Then he shook his head. "She's gone."

"Good. If the voice comes back, let me know at once. Will you do that?"

"Yeah." An awkward hesitation, and then an even more awkward, "Thanks."

I wanted to tell him not to thank me. I wanted to tell him it was no more than what I ought to do, and I should have done it two weeks ago in any event. I wanted to tell him I loved him. I wanted, very badly, to kiss him. I said, "It wasn't difficult. Are you . . . all right now?"

He gave one of his half shrugs. "I'm okay."

"Truly?"

He met my eyes—only for a moment, but enough that I knew we saw each other, as we so rarely did, plainly. "Good enough to get by on." He hesitated again, then gave a slight, defeated sigh, and said, "You can't mend everything, Felix. But thanks for wanting to."

"Anything I can . . ."

"I know." And that sweetness entered his face that was not a smile, because he did not smile. "And really, thanks. But some things are past fixing. Even with magic."

The truth of that hurt. I covered my flinch by standing up and saying, "We should get to sleep. It's late." And then, the thought occurring to me belatedly, "Have you eaten?"

"Ain't hungry."

I bit back my first response: *That's not what I asked.* I said, "If you're looking for a hobby, may I suggest wood carving rather than starving yourself to death?"

"I'll get something tomorrow." He turned away from me sullenly and started unbuttoning his waistcoat. Somehow, I had said the wrong thing despite myself.

And there was a limit to how much caretaking either of us could bear from me. Better not to push my luck. The important thing tonight was that the last of that horrid spell had been dispersed; perhaps from here other things might improve without my interference.

We undressed and prepared for bed in silence. I did my best not to look at him, at the strong muscles of his shoulders and arms, at the ugly shine of scars on his lame leg, at the fox-red river of his unbraided hair.

Stop it, I said to myself. Just stop it.

We climbed into bed, one on each side. I snuffed the candle and then, in the dark, dared to ask, "Would you like me to ward your dreams again?"

What felt like a year later his whispered answer came back: "Yes. Please."

🜲

I did not intend to dream of the Khloïdanikos and its beautiful ghost-infested paths. If anything, I'd meant to stay away from it. But finding myself among the perseïdes was not a surprise. It felt somehow inevitable.

I avoid the Omphalos, but otherwise I simply wander, exploring. There is a stream, clear and peaceful and nothing that exists in the waking world, canopied by willows that lean to trail their branches in the water. I cross it one way on a set of stepping-stones, each carved with a different flower: a lily, a rose, a chrysanthemum, a snapdragon, a branch of cherry blossoms.

A little later, I cross the stream again, this time on a graceful bridge, arched like the back of a cat demanding to be petted. I walk through a rose garden, the roses blazing in shades of red and orange and yellow. There is a sundial in the middle, but its gnomon casts no shadow. The path changes from warm red brick to squares of glossy black slate, and I find myself in a water garden, boasting small artificial waterfalls and a great green pond, with water lilies the size of my two fists floating on it like the barges of ancient queens. I catch a flash of red-gold beneath the surface of the water, and realize that there are koi in the pond, massive, serene, and I wonder: are they dreams of fish, or fish who dream?

I investigate the windings of a path tiled in white and blue. Perhaps it is the nature of the Khloïdanikos, as it is of the Mirador, to encourage meetings, and most especially with the people one most wishes to avoid, for I come around a stand of perseïd trees, and there, sitting on a bench amid the heartbreakingly verdant grass, is Diokletian. There is another man with him, younger, with eyes like gold coins in his paper-white face. I recognize him as the diviner who nearly killed Mildmay, and after a moment remember his name: Thamuris.

If I were able to break the dream, I would. But as I did not choose to enter the Khloïdanikos, so I cannot choose to escape it. True-dreaming is not like magic; it has its own rules and its own rhythms. And the Khloïdanikos—I cannot even begin to guess what powers the Troian oneiromancers might have used to create it, or to maintain it. I am becoming more and more aware that it, too, has its own rules, perhaps even, in a nebulous way, a set of priorities that no one now alive understands.

Diokletian leaps to his feet. "YOU!" he cries, as dramatically as any pantomime hero.

I know I should not, but I cannot help laughing. "What? Will you forbid me the Khloïdanikos?"

"Could you?" the other man asks Diokletian.

"Thamuris!"

Thamuris's tone is one of scholarly interest; he seems not at all threatened by my sudden appearance, nor disturbed by the hostility between Diokletian and me. I look at him more carefully, seeing in his dream-self the sharp and questing intellect that in the waking world is debilitated by his disease and deadened by laudanum. Here is one who will share my interest in the Khloïdanikos for its own sake, and that thought—the thought of having someone I can talk to as an intellectual equal—is like rain after a long drought.

I say to the diviner, "I don't think he can. I certainly wouldn't know how to go about such a thing."

"It is not a private world," the diviner says.

"No, clearly it was not intended that way."

"Thamuris!" Diokletian says again, strident with jealousy and anger.

The golden eyes, dispassionate as a lion's, turn to him. "Yes, celebrant?"

I remember that Thamuris is a Celebrant Celestial. He outranks everyone in the Gardens of Nephele, including the Arkhon. The consumption does not care.

"This man," Diokletian says and flounders to a halt.

"Is what?" I say. "A foreigner? An ungrateful wretch? The low and sordid child of a fabulous mother?"

"Is not to be trusted," Diokletian says, giving me a triumphant glare.

"Nor am I," Thamuris says. "As he knows. But I do not think that, in the Khloïdanikos, we can do each other any harm."

It is the nature of the Dream of the Gardens that I can see Diokletian's hurt around him. I say, "I do not wish to drive you away. Nor to quarrel."

"What right have you to speak of driving me away?" Raw, thwarted fury, and in the waking world he would never show it—would barely even know he felt it—but here, dreaming, it is a palpable presence. It is not about Methony any longer, except insofar as he sees me as a betrayal of her memory. This is the wizard's occupational disease: envy. Deadly, grinding envy, which looks at my power and my person and argues that the one does not deserve the other. I have heard it, seen it, felt it, ever since the moment at which I first learned I was a wizard at all. I reveled in it in the Hall of the Chimeras, flaunted my looks and my tastes and my cruelty. But I was powerless for over a year, powerless and helpless and frightened, and somewhere along the way I lost my appetite for this particular poisoned feast.

I say, "None. But since you cannot drive me away either, cannot we . . . can't we just let this rest?"

"What possible reason can you have to stay?"

"I made no secret of my interest in the Khloïdanikos. And I would like to hear Thamuris's opinion of it."

I see Thamuris's surprise, just as I see Diokletian's anger. Here at last, in this lion-eyed diviner, is someone who believes that I care about Mildmay and believes that I should—someone who recognizes his own mistakes, his own thoughtlessness. He knows too much about his own flaws to sit in judgment on others. I realize, or perhaps the Khloïdanikos shows me, that I wanted Diokletian to be that person, wanted him to be the wise teacher he seemed. But that is not what he is, any more than I am a version of Methony who can be tamed.

I sit down beside Thamuris. He looks at me curiously, sidelong, and I know he sees something of what I feel, just as I can see his feelings not quite staining the air around him.

Diokletian is blind to this other not-quite-sense. He does not have the openness to which Thamuris has been trained and into which I was forced by Malkar's terrible working. It is not a matter of power, although I know he would never believe me if I tried to tell him so, nor a matter of willingness or interest or anything else that can be explained or understood. It is what the Khloïdanikos demands, a token of surrender. And thus, entering the Khloïdanikos from a controlled trance, I was as blind to it as Diokletian was. I wonder how and why the Khloïdanikos acquired that quality, and if it was any part of the original creators' plans.

Diokletian struggles with his anger and wins. He sits down on Thamuris's other side and says, "If you would have the kindness not to interrupt . . ."

But before I can say anything, sarcastic or otherwise, the Khloïdanikos dissolves in a wash of green around me, and I wake.

✼

Gray streaks in the darkness showed me where the shutters were, and that beyond them the sun would be rising soon. Mildmay was a huddled mass beside me; he slept always as if he had had to be beaten into submission. He snored, very slightly, a legacy of the times his nose had been broken; I did not know if he knew that, and I was reluctant to tell him. I was afraid it would embarrass him, and I found myself curiously protective of that slight rattle. It was a comfort, when I woke in the middle of the night from one or another of my bad dreams, to know that there was a living person beside me in the bed, that if I had to, I could wake him.

I lay, watching my brother sleep and wondering about the Khloïdanikos, until the sun came up.

Mildmay

We'd been hearing for most of a decad about the hocus they were going to burn in Aiaia to start the Trials of Heth-Eskaladen. Even with my head full of Ginevra's voice I hadn't been able to miss it, and once Felix cleared that out, powers, it seemed like that was all people were talking about. And not just the players, neither, although they gossiped like a pack of old ladies, but hotel clerks and guys getting drunk in the bars and the people who came to watch the plays—*everybody* talking about this poor fuck that the Duke of Aiaia was going to burn at the stake.

Nobody seemed to mind very much. Or to care what he was being burned *for*. It got to the point—well, I ain't as bad as Felix, but I did get to where every time the thing came up, I said, "So what'd he do?" Hard and bright and a little nasty, and even though nobody ever answered me, it took the edge off the conversation a little, and I was glad of it. I'd seen a hocus burned at the stake. Least the sanguette's clean.

But nobody knew. He was a hocus, and the southern duchies hated hocuses, and apparently that was all there was to it.

There was a whole bunch of other stuff the southern duchies hated, including molls and people with funny religions and most all foreigners. Felix was getting twitchier and twitchier by the day, and I couldn't blame him. All it would take was somebody wondering about whether *maybe* they should suspect him—hocus or moll, either way, and he'd end up decorating a woodpile himself. He wasn't flirting. He wasn't hardly talking to nobody but Mehitabel Parr, although the manners on him when he decided he had to use them—powers, it was a sight.

And we were at least a little safe—safer than we'd've been if we hadn't had Miss Parr along, and you can imagine how much I hated having to admit that. But I'd thought we'd seriously been hung out to dry, after we reached Mukenai with Mr. Gauthy's caravan. They were going on south to Lunness Point, and it was pretty clear from what the caravan guards told me that they thought we were completely fucked in the head for going west.

And I was getting to where I agreed with them. I know it was my idea and everything, but the longer I thought about it, the more I couldn't believe we'd made it across the Grasslands *once*, and crossing it again felt like walking back into a lion's den, only this time with a slide trombone.

I was a little nervous, thanks for asking.

But then Miss Parr played her trump—I figured she'd been saving it until she was sure she wanted to be stuck with us for the long haul. Turned out she'd been born in a players' troupe and was related to half the actors in the Empire. And since even in Kekropia, people are glad to see actors most everywhere, there weren't no problems finding troupes going the direction we needed. And what was even better, they took me and Felix along without even blinking. Friends of Miss Parr seemed good enough for them.

And if you're going to be stupid enough to try to get across the duchies with a brother who's a hocus and has the tattoos to prove it, then a players' troupe turns out to be right exactly what you want. They all dressed funny themselves, and it seemed like half of them were redheads. Which, the farther west we got, was a bigger and bigger favor.

I hadn't thought there was anything about Troia I'd liked, but that was one, not having to worry that my red hair would get me into trouble. I'd dyed it for most of two septads, until Mr. High-and-Mighty Mavortian von Heber—who was probably dead and I should quit being nasty about him— had made me stop. If I'd been thinking in Klepsydra, I would have dyed it again, and made Felix dye his, too, no matter *what* he said, but I hadn't been thinking, and the kind of hair dye we needed was just not something we were going to find out here in the absolute ass-end of nowhere. So the fact that a lot of actors apparently had Troian and Merrovin blood—well, it didn't exactly make us inconspicuous, but it did at least make us less of a target.

And actors don't ask questions. This is the thing I learned about them, and I had days where I wanted to kiss them for it, every man, woman, and child. I mean, they gossiped and all, but if you didn't bring up the subject of what you'd done with your life or why you were so interested in getting across the Grasslands, they didn't either. I returned the favor and didn't go prying around myself, even about Miss Parr, although my curiosity on that subject was getting pretty fierce. Especially on how a gal like her had ended up a governess in Klepsydra. But she wasn't telling, and it wasn't like it was any of my business anyway.

We didn't stay with any one troupe for long. They had their little territories, like the alley cats in the Lower City, and we'd generally end up walking for a day or two from where one troupe wasn't going no farther west to where we could find the next one. And it was okay—the walking, I mean— but I had to admit it to myself, I couldn't have walked all the way to Mélusine. Crawled, maybe, but not walked.

And of course, the more that got hammered into my stupid thick skull, the more I worried about what I was going to do with myself when I got back home. And I don't know how long it took me, but one day it was like I woke up and thought, Fuck me sideways. Why didn't *I* go to Aigisthos?

The answer came back, quick as a smart remark: because Felix couldn't. And then I spent the next half mile or so trying to pretend I hadn't thought that.

You ain't nothing to him, Milly-Fox, and don't even try to make like you are. You think he's going to take you to the Mirador with him when y'all get back to Mélusine? Do you even *want* him to?

And, of course, no, I didn't. Didn't want to have nothing to do with the Mirador. Ever. But if we were both in Mélusine, there was a chance maybe we could see each other occasionally. I tried to imagine going out to a bar with Felix, say the Hornet and Spindle or the Green Pig, and then thought, Who the fuck do you think you're kidding?

So bail, stupid. Go to St. Millefleur. Or Cypriot.

And then what?

That was the bitchkitty, and it had been the bitchkitty for . . . I didn't even know how long. I couldn't reckon the months. Since Ginevra had died. I'd let myself be carried along, first by Mavortian and his plans and then by Felix needing me so bad, and there'd always been something else to worry about, some new horrible thing. And no time to think. But now I had all the fucking time in the world.

So what do you want to do, Milly-Fox?

Keeper's voice, pretending to be interested. And of course I didn't have an answer, the way I'd never had an answer when Keeper asked me something. I'd never imagined I'd end up lame, never thought about what I'd do if I couldn't do what I'd been trained my whole life for. And now that I was thinking about it, it didn't seem like there was anything I *could* do. Be hired muscle. Be somebody's errand boy. Let somebody else tell me what to do and where to do it. Fuck, at that rate, I might just as well go and see if Keeper would take me back. Because it wouldn't be all that different. And something sick and cold in the pit of my stomach knew that she would.

Up ahead, Felix laughed at a comment of Miss Parr's. I thought helplessly, He'll leave. And it seemed like just too much to bear. It would be like bleeding to death, only nobody else would ever see the blood. And there'd be nothing to keep me from crawling back to Keeper like a half-dead dog, nothing to keep her from using me, using me up. Nothing to keep me from dying for real.

But I didn't see what else I could do, and the more I thought about it, the less I knew anything, and within a couple of days you could've dyed all the laundry in Lyonesse black just with the mood I was in. I fought it as much as I could, at least to where it didn't show. And I was pretty sure Miss Parr didn't notice anything wrong. Felix was starting to look at me funny, but he didn't say nothing, and that was just fucking fine.

So that's where we were at, the day I got all the information I wanted and more about the Duke of Aiaia and his plans. We were walking into a town called Ogygia, a couple days north of Aiaia. I'd just been congratulating myself on how we weren't going to have to get any closer to Aiaia than this, and I should've known better. Should've felt Kethe leaning over my shoulder and laughing.

If it'd been just me, I wouldn't even have noticed it. A handbill, stuck up on one of those damn milestones. Miss Parr didn't notice it, either, but Felix—well, I'd figured out by then that if there was words on something, Felix would read it. Nothing weird about that. What was weird was the way he stopped dead in his tracks, went back half a step, and ran into me nearly hard enough to knock us both on our asses.

"Sacred *fuck*," I said, but Felix wasn't even paying attention. He was staring at that fucking handbill like it was a swamp adder.

"What?" I said.

"Felix?" said Miss Parr.

He waved at us to shut up without even looking around. Miss Parr gave me a *what the fuck?* look and I gave it right back to her. And we stood there and waited for Felix to get back on board with us.

I think he read it twice before he turned around, and when he did turn, he looked like a man having a good close gawk at a ghoul's teeth. He said, in a jittery little voice that was mostly breath, "Mildmay, you said . . . the Kekropian we knew before . . . before . . . never mind. You said his name was Gideon Thraxios?"

Oh fuck. Everything in my head went cold and sick. Oh fuck oh fuck oh fuck. "Yeah."

Felix jerked his thumb back at the handbill.

He didn't say a word. He didn't need to.

Felix

We found a hotel in Ogygia, booked our rooms. Without discussion, we crammed ourselves uncomfortably into the room Mildmay and I would share, which would not have been generous for one person and verged on the morbidly claustrophobic for three.

Then I said, my voice harsher than I wanted, "Is there anything we can do?"

Mildmay, sitting on the bed with his lame leg stretched out, looked up at me. "You know what they'll do to you if they catch you? It'll make whatever they got planned for Gideon look like a hangnail."

"Are you saying we should just leave him to be burned?"

"They'll *kill* you," he said, as if I didn't know that.

Mehitabel said, with heavy patience, "Would one of you like to tell me what's going on?"

Mildmay and I stared at each other. I'd grown so accustomed to Mehitabel as a traveling companion, so used to the idea that she knew the secrets we were guarding, that I had forgotten there were things she did not know. Mildmay, who still did not like her and did not trust her, had of course not forgotten, but he had stopped fighting with me about it. I knew that look, that very slight hitch in his eyebrow that said he knew I was going to do what I wanted anyway, and he wasn't going to waste his breath on me. I did not care for that look, but it was better than another quarrel.

I said to Mehitabel, carefully, picking my way around the things I did not want to discuss, "When we started east, we had traveling companions. We were separated from them. One of them is the man whom the Duke of Aiaia apparently plans to burn in a week's time."

Mehitabel nodded, her pretty, deceptively childish face unreadable. "The perverted cultist Eusebian defector described in that handbill, you mean?"

I winced.

Mildmay said, "So what?"

"I just like to be clear," she said, although her face was still stony. "And you want to rescue him?"

"Yes," I said.

"*Can* you?" she said, looking past me at Mildmay.

He shrugged.

"Well, it wasn't an outright no," she said, and he gave her a flat look that I could read as bottled murder.

"We can think of something," I said.

"Hold on," she said. "Not 'we,' sunshine. He's right about that."

"But—"

"No. I've seen witch-hunts in the duchies. They'll *smell* you. Mildmay and I will be safer on our own."

"Who said you were going?" Mildmay said.

"Don't be an idiot," she said. "Whether you can rescue your friend or not, you certainly can't do it by yourself."

"It ain't right," he said.

"Worried about my reputation?" she said. "Or yours?"

He flushed an unattractive brick red that clashed with his hair, and I said quickly, "But how will I find you again?"

"We pick a place to meet," Mehitabel said. "The next big town west of Aiaia is Julip. Get there however you can."

"And then?"

"Pick a hotel near the east gate," Mildmay said. "I'll find you."

"If we get there."

"It's your fucking plan."

"I don't like indulging in undue optimism," said Mehitabel Parr.

Mildmay

We left the Grass-Widow's Harp in the middle of the night. I still felt sick about the whole thing, but both Miss Parr and Felix had laughed at me for trying to argue. I didn't want her to think I was any stupider than she already did.

Miss Parr and Felix had worked out the story, and I was sure Felix could carry it off. He could carry off most anything when he wanted to, not just how come the people he was traveling with had up and left. I did what I was told and followed Miss Parr south out of Ogygia. Shank's mare through the Grasslands again, and I wished it was Felix with me this time. Felix thought everybody was stupider than him, not just me.

We didn't say nothing for a couple hours, but then out of nowhere Miss Parr said, "Why'd you let him bully you into this?"

"What?"

"You didn't want to do this. Do you always do what he wants you to?"

"I don't remember you saying nothing against it. Seems to me you was raring to go." Kethe, Milly-Fox, could you mind your fucking grammar? I could feel the wallop of Keeper's hand across my ear.

"Oh, so it's my fault?" Miss Parr said.

"Just leave me the fuck alone," I said.

"Gladly," she said like a mousetrap snapping shut.

We had to stop when the moon set—there was no point walking into a ditch. We sat by the side of the road. I stretched my bad leg out and wished I was back in Ogygia with Felix.

Miss Parr sighed loudly and said, "We need a cover story."

I hated the fact that she was right. "So I guess you're my wife then." Because nobody but a blind man would believe we were related.

"Dearest," she said, and she probably batted her eyelashes at me, too, although I couldn't tell in the dark. "Now why are we going to Aiaia? Aside from the execution, that is?"

I didn't say nothing.

"A wedding," Miss Parr said. "People always like a wedding, and the end of the Trials is a good time for them. My sister, I think. Girls with your coloring have a hard time getting married in the far southern duchies. And maybe . . . yes. You're looking for work. It'll give you an excuse to be surly and not say much. And for goodness' sakes, mumble! We'll be completely in the soup if anyone recognizes your accent. Besides, it will give me the chance to hint about *other* reasons I might have to want to be near my family, and that should distract anyone who gets curious."

I hadn't meant to say nothing, just let her run the whole show since it was what she wanted, but I couldn't stand that. "Kethe!" I said. "Miss Parr, I can't . . ."

"I'm not asking you to *beat* me," she said.

"No, but . . ."

"And I won't *tell* anyone you beat me. I do wish I had a bruise or two to show, but I can manage without. Why on earth are you so shocked? Does it go against your principles to hit a woman?"

"Not one that deserves it," I said before I could stop myself. "Oh, powers, I'm sorry. I didn't mean . . . I wouldn't ever . . ."

She was laughing at me again. "It's a good story," she said. "People will believe it."

Yeah. People will believe anything of this fucking scar. I kept my mouth shut.

"We need names," she said. "It adds conviction." She lay back, staring up at the stars. "Zenobia, I think. Zenobia Wainwright. That sounds convincingly uneuphonious—especially as all the girls I've known with the name Zenobia have gone by the unfortunate nickname of Nobbie. Nobbie Wainwright sounds like the downtrodden wife of a ne'er-do-well to me. What about you? What shall we call you?"

She was talking like it was a game, and she wanted me to play along. "I don't care," I said.

"Ananias, then," she said, like she'd had it waiting. "Ananias Wainwright. Will it do?"

"Sure," I said. In the Lower City, any kid named Ananias would've been called Nanny and bleated at. But I just wanted her to shut up and leave me the fuck alone.

When it was light enough to see, Miss Parr started in on her clothes the same way she'd done on our names, ripping loose the ruffle from her cuffs and writhing out of her two petticoats. Her dress sagged without them. She took her hair down, and then pulled a palm-sized mirror and a comb out of her skirt pocket and put it up again in a different style, wound in two braids around her head. She tugged off the blue satin ribbon that had trimmed one of her petticoats and caught the ends of her braids with it at the nape of her neck. Then she took her spectacles out of her pocket—the ones she hadn't been wearing since we left Klepsydra—and put them on, pushing them up on her nose with an awkward gesture I had absolutely never seen from her before. And she did look like a different person. The brown dress looked dowdy instead of smart, and her heavy braids practically made her chin disappear. There was something different about the way she was wearing them spectacles, too. She didn't look teachery at all, more like a not-very-bright gal who was blind as a mole. Even the blue ribbon helped. It was the kind of thing women did when they were too poor to buy a new dress.

She gave me a once-over that made me want to hide. "You don't grow a beard, do you?"

"Nope."

"No matter. People round here are used to what they charmingly call the Taint, and that scar would make up for any amount of good grooming. But I'm afraid your clothes are simply too tidy, and Ananias just wouldn't have your nice taste in waistcoats. In fact, Ananias and Nobbie probably have only the vaguest idea of what a waistcoat is. Out here they're called vests and sneered at as things for sissified cityfolk to wear."

Felix had picked that waistcoat out. I unbuttoned it and took it off, remembering at the last second to save Florian's letter. Miss Parr watched me stuff it in my trouser pocket, but she didn't say nothing about it.

Instead, she had more orders: "Unbutton the top two buttons of your shirt and roll up your cuffs. The shirt really should be older, but at least it does look lived in."

"Just say I stole it."

"Unnecessary, I assure you. Ananias is a well-recognized type in the Grasslands." She looked me up and down. "I believe you'll do. Just remember to glower."

"That won't be hard," I said, watching her dump her petticoats and ruffles, and my waistcoat, into the drainage ditch, where they sank into the muck.

She ignored me. "Now, come on. There'll be people on the road soon."

"Yes, ma'am," I said, but enough under my breath that she could pretend like she hadn't heard that, either.

About two miles later, we were taken up by a farmer on his way to Hyle, the next big town along the southern road. I sat in the back with the bags of turnips and listened to Miss Parr being Nobbie Wainwright. She was an actress, sure enough, and a good one, although I would've eaten coals rather than tell her so. She had the local dialect nailed—she could have been the farmer's sister, they sounded that much alike—and she chattered away to him like she'd known him all her life.

She didn't tell him much of that story she'd made up, but I could see her using it and sort of understood why she'd insisted on having it. It was there in everything she said, and every so often she'd look back over her shoulder at me, like I made her nervous. Which I fucking hated. But I held up my end. When the farmer looked back at me, concern for Miss Parr all over his moony face, I gave him the worst glower I could. He actually went pale.

The farmer set us down in the market square of Hyle. We bought sausages there from a street vendor and ate them walking south. We left Hyle just as the church clock was striking the septad-day, though with the wrong number of strokes, of course, and walked for most of the afternoon. Near sundown, we were overtaken by a traveling tinker, and he gave us a ride to Merops. We couldn't afford lodgings, so Miss Parr said good night to the tinker, and we walked another mile or two until we found a haystack that it didn't look like nobody cared too much about.

I hadn't done much acting—it wasn't hard to look like I was thinking of beating Miss Parr black-and-blue—but I was glad to be shut of the characters she'd made up until the morning. I asked her how far she thought we were from Aiaia.

"Probably another day or two," she said. "Thank goodness you *aren't* Ananias." She was asleep almost as soon as she said it. I stayed awake for a while, wondering if that meant she sort of liked me a little, but I was too tired to really care. I fell asleep worrying about Felix.

Felix

The Khloïdanikos is beautiful at night, drenched in moonlight, leached of color. I find Thamuris standing beneath an arbor of clematis. His hair, almost black in this light, hangs loose past his hips; his lion-colored eyes are wide with delight. He folds his hands and bows when he sees me; I bow in return.

I say, not quite idly, "Where is Diokletian?"

There is a smile deep in Thamuris's eyes. "He does not know that I do not need guidance to find the Dream of the Garden. Were he to ask, I would tell him, but . . ."

"You are serpentine," I say.

"I have few other amusements." He looks away, up at the brilliant stars. "These are the wrong stars, you know."

"They are?" I look up. "I've never seen the Khloïdanikos at night before."

"Really?" He looks back at me. "That's odd. I find night here more often than not. Except with Diokletian. It's always daylight when he's here."

"Strange," I say. "But you're right. These stars are very odd."

"I know parts of the Khloïdanikos itself do not match up with the waking world, but astronomy has been a study in Troia for millennia. The oneiromancers would not *merely* get it wrong."

"They would have a purpose, you mean?"

"Yes, but I can't imagine what it would be."

"Well, what was the purpose of the Khloïdanikos?"

"I don't know that, either. Oneiromancy is a lost art in Troia."

"So Diokletian said. But surely there are records. What good is having a library if it doesn't keep *records*?"

He laughs, and I am reminded that he is closer to Mildmay's age than my own, for all the power and death that surround him. "Oneiromancy was starved out," he says. "Chipped away over decades. And I'm sure you know that the most fiercely contested resource of any library is shelf space."

"Yes." I think of the libraries of the Mirador, shoved in, like stickpins adorning a bloated dowager, wherever room can be found. "Yes, I do."

"So the texts were culled. Gradually. And then, when oneiromancy was abandoned, and the oneiromancers retired, or died, or went into exile—as some of them did—there was no one left who cared, and many who feared to be accused of caring. The House of Hakko . . . has ways of making its displeasure felt."

The House of Hakko killed him, I remember, even though he has not yet died, and I do not wonder at the slight tang of bitterness in his voice.

"But the Khloïdanikos has survived," I say.

"Yes. Baffling, is it not?" His smile is wide with delight.

"Completely," I say, and my delight answers his.

Mildmay

The walls of Aiaia scared the living daylights out of me.

They were huge fuckers—not so much with the height, where they weren't a patch on Mélusine, but just the thickness, and blessed saints the size of the blocks. Each block was bigger than me. I wondered if the walls had been put up by giants or hocuses.

We came to Aiaia in the back of another fucking wagon, this one with a family. The father was looking for work, although I didn't think he was going to find anything, and his wife didn't think so, either. I hated having to be Ananias Wainwright around them, because I was scaring the kids, but the walls bulking up closer and closer made it easy to glower at everything. When we got into their shadow, I felt like I was walking into the Boneprince to meet Vey Coruscant all over again.

I helped Miss Parr down from the wagon in the market square just beyond the gates, and I wasn't liking the city no better than I'd liked the walls. It was mud and garbage underfoot more so than cobbles, and the buildings were all tall and narrow and made of a wood I didn't recognize. It weathered to a muddy purplish brown that was just as purely ugly as sin. Here and there, somebody'd tried to do something with whitewash and flower boxes, but really I think it just made things worse. The streets were narrow and crooked and looked like they'd been laid out mostly to keep rioters from getting any bright ideas.

But we didn't have no trouble finding the kind of hotel we needed, with slatternly maids and a desk clerk so fucking drunk he wouldn't have noticed if Miss Parr had been the Queen of Tambrin and me her dancing bear. The room he gave us was filthy, and the door didn't lock.

"I love your taste in accommodations," Miss Parr said to me.

"I been in worse," I said and decided to save sitting on the bed for when I felt braver.

"I'm sure you have, but that wasn't my point."

"Nobody'll bother us, and they won't remember us two minutes after we're gone."

"The rats might," she said, and flung the shoe in her hand at the wall. Something squeaked and skittered away.

"We ain't gonna be here long enough for it to matter."

"I'm glad to hear it. What do we do now?"

I looked at her.

"What?" she said.

"I thought you had a plan."

"I had a plan to get us here."

The whole hotel would hear me if I yelled at her. And there was no point in it anyway. Now that we were here, we had to go forward. I said, "Gotta find out where he's being held, then. You'll have to go scout."

"Have to what?"

"Scout. Look around. Find stuff."

"Me?"

"*Look* at me," I said.

"Of course. Whereas I am drab and unremarkable. There are probably hundreds of women in this city just like me."

"That ain't what I said."

"No, it isn't. I'll go scout." She shoved her shoes back on, then jerked the ribbon out of her hair and started undoing the braids, throwing the pins down on the table like she could hurt them.

"I don't like it no better than you do," I said. "Rather go myself."

"You don't trust me?"

"Oh fuck this for the emperor's snotrag." I did sit down on the bed. It sagged under me most of the way to the floor. "You know that ain't what I meant."

"Be damned if I do! You've made no secret of the fact you don't like me, and you didn't want me with you."

"You're the one wanted to come play hide-and-seek with the duke anyway. Wasn't my idea."

"You wouldn't have done it, would you? You would have left your friend here to die."

"Ain't my friend. He's a hocus."

"So is Felix a 'hocus.'" She dragged the comb through her hair, fast and hard, the way Keeper had combed Christobel's hair. It had made Christobel cry. I couldn't see Miss Parr's face.

"That's different."

"Really?" she said. "You mean you wouldn't leave Felix here if the Duke of Aiaia had him?"

She thought I would. She really did.

"Why do you care?"

She turned on me. Her face was like Margot's had been on the roof of the Judiciate with all her little Badgers dead around her. "I had a lover," she said and slammed the comb down on the table. "He was a wizard in the Bastion, and he tried to run. I couldn't stop him, and I couldn't save him. And I had to watch what happened to him when they brought him back. It took *all day*." She turned away from me, because she was starting to cry, and she didn't want me to see.

There was nothing I could say that wouldn't be the wrong fucking thing.

"What?" she said after a minute and started pinning her hair up again. "Nothing to say? As usual?"

"I don't know what you want from me! I'm sorry? I am, but that's no fucking good, is it? D'you want me to say I wouldn't leave Felix here? I wouldn't, but you don't believe that anyway. Why can't you leave me the fuck alone?" Shit. I was shouting. I stopped and clenched my hands together and stared at the floor.

"You know," she said, "I think that's the most words I've ever heard you say at one time."

"*Fuck,*" I said, and put my fist into the wall.

There was a long silence. I wrapped my handkerchief around my bleeding knuckles and sat and wished she'd just go away.

"I'm sorry," she said. "I was raised by men who thought bear-baiting was the epitome of spectator sports. We don't have to like each other. What should I be looking for?"

She'd put her hair up. It was in a kind of a coil, like Ginevra'd used to wear to work, and she'd pulled some little tendrils forward around her face. She didn't look like Nobbie Wainwright anymore, and she didn't look like Mehitabel Parr, neither. She looked like a tired shopgirl, the kind that's a septad to the centime in a town as big as Aiaia.

She was right. We didn't have to like each other at all. "We got to find out where he's being kept."

"Right," she said, and added in the most teeth-grindingly sweet voice I'd ever heard out of her, "Don't wait up, dearest." She left. I kept ahold of myself and didn't put my fist into the wall again.

She came back four or five hours later, looking like a thundercloud. She swore under her breath the whole time she was jerking the pins out of her hair. Didn't repeat herself much, either. When she ran down, she said, "There's a man in the pillory as a collaborator—I think he tried to rescue your 'hocus' a couple days ago."

"He did *what*?"

"As you may be able to imagine, I didn't want to seem unbecomingly curious. But apparently he tried to free the wizard who's going to be burned. And another wizard who was imprisoned with him, although I don't know what they're planning to do with him."

"Fuck me sideways," I said. "The guy in the pillory. Big blond guy? Braided mustaches?"

"Yes." She was giving me the hairy eyeball in a serious way, but I didn't even care.

"Sacred bleeding fuck, that's *Bernard*."

"And who is Bernard that we should care?"

"Him and his brother were the other people we were traveling with before we got . . . never mind. But the other hocus is probably Mavortian. His brother."

"So we're now rescuing three people instead of one, and two of them wizards?"

"If we're gonna do it, we might as well do it right."

She stared at me for a moment, and I thought I was in for a chewing out like Felix would've been proud of, but then she laughed. "Your logic is impeccable. All right."

"Did you find out where they're holding Gideon?"

All the light went out of her face. "I did."

"And?"

"I found out some other things."

"Like?"

"I didn't want to say anything until I knew, because—well because it's so horrible. But, the cult that your friend is part of, when they catch them . . ." She couldn't seem to find the words she wanted; her face had gone almost gray, and she was wringing her hands.

"Cough it up."

"They cut out his tongue."

"Kethe," I said. I was glad I was already sitting down.

"Yes, and he's only in Aiaia because the Bastion didn't want him back."

"What?"

"Usually, they drag defectors back to the Bastion. But they couldn't be bothered. They let the duke have him."

"Might be the worst thing they could think of to do to him."

"God." She shuddered, then turned away and started dressing her hair again. "The other wizard—Mavortian, you said?"

"Yeah."

"He's being kept in the duke's house. I'm not quite sure why. Nobody seemed to know."

"Well, he's crippled. So they don't have to worry about him running off."

She wasn't buying. "Somehow I did not gather the impression that the Duke of Aiaia does anything out of the kindness of his heart."

"About all we can do is go find out."

She turned and gave me something that was almost a smile.

"Right," I said. "How long we got?"

"The execution's in three days."

"First day of the Trials." And a fuck of a way to celebrate it, too. I didn't like this—I hated the shit out of it, to be perfectly frank—but I could feel the old excitement starting to kick in. It was like having a commission, only this time I was trying to *keep* somebody from getting killed. Thinking about it like that made things sort of okay.

"I don't figure we want to wait around," I said.

"No, I don't think so. I'm not quite sure what the authorities have planned for your friend Bernard, but the things I was hearing suggest that the good citizens of Aiaia may not wait for justice to be served."

Fucking perfect. A lynch mob. "Better spring Bernard tonight, then."
And this time she did smile. "I didn't like this room anyway."

✂

I had to hand it to her: she knew about disguise. She'd bought a black scarf
while she was out, and before we left, she got my hair covered by it and put
soot in my eyebrows. "You look like a pirate," she said. "You'll fit right in."

I thought that had been sort of a joke, but she wasn't far wrong. There
wasn't anybody out on the streets that I would have trusted to watch a baby
for as much as a second. After I saw three guys with uglier scars than mine
on their faces, I quit counting.

The pillory was in the main square, with the duke's house fronting it on
one side and the jail on another. Very fucking convenient, and I wasn't a bit
grateful. The pillory was up on this sort of platform. Pillories, I mean, because there were four of them, and all the same ugly muddy purple-brown
color as the buildings. Only one occupied, and it was Bernard sure enough.
He had that look on his face, the one he got when I said something to Mavortian he wanted to strangle me for. It was all over his face that he
wouldn't have asked an Aiaian to piss on him if he'd been on fire. He was
too mad to notice me in the crowd, and that was just fine. We went and got
something to eat while we waited for it to get dark.

Aiaia had a curfew—no big fucking surprise there. But it wasn't hard to
dodge out of sight if you had a mind to, and two hours after sundown, the
main square was as deserted as anybody could ask for. Next door to pitch-
black, but I didn't mind that near as much as I'd minded the thought that
there might be guards. Which there weren't, and I wondered if that was to
give any mob that might be hanging around a clear shot.

Bernard heard us coming. He'd been sagging lower and lower, but I saw
him get his feet under him, and I knew what he was thinking.

"Bernard," I said, quick, in that flat whisper kept-thieves learn real
young, and I wished there'd been enough light I could've seen his face. I did
see the way he tried to straighten up, all in a rush, and just about killed
himself with the yoke of the pillory.

I swung up onto the platform. I'd noticed earlier that the pillories were
held shut with padlocks that looked basically homemade, and I'd got Miss
Parr to give me another hairpin. Standing there in the dark in the middle of
Aiaia forcing that lock with nothing but a hairpin ain't nothing I ever want
to do again, but it could've been way worse. And, powers, that lock was just

embarrassingly bad. Probably could've pried it apart with my bare hands if I'd had to, but Miss Parr's hairpin did the trick. I lifted the yoke and Bernard backed himself out of it. And sat down hard, like anybody would after being stood in a pillory all day.

Me and Bernard both quit breathing for a second, but I don't suppose the noise was anywhere near as loud as it seemed like. Leastways, nobody came to check on what was causing the ruckus, and, powers, that would do to get by on.

Bernard sort of crawled to the edge of the platform, and me and Miss Parr between us got him off it. And then he sat there, trying to breathe quiet, and I tried to figure out what the fuck we were going to do next. Finally, I got myself down next to him, as best I could, and said, real low, "We got to get Gideon out."

"Yeah. And Mavortian."

"Yeah, okay. But Gideon first. He's the one they're fixing to barbecue."

Bernard said something nasty in Norvenan, aimed at the Aiaians, not me.

"How'd you get caught?"

"Bribed a guard who didn't stay bribed. Fucking Aiaians. But I know how to get into the jail."

"Can you move?" Miss Parr said.

"I don't have a choice, do I, miss? Come on."

Short of stuffing him back into the pillory, we didn't have a choice, neither. So we got Bernard on his feet and headed out. By the time we'd gone a couple of blocks, he'd even quit leaning on us to keep himself upright.

᛭

It goes against the grain to say anything nice about the Kennel, but I'd rather be locked up there than in the jail of Aiaia. It stank of piss and shit, which you expect in a jail, but it also had that horrible sweetish smell you get when something's died and rotted, like the Aiaians didn't bother dragging out the prisoners when they croaked. The rats we met were the size of small dogs, and they watched us go by like they'd figured out that what people were for was feeding rats. All those little bastards had to do was wait. The hallways were low and dark and probably made the rats feel right at home. The floors were sticky—Kethe might know with what, but I don't want to.

We'd got in the easy way, by staking out the latrine and borrowing the keys from the first guy unlucky enough to need to take a piss. The jail was either undermanned or sloppy, because we didn't meet nobody else until we got to the door that led, Bernard told us, to the cell where Gideon was being kept. I figured the guy there was the guy who hadn't stayed bribed, because Bernard went after him like a gator after a pig and laid him out cold with a broken jaw before he even knew we were there. Bernard busted his knuckles, but he didn't seem to mind.

Used the second guard's keys to get through the door. Dragged him in with us and tucked him away in an empty cell, nice and tidy where he wouldn't bother nobody. Miss Parr stayed to keep watch, because even if they were both sloppy *and* undermanned, there had to be more than just two guys ambling around. Me and Bernard went after Gideon.

"Too easy," I said. "Too fucking easy."

"Wait until you've seen Gideon before you say that," Bernard said. "He's down there."

There was a trapdoor in the floor of the hallway, with another of those big clumsy padlocks the Aiaians seemed to like so much. "Down *there?*" I said.

"I wouldn't treat a dog that had bitten me the way they've treated him. Why do you think I was caught here?"

Which I hadn't expected from Bernard any more than Miss Parr had expected it from me. So I didn't say nothing, just got myself down on the floor and started trying keys in the padlock.

"Hurt your leg?" Bernard said, more curious than sympathetic.

"Long story." The padlock groaned open in a shower of rust. "Powers," I said.

"Some kids just don't look after their toys," Bernard said, straight-faced, and there was a moment where we both nearly lost it. I got my fingers under the trapdoor and heaved. Bernard caught it as it came up, and we laid it over on the floor quiet-like.

Bernard lifted a short ladder down off the wall and let it down into the hole. We looked at each other. "Can you manage that ladder?" he said.

"Can you?"

I could see it chafed him raw to admit he couldn't, but he wasn't stupid—least not all the way down. After a second, he shook his head. "One of us better stay up here anyway."

"Okay." And I climbed down.

As cells went, it would have made a cramped coffin. The smell was enough to knock you flat, and it was cold and damp, and it was half a second or less before the only thing I wanted in the world was to get the fuck back up that ladder.

It took me a moment to see Gideon. No, that ain't it. What I mean is, it took me a moment to realize I was looking at him and not just a lump of filthy straw. He was hunched up in the corner with his hands up to protect his face. I didn't see bruises or nothing, but fuck, what more did the Aiaians need to do to him once they'd cut out his tongue? There was a cuff around one ankle—same fucking blacksmith as made the padlocks. I said, "Gideon? It's . . . it's Mildmay."

His head came up at that. There was an old story I'd heard from a whore in Pharaohlight about an angel King Philemon had kept chained beneath the Mirador for a Great Septad. That was what Gideon looked like to me, his choirboy face gone to a skull and his hair hanging in dreadlocks around his shoulders. And there was no mistaking the look on his face. He was purely fucking horrified. And it wasn't because he didn't recognize me. It was because he did.

"Powers," I said. "I'm sorry. But, I mean, d'you *want* to let the duke burn you at the stake?"

His head dropped back into his hands and his shoulders started shaking. For a second I thought he was crying, and then I realized he was laughing, just not making no noise about it. And then he stuck his leg out, with that lump of iron on it, and I figured that was his answer.

I wrenched the cuff open, and just barely kept myself from throwing it at the wall. See which one of them broke. But I put it down, and said, "D'you . . . can I give you a hand up?"

He actually smiled at me. He'd lost teeth. And he pushed himself upright and took a step out of the corner. His knees buckled, which I'd been expecting even if he hadn't, and I caught him.

I swear I could feel the shame baking off him. I didn't know what to say about it, so I just said, "Come on. We've still got to spring Mavortian and get the fuck out of town before dawn."

It was a good thing he wasn't a big guy to start with and that he'd lost weight, or we'd never have done it. As it was, it took both me and Bernard to get him up the ladder, and we all three almost fell back down it on our heads, because the torchlight was just more than Gideon could stand. He kind of rolled over on the floor with his hands over his eyes, like a mole me and Cardenio had seen once in Richard's Park. Cardenio'd put his hat over it until it got itself back underground.

Neither me nor Bernard had anything that would make a good blindfold, so I went back to the guard Bernard had coldcocked. He was still out. Small favors. I stripped him quick as a Losthope thief. Didn't figure Gideon would want his underclothes—and I didn't want to touch 'em anyway—but shirt, jacket, trousers, and boots were all clean enough, and that way we could turn the ratty sort of nightshirt thing Gideon was wearing into a blindfold.

Gideon was trying hard not to go to pieces, but he wasn't doing so good at it. Me and Bernard basically manhandled him into the guard's clothes on account of not having time to be nice about it, and I know I knotted some of his hair into the blindfold. But, powers, we were doing the best we could. And he didn't complain or nothing. I just knew we were hurting him.

"What about the trapdoor?" Bernard said when we'd got Gideon fixed up about as well as we were going to.

"I'll get it," I said. Anything to buy us time. I hung the ladder back on the wall and heaved the door closed. Locked it, too, and I hope it confused the fuck out of them.

We collected Miss Parr and got back out of the jail about as quick and easy as that makes it sound. Not even any close calls. Got the blindfold off Gideon again. Scrambled over the wall, with Bernard boosting Gideon and me dragging. And then we just kind of stood there, Bernard leaning against the wall, me holding Gideon up, and Miss Parr looking cool as well water, waiting for us to get our shit together. She was the one who said, "What now?"

There always comes a point on a job where no matter how fucked up things are, no matter how much you wish you weren't doing this, you just don't dare stop, because you know where the pieces are *right now,* and they ain't going to stay put while you sit down and think things over. You just have to keep going and hope like fuck you can dodge faster than Lady Fate can throw things at you. That was where we were. We had to keep going, or the whole fucking thing was going to come crashing down around our ears.

But Gideon was in terrible shape and Bernard not much better. And this next bit seemed all too likely to turn around and bite us. In which case, we wanted Gideon out of the way, where they maybe couldn't get their hands on him again. I said to Bernard, "Can you get Gideon out of town?"

"What about—"

"I'll go after Mavortian. But I want Gideon gone."

He wanted to argue, but didn't. "All right. Mavortian's in the duke's house. In a bedroom and everything, like a guest instead of a prisoner. You'll want to use the smugglers' tunnels to get out—nobody watches them because it's half the damn economy. The safest one is in the city wall, two blocks south of the west gate. It looks like a bricked-up gate itself. You press the fifth brick up from a bright blue brick."

"Right. You take Gideon and get the fuck out of here. Find someplace safe along the western road and wait. If we ain't there by sunrise, go to Julip. Felix'll be in a hotel near the eastern gate." *I hope*, I added, but not out loud.

Miss Parr said, "Do you want me to go with them?"

I just about swallowed my teeth when I realized *she* was asking *me* what to do. "No," I said. "Unless . . ."

"I can manage," Bernard said. "And you may want backup."

"Yeah." I hoped I wouldn't, but, well, I wasn't feeling like trusting my luck.

Gideon was shivering like an overworked horse, and I said to him, "I'm sorry. I know this ain't no great rescue." His hand found mine, and he squeezed, which I figured for *it's okay*. And it was the best we could do.

Bernard pushed himself off the wall and said, "Come on, Gideon." There was a pause, and he said, "Good luck."

"Thanks."

And they went off one way, and we went another, and I just hoped we'd all see each other again, and not on a bonfire, neither.

The duke's house was a three-story affair with gilded pillars and marble facing, and it was as ugly as a gator in a pink satin ball gown. Our business wasn't with the front, and I was just as glad. We worked our way round to the back, climbed another fucking wall, and found ourselves in the duke's private garden.

He had trees trained against the walls and rosebushes fucking *every-where*. Miss Parr's dress kept snagging, and my hands got scratched up pretty bad from saving myself at the last second from taking a header into the biggest bush. We didn't make much noise about it, at least, so we fought free to the clear space along the back of the house without nobody sticking their head out to see what the fuck was up.

I took a gander up the back side of the house. It had one of those dumb ornamental balconies that ain't wide enough for a cat, gilded like the front—the balcony, I mean, not the cat. Jam for cat burglars, balconies like that, even covered with climbing roses the way that one was. I left Miss Parr playing lookout and shinnied up one of the balcony's supporting columns. My leg didn't like it much, and neither did my hands, but I was right out of options. The windows on the ground floor were all curtained and dark, and the main floor was where the servants and guards and shit were likely to be. And anyway I was banking on Kekropian houses being like Marathine houses with the bedrooms on the third floor. And it would have been a real funny joke on me if I'd been wrong.

But the first window I got to was a bedroom, sure enough, with the mosquito netting across the windows but the drapes not drawn. Looked like a spinster cousin. I had a fuck of a time getting past without either being seen or falling off the balcony, but I managed it somehow. The ache in my bad leg was getting worse. Should've risked the door, Milly-Fox. But it was too fucking late now.

The next window had the drapes drawn, and I figured it was the best chance I was going to find to get myself in the house. Window was locked, but the lock was for crap, like every other lock in Aiaia. I didn't figure Miss Parr was going to want this hairpin back, but it got me what I wanted.

Casement window, opening out just to keep me from thinking I was doing okay or anything. I got clawed across the back of the neck by one of those fucking rose brambles, but I got it open. And the first thing I heard was Mavortian's voice.

"No, your Grace, I am afraid you will not change my mind."

He sounded about as pissed off as he'd been the last time I'd heard his voice, the better part of an indiction ago. Of course, then he'd been pissed off at Felix—I couldn't even remember for what—and now it sounded like he was pissed off at the Duke of Aiaia.

Another voice, deep and kind of slimy somehow. I couldn't make out what he said—he was farther from the window than Mavortian. But Mavortian came right back with, "Then go ahead and burn me. I would prefer it."

Oh fuck, Mavortian, don't get your stupid self killed *now*. He'd got the duke mad enough to raise his voice: "Do you think I won't?"

"I don't care. Good night, your Grace," and I heard a sound I knew for Mavortian rolling to face the wall.

There was a pause where I could imagine the duke trying to think of something to say. What he came up with was, "This is not over," which didn't impress me none and I was sure didn't impress Mavortian, neither, and then the door slammed.

No fucking time, since it could be two days or a minute before the duke thought of what he wanted to say and came back. I went through the window like a sack of potatoes—no grace or nothing—and scared Mavortian half to death. He came bolt upright on the bed, and there was a second where he almost shouted. But he recognized me, and his jaw sagged open without any sound coming out.

He didn't look as bad as Gideon, but he hadn't been living no life of luxury up here in the duke's palace, neither. He looked sick—kind of gray and with lines in his face I didn't remember. And his pupils were shrunk down into nothing. They'd got him drugged on something, which wasn't surprising when I stopped and thought about it. Kethe, I was hating the Duke of Aiaia and I'd never even laid eyes on the fucker. Didn't want to, neither.

"Mildmay?" Mavortian said, and he sounded like he was figuring it for a drug dream.

"Yeah. Jailbreak. You game?"

Some of the ugly lines seemed to smooth out of his face. "You have to ask?"

"Polite. You know. Can you hang on to me?"

"If you're getting me out of here, I can do anything you want."

"Okay then." I was already on the floor, so I just kind of scooted myself over to the bed and let Mavortian get his arms around my neck. And then I stood up, and that was no treat, let me tell you. I was pushing right along the ragged edge of what my bad leg was going to let me do. But I stood up, and I didn't fall over, although there was a second or two where it was pretty close.

But I got my balance, got my weight on my good leg as much as I could, and said, "Can you hang on with your legs?"

I'd never asked him that kind of question, because him being crippled was this thing that somehow nobody ever talked about with him. You just didn't. But looking at getting back down that damn balcony with Mavortian's extra weight to fuck me up, I wasn't feeling real nice about other people's sore spots. And he didn't give me grief for it, just said, "Yes, although not well." I could tell it hurt him to say that, but, you know, not as bad as being burned at the stake. And he brought them up around my waist. Wasn't much of a grip, but it'd make things easier.

"Let's fucking well do this, then," I said, and went back out the window.

I would've liked to close it behind me, same way I'd closed the trapdoor in the jail, but that was just asking for me and Mavortian to both end up dead in the duke's fucking rosebushes. So I checked over the balcony for the nearest pillar and started climbing.

And halfway down, my leg went. I'd been okay—I mean, it hurt like a motherfucker, but it was working—and then I went to brace against the pillar and there was just nothing there. Except for all them hornets I thought I'd gotten rid of back in Troia.

We were still way too high up off the ground. I did the only thing I could, in the split second where I could do anything at all, and grabbed the lip of the balcony in both hands, getting a double handful of rose thorns along with it. I felt the jolt in my shoulders as my hands took our full weight, and then I was hanging there with my palms bleeding into the roses and my leg burning white with the pain.

"Mildmay?" Mavortian said, real soft and real scared, in my ear.

"Bad . . . leg," I said, my teeth clenched like grindstones. "Just . . . hold . . . still."

And he held still like a champ, I'll give him that. I found the pillar with my left leg and hooked my knee around it, right on out the other side of glad that I'd talked Felix into the corduroy trousers instead of the lightweight stuff he'd wanted.

I could do this. I'd been an assassin and a cat burglar, and I'd done harder things than get down a pillar with two arms, one leg, and a crippled hocus on my back. I was sure of it, even if I couldn't right then think of none. But I was hating those roses in an up-front and personal way.

One arm around the pillar, then the other. Shift the leg down, grip again. One arm, then the other. I actually got annoyed by the second-floor balcony, because it fucked up my rhythm.

"We could stop," Mavortian said. "Do something . . ."

"Only get worse," I said. From the way my hands felt, the skin was hanging off my palms in strips, and I knew once I let go of the pillar, I'd never be able to make myself grab it again. I kept going, not thinking, just moving, and the first I knew about the ground was my right foot hitting it, and I just barely kept from howling like a mauled coyote.

And thank the powers, Miss Parr had realized something was wrong, and was there, holding me up while I got my left foot planted and finally let go of that fucking pillar. She smelled a little like lavender but mostly like sweat, and right then I would have sworn any oath you liked that she was the most beautiful woman in the world.

"Got to . . . sit down," I said, panting.

"Can we get farther from the house first?" she said.

"Yeah. Good idea." And I managed it somehow, leaning on her. We got back behind the rosebushes, and I said, "Fuck," through my teeth, and went down on my left knee and both hands, my right leg hanging off to the side like a dead thing.

Mavortian let go of my neck and rolled himself off me, and powers that was a relief and then some. I twisted myself around so I could sit down without bumping my right leg, and then I just sat there for a while, thinking all the worst swearwords I knew and rubbing at my thigh with both hands. Miss Parr sat beside me, and I was grateful to her—more than grateful—for keeping her mouth shut and letting me be.

When I finally straightened up again, with the worst of the pain backed off, she said, "What happened?"

"Bad leg went worse," I said.

"Are you going to be able to . . . ?"

"Well, since it's that or stay here—yeah. Think I am."

"What about—"

"Mavortian," said Mavortian. "Not that I'm not grateful, mind you, but escaping the bedroom to end up in the garden is not really what I had in mind."

"Me neither," I said, instead of something really nasty. "Long as I don't have to do any more climbing, I think I'm okay. If I can get over the wall. But I need something to wrap my hands with."

"The roses," Miss Parr said, like she was catching on to something she'd been missing.

"Yeah."

"Here." I heard cloth tear, and she handed me two pieces off her dress. I wrapped them around my hands—sloppy but it would do—and got back to my feet. "Fuck," I said.

"Are you sure you're all right?"

"Have to be, don't I? But I can't get down again. Can you help Mavortian get up?"

She did it somehow, and I bent over, and then Mavortian's arms were around my neck again, and I hoped I didn't dream about being strangled tonight. Hoped we got out of Aiaia and nightmares were something I'd even have to worry about.

I got over the wall on pure cussedness and a lot of help from the fruit trees and Miss Parr. And it was purely Miss Parr's doing that I ended up on the other side still on my feet. "Fuck," I said again, because I wanted to scream and couldn't, and started for the western wall and the door Bernard had told us about.

We were about two blocks away from the main square when the hulla-baloo began. Fuck. We ducked into a shrine to a fat cross-eyed goddess and just barely avoided a squad of guards galloping toward the duke's house. And then we ducked back out and kept going. Because it was down to a race now. Either we made it to the tunnel before we got caught or we didn't.

Kethe, I would've given most anything to just be able to *run*. But I couldn't. I couldn't even walk fast, although the cramp was working itself out a little and I wasn't almost falling down with every step. Mavortian's grip on my neck was probably leaving bruises, but I was grateful even for small backhanded favors. If he hadn't lost a bunch of weight since the last time I'd seen him, I couldn't have managed at all. Miss Parr played scout, and that saved us from at least one more group of guards. I gave up on cussing—I'd run out of words filthy enough—and just started praying. Kethe probably wasn't listening, but there wasn't nothing else I could do.

But we got to the spot along the wall Bernard had said without nobody seeing us, and the brick worked just like he said it would. I was thinking the Aiaians really were stupid enough to just let us waltz out of the city with all three of their prisoners, when we heard people running our way. The guards in Aiaia don't sound that much different from the Dogs in Mélusine.

"Somebody caught on," I said and swung Mavortian into the tunnel. "Go on, Miss Parr."

"Don't be an ass," she said and kicked the door shut, grabbed me, and dragged me down into a clinch.

Kethe, I'm about as dumb as a rock. It took me *forever* to realize what she was doing, but then I played up for all I was worth. I dug my fingers into her hair pretty vigorously—that neat shopgirl's hairstyle wouldn't do for any lady who'd be out along the wall this time of night. By the time the guards got close enough to see us, we'd got into the swing of things. So if we looked guilty, well, there was a reason.

"Hey, you!"

Me and Miss Parr kind of jumped back from each other, like we hadn't even heard the guards coming.

"What the fuck are you guys doing?" And now she sounded like she could've been the sister of one of the slatternly maids at the hotel.

"Does either of you have a license to be out this late?" the captain said.

Miss Parr's breath hitched a little. "Left it in my other pants," I said, and let my scar do what it wanted to the way the words came out. "What gives?"

The captain pulled himself up, all stern and shit. "The wizard has escaped."

Miss Parr gave a little screech and shrank back against me.

"Have you two . . . seen anything?"

Another time, I might've made him eat that smirk. But Miss Parr said, "I thought I heard voices down toward the gate about ten minutes ago." She did it just right, too, not helpful, exactly, but like she'd thought there was something funny about it at the time.

The guards all perked up like dogs catching a scent.

"I'll let you off with a warning this time," the captain said, like it was some big favor he was doing us and not that he wanted to be the guy to catch poor Gideon.

"I hope you guys get him," Miss Parr said.

"Oh, we will." And they sprinted off.

The instant they were out of sight, I pushed the brick and we fell over each other through the opening.

"I thought I'd seen the last of you," Mavortian said.

"We haven't time," Miss Parr said. "They'll realize."

"And soon," I said, and between the three of us we got Mavortian on my back. "Tell you later. Did I hurt you?"

"Not as much as they would have. Let's go."

We came out of the wall in the middle of a cemetery. Like the Ivorene back home. Picked our way to the gate, which was rusting right off its hinges, and got out onto the road.

And then walked the fuck away from Aiaia.

Chapter 8

Felix

The hotelkeeper in Julip took a liking to me, even to the extent of running her own errands. One sunny morning, a fortnight after I'd signed the register of the Duelling Hares, she came up to my room and said that a person wished to speak with me.

"A person?" I said, and then I knew, like a sunrise, who she meant. "Red-haired, this person? Scar on his face?"

"Yes, sir," she said, very dubiously.

"My brother," I said, grinned at her expression, and breezed past her down the stairs.

Mildmay was waiting in the lobby. He looked considerably the worse for wear; his clothes were shabby, ill fitting, and not what he'd been wearing when he left Ogygia, and he didn't look like he'd been getting much sleep. I did not wonder that the hotelkeeper had designated him as a "person."

But he was still in one piece, and there was nothing about him to suggest that he felt himself to be in any imminent danger. When I said,

"Hello," my voice was steady, not betraying any of the nightmares that had haunted the past week.

He turned and said, "Glad to see you."

"Have you been looking long?"

"Nah. I know you."

That was pure Mildmay and gnomic in the extreme. I decided I didn't want to know exactly what he meant. "Where are the others? There *are* . . . that is, they are with you, aren't they?"

"Yeah." He tucked his hair back behind his ear on the right side, and my other concerns were immediately eclipsed.

"What happened to your hands?"

"What? Oh." He looked at his hands, at the scabbed lines and pink new skin, as if they simply perplexed him. "Roses."

"*What?*"

"It's a long fucking story. And not here, okay?"

I wanted to press the issue, wanted to find out the extent of the damage and what had happened. But the harder I pressed, the less Mildmay would tell me. So I said: "Which brings me back to, where are the others?"

"Baths."

"That has a certain pragmatic logic to it."

"Mavortian wants—"

"*Mavortian?*"

"Yeah. We found him and Bernard, too. And, you know, we were already doing a rescue, so it seemed a shame to leave 'em."

His version of a joke, I thought. There were suddenly more questions than I could even find the words to ask. And Mildmay was not the person to give me useful answers. "Why don't I come with you to the baths?" I said. "You could use one."

He made that face at me that was as close to a smile as he came, and limped ahead of me out of the lobby.

The public baths of Julip were new, a pet project of the current duke, full of air and light. The water was heated by an enormous bank of furnaces, roaring like lions beneath the earth. Mildmay stripped in the changing room with a serene lack of self-consciousness; I stayed fully dressed. Like the various public baths in Mélusine, these were as much a place for meetings and commerce as they were for bathing; no one commented. Watching Mildmay pad through the high-ceilinged rooms, I was reminded of a panther I had once seen being portaged through Mélusine to be shipped up the Sim to Vusantine. That same sense of imprisoned power, although Mildmay's cage was the twisted bone of his right thigh, not a structure of iron bars. And his cage was the worse, because there was no door I could open to let him out.

The baths were arranged in a cross: calder to the east, tepidary to the north, froy to the west, with the changing rooms and offices to the south. The center of the cross was an impluvium, with koi in the circular pool and benches all around.

"You wanna stay here?" Mildmay said. "Or come along?"

"I'll stay here." The realization was hammering home now that these people whom I barely remembered—Mavortian, Bernard, Gideon—were people who had last seen me at the height of my madness. That had seemed safely unimportant when it was only Gideon being rescued, and being rescued from something so dire that there was not even a thought of weighing options, consequences, benefits and deficits. Now, about to be faced with men I remembered only as monsters, I was conscious of a desire to turn tail and run, to deny that they had any connection to me. But I had tried that in the Gardens of Nephele when I was first healed, I remembered bitterly, and it had not worked. It had only hurt Mildmay. I would have to face whatever was coming.

I did not sit down, wanting the advantage of height if nothing else. It was an effort not to let my fingers knot together, but Malkar had taught me, via his own brutal and unscrupulous methods, to counterfeit a nobleman's poise, and the old instincts were not lost.

I can do this, I thought, and that was when a short, skinny Kekropian emerged from the calder, wrapped in one of the togas Mildmay had disdained. My knees all but buckled, and I was lucky to end up sitting on one of the benches rather than on the floor. For a moment, all I could see was green, and there was the sound of a river in darkness and the smell of cloves. I locked my hands against the edge of the bench and held on grimly, held on to the cool marble and the slight pain of my stiff finger joints, to the sunlight on the water and the lazy, circling shapes of the koi. A voice said, in my memory, *He began to draw mazes that could not be solved,* and I knew now that it was the voice of Gideon of Thrax.

And then, as if in answer, a voice in my head that was not a memory, :Felix?:

I blinked, then squeezed my eyes shut hard and opened them again. The Kekropian, standing in front of me, dark eyes intent in a too-thin face, long

wet hair like ink against the whiteness of the toga. He did not look familiar, except that somewhere in the darkness inside my head, I knew him. I
knew him.

I could not find my voice, my composure. Could seem to do nothing
but sit and stare at him. And then there was that voice again, :Felix? Are
you . . . :

Neither memory nor imagination. In a sudden clutch of panic, I scrambled up, getting the bench interposed between us. "Is that you in my head?"
I did at least keep my voice down, but I saw the vicious flatness of my tone
hit him like a blow. He took a step back, raising his hands in a gesture that
was half defense, half apology. :I'm sorry. I can't . . . I can't speak. Out
loud.: The dark eyes were wide, pleading.

For a moment, I was on the verge of lashing out; I did not have to remember this man to wound him, and I knew it. But I caught myself, controlled myself. That I associated this particular wizard's trick with Malkar
was no fault of Gideon's. I managed half a smile, said, "You startled me.
Mildmay didn't mention . . ." Anything, really.

:It does not work with annemer. And I cannot . . . : Another gesture, this
one of frustration. :The Fressandran disciplines are too different, and too
controlled. Even if I wished to speak to Mavortian in this way, I could not.:

"Are you . . . ?"

:All right?: His mouth quirked. :I am both alive and sane, which is
more, I think, than I had any right to expect. So, yes, I am 'all right.':

"Gideon, I—"

:And you are also alive and sane.: He raised his eyebrows, inviting an
explanation that I did not particularly want to give. I remembered Mildmay
saying, *It's a long fucking story,* and found myself suddenly more sympathetic to his point of view.

"The celebrants of the Garden of Nephele are both learned and skilled,"
I said as neutrally as I could.

But his reaction was not what I had hoped for. :Then you *did* find
them!: he said, his eyes lighting up.

I didn't want to talk about this. And he saw that, for his face was suddenly shuttered again, and he said, :I beg your pardon. I did not mean to
pry.:

I could not lie and say it was no matter, and we were still staring at each
other in bitter awkwardness when Mavortian von Heber and his half
brother Bernard came into the atrium.

I remembered Mavortian von Heber far better than I wished to. I remembered those bright, cruel blue eyes; I remembered, before he opened his mouth, the sound of his harsh Norvenan accent.

He for his part seemed momentarily struck dumb by the sight of me, a reaction that I was beginning to find tiresome. Then he came limping forward on his canes—new, I could tell, by the pale rawness of the wood—and said, "So. Messire Harrowgate. I did not think to see you again, and certainly not to see you thus."

"I have been fortunate," I said, with a quick, insincere sliver of a smile.

"As have we all," Mavortian said. "We should talk soon. And privately."

"I'm staying at the Duelling Hares," I said, "and we can hire the private parlor."

"Excellent. Once we've cleaned up, we'll meet you there."

I found I did not like him better now that I was sane. I smiled again, slightly wider but with no greater sincerity, and said, "I'll wait here for my brother, thank you."

He made me a slight, mocking bow. "As you wish." And by some art that I could not quite decipher, contrived to collect both Bernard and Gideon in his wake as he headed for the tepidary.

No, I did not like Messire von Heber. Not in the slightest.

༄

We were a motley convocation that gathered in the private parlor of the Duelling Hares: Mehitabel, Mildmay, and myself on one side of the room; Mavortian and Bernard on the other. Gideon, looking uneasy and unwell, perched on the window seat, his gaze shifting restlessly between Mavortian and me.

Mavortian had wanted this meeting; I would let Mavortian open the conversation. I leaned back in my chair, steepled my fingers in front of me, and waited. The spark of annoyance in Mavortian's eye said that he'd recognized what I was doing and didn't appreciate it; I smiled back at him sweetly.

"Let me say, Messire Harrowgate, how very gratified I am to see you well," Mavortian said with a smile as insincere as my own.

"Thank you, Messire von Heber," I said, matching his formal cadences as if we were two knights in a Tibernian romance. If he thought it gave him an advantage, he was wrong. "I am gratified likewise to see you . . . alive. But I understood that you had something you wanted to say to me."

One dark eyebrow went up. "Yes, indeed. I wished to ask you, since we have all been so fortunate, what you intend to do now." Irony and condescension slashing like knives behind his words.

I shrugged in a way I'd learned from Mildmay. "I am returning to the Mirador."

"Are you sure that is wise?"

He knew the conditions under which I had left the Mirador, of course. I kept myself from snarling at him. "Before I answer that question, I would appreciate it if you would tell me what right you have to ask."

The room was perfectly still. Gideon had gone an even more unattractive color, and Mildmay gave me a black look.

"We do have a history together." I could not tell whether he was affecting to remind me of something he thought I already knew or whether he had guessed that I had essentially no memory of him.

"And my debt to you is not canceled out by your rescue from certain and unpleasant death?" I said mildly, as if I were only curious. He went blotchy red and said nothing for a moment. Bernard gave me a look even blacker than Mildmay's.

"Messire Harrowgate," Mavortian said, with the air of a man who has gathered his patience together with extreme care, "I am hoping that you may be the answer to a problem that has been troubling me for a good many years. I believe you know a man named Beaumont Livy?"

And all I had to do to vex him to the greatest possible extent was tell the truth. "No, I don't."

Mildmay

People talk about being able to cut tension with a knife, and I've always thought it was a stupid sort of thing to say, but right then I knew exactly what it meant. Because things were that fucking thick. Mavortian was staring at Felix, and Felix was staring right back, looking pleased with himself. Powers, I wished they hadn't decided to hate each other on sight, but I'd known it was coming—or would've if I'd had the basic brains to stop and think about it. You put a guy who wants to control everything in the same room with a guy who'd rather walk into a bonfire than listen when somebody tells him not to, and it's your own damn fault if you're surprised when things get ugly. Stick to the heavy lifting, Milly-Fox. All you're good for. And I thought I might also keep an eye on Bernard, be-cause, Kethe, the look on his face. If Mavortian decided he wanted Felix dead, Bernard was going to be more than happy to oblige. It was almost funny, how fast Felix had managed to get on the wrong side of both of them.

Of course, Mavortian had gotten on his wrong side first. I'd known that as soon as I came out of the calder and saw him standing there glar-ing red-hot murder at Mavortian's back while Mavortian and Gideon and Bernard went into the tepidary. He didn't say nothing about it, and I didn't like to ask.

I knew what the real problem was here anyway, even if neither me nor Felix was ever going to say it. Mavortian had seen Felix when he was crazy, and Felix felt about that whole thing like a cat about a mud puddle. And would have even if he'd remembered it. I didn't know if him getting that part of his memory back would make things better or worse, but it for sure gave him fits that he couldn't remember and other people could. And being Felix, he liked to hand his fits around.

Which Mavortian needed to catch on about pretty fucking quick, or his life was going to be a misery to him. I wanted to tell Felix to quit running Mavortian and Mavortian to quit letting Felix run him, but it wouldn't help none and would get them both mad at me to boot.

So I waited and everybody else waited and Felix just sat there, not smirking exactly—or not so as you could call him on it—but clearly happy with how unhappy he'd managed to make all of us. And finally Mavortian took a deep breath and said, "Are you quite sure?"

"Absolutely," Felix said, and I thought he was even telling the truth. "I don't know anyone by that name."

"But the strong divination . . ." Mavortian sounded a little dazed now.

"The what?" Felix leaned forward, and he had that look on his face that could be real interest, or could just be him deciding to yank your chain.

"I did a strong divination at the death of the year, and it gave me your name."

"What did you ask it?"

"The name of the man who could help me find Beaumont Livy. So how can you not know who he is?"

"Perhaps," Felix said carefully, like now he wasn't sure what kind of gator pit he'd fallen into, "you should start from the beginning and tell me who Beaumont Livy is and why you want to find him."

I'd heard it before, but I listened anyway. Wanted to know if Mavortian's story would change now that he was telling it to somebody who mattered. It didn't, though. The gal in the miniature—except he didn't have it anymore, the Duke of Aiaia or his goons must've taken it—Anna Gloria Pietrin. Mavortian's fiancée. Seduced and abandoned by this Beaumont Livy that Mavortian wanted to find so bad you could practically see him drooling. Her committing suicide in some half-horse town up in Skaar. Livy being a hocus, being the one that'd crippled Mavortian up so bad he couldn't stand on his own no more. And Felix listened, taking it all in, and when Mavortian was done, all he said was, "Now tell me about strong divination."

The rest of us sat and listened while him and Mavortian got into it. Me and Bernard and Miss Parr just kind of shrugged at each other. We were annemer, and we didn't expect to get it. Gideon was listening hard, though, and I wondered what was going on upstairs with him.

I'd been wondering that a lot, the past decad.

He wasn't crazy. That much I was sure of, although powers and saints I wouldn't've blamed him if he had been. But, no, his eyes were the same as I remembered them, sharp and bright and watchful. More watchful even, but I sure as fuck understood where that was coming from.

If I'd been him, I wouldn't've taken my eyes off Mavortian von Heber either.

He didn't want to talk to us. When Mavortian had offered him paper and a pen, he'd just *looked* at him, like he wasn't just an asshole, but stupid as well, and somehow Gideon'd thought better of him. Fuck of a look, and that was the last time anybody tried to get him to tell us what was going on in his head.

Now he was watching Felix, with this little line between his eyebrows, and I remembered how most of an indiction ago I'd thought maybe Gideon was in love with Felix a little bit. Hadn't understood it at all, mind you, but I figured if it had been true then, it had to be like a septad times worse now.

But he wasn't mooning over Felix just then, don't get me wrong. He was *listening*. He understood what Felix and Mavortian were talking about, no question. Understood—and didn't much like it. Which I figured wasn't good news, because no matter how you looked at it, of the three hocuses in the room, Gideon was the only one with enough common sense to be trusted to cross the street on his own. That was something else I remembered about him.

Felix was frowning, too, and his frown was getting blacker and blacker with every word Mavortian said. Which was some comfort. I hadn't realized how nervous I'd been about Mavortian talking him into something.

Just because *you're* a pushover, Milly-Fox.

Mavortian must've noticed Felix's expression, because his sentence kind of trailed off into nothing, and he said, "Messire Harrowgate?" like he thought Felix was going to bite him.

"No," Felix said.

Everybody in the room twitched.

"What do you mean by that?" Mavortian said.

"Exactly what I said. No. I don't know Beaumont Livy, and I am not going to help you find him."

"Why not?" Mavortian had his voice mostly under control, but something pretty raw was leaking out around the edges.

"Oh, I could list you my reasons, but perhaps you should answer this instead: why should I?"

And Kethe that just *sat* there. Me and Bernard met each other's eyes by accident and looked away in a hurry. And then Mavortian said, "I can help you."

"You? Help *me*?" Felix snorted. "And just how do you think you can do that?"

"I know what you want to do."

Another silence, this one big enough to swallow a small dog. I don't know about anybody else, but I was staring at my hands. Because I didn't want to risk catching Felix's eye by accident.

"Enlighten me," he said in that smooth, purring, mocking voice that I hated more than just about anything. "Tell me what it is I want to do. Since clearly you know that better than I."

And Mavortian rapped right back at him: "You want to mend the Virtu."

ЗѦ

We cleared out. Us annemer. Gideon wouldn't come, but the air in that fucking room was getting too thick to breathe, and it wasn't like Felix and Mavortian needed us around. They barely even noticed when I got up and jerked my head at Bernard and Miss Parr and we got the fuck out of there.

We didn't go far, just down to the hotel's back garden, where there were rosebushes and a bench and I could sit down and wait for the whole fucking thing to make sense.

Felix wanted to fix the Virtu.

I couldn't even *start* to explain how fucked up that was.

Which was bad, because Bernard and Miss Parr both wanted to know. I did my best, but Kethe knows how much of it made sense to them, because I'd be fucked if I understood it myself.

Here's what I knew. The Virtu was a big blue ball made out of something that looked like glass. Down in the Engmond's Tor Cheaps you could buy bad reproductions of Clementine Nesbitt's painting of *The Cabal Creating the Virtu*, with everyone looking all mystical and uplifted and shit. The Virtu was magic, no fucking question about that, but what exactly it did . . . powers, I ain't no hocus, and some days I think it wouldn't make sense even if I was.

Before it'd been broken, every hocus in the Mirador had sworn oaths on it every day. I didn't know what kind of oaths—and I wondered if Felix would tell me if I asked—but I knew they were part of why there hadn't been no more coups like the Cabal's and why the Empire hadn't rolled over us like a fiacre over a frog. After the Virtu was broken, the Lord Protector had held things together as best he could, but things had been bad in the city, even before the Mirador got set on fire, which was one of those things that wasn't supposed to happen. Ever.

And there was one other thing I knew about the Virtu. Felix was the guy who broke it.

Or, to get at the story behind the story, some motherfucker of a hocus named Malkar Gennadion had used my brother to break the Virtu and sent him crazy doing it. And if I ever got my hands on Malkar Gennadion, we were going to have words about that. But I knew, the way Felix felt, it might just as well have been him that did it, and thought it out for a decad beforehand. So what Mavortian said made sense—except for the part where I couldn't get my fucking head around it, the idea that somebody was going to *fix* the Virtu. Like somebody saying they were going to fix the sun after it went out.

I don't think Bernard and Miss Parr understood that part at all, but they got the idea that this was big witchery, and they didn't like it any more than I did. I thought about asking Bernard if there was anything he could do to shut Mavortian up, but a look at his face told me there wasn't.

Shit, I thought, and we sat there not talking for a while.

It was getting dark by the time Felix came out to find us. We were still sitting there not talking. I don't know about the other two, but I couldn't think of a thing in the world worth saying. Me and Bernard both knew how things were going to play out, and we didn't want to talk about it. And I guess I could've asked Miss Parr what she was going to do, but I couldn't get up the gumption.

So Felix came out and she was the one who stood up and said, "Well?"

He looked past her at Bernard and said, "Mavortian wants you."

Bernard kind of grunted and got up and went inside. Felix looked at me a moment, but I didn't have nothing to say, and he looked back at Miss Parr.

"As I told you, I am returning to the Mirador. You are welcome to continue traveling with us if you wish."

Like I was so much stew meat. But that wasn't telling me nothing I didn't already know.

"What about Messire von Heber?" she said. "And Messire Thraxios?"

"Gideon has been granted asylum by the Curia. And I do not believe he has anywhere else to go."

Poor little fuck, I thought.

"And Messire von Heber?"

Felix gave her a look, but she wasn't impressed. He sighed. "Messire von Heber claims he can help me with my problem, and he seems to know what he's talking about. Anything more will have to wait until the Virtu is mended."

"You really think you can?"

My voice came out ugly and made them both jump.

Felix looked at me without answering for a second, and then said, "Yes."

As simple as that.

Felix

I waited for Thamuris in the Khloïdanikos.

We had agreed to meet on my schedule. The only hostile country he was trapped in was his own body; no one would remark or wonder if he kept strange hours. And he could feel the Khloïdanikos far more clearly than I could. Even awake, he could feel my presence in it.

Our small experimentations had kept me from driving myself to distraction while I waited for Mildmay and the others to reach Julip, and for that alone—and for the fact that he never commented on my anxiety although he was certainly aware of it—I would have counted Thamuris as a friend.

And he had rapidly become a friend in other ways. It was rare to find a wizard whose intellectual curiosity was stronger than their ambition, than the desire for power that gripped us all like a disease. Malkar had hated my curiosity and had done his best to beat it out of me, but all he had been able to do was teach me to hide it from him. Once I escaped his hold, it all came surging back. I was the most powerful wizard the Mirador had, the lover of the Lord Protector's brother; I had all the material for power games I needed. My research, my *work*, was bounded by nothing but my own intellectual abilities, and many wizards looked at me askance for it.

My friend Sherbourne Foss understood, before I betrayed him. Before the Mirador's wards were broken, and he was killed by the dead things those wards no longer bound.

I doubted that Thamuris had always been this pure a scholar. In fact, between what Xanthippe had told me of his past and what he had said himself, I was quite sure he had not been. But, his health shattered and his chosen life closed to him, he had accepted the new path opening up before his feet, even knowing he might not have very long to walk it.

I admired him quite dreadfully for that.

We had explored the Khloïdanikos together over the past few weeks. Diokletian did not join us; I had not asked why and didn't intend to, any more than I had asked how Diokletian had come to show Thamuris the Dream of the Gardens in the first place. Thamuris and I had found many ways in which the Khloïdanikos was not the same as the Gardens we both knew in the waking world, and one strand of our research—perforce almost entirely Thamuris's alone—was in trying to discover if those differences were due to changes in the material Gardens over the centuries. He promised me that he was not overexerting himself; apparently, Khrysogonos was a willing assistant.

"*Khrysogonos?*" I'd said when he first told me.

And Thamuris shrugged and smiled his slow, laudanum-drenched smile. "We both miss Mildmay," he said as if that explained everything, and I made a spur-of-the-moment decision not to broach the subject of Mildmay's feelings about Khrysogonos.

In the Khloïdanikos, Thamuris had nearly the stamina of a healthy man. We spent most of our time together walking, exploring the reaches of this strange little world. And because we were wizards, we talked about thaumaturgic theory, deeply, obsessively, and without any signs of the topic's being exhausted. Some nights I could almost see Mildmay rolling his eyes.

I always entered the Khloïdanikos through Horn Gate, even if my dreaming mind had not fully visualized my construct-Mélusine. But as Horn Gate never led me to the same place in the Khloïdanikos twice, Thamuris and I had decided the sensible thing to do was to choose a meeting place so that we would not waste precious time trying to find each other.

I did not like the Omphalos, although it was the Khloïdanikos's most obvious landmark. For reasons I did not fully understand, it reminded me of Nera—and of course I did not care for the memory of the tawdry and embarrassing confrontation between Diokletian and me. Thamuris did not like it, either; it worried him because it was so aggressively unlike the real Omphalos and because the differences did not (he said) entirely make sense. We met instead in a stand of perseïd trees, which was distinct from its waking counterpart only in that the trees were younger. There was a bench to sit on, and the scent of the trees was like the blessing of some faded and forgotten god.

I sat on the bench, and after only a few minutes, I caught sight of Thamuris wending his way through the trees. He smiled as he came up to me, and said, "Shall we walk?"

"Yes, let's."

For a long time, I did not speak, and Thamuris let me hold my silence. It occurred to me that he and Mildmay were the most patient men I had ever met, though they came to their patience in very different ways. I wondered sometimes how much of Thamuris's patience was laudanum, but it would have been cruel and unjust to ask.

And in the end I sighed and said, "How much do you know about the Fressandran school of divination?" I was a little uneasy at broaching the subject of divination with him, but there was no one else I could ask. I did not trust Mavortian von Heber to tell me the full truth.

"Fressandran," Thamuris said, searching his memory. "A discipline of Norvena Magna, is it not?"

"Yes. They practice something called strong divination." I said it in

Midlander and offered the three different Troian translations I had been able to think of.

The third one was right. Thamuris's eyes widened a little. "You know it," I said.

"I know *of* it. We don't practice it."

"Then it isn't the same as pythian casting?"

"No."

"Can you explain the difference?"

"I can try." He frowned, thinking. "How much do you know about divination?"

"Very little. The Mirador does not practice it." It was not heresy, but it was considered vulgar and largely the province of foreign charlatans.

"Very well," Thamuris said. "I will tell you the explanation I was given when the Celebrants Terrestrial were first teaching me augury."

"Augury?" I said, because I was not quite sure of the connotations of the word in Troian.

"Even in the House of Hakko, we did not perform pythian casting *all* the time," he said with a rueful smile. "Augury is closer to a form of meditation, except that what you meditate on is the huphantike."

"The huphantike?"

"The pattern of the future. In the older texts, it's called the labyrinth of fortune."

"Of course it is." I was becoming resigned to the idea that I was cursed with labyrinths.

"Beg pardon?"

"Nothing. Please continue."

"What we learn when we are taught augury as novices is that the future has a pattern. The huphantike. We cannot know the future, but we can see the pattern."

"When you say 'pattern,' what does that mean?"

"Every scholar has a different metaphor. Many of them are contradictory."

"You're a Celebrant Celestial. Surely you have a metaphor of your own."

He blushed, the color rising in his pale face like a fire. "I am not a scholar."

"I don't care. Tell me how *you* think about it, and leave the scholars to quarrel amongst themselves."

His smile was shy, uncertain, as if he thought I was teasing him. I made an encouraging gesture, and after a moment, he said, "To me it always seems like looking at a map." He stopped short, staring at me anxiously.

"Go on," I said. "It doesn't make sense to me yet, but I don't despair of it doing so eventually."

"A map," he said, with a better smile this time. "A map of a country you do not know. Most of the map is—not blank, but in darkness, illegible. But there are a few landmarks that show up clearly, and they indicate the path the future will take."

He paused, looking at me again, and I nodded to show I had followed him that far.

"But just as the symbol on the map gives you no sense of the actual, material city you will enter, so too the landmarks—the *semeia,* the scholars call them, both markers and omens—do not tell you what will happen."

"No?"

"We cannot know the future."

"Now I'm lost. If you can't know the future, then what's the point of divination?"

"You misunderstand me. We cannot know the future, but we can know the pattern."

"What's the difference?"

"I am explaining this badly," Thamuris said, downcast.

"No, you're doing splendidly." I reined in my impatience. "Just tell me: what's the difference between 'the future' and 'the pattern'?"

He thought about that for a while, then said slowly, "The future is the events that will happen, just as the past is the events that have happened. We cannot know the future until it becomes the past."

"All right. Then what's the pattern?"

"The range of possible events that may become the future. Given the past, there are only so many different directions the future can take. The landmarks in my map metaphor are those events that have the strongest likelihood of occurring."

"But you don't know what they are."

"No, but I can know their shape."

"Their *shape*? Perhaps if you gave me an example?"

"All right." He hesitated, his face reddening again, then said grimly, "The pythian casting I did with your brother. The huphantike was spoken through me." He tilted his head back, shutting his eyes, and recited, "Love and betrayal, the gorgon and the wheel. The dead tree will not shelter you, and the dead will not stay dead. Though you do not seek revenge, it will seek you all the same."

"*That*'s the huphantike?"

"That is your brother's huphantike. That is the pattern his future has. But what events make up the pattern, that we cannot know until they occur."

It sounded so horrible. I said, "You said the huphantike was the range of possible events. It may not reflect what will actually happen, correct?"

He lowered his gaze, becoming apparently fascinated by the square red tiles of the path we were following. "The nature of pythian casting," he said and stopped.

"Yes?" I said, too anxious now about Mildmay to care about Thamuris's feelings.

"The nature of pythian casting—the reason that it is such a powerful tool—is that by the act of divination, one increases the strength of the huphantike as one sees it."

"You mean you make it happen?"

"Nothing so simple as that. But the pythian casting sets the pattern, like cold water sets a dye."

And you did that to my brother? For no better reason than you *wanted* to?

I wanted to scream at him, curse him, but it would do no good, and there were too many ways in which it was not his fault. I pushed the anger and fear aside and said, my voice calm, if rather cold, "Then if that's what pythian casting does, what is strong divination?"

"Some scholars think it isn't properly divination at all," Thamuris said, his gaze still fixed on the red tiles beneath our feet, "but a kind of sorcery. In strong divination, once you've cast for the huphantike and gotten a sense of its variances, you cast again to ask what you must do to make the future follow the huphantike as you wish it to."

"And how is that different from pythian casting?" My anger escaped my control to become clearly audible.

"I didn't—!" He stopped, backtracked, recast his response impersonally: "In pythian casting, the diviner has no control over the huphantike they receive. They simply set it. But in strong divination, the *point* is to control the huphantike. To make the future be what you want."

"I see," I said, and I did. I wondered why this future that Mavortian von Heber wanted so badly had led him to me. It was not a comfortable question.

"I'm sorry," Thamuris said after a while. "I really didn't know."

"Then why did you do it?" I asked and was astonished at how mild I sounded.

"Have you ever been the channel through which the future speaks?"

"No."

"Then I cannot explain it. But I understand why early pythian casters made a practice of castrating themselves. And I understand why I let it kill me."

There was nothing I could say in response to that, but the silence between us was amicable again, and we walked along the red-tiled path together until it was morning in Julip and Mildmay was telling me to wake up.

Mildmay

We headed out the next morning, along of not really wanting to wait and see if the Duke of Aiaia was going to catch up with us or not.

We'd staggered into Julip with Bernard carrying Mavortian, and Miss Parr more or less carrying me, and Gideon carrying himself but only barely. I'd been dreading the fight about how we were going to get ourselves *out* of Julip again, and was just about knocked sideways when it turned out Felix had already thought of that and arranged to hire transportation from Julip to the next big town, which was Wassail. He hadn't been banking on two extra people, but since the only thing he'd been able to get for what was left of the money Mr. Gauthy'd paid him was a broken-down old diligence, it turned out to be just fine. Only two horses, but seeing as how I was the only one knew anything about driving, and I wasn't sure I could've handled a team, that was okay, too. So Bernard and Mavortian and Gideon got stashed inside where nobody could see 'em to remark on how much they looked like the Duke of Aiaia's escaped prisoners, and Felix and Miss Parr climbed up on the roof behind me.

And I drove, trying to pretend like I wasn't nervous about the Duke of Aiaia's goons and wasn't nervous about going back to Mélusine and wasn't even a little bit nervous about what was going to happen to me when I did. Too much time to think and too much to think about, and Felix behind me where I couldn't see him, but I could hear him, and, powers, it seemed like I could *feel* him, and everything I thought came back around to: I don't want to leave him.

Which was stupid and useless and embarrassing besides, but it was the truth. He was all I had anymore, the only person in the world who cared about me even a little—the only person left that I . . . loved.

Going molly, Milly-Fox? Keeper drawled in my head. But I wasn't. I didn't want to fuck him or nothing like that. I just kept remembering how it had been going across Kekropia the first time, just him and me and the batfuck crazies. And mostly it had been pure Hell, don't get me wrong. But he'd needed me, and he'd trusted me. He'd saved my life, too, because if he hadn't come and got me out of that farmhouse cellar before the hired man got back with the sheriff, I would have been hanged for sure and certain. And it had broken my heart, all the way across the Grasslands, watching him trying to cope with this thing that was tearing him up from the inside out. It had been a losing battle all the fucking way, but he just wouldn't lay down and let it walk over him. I loved him for that. I loved him for helping the dead people in Nera. I loved him for all the times he'd made some smart-ass remark like him and me were really brothers, like we'd grown up together and knew each other and had that thing between us that there ain't no good words for.

I loved him. I loved him the same way I'd loved Christobel and Nikah and the other kids I'd grown up with, the ones who were mostly dead now. And I wanted to be with him, to get up in the morning and know that whatever shit the day had waiting for me, at least he'd be there, too.

But there was no fucking way I could have that. He was going back to the Mirador, and even if I'd thought I had the right to, there was no way I could stop him. And if I went with him, it'd take a decad tops before the Mirador found out who I was and hanged me. And not that I didn't deserve it, but I didn't want to die. And I couldn't bear the thought of Felix being in the crowd watching.

I shoved the whole mess away again, the way I'd been doing for days, and concentrated on the horses and the road and not listening to Felix and Miss Parr laughing at each other.

But I knew it would come back.

That night, I didn't dream about Keeper or Ginevra for a change. I dreamed about Porphyria Levant.

Porphyria Levant was a blood-witch, the woman who taught Brinvillier Strych everything he knew. I don't remember much of that dream—just remember coming awake and laying there, staring up at the ceiling and breathing like I'd been in a fight. And thinking about Porphyria Levant. Remembering that old story about her and Silas Altamont and the obligation d'âme and what she'd used it to make him do.

Please, let me stop or I'm going to go out and slit my wrists.

Silas, I forbid you to kill yourself.

And after a while I figured out what the dream was trying to tell me.

I didn't sleep the rest of the night, and all the next day I was watching Felix like a first-time pickpocket watching the mark. Felix noticed—of course Felix noticed, and of course it pissed him off, but Kethe I couldn't help it. Because things were lining up in my head.

If I went back to the Lower City, I was going to end up dead. I could feel it, the way sometimes I'd felt when a job was going to go bad and known not to take it. Couldn't explain it, couldn't argue with it. Sometimes I just knew. And that was the way I knew this. The Lower City would kill me. Someone with a grudge would come after me, or give me to the Dogs, or I'd go to Keeper, or I'd starve to death or kill myself or just plain *die*.

I hated myself for it. Hated myself for being so fucking weak. Hated myself for having got into this situation where somehow there wasn't nothing I could do that wasn't stupid. But there was only one choice that didn't seem to lead straight to the Ivorene—or worse, if the Dogs got me, the Boneprince. And that was Felix and that old story about Porphyria Levant and Silas Altamont. The moral of which was, don't do exactly what I was thinking about doing.

Everybody was looking at me squiggle-eyed by the end of the day, and I didn't blame them. I hadn't been able to eat, hadn't been able to put two words together in a row, hadn't been able to quit watching Felix. I felt like a rope, stretched too tight and starting to fray.

I went upstairs early. Way early. Because I'd caught myself just about to buy a second glass of gin, and I hate the stuff. And then I sat there on the edge of the bed me and Felix were going to be sharing and clamped my hands together and tried to quit shaking. I didn't figure there was much else I could hope for, but I wanted to start this conversation with Felix *not* shaking like a virgin on her wedding night.

Oh, bad bad comparison. Because we hadn't talked about that weird thing that had happened in the river, and I didn't want to be Silas to Felix's Porphyria. And, fuck, that was an even worse comparison. Quit thinking while you're ahead, Milly-Fox.

Felix being Felix, he didn't make me wait long. I'd about got my breathing steadied out when I heard the hotel stairs creaking. And then I was panicking all over again, like a virgin being married off to an ogre or something.

"Fuck this for the emperor's snotrag," I said and threw myself backwards on the bed. Not that it helped, but it was better than sitting there all hunched up like a hedgehog. Felix opened the door just as I was laughing at the idea of a hedgehog-bride.

"What?" he said, shutting the door behind him.

"Nothing. Not about you, I mean. Just . . ."

He sighed. "You don't tell anyone even a quarter of what you think, do you?"

"Um," I said and sat up again. "I don't know. I mean . . ."

"Never mind." He sat down on the other side of the bed. "You've clearly wanted to say something to me all day. What is it?"

"Oh. Powers. Um."

"What? That *wasn't* why you were staring at me every time I turned around?"

"No. I mean, yes. I mean . . . I mean, yes. I got something I need to say. To ask."

He waited, his eyebrows going up. "Well?"

I was shaking, and I could feel myself going red. But he was here, he was listening, and I just spat it out: "D'you know how to do the obligation d'âme?"

"Yes. But why . . . Oh." He folded his hands together carefully and calmly. "Mildmay, please tell me that you're not asking for the reason I think you are."

"Yes. I mean . . . fuck it, you keep getting me all twisted. I mean, yes, I need you to do it, the binding-by-forms. With me."

"Why?" he said, real quiet, real controlled, and I wished he'd been yelling.

"Because . . ." I'd tried to work out what to say, but none of the words would come, and I ended up just saying the truth: "Because otherwise I'm gonna end up dead."

It rocked him. Whatever he'd been going to say, he didn't. He just sat there for a moment, and then he pushed his hair back from his face and said, in a completely different voice, "Why?"

"You know what I done. About . . . about the Witchfinder Extraordinary."

"Yes."

I swallowed hard. "You ain't the only one who knows. I can't work no more, not with my leg like this. And if I can't work, I got nothing to trade, nothing to make me more useful to people than the gorgons they'll get for telling the Dogs where to find me."

"But I don't see—"

"*Please*. I know it's crazy, but I can't . . . there ain't . . ." I looked down at my hands, where they were clenched together over that ache in my right thigh that was never really not there, even when I wasn't thinking about it. "There ain't no other way."

"Of course there's another way. Don't be an idiot."

"Felix, there *ain't*."

"There's no reason you have to come back to Mélusine," he said, and he sounded so matter-of-fact about it, so fucking *cheerful*, that I wanted to strangle him.

"I can't . . ."

"Can't what?" He was frowning at me, not like he was mad, but like he really didn't understand the problem.

"I just *can't*. Okay?"

"No. Not 'okay.' You can't ask me to do something like that and then not tell me why."

"Fuck," I said. I unclenched my hands, rubbed my face. Didn't really feel it on the left side, but that'd been true so long I couldn't remember what it'd been like before. " 'Cause I have a feeling."

"A feeling," he said, like he thought he'd misunderstood me.

"Yeah. I got 'em sometimes, about jobs. About jobs I shouldn't take. And I got one now."

"And this feeling is telling you what? That I have to commit an act of the grossest and most blatant heresy to save your life?"

"Not like that."

"Then what is it like?"

"Look," I said, and my voice was starting to shake with something that was partly anger but mostly not. "If I go back to the Lower City, I'm gonna end up dead. But if I . . . if I . . ."

"What?" he said, more gently.

I could only meet his eyes for a second. Having his full attention was like getting a sword through the guts. I gulped and said, "If I got to leave you, then I don't know why I should bother to stay alive."

I saw it hit him. His eyes widened. He went red, and then white, white as his shirt. He said, his voice barely a whisper, "You don't mean that."

"I do," I said. "I swear to you, I mean it."

His hands moved like he was trying to push the whole idea away. "You can't. You can't mean . . . do you know what the obligation d'âme *does*?"

"Yeah."

"Mildmay, I can't . . ." His fingers were pressed against his mouth. "I can't do that to you."

"You ain't. I'm *asking*."

He shook his head, but not like he was disagreeing. It was like he didn't even know he was doing it.

And then I thought of something else. "Don't you . . . I mean, if you don't want me to stay, I'll leave tonight. Head for St. Millefleur or something."

"No!" He reached out before he even knew he was doing it. His fingers were cold on my wrist. "Don't go."

And then we sat there staring at each other. Finally, I said, "I don't want to go. But if I go to the Mirador with you." I had to stop for a second, just out of being purely unable to believe I'd said it. "If I do that, I'll end up hanging from Livergate in a decad, tops."

"But no one knows."

"Nobody in the Mirador knows. There's plenty of people know. And they'll tell."

"But . . ."

"You got oaths you swore, right? To be loyal and shit?"

He nodded, his eyes big and spooked, like he was halfway back to crazy again.

"I know the stories. I know the binding-by-forms is the only thing can trump them oaths. And so that's the only way."

"But, Mildmay—"

"It's either that or I go to St. Millefleur. The Mirador'll kill me one way, or the Lower City'll kill me the other." I pulled, gently, and he let go of my wrist. "I may not last the winter in St. Millefleur, but that ain't on your head."

I started to get up, and he said, in a funny, breathless voice, "I'll go to St. Millefleur with you."

"The fuck you will," I said, dropping back down and staring at him. "What the fuck are you gonna do in St. Millefleur?"

"I don't know. What are *you* going to do?"

"That don't matter. I ain't a hocus. Don't you get it? You got something to go back to. I don't."

"But you—"

"It's *over*." I hit my right leg, maybe a little harder than I should've. "Can't be a cat burglar with a bad leg. I ain't gonna be a pusher or a pimp, can't be a fence. And I don't want to be just hired muscle."

"Those aren't your only options," he said through his teeth.

"I can't go straight. That gets me right back to the Dogs and the Kennel. And the spikes over Livergate. I need protection, Felix. And you're the only one can give it to me."

"What you're asking me to do is monstrous."

"So? Ain't we both monsters?"

He just stared at me. Then he turned away, managed this shaky sort of laugh, pushed his hair back. Said, "You've got to give me some time to think about it. I can't just . . ."

"Why not?"

"It's *heresy*."

"Will they burn you for it?" I hadn't thought of that. I'd kind of figured once you were in with the Mirador you could do whatever the fuck you liked. But if it was going to get Felix in that kind of trouble . . . I'd go to St. Millefleur or wherever, and if I died of it, that was fine.

His mouth opened, then closed again, and he got this weird look on his face, like he was looking at something a long ways away and he couldn't decide if he liked it or not. "Technically," he said in this dreamy kind of voice, "at the moment I am not a wizard of the Mirador."

"You ain't?" Fucking news to me.

"No." And now he was smiling, sort of bitter and dreamy all at once, and the hair was trying to stand up on the back of my neck. "They stripped me of my rank and privileges."

I didn't say nothing because I was afraid the next time he looked at me it'd draw blood.

"They cast me out themselves. They can't accuse me of heresy when they've already declared me anathema." His smile sharpened. "An object lesson."

Then he did look at me, and somehow, powers, I didn't flinch. "Is this what you want?" he said, hard and sharp and bitter like an iron knife. "Are you sure?"

"Yeah," I said and swallowed hard. "I mean, yes. I am."

"You understand what it entails?"

"I know the story of Silas Altamont."

A flicker of darkness in his eyes. "Then may we both be forgiven for this. Give me your hands."

Too late to back out now, Milly-Fox. I held out my hands. He stripped off his gloves and laid them aside. His hands were smooth, soft, not like mine with the scars and the calluses and the lumpy knuckles, but I could feel the stiffness where his fingers had been broken and hadn't healed quite right. He traced over the scars on my hands, and then his grip firmed and I gripped back.

"You're sure?" he said and was more himself again. He sounded like he cared about the answer.

"Kethe, just get on with it!"

He nodded and bowed his head over our hands. He said something I didn't understand, and then he looked up—looked me square in the eyes—and leaned in and kissed me.

Hard.

With tongue.

And that was when I felt the obligation d'âme take hold, like a lightning bolt, like falling down a staircase you didn't know was there. And it was all tangled up with the taste of him and the way his lips felt against mine and powers and saints the things he was doing with his tongue. Some stupid part of my brain was going, So this is what a Pharaohlight whore is like, and even though I didn't know why he was kissing me and didn't want him to be doing it, neither, I couldn't help, just for a second, wondering what it would be like with him.

And then I could move again, and I pushed away from him and said, "What the *fuck*?" My voice was unsteady and mostly breath and slurred worse than ever, and I couldn't seem to get my eyes to move away from him.

"Magic is symbolism," he said. "The obligation d'âme binds us closer than lovers."

"Symbolic kissing?"

"I thought you would prefer it," he said, and when I figured out what he meant I went red clear up to my scalp.

"You could've warned me."

"I could have," he said darkly. "In any event, it's done, and I wish you much joy of it."

"Better'n being dead," I said, and my voice broke on the last word.

He didn't have an answer.

Felix

Once Mildmay was asleep, I got up and slipped out of the room. I could not sleep, and I did not want to be alone with my thoughts and the quiet rasp of his breathing.

I felt as I had the night I had lost my virginity, only this was in some indefinable way worse because I had *done* this, I had *chosen* it. I had used my magic on an annemer, and it did not matter that he had asked me to, that it had been his idea to start with. And I had kissed him. That had not been his idea, and I was trying very hard not to catalogue the reasons I had not warned him it was part of the deal.

I felt feverish, nauseated. It was with no clear idea of what I was doing that I found and ascended the stairs to the roof. It had rained earlier, but the sky now was clear, the air smelling damp and clean. I stood and tilted my head back to look at the stars, calming myself with their names and constellations.

He had called me a monster, and I knew he was right. But he had also said he did not want to leave me. He would rather endure the obligation d'âme than leave me, monster that I was. I could not make sense of it, of this unwarranted devotion, no sooner admitted to than betrayed. In a choice between committing an act of grievous heresy—possibly even an act of evil—and losing my brother, I had chosen to commit heresy. And no matter how much it sickened me, I knew I would make the same choice again.

I could still feel his lips against mine, the strange stiffness of scar tissue, the surprised softness of his mouth. The harsh bite of gin on his tongue, the hard edges of his teeth. The way that, for a moment, a bare breathless moment, he had not been unwilling.

And then he had pushed me away.

A noise behind me, a foot scuffing against the shingles. I turned: Gideon Thraxios, his eyes like night-filled holes in his sallow face.

"Oh," I said, letting my breath out in a sigh that was half relief and half exasperation. "It's you. What are you doing up here?"

He hesitated, his dark eyes searching my face.

"Go ahead," I said tiredly. "You might as well."

:I did not mean to disturb you. Or to intrude.:

Well, you did. I kept from saying it, although it was an effort, and said instead, "It isn't my roof. You have as much right as anyone to be up here."

He almost seemed to flinch although it was hard to tell with only the moon and stars for light. He said, his mental voice as carefully neutral as my spoken voice had been, :I was looking at the stars.:

I tilted my head back, contemplating those distant brightnesses, and said, "And what do the stars tell you?"

:Nothing. The stars have no voice that I can hear.:

Pain, bitterness, loneliness. It was my turn to flinch, and he said, :I am sorry. I should not—:

"Who else do you have to talk to?"

:You do not want to talk to me.:

"I do not want to talk about certain subjects. I have no objections to talking to you."

His body language was doubtful, wary, but he came a few steps closer. :If you are sure you do not mind . . . :

"As long as you don't want to talk about me," I said and gave him a wry smile, "I'd be glad for someone to distract me from my thoughts."

He was close enough that I saw him return my smile. :Then what should we talk about, Messire Harrowgate?:

I hesitated, but there were only two topics that could hold my attention at the moment, and I did not want to discuss Mildmay. With anyone. "What do you know about divination?"

:You are worried about Messire von Heber's rather remarkable story?:

"Yes—well, not so much the divination itself, but do you think he can help me mend the Virtu as he says?"

:This is truly your goal?:

"Yes. It is."

:Frankly, I don't know if such a thing is possible at all. If it is, I would imagine you will need all the help you can get.:

"Granted. But what he said—"

:I am neither Cabaline nor Fressandran,: he said with some asperity.

"You're a wizard, and unless I am very much mistaken, there is no love lost between you and Mavortian von Heber."

:Are you asking me to choose sides?:

"There are no sides to choose thus far. But I do not wish to believe things merely because Mavortian tells me they are true."

:Yes,: Gideon said. :You are wise in that.: Old bitterness in his voice, but I could not ask without revealing that I did not know, and I was not entirely prepared to trust Gideon Thraxios, either.

He shed that dark mood like a snakeskin and said, :Explain to me what the Virtu is and how it was broken.:

My horror felt like the building lurching beneath my feet. But he was right. He couldn't offer me any kind of opinion until he knew the parameters of the question. And I supposed, distractedly, that I should be grateful for the chance to practice my lies before I had to tell them to Mavortian.

Now if only I had had a chance to work out what my lies were going to be.

Reflexively, I stalled for time. "The Virtu was created by the Cabal in 2101, not quite two hundred years ago. They were trying—among other things—to find a way to convince the wizards of Mélusine to work together rather than preying on each other as had been their wont."

:And did it work?: Gideon asked, dryly enough that I knew he knew the answer.

I thought of what I had done to Mildmay that evening, exactly the sort of thing the Cabal had been trying to eradicate; I remembered the look in his eyes when he'd said, *You could've warned me.* "As well as anything ever can, with wizards. The Virtu was—*is*—a thaumaturgical device with a dual purpose. It collects power from each wizard of the Mirador and uses that power to maintain a number of defensive spells, some attuned to the individual wizards, some guarding the fabric of the Mirador, some guarding other things. It would be heresy if they tried to do it now, of course." Though not as unforgivable a heresy as performing the obligation d'âme.

:It sounds like a monumental work of magic.:

"There's a reason the Cabal all died young. The problem, though, is that the Virtu has never failed in all this time."

:The *problem*?:

"Let me finish. You see, as long as everyone swears their oaths and contributes their power, the spells don't erode and the structure maintains its stability. The Curia is nominally responsible for the Virtu's maintenance, but we've never needed to *do* anything."

:We?: Gideon said, and I saw his eyebrow rise.

"I was a member of the Curia," I said stiffly.

:Yes, and now you are not. Which I believe is also part of this explanation.:

I very nearly cursed him to his face for being so damnably right. As it was, I knew I had been silent too long before I said, "Yes, I suppose it is."

:You did ask for my opinion.:

"Yes, I know that. Very well." I looked out at the horizon, because it was the only way I could keep my head up. "The Virtu was broken via a working done on me by Malkar Gennadion." That much was common knowledge; he must have known it before he made me say it.

:Specify,: Gideon said in the cool, dispassionate tones of a scholar.

"He found a way—he put together a working that allowed him to use my magic as if it were his own." My nails were digging into my palms with the effort it took to keep my voice level. If I closed my eyes, I knew I would see the louring walls of Malkar's workroom, the evil shine of the pentagram laid into the floor.

:I thought the Virtu protected the wizards of the Mirador against such spells.:

I felt like a man who had backed away from a bear trap only to fall onto a bed of swords.

:Well?: he said after a moment, when I still had not managed to speak. :How did Messire Gennadion do it?:

"I . . . I was . . ." His molly-toy, a cruel voice in my head finished, the voice of the teenage whore I had been. "He was never Cabaline," I said, lamely and too quickly.

:Surely *that* shouldn't make any difference.:

"No, no, it—I just meant, it wasn't heresy to him." And he wouldn't have cared if it was. I was babbling and I knew it, but seemed entirely helpless to stop myself.

Gideon's head tilted; I was puzzling him. :What has heresy to do with it?:

"Nothing." I turned away from him, pushed my fingers savagely through my hair, bit my lower lip until I was focused on that small pain instead of the panic baying in my mind.

:Messire Harrowgate?: I felt Gideon coming closer. :Felix?:

I turned, sharply enough that he stepped back a pace. "Unpleasant memories," I said and managed a thin smile. "And I am more tired than I realized. Malkar Gennadion was my teacher in magic before I swore my oaths to the Mirador. Doubtless he found some occasion to cast a spell that would circumvent the Virtu's warding." Doubtless while he held me with the obligation de sang, but I did not want to talk about that, either, nor think about its kinship to the obligation d'âme. Thus, I did my best to make circumventing the Virtu's warding sound like a simple matter rather than something I had no idea how Malkar had accomplished.

Gideon's disbelief was palpable, but he said nothing, simply stood and waited. His air, that of a schoolteacher faced with a recalcitrant pupil, was enough to push me from fear to anger, and somewhere underneath the wave of fury, I was glad of it.

"That part doesn't matter," I snapped. "What matters is that the Virtu was broken by the raw application of thaumaturgic force. I was only the hammer."

:You're saying he just . . . hit it?:

And now I was angry at Gideon for so readily dropping the subject of what Malkar had done to me. "There was no subtlety in that spell. Trust me. I was there."

:I suppose that *is* the easiest way to deal with something one does not fully understand,: Gideon said thoughtfully, as calm and conversational as if he had not noticed my hostility. :Not the safest, but the easiest.:

I could feel myself floundering, so wrong-footed that there seemed no response I could make. It was a mercy that Gideon did not wait for a reply from me. :And that being the case—it explains why the physical structure was shattered. And if the thaumaturgic structure was shattered in the same way . . . then a wizard trained to read patterns, as Fressandran diviners are trained, might indeed be very useful to you.:

Mavortian. Yes. We had been discussing Mavortian. "Do you think . . . do you think he understands how it happened? What Malkar did?"

:I doubt it,: Gideon said. If there *were* sides to be chosen, Gideon of Thrax had already made up his mind. :But his techniques may help *you* to understand it.:

"Oh," I said, with woeful inadequacy, realizing clearly for the first time that here was another, like Thamuris, who could keep up with me intellectually, and possibly even outdistance me.

:I do not know what Messire von Heber imagines he can offer you, Messire Harrowgate. But I do think he may be useful.:

To which I said the only thing I could: "Please. There's no reason for you not to call me Felix."

Chapter 9

Mildmay

You want to know what the obligation d'âme is like?

I only wish I could tell you.

In some ways, it didn't feel like anything had happened at all. I mean, I was still me, and Felix was still Felix—powers and saints was he ever—and sometimes I could almost think I'd dreamed the whole fucking thing.

But then there was the stuff that *did* change, and that's the stuff I don't got the right words for. All I knew about the obligation d'âme, the binding-by-forms, was what I'd learned from stories, and stories didn't help. Stories didn't talk about what it was *like* to be bound by the obligation d'âme. They just talked about why you shouldn't do it, and fuck I knew that part already.

So the stories didn't give me words for the way my heartbeat seemed to have picked up an echo, or the way I'd find myself looking at Felix all the time, even when I didn't mean to be. The stories didn't tell me what to call it when Felix told me to do something, and I could *feel* it like a fucking lead weight in my head. The stories didn't tell me about the dreams.

Now, don't get me wrong. Compared to the nightmares I'd been having, these were nothing, and I knew it. But they were spooky. And it wasn't nothing as simple as me dreaming about Felix or dreaming Felix's dreams or anything like that where I could've explained it. It was just that no matter what I was dreaming about, there was this kind of *muttering* all through it. It was Felix's voice, but no matter how hard I listened I could never make out the words.

Spooked me right the fuck out, let me tell you.

I'd already given Felix all the power over me he was ever going to need, and I figured whatever the fuck was really causing those dreams, I could take them as a reminder not to give him more. So in the hotel a couple days' ride from Mélusine, when I shoved my hands in my pockets and found Florian's letter *again*—I don't even know how often I'd done that since we'd sprung Gideon and them from Aiaia—and thought, Well? What *are* you going to do about this fucking thing?, it wasn't Felix I went to.

It was Mehitabel Parr.

⁊⁊

We'd been doing better with each other since Aiaia. Since she'd kissed me. And it wasn't nothing as simple as what that sounds like, neither. It was just . . . well, I don't know what it was, and that's the truth. But I'd started to like her a little, and I thought maybe she was sort of starting to like me back.

And I also thought, because she hadn't told nobody about her kissing me—not even Felix, who was way more her friend than me and would've thought it was the world's best fucking joke—she hadn't breathed a word, and I thought I could maybe trust her to keep her mouth shut about this, too.

At least, I hoped so.

Money was tight, but between Mavortian telling fortunes with his Sibylline cards—which apparently he'd managed to hang on to by telling fortunes for all the Aiaian guards, and, no, don't ask me to explain it either, 'cause I can't—and the Long Tiffany players who thought they were something special, we were doing good enough so as Miss Parr could have her own hotel room. Then Mavortian and Bernard shared one, and me and Felix and Gideon shared one, along of Gideon not wanting to be alone with Mavortian and Bernard, and me not wanting to be alone with Felix—not that either of us ever came right out and said so. And, I mean, not a great arrangement, but at least I knew I could talk to Miss Parr in private.

I knocked on her door.

"Who is it?"

"Me. Um, Mildmay."

She opened the door. Her braids were hanging down her back, and the top buttons of her dress were undone.

"Oh, powers. I'm sorry. I didn't mean to bother you."

"You aren't. What is it?"

"I wanted to ask . . . I mean, I need a favor."

"Of course," she said, like it was obvious. "Come in."

I was starting to feel really stupid, but I went into her room, and then stood there like a half-wit dog while she closed the door and sat down on the bed and looked at me. Then she smiled a little, I guess 'cause she'd figured out I wasn't going nowhere without a push, and said, "What can I do for you?"

"I . . . it . . ." I knew exactly what Felix would've said and *how* he would've said it, too, the smug fuck. My Kekropian's a little rusty, and smile at her and hand it over. But I couldn't do none of that. Couldn't lie and couldn't act like it was no big deal and especially couldn't smile.

"I won't bite you," she said, "unless you ask me nicely. What do you need?"

"I . . . I got this letter." I pulled it out of my pocket and kind of shoved it at her. "I can't . . ."

She took it, opened it. "Read Kekropian," she finished for me, and I nodded.

She smoothed the letter out. "Gracious. I didn't think there was a force in this world that could drive Florian Gauthy to write a letter more than two lines long. You have hidden depths, Messire Foxe."

"Mildmay," I said.

She looked up, and I felt like a bug pinned to a card. "Only if you call me Mehitabel."

"What?"

"My name. Mehitabel. Or if you find that too cumbersome, I also answer to Tabby."

"I, um . . . okay. Mehitabel."

"Much better. Mildmay." And she smiled at me, bright as sunshine.

She fished her spectacles out of her skirt pocket, settled them on her nose, and started reading:

*To Ker Mildmay Foxe, greetings. I am writing to you to
acknowledge that I am in your debt. You saved my life, and
although I don't think I will ever see you again, I had to write
and tell you that I am fully sensible of the debt I owe you.*

"I see Jeremias taught the boy nothing about prose style," she said, and
continued:

*I wish there were something I could do for you in return, but
Delila cannot think of anything.*

Mehitabel looked at me over the tops of her spectacles. "That isn't as
limp an excuse as it sounds. Delila is the only one in that family with any
sense at all."

"Powers! I didn't think . . . I ain't . . . Florian don't owe me nothing."

"No? You did, as he points out, save his life."

"Yeah, but—Kethe. That ain't why I did it, so he'd *owe* me or nothing."

"I know that," she said, "and I would wager Florian does, as well. Shall
we continue?"

"Yeah," and fuck me sideways if I wasn't blushing again. "Please."

She cleared her throat and read:

*I also want to thank you for trying to save Ker Tantony. My
mother says that Ker Tantony deserved his death, and I ought not
to be sorry for him, but he was my tutor, and I liked him, and I
know you would have saved him if you could.*

"Kethe," I muttered. I figured my face was probably as red as my hair
by now.

"Florian is an idealist," Mehitabel said.

"A what?" I said and then winced.

But she took it in stride. "Someone who always thinks the best of people. I fear in this case Keria Gauthy comes nearer the truth."

"Sounds like you didn't much care for Ker Tantony," I said, half-
expecting to get my head snapped off for it.

But she just made a face. "No, I didn't. But he was very good in bed."

"Oh," and Kethe, Milly-Fox, can't you say nothing better than that?

She gave me a wicked grin. "You don't think governesses should fornicate, Messire Foxe?"

"Mildmay," I said, mostly on reflex. "And you ain't really a governess anyway, are you?"

"What makes you say that?" she said, all light and good-humored but also just a little bit watchful.

"Dunno." I did know, but I didn't want to say it. There was the way she moved and the way she looked at people and the way she'd turned herself into Nobbie Wainwright on the way to Aiaia. She'd been playing a governess when we met her, but that wasn't what she was.

She looked like she wasn't real happy with my answer, so I said quick, "Was the fucking worth the not liking him?"

"It was better than not fucking at all. And there were advantages to having Jeremias Tantony as one's ally in the Gauthy household. He was the sort of man who knew how to get what he wanted. I suppose you could call us kindred spirits." And her smile got thin and kind of bitter.

"You wouldn't've taken Florian down into that maze," I said, because it was true, and she blinked but didn't say nothing, and then she just went back to the letter:

Ker Vilker says the Antiquarian Society is very excited about the labyrinth and are trying to convince Father to endow a lecture in Ker Tantony's memory.

"Keria Gauthy will never agree to that," Mehitabel said, mostly to herself, then looked up and skewered me before I was ready. "What was there between Ingvard and Felix?"

"Nothing," I said, and after all it was mostly the truth. But I said it too late and not quite casual enough. And she just gave me this look said as how she wasn't buying it, not even with a free pound of tea.

"I don't know," I said, which was also mostly true. "Felix won't talk about it." And that part at least was true all the way down.

Mehitabel just said, "Indeed," in a way I didn't much care for, and read:

I am very well and do not want you to worry about me. I hope that you are well, too. I am sad that I will probably never get to see you again.

"And he's signed it, *Your friend, Florian Gauthy*," Mehitabel finished and handed me back the letter. She watched me fold it and put it in my pocket. "Were you expecting bad news?"

"Um, no. Why?"

"You seemed anxious. I thought maybe . . ." She shrugged.

"Just embarrassed," I said before my mind could catch my mouth and get it to shut up.

"Embarrassed? Because you don't read Kekropian?"

"Can't really read Marathine either," I said, only it was a mumble, and I don't know how she understood me. It was nice of her not to pretend it was any big surprise. She just sort of nodded and said, "Well, I'm happy I could help." And then she gave me another one of her looks like a skewer. "Does Felix tease you about that?"

"Only a little." Keeper'd been way worse. She'd quit trying to teach me when it got obvious I was too stupid to learn, but she *never* quit bitching about it.

"God, he can be insufferable. Why do you put up with it? You don't have to, you know."

"Don't hurt me none."

"Are you sure?" she said, and before I could find an answer to that, she followed it up with an even worse poser: "He did something to you that night in Farflung. What was it?"

Powers and saints, I fucking near swallowed my tongue. She said, "I've traveled with the pair of you all the way across the Empire. I know something's changed, and I don't think it's for the better."

I didn't say nothing—Kethe, couldn't've said nothing if she'd offered me a septagorgon—and she leaned forward to touch my arm, almost the way you'd pat a skittish horse. "You don't have to tell me anything, but if I can help . . ."

"It ain't the sort of thing you can help with."

She frowned at me, a stern, teachery sort of look, and said, "Did he hurt you?"

Well, how the fuck was I supposed to answer that? Yes, but I asked him to? I said, lame as a three-legged cat, "No, he . . . he didn't do nothing to me."

You know, I wouldn't've bothered giving that an answer either. She just looked at me and next thing I knew, I was saying, "It's called the obligation d'âme, but it's okay. Really. It was my idea."

"I'm sorry. *What* was your idea?"

"The obligation d'âme." I said it slower that time, and she understood me.

"That doesn't sound like anything terribly pleasant."

"It ain't so bad, and it was the only thing we could do, anyway."

"The only thing you could do. Why?"

"I can't explain it."

"Then you had no business doing it."

"It's a spell, okay? And it binds us together. He protects me, and I . . . serve him." I almost couldn't get it out, but there was no sense trying to dress it up pretty. There's a reason the old word for the guy on my side of the bargain is *esclavin*. Slave.

"*Protect* you? From *what*?"

"Consequences," I said.

Felix

Gideon and I were discussing divination again when Mehitabel found us, her expression not merely stormy, but wrathful enough that I half expected to be hit by a bolt of lightning.

"Keria Parr," I said, not best pleased to be interrupted. "What may we do for you?"

"Tell me," she said, "about the obligation d'âme."

"I beg your pardon?"

"I asked Mildmay what you'd done to him, and he told me." She folded her arms and gave me an openly implacable glare.

"Oh," I said uselessly.

"So 'fess up, sunshine. What is it exactly that you *did*?"

"Nothing he didn't ask me to," I said and hated the sullenness I heard in my own voice.

"That's what *he* said, and I believe him. But just because he asked you to do it doesn't mean it was a good idea."

"I know that! But he didn't leave me much choice."

"No?"

Damn her for sounding so skeptical. Damn her for knowing me so well, so quickly.

"He said it was either that or watch him die."

"A stringent ultimatum, to be sure." And I damned her again for saying it exactly the way I would have if our positions had been reversed.

"He wouldn't leave!" And I realized only after I'd said it that I was on my feet and shouting.

Mehitabel Parr didn't even blink. "And what does that mean?"

I sat down, folded my hands stiffly. "I can't tell you Mildmay's secrets. But he said he would not leave me, and this is the only way he can stay with me without the risk—the near certainty of death."

"God, he just handed himself to you on a platter, didn't he?" Her tone was exhausted, disgusted, deeply cynical. "You're going to eat him alive and never even notice."

"I—"

"Isn't that what this 'obligation' does? Because that's certainly what it sounded like to me."

"I wouldn't—"

"Yes, you would."

"*I'm doing the best I can,*" I said and forced my hands to unclench from around each other.

"Then we will have to hope your best is good enough." She pinched the bridge of her nose and sighed. "Good night, gentlemen," and she was gone before I could muster a counterattack, leaving me alone with Gideon.

He regarded me thoughtfully for some moments before saying, :Isn't the obligation d'âme gross heresy?:

"Yes."

:Then how—:

"At the moment," I said and gave him a mirthless smile, "I am not a wizard of the Mirador. They stripped me of my rank and privileges directly after the Virtu was broken. Thus I am not bound to follow their laws, and, moreover, we are not in their jurisdiction. The act of casting the obligation d'âme is heresy, but they can't prosecute me for it. And if they want the Virtu mended—and I can guarantee that they do—they'll have to accept the fact of it."

:You seem awfully certain.:

"I was a member of the Curia for five years. I *am* certain."

:Is that why you did it?:

"What?" I said, although we both knew I'd understood him perfectly.

:You have every right to be . . . angry at what they did to you. And this seems to me a very cunning piece of blackmail. He did murder the Witchfinder Extraordinary, after all.:

I was assailed by a sudden burst of memory, like the punishing cacophony of a fireworks explosion. Mildmay, his eyes wide and his face white with pain, surrounded by a roiling, writhing cloud of black briars. The Mirador's curse. The curse that had lamed him. "Yes, I know," I said, and Gideon looked up sharply, hearing the waver in my voice.

:Felix?:

"I'm all right," I said although my voice was no steadier.

:What's wrong?: He leaned across the table to touch my hand. I looked at the delicate bones of his fingers, the sallowness of his skin, the contrast against my own pallor and the brightness of my tattoos.

He jerked back as if I'd burned him just with my gaze. :I'm sorry. I didn't think . . .:

I looked at him and discovered in his face something that, in retrospect, I knew I should have expected to find.

"Gideon?" I said.

He flushed a miserable red. :Truly, I am sorry. I didn't mean . . .:

It was so easy to reach across the table, to tilt his chin up with one finger. So easy to read the desire and fear and embarrassment in his eyes. So easy to smile, to see his face light up in return, to lean across the table and kiss him.

For a moment he seemed petrified, and then his lips parted eagerly against mine, and I felt the soft, shy touch of his fingers stroking my hair.

I broke the kiss, leaning back, and was pleased when he neither protested nor attempted to claim the initiative. He merely looked at me, his wide eyes dark as night, and I could see that he was breathing a little faster than he had been. I knew, without having to ask, or even wonder, that he would be a compliant, submissive lover, as eager to please in bed as he was intransigent normally. He would not try to take before I was prepared to give, would not crowd me as Ingvard had done.

I smiled at him again, putting every ounce of charm I had into it, and said, "Shall we find somewhere more private?"

He looked away, clearly ashamed of his own reaction, but nodded.

"Good. Wait here a moment." I had no fear that I would be disobeyed.

Mildmay was in our room, lying staring at the ceiling with his hands interlaced behind his head.

"Out," I said.

He sat up. "Sorry?"

"Out. Go tell Mehitabel some more of your life story if you want."

"Oh, powers. She didn't—"

"Yes, she did, and right now I don't want to discuss it with either her *or* you. *Out.* I'll tell you when you can come back." And it took only a featherlight touch on the obligation d'âme to convince him I meant it. He fled—for all his dour stone face, he was ridiculously easy to hurt—and I went to fetch Gideon, knowing I was being cruel and in that moment not caring.

Gideon was waiting, anxiety clear in the stiffness of his posture and the frown line between his eyes. "Come on," I said. "Our room is free."

He stood up, still anxious. :Mildmay?:

"Taking a walk," I said and smiled at him reassuringly. "We won't be interrupted."

He colored and looked away. :I'm sorry. It has been a long time since I've had any part in this sort of . . .:

"Exploit," I suggested and got a small smile. "Look—don't worry. And don't apologize, either. Just come to bed."

It was a calculated risk, and it paid off splendidly. He seemed stunned momentarily, but then his answering smile transformed him nearly into the beautiful boy he must once have been, and he came willingly around the table and into my arms.

I kissed him quickly, as a promise, then guided him to the bedroom, where I shut and locked the door behind us. For once, I did not need elaborate explanations or persuasions to convince my lover to blow out the candles; Gideon, an easy fifteen years my senior, was no more eager to be seen in good light than I was.

We undressed in the dark, and when I touched him, he was shivering.

"What? What's the matter?"

:Nothing.: A shaky, soundless not-quite laugh. :It's just—it has been a *very* long time.:

I answered him mind-to-mind, as he had to speak to me. :We don't have to—:

:*No!*: With unexpected force, and his hands were gripping mine tightly. :I've wanted you quite desperately since the first time I saw you, but I never believed, never *imagined* . . . I'm not going to back away now.:

I had more power over him even than I had thought—and I had an unwelcome memory of Mehitabel saying, *He just handed himself to you on a platter, didn't he?* I pushed it away. Gideon had been there, too. Gideon had heard Mehitabel's scathing indictment of my character, and the fact that he was here with me now . . .

I bent my head and kissed him carefully, lingeringly. He was as responsive as he had been before, and when my tongue slipped into his mouth, into that emptiness the Aiaians had created, he made a noise deep in his throat that was half gasp, half sob, and his hands came up to clutch at my shoulders so tightly I was afraid he would leave bruises.

I guided him backwards to find the bed, pushed him down gently. He went willingly; the only protest he made was when I moved my mouth away from his, and that was more of a sob. :Please.:

:Please, what?: I asked, teasing, testing.

:*Please.*: His hands found my face, and he dragged me down into another kiss, his mouth open, begging.

I gave him my tongue again; we kissed fiercely, languorously, while my hands explored his body, all ribs and hipbones under dense curly hair. His erection was already hard with need when my fingers found it. A few strokes had his hips rocking, and then I plunged my tongue into his mouth and tightened my grip, and his climax arched him off the bed like a bow. He had not been lying when he said it had been a long time.

I kissed him through the aftermath, and he clung to me with mouth and hands. He might have been crying; in the darkness I could not tell, and I did not care to know. I could leave him some privacy, some remnant of pride.

After a while, he said, his voice dry and calm, as if by force of will he could deny his body's abject capitulation to my control, :I believe the correct expression is, 'Turnabout is fair play.' What do you want me to do?:

:You know what I want,: I said, letting my fingers slip between his thighs.

:Yes.: A shiver, quickly repressed.

:You don't have to,: I said, as my fingers traced a slow path along scrotum and perineum.

:I want to,: he said stubbornly and then made a tiny, needy moan as my fingers found and caressed what they sought.

:Perhaps you do, at that,: I said and let him hear my amusement. :Roll over.:

He did, still obedient, and I left the bed briefly to find the herbal oil that Mildmay used to keep the scarred skin of his leg pliant. I'd observed weeks ago that it was well suited to other functions, but had not expected to have the chance to prove it.

I lay down beside Gideon again and said aloud, possibly more for my benefit than his, "If you tell me to stop, I will."

Gideon made no reply. I uncorked the oil and began to make my preparations, trying not to pretend that this was Mildmay's body beneath my hands, Mildmay's back arching with pleasure, Mildmay's breath catching in that little sigh. Gideon's body, half-starved and middle-aged, was nothing like Mildmay's; there was no difficulty except in my own useless desire for what I could not have.

And Gideon was beautifully responsive, delighted, coming to this pleasure almost like a surprised virgin.

:Has no one ever bothered to make this good for you before?: I asked.

:Not like this,: he said and moaned—a soft noise, but the loudest I had heard him make since we had met again in Julip.

I thought of Malkar, who always preferred sex to be accompanied by pain—mine, not his. And I thought of Shannon, and even of some of the patrons of the Shining Tiger, who had cared enough to go about this activity properly. And I was finally able to forget Mildmay in my desire to give Gideon pleasure. He climaxed again before I was done, and from the stunned undertones to his postcoital comments, I could tell that not only had he not expected to, he hadn't believed it was possible.

Maybe that was something I could do, I thought, kissing Gideon one last time before I got up to find Mildmay and tell him he could come to bed. I could give him pleasure in return for everything I took.

Mildmay

Before you ask, yeah, I knew what they'd been doing. I would've had to be deaf and blind to miss it. And I know what sex smells like.

Poor Gideon couldn't even look me in the eye. I wanted to tell him it was okay—I knew how he felt about Felix, and it had only ever been a matter of time before Felix figured it out. And it wasn't like I had any problem with the two of them fucking if that was what they wanted to do. But I couldn't think of a way to say it that wouldn't embarrass the fuck out of both of us and make everything about a septad times worse. So I just pretended not to notice as best I could and hoped that was what Felix wanted. I couldn't tell, and he wasn't giving me nothing.

Of course, he wasn't giving nobody nothing the next couple of days. He was pissed off at me and pissed off at Mehitabel, and the closer we got to Mélusine, the more like a Cabaline he acted. If we'd run into trouble crossing from Kekropia to Marathat—which we didn't—we could've sailed through on his brass alone.

There's this old law on the books in Mélusine about the ways hocuses can and can't enter the city. They have to declare themselves at whatever gate they come in through—no sneaking around not telling the Mirador they're back—and they have to come up the city openly. "No more gloves," Felix said, and I really think he would've burned his if me and Gideon hadn't convinced him to put them in a church donation box instead. He put his rings on like he was daring somebody to try and stop him.

The law don't say nothing about how the hocuses travel, but Felix told me there was a tradition in the Mirador that you didn't walk unless you were in some kind of serious trouble. And he said, with a smile that scared the shit out of me, that he might be in that sort of trouble, but he wasn't about to admit he knew it. I didn't like to ask how much of the trouble was my fault.

So we hired horses from one of the livery stables along the Road of Chalcedony, out past Chalcedony Gate where it was starting to settle down to be just a road again. The ostler who came out to see what we wanted did a pantomime-perfect double take at Felix's tattoos, stammered, gulped, turned three different shades of red, and bolted like a rabbit to find the head ostler.

And I knew I was back in Mélusine.

We'd all done the best we could with clothes, although the secondhand shops in Julip and Farflung and Wassail were nothing to get excited about, especially compared to what you could find in the Engmond's Tor Cheaps, and that was another thing Felix was biting everybody's head off over. He had some kind of picture in his head about how he wanted us all to look— *Felix Harrowgate Entering the City* done by one of the flash painters in the Mirador if I had to guess—and it was driving him absolutely batfuck that he couldn't have it. I mean, everybody was decent, but we were all shabby and out-of-date and riding job-horses to boot.

And he was especially pissed off at me, riding up to Chalcedony Gate, because I was wearing black and he couldn't honestly tell me I shouldn't. No matter how much he wanted to.

I said as how the old stories weren't much use in dealing with the binding-by-forms, and they weren't. But one thing they were real clear about was that the annemer half of the thing, namely me, dressed in black. I think it was mostly meant to be instead of livery, so people would know they weren't dealing with an ordinary servant, but that's really just a guess. For all I could tell, it had some sort of important magical meaning, and anyway it was about the only fucking thing I knew about how I was supposed to behave.

So I'd sorted out plain black trousers and a plain, high-collared black coat, a plain black waistcoat and a plainer than plain unbleached linen shirt to wear under it, and black stockings with some seriously lumpy darns and a pair of black boots that were probably a septad older than me. And Mehitabel got into the spirit of the thing and found me a black ribbon so I could queue my hair back like a gentleman.

Kethe, the kids I grew up with would've been laughing so hard they puked.

Felix just about had a fit. But he couldn't argue with the part where it was what I was supposed to be wearing, and that pissed him off worse than anything else.

Of course, I don't know why he bothered getting so worked up over it. The guards at Chalcedony Gate weren't looking at nothing but him and his tattoos and his spooky skew eyes. They knew who he was. You could see it as loud as if they'd said it. I laid a private bet with myself that they'd be sending a boy up to the Mirador as hard as he could run. If he was fast and smart, he'd be there well before we were, and the Mirador would have time to decide what they wanted to do about it.

That wasn't no nice thought, and I wished I hadn't had it.

I'd been trying all that morning not to look at the Mirador, but we came through Chalcedony Gate and it just hit me right between the eyes like a fucking crowbar. I don't know if I can explain how it was. I mean, I don't like the Mirador. They burned my friend Zephyr, and there ain't been a single thing in my life that's been better for the Mirador being a part of it. But then the Mirador sure as fuck beats the alternative, that being the Bastion and the Empire and being ruled by greedy fuckers like the Duke of Aiaia. The Bastion would've burned Zephyr just like the Mirador, only they would've taken all day about it.

And the Mirador itself—the fortress, I mean, with its towers and walls and banners and gates. It was just *there*. It had always been there. For me and for everyone I knew and their parents and their parents' parents, all the way back farther than I could count, maybe farther than I could even imagine. I could remember staring at it when I was a little kid, trying to make out the pictures on the banners and bugging the shit out of Nikah to tell me what they all meant. And the Mirador looked the same then as it looked in pictures from ten Great Septads ago, and the same as it looked ten indictions later when I was going up the city to kill Cerberus Cresset, the Witchfinder Extraordinary.

But that wasn't how it looked now.

It was like the difference between an ugly old man and his corpse a decad and a half later when the resurrectionists dig it up.

And I don't got the words to explain how fucking *wrong* it was, seeing the Mirador like that, all scorched and sooty, and with its roofs still only half-mended because, powers, it had fucking *acres* of roofs and I didn't like to think about how many days in the indiction the roofers wouldn't be able to go up, even with the best will in the world.

And I knew it was my imagination, but I felt like there was still smoke hanging over the city, like I would still taste ashes if I breathed too deep.

I kept on following Felix, because that was what I did now. But no matter how hard I tried, I couldn't stop staring at the Mirador, and even when I managed to drag my head around to look at something else, I couldn't stop fucking *seeing* it. So I was only sort of noticing all the people coming to gawk at us, thieves and citizens and peddlers like a bunch of fucking pigeons, and I hoped there was a thief-keeper or two out there with the sense the powers gave a pineapple, because it seemed like *somebody* should be getting some good out of this.

I hate being stared at, as I may have mentioned, and although mostly people were gaping at Felix—and he could not have been happier—I was riding right next to him and I had the matching hair and everything and I should have gone out and got my stupid self eaten by a ghoul before I let Mavortian nag me into stripping the dye out. Although at least nobody who'd known me knew my hair was red—except Keeper and oh blessed saints and merciful powers *please* don't let Keeper be in this crowd—so I supposed it meant people were less liable to recognize me, and that would be just fucking fine.

And I went right on supposing it until Rindleshin shouted my name.

We were almost out of the Lower City by then. Not close enough that I'd relaxed or nothing—although honestly I'd pretty much given up on relaxing anytime this side of the end of the world—but far enough up the city that the only person I was even a little bit expecting to hear was Cardenio, and that was mostly just wishing.

So at first I didn't even recognize the voice. I just turned and saw him and felt my lungs cramp up in my chest like I'd been punched.

I reckoned it up later, and it must've been one indiction and two-thirds of another since him and his pack chased me from the Corandina to Ver-Istenna's. And whatever they'd been doing since then, it hadn't been no fun and hadn't paid for shit, neither.

Rindleshin looked crazy. Skinny and dirty and sick, but mostly just crazy. The kind of crazy you can smell. He looked like those guys who stand on street corners in Engmond's Tor and Dragonteeth and shout at people passing by.

And right now he was shouting at me.

I could see a couple of his pack members behind him, and the guy must've had something going for him because fuck those kids were loyal. They didn't know how to stop him, because you could tell, clear as daylight, they would've if they did. They were only barely past their second septad, and they looked shit-scared. I didn't blame 'em. They couldn't've seen this coming any more than I had.

Rindleshin'd elbowed his way to the front of the crowd. He was still shouting and people were getting the fuck out of his way. Didn't blame them, neither. I was getting some words out of his yelling, "death" and "fire" and "hungry" and "motherfucker," enough to know that, yeah, Rindleshin and his pack had pretty much been fucked over the last indiction and a half, and what had him pissed off right now as well as crazy was me looking mostly okay and like I'd had a bath anytime in the last three months.

I wanted to lie down in the road and howl like a dog. Either that or smack Rindleshin upside the head and tell him to just fucking forget about me. I was not the fucking problem, and even crazy as a drunk flea, I thought he knew that. But all I could do was try to keep my horse collected—it didn't like Rindleshin, and I couldn't blame *it*, either—and pray kind of hopelessly for some way out of this fucking mess that wasn't me bleeding all over the Road of Chalcedony. And wondering how many other people I knew were in this kind of shape. How many people I knew had died.

Rindleshin was out in the road now, his knife in his hand, and if it'd been a throwing knife, I would've been dead already because I couldn't get my brains to work, couldn't get past how Rindleshin looked and the kids behind him and all the people along the road and the fucking Mirador up there like the world's worst wart, and I was so fucking *sorry* even though it wasn't my fault, and there was nothing I could do, and Rindleshin was shouting at me to get down off my fucking horse and face him, face him like a fucking man, and let's settle this, you fuck, right now, let's see who's really got the fucking balls—

Felix nudged his horse sideways, flash as could be, so he was between me and Rindleshin, and said, "I must ask you to leave my brother alone, or you will not like the consequences."

Kethe, never mind lying down or screaming or nothing. Right then I wanted to die. A nice plain apoplexy would do me just fine. Rindleshin was staring at Felix and staring at me, and then staring at Felix some more. And he wasn't the only one, neither. Eyes as big as bell-wheels all up and down the fucking road, and if this hadn't spread from one end of the Lower City to the other by the septad-night, I'd eat Felix's waistcoat, brass buttons and all.

Fuck me sideways, I thought in pure despair, and Rindleshin snarled at me like a dog and said, "Hiding behind a hocus now, Mildmay? Hope you're proud of yourself." Anybody else—anybody who wasn't completely crazy, I mean—would've backed off then. Made another couple cheap sneers, talked big, but, you know, got themselves the fuck off the road and into the crowd quick as they could without looking yellow. But Rindleshin, being—like I said—stark barking batfuck, ducked around Felix's horse and made a lunge at me with his fucking knife.

My horse, not being a fool, shied away pretty hard, and I was busy not getting dumped on my ass, never mind something fancy like reaching for the knife in my boot. But all the same, I saw what happened next.

Felix had turned, keeping his good eye on Rindleshin, and what happened was, he said something, just a word or two under his breath, and made this tiny nothing of a gesture with his left hand.

And Rindleshin screamed and dropped the knife.

Which hit the ground and lay there, the wooden hilt smoking a little and the blade glowing red.

And Felix said, mild as mild, "I *did* warn you."

Rindleshin screamed again and kind of staggered past me and into the crowd on the other side of the road. His pack kids gave each other this oh-powers-we're-so-fucked look and bolted after him.

I got my horse under control again and said to Felix, more or less under my breath, "Thought that was heresy."

The others bunched up with us in time to hear him say, "I cast a spell on the knife. It was entirely up to him whether he let go of it or not."

"Casuistry," Mavortian said. Which was a word I didn't know, but I figured I had a pretty good guess what it meant.

And all the more so when Felix gave him a smile fake as a gilt gorgon and said, "Nature of the beast, my dear Mavortian." Then he clucked at his horse, cool as if there weren't Kethe knows how many people watching, and started on up the road to the Mirador.

I followed him because there wasn't a fucking other thing in the world I could do. Between us, me and him, we'd seen to that.

Felix

I remembered the last time I'd been on this road, after Malkar had broken the Virtu, remembered being led along it on a rope like a wild animal. Probably, some of these same people had been watching then, jeering and shrieking and throwing things. They would have torn me apart limb from limb if Stephen had let them, and I could still taste their hatred, thick and cloying in the back of my throat.

It was a relief to be able to release some of that anger, even if it was only on a wretched creature like the boy who accosted Mildmay. It did not entirely exorcize my urge to burn the whole filthy gawking mob of them to ashes where they stood, but it made it possible to bear. Made it possible to keep my back straight and my expression pleasant, to behave like a wizard of the Mirador instead of the Pharaohlight whore I once had been.

I was aware of the others behind me, aware particularly of Mildmay in his self-decreed black, his face white and set and as expressive as a block of stone. I would have to ask him later about the boy who hated him, ask him about the history that lay between them. I knew so little about him; my long madness had given me trust but not knowledge.

We were approaching the Mirador: Livergate, where Mildmay had expected to be hanged and where I would be burned if I was not careful. I wondered what they would do to Mildmay then and thought bitterly that Mehitabel was right about me. Only the vilest and most egregious kind of selfishness could have made me agree to anything that would bring Mildmay within the Mirador's reach. The spikes above Livergate were a cruel reminder that his life now depended on mine, and it was by no means a foregone conclusion that I would live to see sunset tomorrow.

I did not know either of the guards on duty at the gate, which I decided to take as an auspicious sign. I was not ready to find out if those among the Protectorate Guard who had once been my friends were friends still, or foes—or even alive. These two were young, barely more than boys for all their hard expressions and long mustaches. I smiled at them and said, "My name is Felix Harrowgate. I seek an audience with the Lord Protector."

They were too young to be able to keep the surprise off their faces. They, like the guards at Chalcedony Gate, knew who I was—I was too easily described for it ever to be wise for me to assume otherwise—and they had obviously expected me to claim honors I no longer had any right to. That, they were prepared to deal with. Simple and relatively honest politeness left them baffled.

I smiled even more brilliantly and waited for them to find a course of action.

After a long, paralyzed moment, one of them said, "Yes, m'lord," only to jump quite visibly when his colleague's booted foot swung into his ankle. "I mean, yes, Mr. Harrowgate. And who are these people with you?"

I said, with bland disregard for the guards' widening eyes, "Mehitabel Parr, late of Klepsydra; Mavortian von Heber, a wizard of the Fressandran school, and his man-at-arms, Bernard Heber; Gideon Thraxios, a wizard of the Bastion granted asylum by the Curia; my brother, Mildmay Foxe." By the strict etiquette obtaining formerly to the obligation d'âme, I ought not to have introduced Mildmay at all; that, however, would involve me in explanations I had no desire to make, and in any event I was, in the old parlance, the obligataire. To a fairly large extent, the rules were what I chose to make them.

The guards gave each other an appalled look, and the same one, either braver or more foolhardy than his fellow—or simply more keenly aware that this tableau vivant had to be ended *somehow*—said, "Thank you, sir. I will go ask the Lord Protector his wishes in this matter."

To have me thrown in the Sim in a sack, no doubt. But I curbed my tongue, and the remaining guard and I, and those arrayed behind me, waited in silence to learn Lord Stephen's pleasure.

The fiacre drivers gaped at us as they drove past, but not more so than their passengers.

I had not replaced the watch that Shannon had given me and that I had lost somehow in the year of my madness; I would have scorned to consult it in any event. Malkar had taught me to play waiting games and to disregard the amount of time spent in waiting. It might have been anywhere from five minutes to half an hour before the first guard returned and bowed rather stiffly, saying, "His lordship will see you."

"Thank you," I said and dismounted. The others copied me, and we led our horses beneath the grim lintel of Livergate.

And it was only by the grace of the powers I did not believe in that I did not immediately stumble and fall to my knees. There was a sound in my head, a song. But I heard it, not with my ears, nor even with my mind as I heard Gideon's voice. I heard it with my blood, with my bones, with the magic that lay coiled within me like a nest of half-sleeping dragons. I heard it with the remnants of my madness that not even all the wisdom and care of the celebrants of the Gardens of Nephele had been able to eradicate, and it was through my madness that I recognized that mournful, broken little melody: the sound of the Virtu singing to itself.

My face must have been ghastly, for Mildmay caught my arm and said, "You okay?" in a tone of sharp concern.

"Fine," I managed, then took a deep breath and straightened, shaking him off. Now was not the moment to admit weakness. "I'm all right."

We both knew he didn't believe me for an instant, but he let it go, let me go, followed me unprotesting into the courtyard behind Livergate, where grooms flocked to take our horses, and Vida Eoline was waiting.

Tall, beautiful, imperturbably soignée, Vida had come to the Mirador from the far southern islands, as her ebony skin and malachite-green eyes attested. Her coldly, ruthlessly rational intellect meant that she and I had often been allies, less often friends. I did not think, looking at the grim set of her features, that we were friends now.

"Felix," she said.

"Lady Vida," I said and bowed deeply enough to be mocking.

Her lips thinned. "Your gall never ceases to amaze me. Why are you here?"

"To speak to Stephen. Did that nice young man not say so?"

"Don't play games. Why are you here?"

I smiled at her. "To mend the Virtu."

It threw her, the only thing I could have said that would. A declaration of undying love would not have fazed her in the slightest; she would have known I did not mean it. This, she knew I meant.

She gave me a searching, almost anxious look. "Do you really think you can?"

"Yes," I said with a confidence I did not entirely feel. If I was going to fail, it was not going to be before I even got within sight of the Virtu.

She stared at me a moment longer and then nodded; we were allies again. "Follow me."

I gathered the others with a look, and we followed Vida into the Mirador.

Mildmay

Kethe. Like being stuck in a fucking nightmare. I mean, I was *in* the Mirador. The only other time I'd been in the Mirador, it was to kill Cerberus Cresset. And I kept thinking about Zephyr. He'd died just outside Livergate, burning, screaming, choking on his own fucking ashes if you want to get morbid about it, which—I was there, so, yeah, I guess I kind of do. And I felt like I should've let them hang me or send me to the sanguette—they don't burn annemer, which is a pretty small fucking favor if you ask me—before I came in here, but I hadn't wanted to die and I still didn't want to die, and somehow that meant I'd ended up in the Mirador.

It's a strange fucking world, and mostly the joke's on us.

So I stuck to Felix like a leech, and we followed the black-skinned lady hocus through a maze of hallways like I'd never seen in my life. Even the Arcane had nothing on this shit, and I kept trying not to think about the maze in Klepsydra and not doing real well at it. And once it occurred to me how easy it would be for somebody to ambush us and stuff our bodies in one of them little rooms that nobody went into from one septad to the next, I couldn't stop thinking about *that,* either.

And Felix just kind of sauntered along like he owned the place, and even though I knew it was an act, it still made me want to smack him. And I guessed from the looks she kept giving him that the lady hocus felt the same.

And then the hallways kind of shook themselves straight around us, and we were coming up on a pair of huge fucking doors, and I had to swallow hard because I knew where we were. I knew what those doors were, and where they were from, and how many people had died to get them here. And I knew what was behind them was the Hall of the Chimeras, and if it'd been an option, I probably would have fainted dead away then and there.

But it wasn't an option, so I kept dogging Felix. Welcome to the rest of your life, Milly-Fox.

Felix told the others to stay in the back, unless they had particular business they wanted to bring up with the Lord Protector, which none of them did. Then he gave me a kind of come-along jerk of the head, and I followed him down the Hall of the Chimeras.

There are paintings of the Hall of the Chimeras. So I knew what it looked like. I knew about the ten-septad-foot vault, and the banners, and the chimeras laid in the floor. I knew about the dais down at the end of the hall and Lord Michael's Chair on it and the Virtu. But the paintings, well, they were just paint on canvas or plaster or what have you. They didn't do a thing to show how it really was. They missed out on all the really important stuff, like how our feet echoed, or how all the flashies and hocuses stood and stared at Felix so I couldn't decide if they were cats staring at a mouse or mice staring at a cat. And the paintings particularly missed out on how fucking dark it was and how heavy the dark was pressing down out of all that space. It took a real effort to keep my shoulders straight. And powers and saints, the Virtu was just smashed to bits.

Felix did that, I thought. I couldn't get my head around it. I mean, it wasn't that I didn't know he was a hocus, and it wasn't that I didn't know he was powerful. But the Virtu was the Virtu. Was supposed to be the Virtu. Not this ugly, spiky lump of glass. And the idea that *Felix* had done it—Kethe, I thought, I should be scared out of my mind just to be standing next to him.

But I looked at him sideways, and oh shit he had that look in his eyes again, the one that said as how he saw a chance to cause trouble and was just loving the fuck out of it, and I was so pissed off I couldn't be scared. Leastways, not of him.

What I *was* scared of was the guy on the dais, sitting there watching us get closer with a look on his face fit to curdle milk. I'd only ever seen Lord Stephen Teverius close-to once before, and that had been in the middle of trying to get the fuck away from him. He was a big guy, bull-necked. Looked a little like something carved out of really hard stone by somebody who wasn't much good at it. And then you got a look at his eyes, and none of the rest of it mattered. Gray eyes, cold and hard, kind of like being stabbed. I couldn't breathe the whole time he was looking at me, even though I knew he was really thinking about Felix. And when Lord Stephen looked at Felix, I did, too, and Felix had this little smirk on his face that I would've counted as grounds for murder. I remembered, from a couple indictions and what felt like three lifetimes ago, the gossip about him and Lord Stephen hating each other, and I couldn't help looking at Lord Shannon.

Now, Felix had said, and said like he meant it, that it was over between the two of them. And I'd been relieved that I wasn't going to have to figure out how to talk to the Golden Whelp, or even just how to be in the same fucking room with him. I hadn't thought about it much further than that. But the way Lord Shannon was staring at Felix said as how he'd never expected to see *this* Felix again, the one who had all his shit together and was sharp enough to cut diamonds. Lord Shannon'd ditched the madman—and I guess you can't even blame him, really, although I can't forgive him for it, neither—but only on the understanding that the hocus wasn't coming back.

And in a nasty, petty sort of way, it even made me feel better to see that look on his face and know there was one person in the Hall of the Chimeras who felt worse than I did. Nice, Milly-Fox. Real fucking nice.

I remembered Lady Victoria, too, but there wasn't no more showing on her face than there was on Lord Stephen's. She was looking at Felix like she'd never seen him before in her life. And next to her on the dais was a guy I didn't know, tall and skinny and near as pale as me, wearing a black tabard worked in scarlet and gold with Tibernia's leopards—his face perfectly blank, like he practiced that expression a lot. So Vusantine had their claws in Lord Stephen. No fucking wonder, and I figured they probably had some fancy word they were using instead of "spy."

Felix stopped a little less than a septad-foot from the dais and bowed. And gave me a glance sideways, so I bowed, too. Because the obligation d'âme said I shouldn't unless he told me to. Felix hadn't showed any signs of wanting to bring that up with anybody, and I didn't want to, neither. Fuck, did I not want to have to explain that. Or listen to Felix explain it, for that matter. So I bowed, and Lord Stephen ignored me, and said to Felix, only just loud enough for Felix to hear him and not loud enough to carry to the rest of the court, "I wasn't expecting to see *you* again."

"I know," Felix said, just as quiet. "But you should have known I'd come back if I could."

"Like a bad centime. What are you doing here, Felix?" He sounded tired and resigned and pissed off all at once, and I had to wonder about the bad history between them, because from the sound there was a fuck of a lot of it.

"I want to be reinstated," Felix said.

"And we're all very flattered, I'm sure," Lord Stephen said. "But considering what you did when you *were* a wizard of the Mirador, I'd really like to know why you think we ought to want you back."

"I can mend the Virtu."

Lord Stephen's eyebrows went up. "That's quite a claim."

"I broke it. Why shouldn't I be able to mend it?"

"As I recall, you said *Malkar* broke it. Are you changing your story?"

"No," and I wanted to tell Felix not to snarl at the Lord Protector, but I didn't dare open my mouth or even look like I could hear what they were saying. "But it was *my* power. Besides, Malkar would never make you this offer, not if you threatened to have him burned."

"I could have *you* burned," Lord Stephen said, like he was thinking maybe it wasn't a bad idea.

"You could, but what good would it do?"

Lord Stephen bared his teeth. "It would be extremely satisfying."

"My lord, let me *try* first. If I can't mend the Virtu, then you can go ahead and burn me with my good wishes. I'll even light the pyre myself. But give me this chance first."

"Redemption, Felix? Somehow I hadn't thought you'd care."

"Call it what you want. But let me try. No one here can mend it, or you would have done it already. So what do you have to lose?"

"Don't ask me that question." Lord Stephen glared at Felix, and Felix lifted his chin and glared right back.

And Lady Victoria said, cold as a dead fish on ice, "You have to consult the Curia first, Stephen, no matter what your decision."

"Powers, do you think I don't know that?" The glare went from Felix to Lady Victoria without missing a beat. "But it *is* my decision, Vicky. I'm the one it falls on."

Felix coughed slightly. Lord Stephen and Lady Victoria ignored him. "You should at least ask the Curia if it *is* possible," Lady Victoria said. "For myself, I doubt it, but I do not know."

"The Curia won't know, either," Felix said, and that got the glare back at him in a hurry.

"Enough!" Lord Stephen snapped. "All right. Clearly you're going to hound me until I either let you do what you want or have you killed."

Felix bowed again, even deeper.

"I'll convene a meeting of the Curia," the Lord Protector said, looking and sounding like a baited bear. "And don't think the threat to have you burned is an idle one."

"My lord," Felix murmured, "I know it is not."

Felix

I had never imagined, when I was a member of the Curia, that there could be circumstances under which I would be glad to see the Lesser Coricopat again. But I could not pretend that the feeling of homecoming was anything other than what it was.

I had told Mildmay to stay with the others and see about getting rooms for them, and about getting my old rooms back. He'd given me a rather baleful look but hadn't argued. Neither one of us wanted him in this room with me now, and he knew it as well as I did.

The Curia sat around that long oval of polished and carved cherrywood, their hands folded, rings gleaming, eyes hooded and watchful. I stood where any petitioner to the Curia would stand, at the foot of the table. Unlike most petitioners, I had sufficient sangfroid to look Giancarlo in the eye.

"Felix Harrowgate," he said, his voice rolling like thunder out of his chest. "I understand that you are petitioning the Lord Protector for reinstatement as a wizard of the Mirador."

"Yes, my lord," I said.

There was a little murmur of shock and disapproval around the table. Giancarlo and I ignored it.

"And I trust that *you* will understand," he continued, "that the Curia feels a certain amount of skepticism about this proposed plan."

"Yes, my lord," I said, and although there was nothing I could do about the blush I felt heating my face, I would be damned if I dropped my gaze.

"Put plainly, Mr. Harrowgate, there are too many questions remaining unanswered from the circumstances of your . . ." He hesitated fractionally. "Your disbarment."

"Yes, my lord." And some of those questions were mine, but they were not questions that could be posed here.

"We must have answers, Mr. Harrowgate, before we can contemplate your petition."

"I understand, my lord."

"We must have answers," said Agnes Bellarmyn, whom I had always hated, "before we can decide whether to carry through on your death sentence."

"Oh, did you sentence me to death?" I said, with my best tone of bright interest. "I'm afraid my memories of my trial aren't too clear. Since I was mad at the time."

As an admission of weakness, I hated it. As a weapon, it worked admirably. Agnes's bosom swelled with wrath, but I saw winces from some of the other wizards around the table—Istrid von Kulp, Hamilcar Nashe, Lindsay Bethonius, wizards who had not made a lifelong hobby of opposing me. Agnes was a lost cause; it was these other wizards I had to convince.

"Your sentence was suspended until such time as we could understand what you had done," Giancarlo said. "A matter that is still very much a mystery, Mr. Harrowgate."

"It isn't what *I* did," I said. "It's what Malkar used me to do."

"Yes, that's your story, isn't it?" Agnes, sneering, the mouthpiece as always for Robert of Hermione. Robert was one of the people I had questions for, but it was just as well he did not sit on the Curia. I might hate Agnes, but that was nothing compared to my loathing for Robert and his for me.

"It is the truth," I said, keeping my voice quiet, calm. "I can't help it if it isn't what you want to hear."

"All we have ever asked of you is the truth," Giancarlo said, perhaps a touch sadly. Giancarlo would have liked to have been my mentor when I had first come to the Mirador, but that was something I had only realized years later. At the time, raw from Malkar's teaching, scared to death that I would betray what he had taught me so carefully to conceal, I had seen Giancarlo only as another threat.

"I will tell you the truth," I said.

"You had better," muttered Johannes Hilliard, another of my foes.

"Lords and ladies of the Curia," I said, letting my voice open out, "my purpose in returning to the Mirador is simple. I believe I can mend the Virtu. All I ask is the chance to try."

It stunned them, as it had stunned Vida. It had not stunned Stephen only because he was annemer and did not truly understand what the task entailed. And hard-minded Vicky had simply not believed me.

I dropped my voice again, said, "But I cannot touch the Virtu if I am not a wizard of the Mirador, if my oaths are not recognized. Please. Ask me your questions. Give me this chance to redeem myself." Stephen's word, and a bitter shard of irony, but it was language even Agnes would understand. In truth, to me, it was not a matter of my redemption; that was, so to speak, past praying for. It was a matter of restitution, but also of rebellion: it was not what Malkar would want.

Giancarlo was the first to recover. He cleared his throat, fussed with his papers, and said, "We believe we understand, in broad outline at least, what Malkar Gennadion did to the Virtu. What we do not understand is what he did to you."

I did not think I entirely hid my flinch. "I beg your pardon?"

"How was he able to put a compulsion on you?" Marius Thatcher broke in. "How did he circumvent the Virtu's protections *before* he broke it?"

"Oh," I said, and did not let my voice shake or become shrill with relief. If that was what they wanted to know, I would not have to describe to them how Malkar used me in the destruction of the Virtu, how he had raped me and driven me mad. This was nothing by comparison, although I knew that the person I had been two years ago would not have thought so.

But then that person, poor silly fool, had thought he had escaped from Malkar for good.

I took a deep breath, said, "I was apprenticed to Malkar when I was fourteen." A statement as much lie as truth, for I knew what these wizards would understand when I said the word "apprentice" and it was nothing, *nothing* like what Malkar had made of me. "I did not then understand the teachings of the Cabal, so I did not understand that what he did was wrong."

"Mr. Harrowgate, you are not on trial for heresy," Giancarlo said. "All we ask is an explanation."

"Yes, my lord. He . . . he cast spells on me."

It was hard to say, partly because it was heresy, partly because Malkar had taught me so brutally never to speak of these matters, partly because what Malkar had done to me was not so different from what I had done to Mildmay in Farflung. Not so different? In all honesty, very much the same. And the wizards all gasped and murmured, like startled doves. I could feel something slowly shredding itself within me at how innocent they were, at how little of what Malkar had done to me they would be able to comprehend, even if I were able to describe it to them. I found that I did not want to hurt them by showing them their own blindness; this was all in the past, anyway, and it would do me no good to shock them with it.

"I don't know what all of them were," I said, and that at least was true. Malkar had not explained himself to me, and by the time I had learned enough to put together what I remembered with what I had read, I was much too afraid of him to ask. "And I thought I had rid myself of all of them before I took my oaths, but . . ." I shrugged helplessly. "It would seem that I was wrong."

"Can you describe these spells in greater detail?" Giancarlo said, although he sounded as if he was ashamed of himself for pressing me.

I hesitated. "Not in any way that would be of help to you. Lord Giancarlo, if I knew how he had done it, I would tell you."

"I believe that you would," Giancarlo said. I felt slightly sick at the knowledge of my own deception, of the obligation d'âme chaining me to Mildmay, but if I confessed it now, they would not reinstate me, and I would not be able to mend the Virtu.

Malkar had taught me the value of only answering the question asked.

"Mr. Harrowgate," said Lindsay Bethonius, "did Malkar Gennadion habitually commit heresy, to your knowledge?"

"He was not Cabaline," I said, "and he did not consider it heresy. But, yes."

They muttered darkly to one another, and I bit the inside of my lower lip, hard, to keep from either shrieking with laughter or giving them the catalogue of the spells Malkar had cast on me that I *could* identify—and cast in my turn.

"Mr. Harrowgate." Lord Selewine, a contemporary of Giancarlo's, a gentle, good-natured old man with an enormous white mustache. "Do you truly believe you can, ah, restore the Virtu to its former state?"

"My lord, I believe I can."

"Which is more than any of us can say," Vida remarked, speaking for the first time. She looked up and down the table. "What do we have to lose?"

"You can't be serious!" Agnes, with all the predictability of a striking clock.

"I'm deadly serious, Agnes," Vida said. "If Felix thinks he can do it, I think we should let him try."

"We have no assurance that this isn't some new trick of Gennadion's," Johannes Hilliard said.

"You have *my* assurance," I said, and he sneered back at me.

"Mr. Harrowgate has less reason to love Malkar Gennadion than any of us," Giancarlo said. He heaved his breath out in something between a sigh and an exasperated snort. "At its simplest the question is: do we believe Felix or not? If we do, then Vida is right. If we don't . . ." He gave me a slow, thoughtful look under his bushy eyebrows.

"If you don't, you might as well carry out that death sentence," I said. "Or exile me to the Myrian Mountains. You won't be able to let me stay here."

"Thank you, yes." Giancarlo collected the other twelve wizards' attention without apparently moving a muscle. "Does anyone have any reasoned arguments against reinstating Felix Harrowgate as a wizard of the Mirador?"

He was a better diplomat than I; he did not stress the word "reasoned."

"How can we?" said Johannes. "We haven't even had time to think. And if you were expecting to have him show up again, Giancarlo, then you must have known something I didn't."

"It is not a complicated question, Johannes."

"But one with very complicated consequences," said Lord Selewine.

"The Virtu won't get *more* broken if you allow the Curia members a day to consider," Hamilcar Nashe said reasonably, and my heart sank.

"That seems fair," Giancarlo said, and I did not say anything because it *was* fair, and my protests would serve only to alienate those members of the Curia who were suspicious but not yet hostile.

I held my tongue and looked pleasant.

There were murmurings of agreement around the table, and when Giancarlo put it to a vote, it passed unanimously.

We would reconvene at two o'clock the following afternoon, and until then, all I had to do was keep from exploding with frustration and pent-up truth.

Mildmay

The Mirador's servants looked at me like I was a two-headed carny freak.

It was the accent mostly—well, and the hair and the scar and me riding in at Felix Harrowgate's tail and all. They knew what I was, and I got to say I didn't care for it, being looked at like I was one of them big Queensdock alley cats—the kind that mostly think people are just really big rats—dropped in the middle of a bunch of house cats. Like I had fleas and probably a septad really nasty diseases.

And those were the ones that would look at me at all.

I let Mehitabel do the talking.

They looked at her a little funny, too, but, I mean, a perfectly nice Kekropian lady or an alley cat? Which would *you* pick?

So she got rooms for her and Gideon and Mavortian and Bernard, and if she thought like I did that Gideon probably wouldn't be using his room much, she didn't let it show. And she did way better than I would've with saying Felix wanted his old rooms back and not making it sound like he'd just assumed they'd been saved for him. Which, if she'd said it, would've been the truth.

And it turned out they had been. I wasn't sure if it was because the Mirador was so fucking big that nobody'd noticed, or just that nobody'd wanted Felix's rooms. In the Lower City, moving into somebody's rooms who'd killed themselves or gone crazy or murdered their wife or something was the worst kind of bad luck and you didn't do it at all without you hired a priest to come and say a blessing. I didn't know if hocuses felt that way or not.

But anyway, nobody was using those rooms, and the head guy—Architrave was his name and he seemed decent enough—sent a couple of gals off to dust and air them out and everything. I almost asked how you aired out rooms in the middle of the fucking Mirador with no windows and Kethe only knows how much stone between you and actual daylight, but I figured the answer was magic and I didn't want to know.

And I was just wondering if there was somewhere I could sneak off to for an hour and just, I don't know, sit still and not have to worry about nothing, when Mavortian caught my eye and said, "We need to talk." And that answered that.

I'd done everything I could not to get stuck alone in a room with Mavortian since we'd made it out of Aiaia. There were too many things I didn't want to talk about with him, and I had this uneasy feeling, sort of like invisible caterpillars crawling up and down my spine, that Mavortian had things he wanted to say to me, and they weren't going to be things I wanted to hear.

But I couldn't tell *him* that, so I followed along to the room him and Bernard had been given and stood and watched while Mavortian got himself settled in the only chair and Bernard started unpacking.

I knew Mavortian was waiting, spinning out the silence to try and make me nervous. But I liked the silence better than whatever it was he was planning on saying, so I just propped myself against the wall and waited him out.

It pissed him off—which, I got to say about Felix, he never let it bother him when he tried something like that and it didn't work. He just tried something else. But Mavortian never liked admitting he was trying to play you, and he snapped at me, "Why did you let your brother cast the obligation d'âme on you?"

"Didn't," I said. "I asked him to."

Bernard had been pretending I wasn't there, but he turned around so quick he nearly fell on his ass. Mavortian went kind of gray and said, "What? *Why?*"

"I got my reasons," I said, and wished it had come out kind of no-nonsense instead of just sullen.

"Whatever he told you, Mildmay, you didn't have to do it."

"He didn't tell me nothing. I made the choice, nobody else." And sure, maybe it'd been a mistake, but that was part of the whole making-a-choice thing. And I thought about how I'd be feeling right about now if I was on the way to St. Millefleur, and I knew it might have been a bad decision, but it hadn't been a mistake.

I added, because they were both still staring at me and I was tired of everybody assuming everything was Felix's fault, "He tried to talk me out of it."

"Bet he didn't try very fucking hard," Bernard muttered.

You weren't there, you prick. But I wasn't going to give either one of them the satisfaction. I said to Mavortian, "What'd you want to talk about?" and, powers, I sounded like I was back at my second septad and Keeper'd been chewing me out for something that wasn't my fault. She did that a lot.

Mavortian leaned back and steepled his fingers and said, like it was all the information I should need: "Beaumont Livy."

No fucking surprise there. I waited.

He said, kind of half-snarling, "Your brother's purposes, while noble, get us no nearer my objective."

"Us?"

"I hired you."

"Yeah. Almost an indiction ago, and you ain't paid me enough to keep a cat alive." It was really satisfying watching him go red. He opened his mouth, but nothing came out right away, and I said, " 'Sides, you know about the obligation d'âme. You know what it means."

He went an even uglier color, and I realized that *he*'d known, but he hadn't thought I did. How fucking flat do you think I am? But I didn't say it. Didn't say nothing, and after a minute he looked at me and said, "I thought you understood."

"Understood what?"

He kept looking at me steadily. "I told you about Anna Gloria Pietrin."

"Yeah. So?"

I knew what he was trying to do, namely fuck me over without lifting a finger. But I've never been real keen on revenge, and it certainly wasn't no good reason to let Mavortian keep using me for free.

"I thought you understood," he said again, sad as a kicked puppy.

"Try it on Bernard," I said, and Bernard gave me a glare that could've melted glass. "Look. Things have changed. I work for Felix now, so anything about Beaumont Livy, you'll have to take up with him. Was that all you wanted?"

"Get out," Mavortian said, and he didn't have to tell me twice.

Out in the hall, I figured I didn't really want to talk to Mehitabel, and there wasn't no point in me trying to talk to Gideon, so I might as well go see if the maids were done with Felix's rooms and if maybe he was back yet. Down to the end of the hall, turned left, and slammed into a little guy in livery carrying a stack of cravats. I just barely kept my feet—and it felt like someone'd run a red-hot wire through my leg—and the little guy ended up on his ass with cravats all around him like big dead leaves.

"Powers, I'm sorry," I said and offered him a hand up. "I didn't hear you—"

I ran out of voice. Because the little guy looked up, and it was Jean-Tigre. I went back a step without meaning to, and my bad leg just went out from under me, and I thumped back against the wall.

Jean-Tigre had run from Keeper just after I finished my second septad. And I'd known he was going and not said nothing, although Keeper would have skinned me alive if she'd caught on. And then it had been like he'd fallen off the face of the world. Not in a pack, not in a brothel, not in a guild. I'd figured he was dead.

But here he was, in the Mirador, in fucking livery. And I'd just knocked him flat.

I'd heard about the Mirador being this way—about how coincidences fucking collected in the hallways—but I'd never imagined it happening to me. And that'd been dumb, but, you know, that was pretty much business as usual these days.

Jean-Tigre pulled himself together first, although his face was as white as the cravats he was picking up. He said in a voice like frozen rain, "I beg your pardon, sir," and looked straight through me like I wasn't fucking there.

I may be dumb, but I can take a fucking hint. I got my bad leg back to where I needed it, went around Jean-Tigre, and headed off down the hall.

And no matter how much I wanted to, I didn't step on none of them nice white cravats.

౫౬

Powers and saints, Felix was pissed off when he showed up. You could feel it coming off him like heat off an oven or stink off a skunk. He said in this tight, cold, furious voice, "The Curia requires twenty-four hours to make up what it claims to be its mind," and slammed into his bedroom like a bear with a sore ass.

I stayed where I was.

I'd had time to myself to explore. He had a big sitting room shaped like a blocky L. The fat end had a fireplace—and I swear to all the powers the thing was big enough to roast an ox—and bookcases along the walls, and a couple of big chairs, old and singed here and there but comfortable. The other end of the room had a big, dark lion-footed table with chairs to match. It was hard to imagine eating off it, but the big sterling teapot in the center said as how that was exactly what Felix did.

The long wall behind the table had two doors. One was to Felix's bedroom, where he had a four-poster Keeper would've envied and two wardrobes big enough that either one could've swallowed me whole. I didn't open them. Figured I'd be getting an eyeful of Felix's clothes soon enough.

The other door off the sitting room was to a narrow little room like a closet with big ideas. I don't know what Felix had used it for before, but Mr. Architrave had had them set up a bed in it, and I guessed that meant it was going to be my bedroom. Which was a huge fucking relief because I'd figured on a lot of nights spent trying to sleep on one of the armchairs while Felix fucked Gideon. And it don't matter how comfortable an armchair is. You're going to wake up with a cramp.

So I'd made the rounds and settled in one of the armchairs where I could stare at the fire and wait for Felix. It seemed safer than going anywhere or trying to guess if Felix would want me to do anything.

Or, to put it another way, I was too fucking scared to move.

So I was glad when Felix showed up, even if he was in a mood to bite a gator. I mean, I was still in the Mirador, but at least I wasn't alone.

He came slamming back out a few minutes later and said, "Where did they put the others?"

"Mehitabel on the Grand-West, and Mavortian and Bernard on the, um, Filigree Corridor. Mr. Architrave said you'd know where that was."

"Indeed. I must remember to thank Master Architrave. And he is *Master* Architrave, not *Mister*."

"Okay," I said, and he shot me this look I'd seen from Keeper so many times I had it fucking memorized: *I know you're stupid, but TRY not to embarrass me, okay?* And, powers and saints, I hated it just as much from Felix as I ever had from Keeper.

Then he said, sharp and brisk-like, "Come on. I want to find company for dinner." And somehow I didn't think he meant Mehitabel and Gideon.

"What're you gonna tell 'em? About me?"

"That you're my brother."

"But—"

"Not until they've reinstated me." And he gave me a smile that had way too many teeth in it. "Not until it's too late."

ᔓᔓ

So I followed him. What the fuck else was I going to do?

I would've thought we walked all over the Mirador looking for the "company" Felix wanted, except that I knew we probably hadn't even covered a tenth of it. It was hard to keep in your head all at the same time how big the Mirador was, and I wondered how anybody could live here and not go completely fucking insane. And then I realized I wasn't sure they *weren't* all crazy, and I tried to think of something else instead of wondering how long it was going to take me to start barking. Didn't have much luck.

Felix told me the names of all the hallways and rooms we went through, kind of over his shoulder like he didn't care whether I heard him or not. I figured, like the old joke says, I needed all the help I could get, so I listened hard enough to give myself a headache.

We passed groups of people here and there, hocuses, flashies, some groups of both, musicians, an artist painting a portrait by candlelight. Felix marched right on past them with barely even a look. He finally found the people he was after in a long room with a barrel vault so low it was walls as well as ceiling. It was a nice room, though, with warm red tiles on the floor and the big grown-up brother of Felix's table down the center. The people there were all hocuses wearing the Mirador's gold sash, and I wasn't a bit surprised.

"The Seraphine," Felix muttered to me and walked in like a parade.

It took a moment before they noticed him, and then everybody got real quiet all at once, except for a big red-faced hocus with gray hair who kept talking into the silence until he realized nobody was listening to him. Then he turned around and saw Felix, and then he was being real quiet, too.

"Well?" Felix said. "Isn't anyone going to lie and say how glad you are to see me?"

Fuck me sideways, I thought and only just kept myself from saying it out loud.

They gave each other these little sidelong looks, and I could see they knew as well as I did that when Felix was in this sort of mood, you'd flap your arms and fly to Vusantine sooner and easier than you'd find the right thing to say. Their expressions went from scared to embarrassed to actually guilty, and I realized these were Felix's friends.

Or had been.

Powers, Felix, can't you be nice just once when it would do you some good? But he couldn't. It wasn't how he was built, and he'd said as much himself. I wanted to strangle him, and I also wanted to just sit down and cry.

Finally, one of them, a lady hocus with a round face and bright brown eyes, figured that somebody had to say *something*, and said, "Hello, Felix." I admired her guts more than her common sense.

"Fleur," he said, and it was that purring voice that made me feel sick. "I'm so pleased you didn't give me the cut direct. This time."

She *was* a friend of his. She knew not to rise to the bait. "It's good to see you looking well."

"And good to see you back," chimed in one of the others, a guy who should've been old enough to know better.

It kind of hung there for a minute while we all watched Felix decide whether to shred the poor dumb fuck to ribbons or not. And then Felix smiled. "Mervyn. Tactful as ever." He started toward them, extending his hands to the lady named Fleur, and I felt something unclench in my chest.

Felix

I went to bed alone that night, although I could have had my choice of companions if I had desired.

I did not desire. I did not want to expend the energy and attention to make love, and I no longer had anyone in the Mirador to whom I could go for something more honest.

And I wanted, badly, to talk to Thamuris. I needed his intelligence. I needed to talk to someone who was neither Cabaline nor Eusebian, someone who had no preconceptions about the Virtu and what it could or could not do. And someone who had no preconceptions about me and what I was capable of. Someone with whom conversation did not have to be a war.

I needed to talk to a friend.

There was more power in my construct-Mélusine here, where it echoed the physical structures and lines of force that grounded my sleeping body. I could feel the need for caution, for care and thought, like the taint of ozone in the air. The jagged, broken magic of the Virtu underlay the whole, and I could all too easily impale myself on it, tear myself to shreds and tatters. The Seventh Gate was like a diseased and gaping maw, and I found myself uneasy about turning my back on it; Iosephinus's warnings about mental constructs were almost audible as I observed the ways in which what had been a simple schematic of the city was changing, becoming in some respects more representational and in others decidedly less. Darkness shrouded the Lower City, with pinpricks of light in Pharaohlight and Simside, while the rest of Mélusine basked under a loving summer sun. The Mirador itself, on whose battlements I stood, seemed to be made of black glass; the sun shone through but could not illuminate it.

I turned toward Horn Gate almost desperately, afraid of what I might see here if I lingered too long. It was standing open, wreathed in white clematis, and beyond it I could see the winding paths of the Khloïdanikos and the twisted perseïdes. I stepped through gladly, gratefully, and found my accustomed place to wait for Thamuris.

I had to wait longer than usual and was beginning to be worried when I felt the Khloïdanikos resonate to his presence like a tapped glass. He himself appeared only a few moments later, hurrying into view at the end of the allée, and he looked much more like his waking self than I was accustomed to. The hectic color of consumption was in his face, and his hair, instead of hanging in burnished waves down his back, was in two fat, homely plaits. His garment was definitely a nightshirt.

I rose to meet him, and he said, "I'm sorry I took so long. The celebrants won't leave me alone." I could hear his struggle for breath and knew that that, too, was showing through from his waking self.

"You're worse."

He waved it aside almost angrily. "It's the nature of the disease. I have been much more ill than this several times."

"That is no excuse for abusing yourself now. You should be resting properly."

"How can I? They won't leave me *alone*."

I wondered how high his fever was, and gave up on the idea of persuading him to forgo this meeting; it would be kinder to give him something to think about that was not his own wretched body. I coaxed him to sit down and told him about my return to the Mirador, the encounter on the Road of Chalcedony, the Curia's deliberations, and especially the singing of the Virtu that I could still hear even though I was no longer mad.

My description of the Virtu distracted him nicely, both from himself and from any questions he might have asked about why I had leaped so spectacularly to Mildmay's defense. I did not want Thamuris's opinion of the obligation d'âme.

"Singing, you say?"

"I don't know any other way to describe it. It's definitely a melody."

"And how long did you say the Virtu had been incorporate before it was broken?"

"A hundred and seventy-eight years. It was the oldest continuous thaumaturgic working on the continent."

Thamuris frowned, and the brightness in his yellow eyes was more than fever. "And its physical foundation?"

I thought of the jagged shards still in the Hall of the Chimeras and shivered. "I believe the correct term is 'temporally coterminous.'"

He nodded. "You called it a loom. Do you think you could also call it a polyphonic fugue?"

"Um," I said. "I recognize 'fugue' as a musical term, but . . ."

"If a tapestry is a picture made by weaving different colored threads together, then a fugue does the same thing with melodies."

"Then, yes, I suppose so. Although it isn't the metaphor I would have chosen."

"Ah, but you did. Because the song you describe is the remaining unbroken strand of the Virtu's magic."

"Is it," I said flatly, hearing the incredulity in my own voice.

"Yes. Our minds have to translate magic into symbols we can understand. That's what the various schools of magic *are*, you know—different sets of symbols for interpreting magic to our minds. Words, objects, rituals, diagrams . . . and your mind chose music."

"How marvelous."

"It should make the task you've set yourself much easier, though," Thamuris said, sensing my lack of enthusiasm and anxious to allay it. "It gives you another, completely separate system with which to analyze the problem and judge your progress."

"I suppose it does," I said, trying to sound encouraged. I did not want to explain to Thamuris how bad the memories were that that song brought back. There were no words, nothing but pain and fear and wretched confusion, and I was afraid of what invoking those memories here might do to the Khloïdanikos if I could not control them.

I smiled at Thamuris and said, "I should stop bothering you with my theoretical puzzles. I'll talk to you later." I left before he could formulate a protest, hoping that the tranquility of the Khloïdanikos would help him rest.

෬

The Curia's decision was a foregone conclusion, despite the best efforts of Agnes and Johannes. They needed the Virtu mended, and I was the first sign they'd had in over a year that such a thing might even be possible, much less achievable. In the end, consensus was unanimous.

I was the second wizard in the history of the Cabaline ascendancy to petition for and be granted reinstatement. The first, one hundred and sixty years ago, had been Damon Esterley, called Damon Turncoat, the only wizard ever to take his allegiance from the Mirador to the Bastion and to return.

I reflected on Damon Turncoat as I prepared for my reinvestiture, as a way of keeping my nervousness at bay. I had felt a certain kinship with him when I was younger and thought myself free of Malkar. He had been ganumedes, as I was; he had been the lover of one of the bright children of the annemer court, as I was. The story of his love for Gabriel Otanius was a favorite with poets and novelists, for a more star-crossed pair of lovers they could not have invented. I had never been fool enough to wish for the trials that beset Damon and Gabriel, but I did remember wondering if it took that kind of suffering to create true love.

By my own example, the answer was no, and I shoved away my memories of Shannon.

My wardrobes had been left untouched, which was both gratifying and faintly disturbing. I found my favorite red-violet coat, my second-best trousers and boots. But not my best boots, and not the trousers that I had bought only two weeks before . . .

A flash of memory, freezing cold water and a monster laughing.

I shuddered, my shoulders hunching involuntarily, and knotted my cravat, shrugged into my coat. My hands were *not* shaking, and I defied them to start. My rings were cold and heavy on my hands; I could wear them because they had not been given to me by the Curia and thus were not the Curia's either to bestow or to withhold. Surrounded by witchlights, I stared at myself in the mirror. My hair was not yet long enough to queue properly, even if I had wished to; my earrings were bare glints of gold, lost in wild curls that were aggressively inappropriate to the sleek decorum of the court. The vivid contrast of my hair against the red-violet coat made my skin look even paler and made my eyes unearthly. That was good. I did not want them to be able to ignore me.

I emerged into the sitting room, where Mildmay and Gideon had been playing Long Tiffany for the past hour. They both turned; Mildmay blinked, and Gideon said, :Isn't that coat a little bright?:

"Very," I said, finding myself suddenly and unreasonably cheerful. "Shall we?"

"Do we got a choice?" Mildmay said, dragging himself to his feet.

"Not particularly, no."

"What I thought." He looked tired, his skin almost gray in the light of fire and lamp.

"Stay with Gideon," I said, invoking the obligation d'âme just strongly enough that he would know I meant it.

"But I thought—" Mildmay started at the same time Gideon said, :I do not need a minder.:

"*After* the ceremony," I said and glared at Gideon. They would reinstate me anyway; they needed me more than I needed them, and we all knew it. But I could not abide the delay that this revelation would cause if produced untimely. I had heard the Virtu singing all night long, even in my dreams.

"Okay, okay!" Mildmay raised his hands in a gesture of surrender and defense. "You're the boss." Gideon made no further protests, either, although his expression when I glanced at him was coldly thoughtful.

We proceeded unhurriedly and in good order to the Hall of the Chimeras, where Mehitabel was waiting.

"May common Kekropians attend?" she asked me, her voice heavy with irony.

I gave her my best smile and said, "No, only uncommon ones. Keep my brother out of trouble, would you?" And leaving her indignation and Mildmay's weary resignation behind, I swept into the Hall of the Chimeras.

The court was out in force, the wizards' gold sashes gleaming among the dark and sumptuous grandeur of the nobles. I'd timed my arrival carefully so that there would be no need for any awkward period of lingering and chatting. I reached the end of the long central aisle just as Stephen took his seat beneath the Virtu and Giancarlo moved into place on the steps of the dais. My bow honoring the Lord Protector matched perfectly with the court's.

The first time I had gone through this, the ceremonies had taken most of a day, and what I chiefly remembered about the investiture was the burning pain of my freshly inscribed tattoos. This time things proceeded in a much more businesslike fashion. I advanced, exchanged ritual words with Stephen and Giancarlo, swore the sevenfold oath that I had repeated so many times I could say it in my sleep—and according to Shannon, sometimes had. Then Giancarlo descended two steps, I came forward, and we clasped hands, left to left and right to right, our rings making cold and hostile music against each other.

I felt it, like a dislocated joint popping back into its socket. Something I hadn't even known was missing returned to its proper place. The Virtu's song was suddenly much clearer; I understood now what Thamuris had been trying to explain to me. I could hear the emptiness where other voices ought to have been.

I must have looked strange, for Giancarlo hesitated a moment before releasing my hands. "Are you all right?"

"I'm beginning to be," I said.

I was beginning to understand what the Virtu needed me to do.

Mildmay

Gideon could talk to other hocuses.

I mean, I'd known he could talk to Felix, but I hadn't realized that he could do it with anybody who didn't happen to be annemer. Between them, him and Mehitabel got quite the little social circle going after Felix had finished with his hocus-thing and the party started.

I faded back—once the ceremony was over, and I didn't have the binding-by-forms breathing down my neck like a hired goon—and left them to it. I wasn't no use at that sort of thing anyway, and I was sick of being stared at. People wanted to know who I was and what the fuck I was doing there, and I didn't blame them.

I just didn't want to be around when Felix told them, and that was past praying for.

So I kind of skulked around behind the busts of the old kings and didn't meet nobody's eyes and tried to keep moving. And wished Felix would come find me and say it was time for bed.

But that wasn't happening neither. He was easy to spot, being so tall and with all that red hair, and every time I looked, he was surrounded by flashies and hocuses and looking happy enough to bust.

I kept moving, kept my distance from the Virtu and the Lord Protector, and after a while I came around to the alcove where they'd stashed the musicians. Glanced in, and fucking near swallowed my tongue.

Hugo Chandler, large as life and twice as natural.

I did have the sense not to say nothing while they were playing, but as soon as the song was over, I said, "Hugo!"

He looked up, saw me, and for a second I thought he was going to pass out on the spot. Then he turned and said something to the gal beside him and edged out to shake my hand.

"Gilroi! I thought you were dead! And what happened to your hair?"

Powers, I was glad to see him. Glad to see anybody from back before my life went to shit. "Quit dyeing it, is all. And my name ain't actually Gilroi. It's Mildmay." I bit my tongue and managed not to say, "Mildmay the Fox." I gave him the name Felix'd come up with and been so pleased with himself about: "Mildmay Foxe."

"Oh," Hugo said, and tried it out under his breath, like he needed to see how it tasted. Then he said, "Everybody thinks you're dead."

"Nope. Just went away for a while."

"Austin is. Dead, you know."

With Ginevra. "Yeah, I know. I'm sorry."

"I'm glad you're not, though. But what are you doing here?"

Fuck, that was a good question. I was opening my mouth to tell him so when somebody cleared their throat, real politely, just behind me. Hugo took one look and melted back into the musicians. My heart sank. I turned around.

It was Felix's lady hocus friend, the one with more guts than common sense. Fleur, her name was.

"Will you walk with me?" she said.

Oh shit. "Yes, m'lady," I said, along of really not seeing that I had a choice, and after a moment I realized she wanted me to give her my arm.

So I did, and we walked, back behind the kings where nobody came. She was about my height, and she smelled good. And after a while, she said, "I am not perfectly sure I understood Felix's explanation. He is so very bad at them. You are his brother?"

"Half brother, yes, m'lady."

"And you met him in Hermione?"

"Yes, m'lady."

"But you're from Mélusine."

Well, fuck, it wasn't like I could hide it. "Britomart."

"I beg your pardon?"

"I'm from Britomart."

"I see," she said, in a way that made it all too clear as how she *did* see. "And you came with him to the Mirador because . . . ?"

"He let me." Which was the truth.

"Not quite what I meant," she said sharply, but I cut in before she could think of a better way to put it.

"Anything else you gotta ask Felix."

I said it too fast, and I was just trying to gather myself to say it again, slower, when the thing happened that I'd been dreading since we rode into Mélusine.

"You *what?*" A man's voice, pitched to carry.

Me and Lady Fleur both turned. A hocus I didn't know, talking to Felix. And from the way he looked, like he'd just swallowed a live frog, and from the way Felix looked, like a cat that's got itself locked into the creamery, it didn't take no genius to see that Felix had just told the whole fucking Mirador about the obligation d'âme.

"Fuck me sideways 'til I cry," I said. And I didn't care if Lady Fleur heard me or not.

Chapter 10

Felix

The temptation had been too great to resist, and the look on Robert's face was all the gratification I could have hoped for.

And then, of course, there were the consequences, which I knew I would be suffering in one form or another for years to come. The most immediate was Giancarlo's sputtering and incoherent fury. For a moment, it was a near-run thing whether he would murder me on the spot, in the middle of the Hall of the Chimeras with all the court as witnesses.

But by then, Mildmay was there, and Giancarlo harrumphed at him and said to me, "You certainly picked an unprepossessing specimen," not as if that excused me, but simply as if it was the final straw and he couldn't even maintain his wrath in the face of my folly.

Mildmay gave me one of his flat, unreadable glares, and that was when Stephen came up behind Giancarlo like a cloud of doom.

"I imagine you must be quite proud of yourself," Stephen said in a mild voice that wouldn't have deceived a child of seven. It certainly didn't deceive

Mildmay, whose face had taken on its most masklike quality, which meant (I had theorized) that he was having to make a conscious effort not to let anything show. But he didn't try to escape or to hide, and it occurred to me that I was proud of him for that.

"No, my lord," I said, even though I was.

"You always were good at that sort of lying by withholding. Did you learn it from Malkar?"

"Probably," I said, making my own effort now to keep my voice level. "He is to blame for most of my bad habits."

"You give yourself too little credit." A different voice, the one voice beyond all others I had hoped not to hear this evening.

The voice of Shannon Teverius.

"I was forgetting your excellent tutelage, my lord," I said.

Shannon went white; Stephen went red.

"In any event," I said, "and irrespective of my morals or lack thereof, the thing is done and cannot be undone."

"You should be burned for heresy," Stephen growled.

"I have performed no act of heresy while a wizard of the Mirador. You saw to that yourselves."

"And even granted that we deserved this petty act of revenge," Giancarlo said, "it is unconscionable of you to use an annemer—your own brother!—to achieve your ends."

"I asked him to," Mildmay said, his voice harsh and abrupt and like the distilled essence of the Lower City. Shannon and Stephen both twitched, and Giancarlo turned toward him with the most thunderstruck look of astonishment I had ever seen on his face.

"You *asked* him to?"

"Yeah." Then Mildmay caught himself and said more carefully, "I mean, yes, m'lord."

"Why? Why in the name of all the blessed saints would you do such a thing?"

Silence. Then, just as I realized what Mildmay was going to do, just as I was opening my mouth to create a distraction, *any* distraction, he said, "I killed Cerberus Cresset." And no matter how slurred his speech, how thick his accent, there wasn't a wizard in the Mirador who could have misheard that sentence.

Mildmay and I were quite abruptly standing in a circle of clear space, and the wizards were staring at us wide-eyed as frightened children.

"He is my brother," I said to forestall the questions I could see forming. I caught Mildmay's arm, said in a fierce undertone, "We are *leaving*," and gave him barely a second to decide whether he would walk with me or be dragged.

They let us go; I supposed grimly that there was really nothing more to say.

At least not in public.

Mildmay

The way Felix tore into me once we were clear of the Hall of the Chimeras, you'd've thought I'd offered to take out the Lord Protector right then and there if they'd pass the hat for my fee. I tried to say as how I hadn't told them nothing they weren't going to find out anyway, but Felix didn't want to hear it. So I shut the fuck up and just tried to keep up with him and not listen all the way back to his rooms.

Where he threw the door open like he was hoping to hit somebody with it, and then stopped dead halfway across the threshold.

"What are *you* doing here?" he said, and I craned around him and saw Gideon standing up out of one of the armchairs looking kind of grim and bloodless but like he wasn't going to let Felix throw him out until he'd had his say. Which of course I wasn't going to be able to hear. But he wasn't here to talk to me, and I wasn't sure I wanted to know what him and Felix had to say to each other anyhow.

Felix was silent a minute—listening to Gideon, I guessed—then said, not even looking at me or nothing, "Go to bed." With the obligation d'âme behind it, just in case I thought I was going to argue.

I wanted to tell him I didn't want no part of his and Gideon's business, but I held my tongue. I did say, "Good night, Gideon," as I went past him, and he gave me a little nod and a nicer smile than I thought I deserved. And then I went into my closet of a room and shut the door with them on the outside and was fucking well glad of it.

I went to bed and dreamed about Cardenio all fucking night.

I knew it was seeing Hugo again that'd set me off. That, and being back in Mélusine and hating the Mirador and all the rest of it. But mostly it was that feeling of being stuck in this place where nobody liked me and nobody was going to like me, especially not now that I'd opened my big mouth and told them all about Cerberus Cresset. Hugo'd be keeping out of my way, too. I wasn't going to lie to myself about that.

Was you born this fucking dumb, Milly-Fox, or do you practice every Dixième?

And Felix might not care so much about Cerberus Cresset for his own sake, but the way the other hocuses felt? That, he cared about, although he would have barbecued me with lemon if I'd been dumb enough to say any such thing to him. Which I wasn't.

But Cardenio knew all that shit already, and we were friends anyway.

At least, I hoped we were still friends, since the last time I'd seen him, I'd done my best to make sure we weren't.

Get your fucking hands off me.

Cade-skiffs had to be used to people being stupid, though. Especially when they'd just got done showing them their girlfriend's dead body. Right?

I woke up with Cardenio more in my head than anything else. Which was just as well, really, since, powers and saints, that morning was fucking putrid.

I guessed from the way Gideon and Felix were looking at each other, and then just about killing themselves not to make eye contact, that they'd fucked but they'd done it instead of talking. Which, you know, means you don't have the argument right then, but it don't really help nothing, neither.

So there was that—which all by itself was enough to curdle milk—and then there was court, and if I'd known in Farflung that that was the sort of thing I was going to have to do, I would've gone straight to Livergate and strung my own self up. Would've been cleaner.

Because, see, the obligation d'âme—and Felix explained it all to me over breakfast, real careful and mean, and I didn't eat much—is particular about how the annemer becomes not just the hocus's servant, and not even really just their property. It's more like part of their *self*. Legally, anyway, and I was just as glad Felix didn't feel like interpreting literally. But it meant I had to go everywhere with him, and I wasn't supposed to talk to nobody without Felix said it was okay first, and I wasn't loyal to nobody but Felix.

Which meant bowing to the Lord Protector during the oath-swearing ceremony—just for an example, can't think why *that*'d come to mind—was right out.

Which, I mean, I'd known. In a general way. But I hadn't really thought about it, because out in Farflung, it hadn't mattered and I hadn't cared. But here in the Mirador it mattered. Fuck did it matter. Because the hocuses had to get up and swear their oaths to Lord Stephen every day, and now that everybody knew me and Felix were bound by the obligation d'âme, we had to act like it. No more finessing the situation by ordering me to stay with Gideon.

So there was Felix with his gold sash and beautiful coat, and there was me like some kind of pox-ugly crow, and there was the Hall of the Chimeras full of people watching us. And of course Felix loved it. He loved being watched. Whereas me, I just wanted to crawl under a cobblestone and die.

But I couldn't, so I followed Felix down the Hall of the Chimeras, and everybody was quiet as quiet, so I could fucking *hear* myself limping, and Lord Stephen sat up there on that dais and watched us coming, the bastard, and Felix stopped and bowed, and I stopped and didn't bow, and the whole time Felix was saying his oath, Lord Stephen was staring me right in the eye. I figured he wanted to see if he could make me blush or embarrass myself somehow. But he could be Lord Protector all he wanted, he *still* wasn't a patch on Keeper, so I just stood there and stared back at him and kept my face still.

He looked away first.

Then back down the hall, and Felix picked a spot next to Lady Fleur, and I stood behind him and wondered how I could get to the Fishmarket to see Cardenio. Beat the fuck out of listening to the goings-on of the Mirador trying to run itself, which I wasn't going to understand anyway and didn't want to.

I had plenty of time to think.

But I hadn't come up with any good answers by the time people finally started clearing out. Felix kind of faded back and let them, so I went with him, and when the Hall of the Chimeras was empty except for us, he said, "*Now* then," like he'd been every bit as bored as me, and went striding down the hall toward the dais.

I went after him because he hadn't told me not to, but when he walked up on the dais like he had a right to it, I stayed on the floor.

"I've been wanting to get a good look at this thing for days," he said, climbing up on Lord Michael's Chair like it was just another piece of furniture, and stood on tiptoe to look at the shards of the Virtu.

I didn't want to ask—didn't want to say nothing—but my stupid mouth opened and I heard myself bleating, "Is it safe?" like some dumb kid who's just barely finished his first septad.

Felix sort of laughed. "Not particularly, but the danger isn't anything you need to worry about." Being annemer, he didn't say, but he didn't need to. We both knew that part.

"Okay," I said and stood my ground.

He smiled at me over his shoulder, a little smile and kind of twisted, but it meant he was glad I was here, and it made me warm all the way to my fucking toes.

Yeah, I'm an idiot, thanks for noticing.

And I couldn't help holding my breath when he reached out to poke at the shards with one finger, like a kid poking a dog to see if it's asleep.

But nothing happened, and Felix muttered to himself while he climbed down off Lord Michael's Chair like he'd been hoping a bolt of lightning would knock him on his ass or something. He straightened his cuffs. And then he looked at me and said like it didn't make him the least little bit happy, "It seems that I must rely on Messire von Heber after all."

Felix

I had been hoping it might unfold like something in a story: Thamuris would give me the insight I needed to mend the Virtu by myself—and preferably with a single lordly wave of my hand.

I had known better, but that hadn't quite been enough to squelch the foolish little voice saying that it *could* be true.

It wasn't.

Knowing that the music I heard was the last unbroken strand of the most complicated thaumaturgical construct the Mirador and its wizards had ever produced helped me to understand what I was hearing. It did not help me to understand how to rebuild the fugue I did not hear.

Mavortian was right. I needed someone who was used to sensing patterns. It galled me to admit it, even to myself—and I intended never to make that confession of *need* to Mavortian—but I did not have time to coddle myself with comforting illusions. I had used up my last scrap of the Lord Protector's most emphatically finite patience. If I crossed him again—or even displeased him—I would be facing the Verpine for certain, and quite possibly the pyre in front of Livergate. Blackmailing the Lord Protector into condoning flagrant heresy was all very well, but it was also not the smartest thing I'd ever done. I had been afraid and angry that night in Farflung, and I had let fear and anger do my thinking.

And, to be fair, my absolute belief that Mildmay meant what he said.

But for all my fine and noble words before the Curia, it was anger that had brought me back to the Mirador. Neither pure nor simple, but the black, cruel rage that I had been fighting against all my life. I had wanted— I *still* wanted—to make them sorry. To prove, viciously, indisputably, that they had been wrong about me. And I wanted it to hurt.

That part, I'd managed, but I had also come much closer to proving them right than proving them wrong.

My resemblance to Malkar was most damnably pronounced.

There was, therefore, neither sense nor reason in putting the unpleasantness off. Stephen and the Curia had agreed to give me full access to the Hall of the Chimeras when court was not in session, and I had a terrible, though sourceless, sense of urgency. It was true, as Hamilcar had said, that the Virtu was not going to get more broken, and I knew it, and yet . . . and yet I kept wanting to look over my shoulder to see what was gaining on me.

We found Mavortian in his room on the Filigree Corridor—and, of course, the ever-faithful Bernard.

Bernard was no different from Mildmay, I reminded myself, except perhaps in that Bernard's loyalty was freely given, not compelled.

"So," Mavortian said. "Messire Harrowgate. I wondered how long it would be before you turned up."

I could not quite make my voice pleasant when I said, "You need wonder no longer," but I kept it noncommittal, neutral.

I felt Mildmay's watchful gaze and knew I wasn't fooling him. But I also knew that if there was one thing in the world I could count on, it was on Mildmay holding his tongue.

Mavortian smiled, showing too many teeth. "What can I do for you, Messire Harrowgate?"

"What do you think? You say you can tell me how to mend the Virtu. I want you to prove it."

"How can I refuse when you ask so politely?"

"Well," I said, "you can't. Not if you want my help with this Beaumont Livy of yours."

"You said you didn't know him."

"And you said your strong divination couldn't be wrong. Which of the two of us are you going to trust?"

"I certainly know which is more trustworthy."

Beside me, Mildmay stirred and subsided; a glance showed him and Bernard glaring at each other. If they'd been dogs, I would have been able to hear them snarling, could have touched Mildmay's neck and felt his hackles bristling. I had not realized before how much he disliked Mavortian and Bernard, and the thought made me recognize how quickly I'd let the situation escape my control.

I pushed both hands through my hair; took, held, released a deep breath. "If you do not intend to help me, please just say so, and I will leave you in peace."

"I never said I did not intend to help you."

Cat-and-mouse games. Malkar had loved them. I liked them myself, but not when cast as the mouse. "Yes or no, Messire von Heber?"

"Of course I will help you, Messire Harrowgate. And you will help me in return."

"Of course," I said and gave him a thin smile, as thin and insincere as the smile he gave me.

𝄞

I had never walked into the Hall of the Chimeras when it was empty. I had never imagined it empty.

No, that wasn't true. I stopped where I was, fighting not to fall down, not to stagger, not to press the heels of my hands against my eyes. Above all, not to cry out.

I heard the thump of Mavortian's canes go past me, but I was staring wide-eyed, blind, at the memory of darkness and brilliant blue-green light, and darkness again in the middle of it, a fracture, a chasm. Blood and shards of stone like glass and pain, pain that was darkness and breath and all the world.

A voice, not part of the darkness: "Felix? You okay?"

I took a breath that felt like a scream, and found the real darkness of the Hall of the Chimeras, candlelit and thick with shadows.

I called witchlight in a blazing crown, as if I could force the shadows to fail and die by nothing more than strength of will. Mavortian glanced back, and I could read the look he gave me; I had seen it a thousand times before: *peacock*. I gave him my best and most infuriating smirk in return.

And Mildmay, still beside me, like Griselde la Patience, said, "Felix?"

"I'm all right," I said, although that was hardly the truth. I groped and came up with something that was at least not a lie: "I don't like the dark."

"Then brother did you pick the wrong place to live."

He surprised me into laughing. The sound echoed strangely among the metal and stone, but I didn't care. When I looked at Mildmay, I saw laughter in his eyes, although his face was as solemn as ever.

Mavortian had come to a halt before the dais; as we came up beside him, he said, "I need a piece of—what *is* it made of, anyway?"

"Stone. At least, that's what it started out as. It responds like glass."

"Does it?" His eyebrows went up; he knew enough about Cabaline theory to recognize how strange that was.

"Actual glass wouldn't have withstood the stresses of the working. You see how friable it made the stone."

"Yes," Mavortian said with something that was almost a wince. "Then I need a piece of stone, and it would help if I had somewhere to lay out my cards."

"Thought they were for fortune-telling," Mildmay said.

Mavortian gave him an indecipherable look. "They can be. They can also be used for other things. In this case"—he turned to me—"I need to cast for the anchor."

"You say that as if it should mean something to me."

"Any pattern meant to hold for longer than simply the duration of the spell-casting has to be anchored. I can tell that the Virtu was anchored by its materials—the . . . stone or glass?"

"Either. Both, thaumaturgically speaking. Call it glass, and the stone of the plinth." Although "anchor" was not the preferred term, it described exactly the purpose that stone served in Cabaline wizardry. It was why the Mirador suited us so well, and why Cabalines outside of Mélusine were drawn to stone towers. Air and glass for working, gems for focus, rock for grounding, water for cleansing. And fickle wood playing each part in turn. Cabaline wizards were never comfortable in wooden houses.

"And by the daily oaths," Mavortian continued. "But that wouldn't be enough to hold it stable. We need to find out what the other anchors are and whether they are still intact."

"And you can do that with your cards?" Mildmay asked.

"Given a focus," Mavortian said and looked pointedly at me.

I sprang up onto the dais, onto Lord Michael's Chair, up onto the arm;

snatched up a shard of stone like a dagger; felt the power jolting up my arm, numbing my fingers. The Virtu was broken, but it was not dead. I jumped down again, demanded of Mavortian, "Do you have your cards with you?"

"Always."

"Then come," I said. "Let us find you a place to lay them out."

It wasn't hard to do; there were a score of small parlors around the Hall of the Chimeras, and that not counting the wizards' antechambers. I found one that contained a marquetry chess table and stared out of countenance the group of young wizards who were in possession. They fled, mumbling something that might have been an apology or a promise of dire vengeance, and I put the shard of the Virtu on the table, rearranged the chairs to suit, with two at the table and the others along the wall where they would not get in the way.

"You are ruthless, Messire Harrowgate," Mavortian said, smirking again.

"I consult no one's comfort but my own," I said, pointing Mildmay emphatically at a chair. He gave me his half snarl, but he sat. "So has it ever been." I sat down myself in one of the chairs at the chess table and looked brightly at Mavortian. "Call me Felix, Mavortian, and show me what your cards can do."

He wanted to refuse, to balk—to put his ears back like a mule and decline to move. But he had no reason to, except our cordial dislike of each other, and I had been careful to be provoking enough that to refuse would be to allow me to win. Power games and manipulation were like air in the Mirador, and despite a new distaste for their childishness, I was breathing deeply.

Mavortian sat, handed his canes to Bernard—who carefully chose a seat that was not next to Mildmay—and then produced a rectangular box from the inside pocket of his coat. It was about the length of my hand, made of a glowingly pale wood, carved in labyrinthine profusion with stylized vines and flowers. There was neither catch nor hinges visible.

"Moonflowers," Mavortian said. I did not see what he did to release the catch, but he lifted the lid. The interior was padded and lined with midnight-blue silk, on which rested the deck of the Sibylline. Mavortian drew the cards out, set the box aside, and began shuffling them, his hands quick and agile. He said, "How much do you know about the Sibylline?"

"It is a method of divination. Believed to come from Cymellune of the

Waters, although I understand there is evidence to disprove that. Not unlike a deck of playing cards, except for the trumps. Rich with symbolism, and thus much beloved of artists and poets." I shrugged. "The Mirador does not dabble in fortune-telling."

That got me a glare from under his eyebrows. He fanned the cards out, facedown. They were old, battered; what once must have been a striking pattern in black and scarlet on their backs was now faded, worn, the black gone to sepia, and the scarlet almost gone entirely. Mavortian ran his hand back along his fan of cards, flipping them faceup. A cardsharp's trick: I glanced at Mildmay, and he rolled his eyes at me.

Mavortian said, "Four suits: staves, wands, pentacles, and grails. As you say, like playing cards. Deuce through ten, the court cards: Lady, Knight, Queen, King." He edged them forward as he spoke: the Lady of Wands, the Knight of Pentacles, the Queen of Grails, the King of Swords. "And the Sibyls. These, you will *not* find in a deck of playing cards."

He pulled them out of the fan entirely and pushed them across the table to me. Wands, Pentacles, Grails, Swords. Four blindfolded women, each with a two-handed grip on the symbol of her suit.

"They are the diviners' cards," he said and motioned for me to push them back. "The alt-cards, both highest and deepest. They stand between the common cards and the trumps."

He drew the entire deck of cards back into his hands, shuffled three times, and began laying the trumps out from the center of the deck. If nothing else, this demonstration was convincing me never to play cards with him for money.

"The twenty-one trumps," he said, "are the cards we will be using, since this is not exactly divination, and we want the cards that respond to patterns most strongly. It would probably be best if you familiarized yourself with them." I looked at the garish, morbid pictures, and could almost hear Malkar laughing at my gullibility. Mavortian named them as he went, but only a few of the images caught in my mind: the Dead Tree, the Beehive, the Nightingale, the Heart of Light. Mavortian did not explain their meanings, and I did not press him. If he needed to keep some superiority, some exclusive knowledge, I did not care, so long as he could do what he claimed.

Instead I asked, "And how are these cards going to help with our particular problem?"

"We're casting to find the anchors," he said with odious patience. "We know two of them." He laid two trumps faceup on the table: the Dog—an enormous shaggy creature, black as night and far more like a bear than any dog I had ever seen—and the Rock, lurid red against its murky background.

"Loyalty and stone," Mavortian said and gathered them up again. "It is the others we want."

"Probably only one," I said. "It would be either three or five, and I cannot imagine maintaining a working like that long enough to lay five foundations."

Mavortian nodded; he pushed the stone shard into the exact center of the table, although I could tell by the way he rubbed his fingers together that he didn't like the feel of its magic any better than I did. Then he handed the twenty-one trumps across the table to me. "Shuffle, please."

"How many times?" The cards felt smooth, slightly furry around the edges, and powerful. I could feel the residue of the magic that had been channeled through them, and there had been a lot of it.

"As many as feels necessary," Mavortian said, and I heard Bernard snort.

But it was not a useless answer, at least not from one wizard to another. I shuffled once, my fingers stiff and awkward, and felt the old power in the cards shift and darken and clarify. The word "awaken" was not quite right, and I was glad of it.

I shuffled again, felt the power move, obedient to my hands. Kept shuffling until the dark clarity ran from hand to hand like water, then gave the cards back to Mavortian.

He nodded, and I did not think I was imagining the slight possessiveness of the way his fingers curled around the cards. He cut the cards twice—and having held them I knew why—and began to lay them out around the shard of stone.

The first two were the Rock and the Dog, and I would have suspected him of more cardsharping tricks except for the fact that there was no point. He could not hope to fool me long-term, and it was the long term he cared about.

The third card was the Dead Tree; Mavortian and I both drew back instinctively and glared at each other.

"The worst-aspected card in the deck," he said, almost spitting the words at me.

"You would know."

We hovered for a moment on the brink of a true quarrel, and then he put down the fourth card.

Death.

I felt myself become cold, as if ice was forming along my spine and in the bones of my hands. Scraps of memory fluttered through my mind: the death of Sherbourne Foss, cold marble roses, a brick-lined tunnel beneath the city, a pale faded boy with inhuman eyes.

I said, my voice steady enough, but very thin, "I know what the third foundation is."

෫෫

Mavortian did not want to believe me. He said it was monstrous, abominable; I said that, yes, it was, but that did not mean it was not true.

"And it explains a great deal," I said. "Including the Cabal's behavior in allowing this knowledge to be lost." I sighed and pushed my hair off my face. "The Mirador has such a troubled relationship with heresy."

"You would know," Mavortian said nastily.

I ignored him. "I don't know very much about necromancy—though I know more than I would wish to—but I can see why they did it."

"And why is that?"

"They were trained necromancers, and what they needed—and needed, moreover, in a dreadful hurry—was stability."

"Stability?" Mavortian was frowning, but I thought that now it was in an honest attempt to follow my explanation.

"That," I said and pointed at the Dog, "takes years, if not decades, to gather enough power that it can truly function as a foundation for spellcasting of any magnitude. And especially in the early days, they couldn't *count* on it. Many of the wizards did not trust them; some paid only lip service to the new regime and were merely waiting for the chance to replace them. And nothing would undermine what the Cabal was working for more swiftly and catastrophically than the failure of their principal and most symbolic working."

Mavortian understood me now. "Expediency."

"Yes. I am sure the Cabal did not intend the Mirador's dead to be a permanent part of their working, but they would have had to wait until the oaths of loyalty had built some strength, and then they would have had to find a suitable replacement, and then find a time when it would be safe to disrupt the Virtu's energies and not have to worry about political unrest or thaumaturgic attacks. And then the members of the Cabal started dying . . ." I let my voice trail off and shrugged dismally.

"And now you are left with the question of how to duplicate their spells."

"No," I said, feeling inexpressibly weary. "Now I am left with the question of whether I *should* duplicate their spells."

The way he stared at me—as if I'd suggested we strip naked and paint each other with woad—did not improve my temper. "Perhaps I missed something," he said. "Did I not understand you to tell me that repairing the Virtu was a matter of the most paramount importance?"

"It is."

"Then how can you seriously be entertaining the thought of leaving it broken?"

"Necromancy is heresy."

"Much you care."

My hands tightened their grip on each other in my lap. "The fact that I have committed heresy does not mean I approve of it."

"A convenient argument. You may do whatever you please while everyone else must toe the line?"

"*No.* I . . . regret what I did." Stiff, ungraceful words, and I was not even sure they were true. "But surely just because I have committed heresy once does not mean you have to imagine me fool enough to commit it twice."

"Leaving the Virtu unmended?"

"No. No, there has to be another way."

"Really?" Mavortian's expression was openly and profoundly skeptical. "If there were, do you not imagine the Cabal might have thought of it?"

"They were trained necromancers," I said, as I had said before. "It was only natural that the necromantic solution would occur to them first."

"But you, of course, can see more clearly than they."

"I didn't say that. But I will not . . . I *cannot* make the dead of the Mirador support this weight. Not unless there is no other choice."

"And if, in fact, there is not?" His blue eyes were bright, unkind, but genuinely curious.

"I will find one," I said and met his gaze squarely, daring him to tell me otherwise.

And whatever his thoughts on that matter were, he had the sense to keep them to himself.

Mildmay

He regretted what he'd done.

He'd said so.

Well, fuck, I said to myself, it ain't like I don't regret it, too. Which, you know, true. But it still hurt, having him say it like that—not even looking at me, like it didn't matter that it was me he'd done it with. Me he'd done it *for*.

We went back to his rooms, and he said something to Gideon that got him out of that armchair like he was on springs, and they both started dragging books off the shelves and spreading 'em out on the table, and Felix got paper and ink out of his bedroom, and they settled in to do hocus-stuff. Something to do with the Virtu, for sure, but I didn't know what, and I couldn't've been any help even if I did.

I watched for a while, but I just felt stupider and more useless by the second, so finally I said, "D'you need me for anything?"

Felix looked up from his scribbled papers. "Why?"

"I want to go visit a friend."

"Well, I certainly don't . . . wait a minute. Since when do you have any friends in the Mirador?"

Yeah, go ahead, slap me in the face with it. "I didn't say it was somebody in the Mirador."

"So where is this friend of yours?"

"The Fishmarket," I said sullenly.

"The . . . ?"

"Fishmarket. In Havelock. The cade-skiffs' guildhall."

"You want to go to *Havelock*? Are you out of your mind?"

"No," I said, even more sullenly.

He put down his pen and heaved a sigh that might've been real, or might've just been look-at-me-being-long-suffering. Because the saints and powers know he's good at that. "Mildmay, you know you can't."

"The cade-skiffs won't give me no trouble. They wouldn't, even if me and Cardenio wasn't friends."

He glared at me. "*You*'re the one who insisted that the Lower City is a danger to you. *You*'re the one who had people come bounding out of the woodwork to kill you."

"That was just Rindleshin. He don't—"

"No. I can't let you go unless I can go with you to protect you. And I can't go."

"*You?* Protect *me?*" I didn't mean it to come out sounding as nasty as it did.

"I protected you from that Rindleshin creature."

I snorted. "Please. Like he had a fucking chance."

"Oh, he had a chance, all right. One good kick and down you'd go."

"You don't know the first thing about it."

"Maybe I don't, but I know one thing. You *asked* for my protection, little brother. So don't complain now that you've got it."

"So it's all my fault?"

"I wouldn't have said that," he said, so sweetly that I knew he also wasn't going to say I was wrong. "Now, if you don't mind, I am rather busy here."

"Fine." I started for the door.

"Don't leave the Mirador without my permission." And the bastard hit the binding-by-forms when he said it, like he thought he couldn't trust me.

"I won't," I snarled and left.

ᔍᔍ

I ended up going to find Mehitabel Parr. I didn't have any real friends in the Mirador, but she was close, and she was annemer, and right then if I never saw another hocus in my life, it would be too fucking soon.

Mehitabel wasn't in her room, and I stood in the hallway feeling stupid. Because if you'd asked, no, of course I didn't think she was going to be just hanging around, hoping that I'd decide to drop by, but I also hadn't thought . . . well, I hadn't thought. Leave it at that.

I was going to give it up as a bad job, just go back to Felix's rooms and sit in my fucking closet and, I don't know, draw rude pictures on the walls or something, when I heard people laughing farther down the hallway. And I recognized Mehitabel's laugh. Or, I guess I should say, one of her laughs. She had two, one that was deep and kind of back in her throat and sounded like sex dipped in chocolate, and another that was more like a real laugh, and you almost never heard it. This was the first one, and that probably meant whoever she was with wasn't nobody I wanted to talk to, but Kethe I didn't even care.

I followed the sound, and figured out what had happened. Mehitabel had just taken over one of the unused rooms along the hallway. Which made sense—I mean, it wasn't like anybody else was even going to notice, and it let her talk to people without having to have them all hanging out in her bedroom.

Three people I didn't know, two gals and a guy, all of them with their hair dressed back and their eyes lined in kohl and none of 'em wearing much more than their stockings. Mehitabel was at least decent, although I'd never seen her in a dress that low-cut before.

"Oh," I said, "sorry, I didn't—"

"Come in, Mildmay," Mehitabel said, although the other people looked kind of doubtful. "These are Jeanne-Undine and Iago and Harriet. They're dancers with the Opéra Ophide."

"Giving a private performance this evening for Lord Paul Corvinius and his friends," the guy chimed in.

"*Very* private," one of the girls said, with a giggle.

"Oh, we hope so. Very much," the guy said, and they all kind of grinned at each other.

"You're shocking poor Mildmay," Mehitabel said. Which they hadn't been—I mean, I was never one for ballet dancers myself, and they wouldn't have looked twice at me anyway, but I heard the stories same as everybody else—but you could never have told it now from the way my face was going bright red. I glared at Mehitabel, and she made a quick, half-apologetic grimace and said, "I did mean it when I said, come in. And I meant, sit down, too."

"I don't like to bother you," I said.

"You aren't. *Sit.*"

I sat. And after a little, they forgot I was there, the way people do if you let 'em, and I sat and listened while they gossiped back and forth, all about the rivalry between the two Pharaohlight theaters, the Empyrean and the Cockatrice, and the things the prima soprano for the Opéra said about the conductor, and what happened to it all when it got down into Scaffelgreen and the pantomimes got ahold of it. And around the edges I caught bits of what had been going on in Mélusine the past indiction or so, and especially how things were in the Lower City. And they weren't as bad as I'd been afraid they were, although powers and saints, they weren't all that good, neither. The Mayor was about as much help as he ever was, but apparently the Lord Protector had been leaning on people to get things rebuilt and make sure the drinking water was clean and stuff like that. Which was more than I'd expected anybody to do.

The Engmond's Tor Cheaps were still open. The Hospice of St. Cecily in Candlewick Mews had been overrun for months, but was getting things sorted. There were like a hundred septad questions I wanted to ask, and I sat there and kept my fucking mouth shut. The Lower City wasn't my home anymore, and I'd better learn to live with it that way.

The clock on the mantelpiece rang the hour. Flashie clock, and I hate doing the math in my head, but I figured it was along about the ninth or tenth hour of the day. "We've got to run, darling," said one of the girls. "Practice."

"And let's hope this lot of musicians can keep time," Iago added. You could tell they were dancers by the way they moved from sitting to standing, like they were water. They made promises with Mehitabel to meet up later, sort of waved to me—awkward, but it was nice of them—and they were gone.

Mehitabel sat down, letting her breath out in a huge sigh, and said, "I've never been in a city like this in my life. *Two* theaters *and* the opera *and* the pantomimes—"

"And that ain't even half of it," I said. "But most of the rest ain't respectable."

"Well, only respectable will do for me, darling," she said, mocking the ballet dancers' languid drawl, and suddenly burst out laughing, her own laugh. "They're like sparrows, aren't they? Twitter, twitter, twitter—all of it malice and nonsense, but it's the only way I can start to understand."

"Understand what?" I said, because I wanted her to keep talking. "What're you trying to do?"

She looked at me a moment, and I'd never been more aware that her wide-eyed childish look was nothing but a lie. Then she said, "You were right when you said I wasn't a governess, you know."

"I was?" I couldn't remember the last time I'd been right about anything.

"Oh, yes. I was born in one of the troupes of players that crisscross the Empire, and I grew up acting. I acted in Aigisthos for a while, but that was too risky. I didn't mean to be a governess when I went to Klepsydra, but a friend offered to pull strings, and I was qualified, and it was . . ." She shrugged. "It was safe. Madly boring, but safe. But now that I'm out of the Empire, I want to be an actress again. It offers a better kind of safety."

That was some friend, but I didn't want to push. "So you're gossiping with the ballet dancers."

Her smile was as bright as a handful of diamonds in the sun. "Exactly! I don't want to make waves, you see, and that means I had better know what's in the pond before I go jumping in."

"Oh."

"As soon as I can find a place to live, I'll get out of the Mirador, too. How do they *stand* it?"

"Dunno." I told myself not to be stupid. I didn't care if Mehitabel stayed in the Mirador or flew to the moon. And she didn't have no reason to care about me, either, or about Felix, or nothing. She had plans, and I could see as how we'd done our bit for those plans by getting her here, to Mélusine—to the Mirador, even, although I didn't blame her for wanting to get the fuck out of it. But if you're going to try to work your way in among the artists or the musicians or the actors or the dancers, the Mirador is the place you want to be hanging out. Because it's where all of them want to get to.

"I love this city," Mehitabel said. "And what I love most is I'm not related to a single solitary actor inside its walls."

"Um," I said. "Okay."

She almost seemed to shake herself, like a dog coming out of the water, and grinned at me. "Sorry. I'm a little . . ." She made a wide gesture with her hands.

"It's okay," I said. "I get it." And I did, a little. I remembered the rush I got from the good jobs, and I figured it couldn't be too far off—although I also figured I'd keep my mouth shut about just what it was I was comparing her to.

Her grin turned into a smile. It even looked like a real one. "And how are you? Did you come hunt me out for a reason?"

Well, yeah, but it wasn't anything I wanted to tell her about. "Nope," I said. "Felix is chasing after some hocus-thing, and I was just gonna get in the way if I hung around."

She heard something in what I said that I honestly hadn't meant to put there, because the smile shifted into a frown, and she tilted her head a little. "And how *is* Felix?"

"Fine."

" 'Fine.' "

"Yeah. He's working on how to fix the Virtu."

"That being the 'hocus-thing' you were getting in the way of?"

"Yeah."

She sighed, made a gesture I recognized after a moment as pushing her spectacles up on her nose, even though she wasn't actually wearing them, and said, "Do you want to play here-we-go-round-the-mulberry-bush for another hour, or do you want to tell me what's wrong?"

Powers and saints, I must've gone red as a bell pepper. "I didn't mean . . . I wasn't . . . I'm sorry, I shouldn't've bothered you." I got up, like a buffalo getting up out of a mud wallow, but I hadn't moved two steps away from the chair before she'd leaned over and grabbed my sleeve.

"I didn't say you were bothering me. You aren't. Sit down, Mildmay. Please. You don't have to talk to me if you don't want to."

Worse and worse. I sat, said, "It's nothing. Just, you know, me being stupid."

"You aren't stupid." She let go of my arm, but kind of slow, like she thought she might need to grab me again in a hurry. "What's Felix done this time?"

"It ain't Felix."

"Don't think I'm stupid, either. Of *course* it's Felix."

"No. It's just . . ." And it kind of fell out of my mouth, without me meaning to say it or wanting to say it or even knowing I was going to say it. "I'm lonely."

And if the floor had opened up and swallowed me just then, I would have said thank you.

"I'm not at all surprised," Mehitabel said.

I stared at her. Couldn't help it.

"I've been thinking since I met you that you're one of the loneliest people I've ever known."

Well, powers, what the fuck do you say to something like that? I stared down at my hands, all scarred and lumpy-knuckled, and it didn't matter how long I was in the Mirador, I'd never be able to pass for flash, not with hands like mine. "I just wanted to go see if a friend of mine is okay," I said, only it came out slurred and jumbled, the way things do if I try to talk too fast, or if I try to say much of anything when I'm upset. But the third time I repeated myself, she got it.

"So why don't you?"

"Felix won't let me." And, Kethe, I hadn't meant *that* to get out, either. Not like that. But it was true, and once I'd said it, you know, I couldn't really try and take it back. Mehitabel wouldn't've believed me.

"Felix won't *let* you?"

"Says it's too dangerous. And, I mean, I guess it is. Kind of. But I just . . ." This was getting me fucking nowhere. I got up, moved away before she could grab me again. "I'm sorry, Mehitabel. It's nothing, and there ain't nothing to be done, anyways. I'll see you 'round."

"Mildmay—"

But I didn't let her say it. It would've been too much like betraying Felix, to let her trash him to my face when I couldn't even get up the guts to disagree with her. I left, and I wasn't running, but I was moving as fast as I could.

Felix

:And what, pray tell,: Gideon said presently, :is a cade-skiff?:

I put my pen down and straightened my back, wincing at the stiffness in my neck. "The Cade-skiffs' Guild is an institution unique to the Lower City of Mélusine." But I didn't have the heart for the grave and rotund oratory of a guidebook. I stretched my neck, first to one side, then to the other, listening to my vertebrae shift and complain, and said, "They drag bodies out of the Sim."

:Ah. 'Cade' then being from Cade-Cholera.:

"Yes. They're very touchy about their mysteries. I've never talked to anyone who knows whether they understand their principal function as the honoring of the drowned dead or simply keeping the Sim clear."

:It is a dark river,: Gideon said, and I knew he wasn't talking merely about its color.

"Yes." And the less I had to think about the Sim, the better. "Are you getting anywhere?"

:Define 'anywhere.':

I gave him a mock-glower, and although he didn't smile back, I could see the laughter lurking in his eyes. :I do not yet know substantially more about necromancy than I did before raiding your bookshelves.:

"And I didn't imagine you would. How about the other end of the problem?"

He shook his head. :I wish your most illustrious Cabal had kept better notes.:

"And I wish you wouldn't call them *my* Cabal. They aren't."

He nodded acknowledgment and said, :But I am beginning to acquire a better grasp of the principles of thaumaturgic architecture, and that, I think, may help us.:

"It's most phenomenally boring," I said doubtfully.

:Then you were taught it badly. It's what the Virtu *is,* a coalescence of the thaumaturgic architecture the Cabal raised in the Mirador.:

"I surrender," I said, raising my hands in token. "Will you explain it again for a backward child of five?"

He tilted his head, giving me a thoughtful, unnerving look. :Malkar Gennadion must have had very narrow views of the usefulness of magic.:

"I beg your pardon."

:Don't bridle at me. He didn't teach you thaumaturgic architecture, did he?:

"He said it was a waste of time, fit only for old ladies and bean counters."

:And of course you follow wherever Malkar leads.:

"I do not!"

He just looked at me, one eyebrow raised. I felt my face heat and dropped my gaze, pushing my hair back with both hands. "I *did* ask you to explain it to me," I said, hearing and hating the sullenness in my voice.

:You did,: Gideon agreed, and had the decency to keep whatever amusement he was feeling to himself. He considered me for a moment, then said, :Probably the example you will find easiest to grasp is that of the labyrinth. I recall that we have talked about them before, in Hermione.:

I did my best to hide my flinch, although probably I was not entirely successful. "I'm afraid I wasn't at my intellectual best in Hermione," I said, with a carefully wry smile, and did not mention the fact that I did not remember that conversation, nor indeed, much of anything that had happened in Hermione.

:No, but you listened well,: Gideon said tartly. He lifted his chin, folded his hands before him on the table, and said, :The doctrine of labyrinths proposed by Ephreal Sand states that the windings of a labyrinth may be used to weaken the boundaries between the material world and the world of the spirit.:

"The world of the spirit?"

:The phrase doesn't translate well. Sand calls it *manar,* which is a word he picked up from reading the Cymellunar mystics. He had no more idea what it properly means than I do.:

"Well, you must mean *something* by it."

He made an impatient double-handed gesture. :Magic exists in two worlds. It is a force of the spirit, which wizards are able to use upon the material world. Cabaline wizards have historically denied that magic is anything *except* a force of the spirit, and that is where their teaching goes grievously astray.:

"I don't . . ."

:You are shockingly ill educated,: he said, but smiled to take the sting out of it. :What Cabaline doctrine fails to acknowledge is the *manar,* the world of the spirit. The world of dreams, of ghosts. The world that diviners, sibyls, and oracles walk into when they go looking for the future. The world you were born with one foot in, as all wizards are. The world that rests upon the material world like the iridescent sheen upon a soap bubble.:

"How very poetic," I said, and he glared at me.

:Thaumaturgic architecture is the art of making the world of the spirit conform to the material world, and architectural thaumaturgy is the reverse, although the distinction is so fine I doubt many wizards notice it.: He acknowledged the confusion I could feel on my face with a nod, and said, :Think of it this way—thaumaturgic architecture makes structures of magic, and architectural thaumaturgy channels magic into material structures. Does that help?:

"A little," I said. "But if the Virtu is a working of thaumaturgic architecture—"

:It's both. That is, the physical object you call the Virtu is the representation in architectural thaumaturgy of a massive working of thaumaturgic architecture. Architectural thaumaturgy is what allows workings to *hold*—it's what anchors them. It is what enabled the Cabal to create a reservoir of magic within the physical object of the Virtu. It is what enabled the Grevillian wizards of Caloxa to create a labyrinth that would collect magic and channel it into an engine.:

"An engine? Gideon, you're making that up."

He shook his head, but the slight smile he gave me did not inspire confidence. :Insofar as I understand the more esoteric reaches of Cabaline philosophy, you are taught that magic working through physical objects is the only way for the world of the spirit to touch the material world.:

"Isn't it?"

:Most decidedly not. It is *one* way, but it is far from the *only* way.

Necromancy chooses a different path, as does divination, and likewise oneiromancy. And there are others.:

"What about the Eusebians?"

His turn to flinch, although he smoothed it out. :Eusebian wizardry tends toward the eclectic. A stance that is epistemologically neither sounder nor safer than the blinkered vision of the Cabalines. Blood-wizardry should be banned, not merely discouraged.:

The grimness in his face showed that he spoke from personal experience; I did not ask for details. I did not need to. Malkar had taught me a great deal about blood-wizardry—even if I had not known that was what it was until years later.

:In any event,: Gideon said with determined briskness, :my point is that what the Cabal seems to have done in creating the Virtu is to combine thaumaturgic architecture with necromancy. Clever and difficult and truly a very bad idea.:

"Not that I would argue with you, but why? Aside from the obvious, I mean."

Gideon made a brief, expressive grimace. :They feed on each other.:

"That was . . . vivid. If a little cryptic."

:Look,: he said exasperatedly, then stopped. Started again. :The problem is containment.:

"Oh." That, I did understand. Even Malkar, blasé about so many things, had not cut corners when he was teaching me the principles of containment.

:Yes,: Gideon said, with a certain amount of satisfaction. :With something like Messire von Heber's cards, the thaumaturgic architecture—the symbols of the Sibylline—contains the magic at the same time that it uses it. But it's a tricky thing to balance. Divination and oneiromancy are simpler, from what I've read, because as disciplines they don't interact with the material world. Necromancy does.:

"Are you saying that the Virtu wasn't containing—"

:I'm saying it wasn't *balanced*. At least, that would be my theory as to what happened when certain of the Virtu's spells were broken.: My incomprehension must have shown on my face, for he continued. :The proper image for the interaction of thaumaturgic architecture and any other praxis is a canal. But the Cabal didn't build a canal. They built a dam.:

That image was also vivid, uncomfortably so. "Then it's a good thing I wasn't planning on rebuilding it," I said after a moment.

:Yes,: Gideon said. :What worries me is what you're going to build to put in its place.:

And to that I did not have an answer.

✋

When Mildmay returned, there was the vertical pin-scratch line of a frown between his eyebrows. For a moment, I thought he was still angry at me, but he limped across to the table and said, "Ran into Lord Thaddeus," and his voice was rather dry, but not hostile. He pulled a folded piece of paper out of his pocket and handed it to me, then sat down next to Gideon.

My eyebrows went up as I looked at the elaborate monogram stamped into the wax. "I see I rated his signet ring. How alarming. I wonder what Thaddeus de Lalage has to say to me that he cannot say to my face."

Mildmay muttered something that sounded like, "Wondered that, too." Gideon looked up from the six different books he was consulting, eyes bright and wary.

I broke the seal, unfolded the paper. "I must ask Thaddeus the name of his stationer." His square, jagged Kekropian hand was unexpectedly, hurt-fully familiar. The thought of him was dark in my head, shrouded with fear and shame and pain. But my *memories* of him, memories that were now seven or eight years old, were memories of a close friend. The disjunct disturbed me, the more so because I knew I should have memories to go with the feelings of fear and misery, and I knew the absence in my head where they belonged.

Mildmay can tell you, a treacherous voice whispered. And if Mildmay can't, Gideon can.

I silenced that voice and began to read Thaddeus's letter.

My friend,

Although I am of course deeply gratified to see you restored to your right mind, and returned to us, I am most distressed that you are continuing to associate with Gideon Thraxios. I must tell you that he is not what he may seem to you to be. I have the gravest doubts of his sincerity in this ostensible "divorce" from the Bastion. He was the longtime confederate and catamite of Major Louis Goliath, the spymaster of the Bastion. Moreover, he is an initiate of a particularly pernicious mystery cult that the government of Kekropia has been trying to eradicate for centuries. He is not to be trusted.

Please believe me: I have nothing but your best interests in mind. I do not want to see you hurt again.

And he signed himself, as most wizards did, with an intricately involved sigil instead of his name.

I stared at Thaddeus's letter for what felt like a very long time, trying to parse what he knew from what he merely believed. And all the while there was a nauseous pounding in my head, not quite physical, as I struggled with the contradiction between my memories and my feelings, struggled to find some basis for my fear of Thaddeus, some reason for this terrible belief that, no matter what he said, he was not my friend.

:Felix?:

I looked up; both Gideon and Mildmay were staring at me anxiously, although I could read my brother's anxiety only by the fact that he was staring at all.

"Thaddeus has some extremely intriguing things to impart about your past," I said to Gideon and passed him the letter.

"Yeah, well, he told *me* you weren't kind to your friends," Mildmay said to me. Peripherally, I noticed Gideon's eyebrows drawing down into a scowl as he read; I said to Mildmay, "And what did he mean by that?"

"I think he was warning me you were gonna treat me like shit." Something that wasn't laughter flickered and was gone from his eyes. "Didn't tell him I knew that already."

"Thank you," I said, midway between irony and sincerity.

:Thaddeus has always been a proponent of telling one things 'for one's own good,': Gideon said, and added something vicious in Kekropian, of which I recognized just enough words to realize that Gideon's gift for invective would turn a sailor's hair white.

"Is it true?"

:Of course it's true. Thaddeus is a self-righteous idiot with a great gift for willful blindness, but he would never demean himself by lying.:

And I would have been convinced by his acerbic, contemptuous tone, except that his hands were restless among his pages of notes, and he looked at my face without meeting my eyes.

"Gideon," I said, "nothing you've done can be any worse than the things I've done, and you already know about those." Some of them, anyway.

:But he is wrong,: Gideon said defiantly. :I am not a spy for the Bastion.:

"I know that, idiot," I said, and when he met my eyes, I smiled at him. He blushed and looked down, but some of the cold misery had lifted from his face.

I was not sure what association of ideas prompted me to look at Mildmay then; he was watching us. There was nothing showing on his face, and I realized suddenly, by the contrast, how much I had learned to read from Mildmay's face, how much, comparatively, he had started to let me see.

And it took only a moment's thought to understand why he might have retreated behind his stone mask now. "Thaddeus alleges that Gideon is a spy and a cultist."

"You mean what the Aiaians said was true?" Mildmay said, with something that might almost be alarm, and looked at Gideon.

Gideon flushed bright red and nodded.

"What kind of cult?" Mildmay said. "I mean, can you talk about it at all?"

"You seem worried about something," I said, and he looked even more embarrassed.

But he said doggedly, "You ain't an Obscurantist, are you?"

:Obscurantist?: Gideon asked me.

"A follower of the God of the Obscured Sun," I said, "whose cult has been extinct in Mélusine for centuries."

Mildmay gave the equivalent in Kekropian, haltingly and with terrible pronunciation. And Gideon's eyes went wide.

:No,: he said, :although I know the god of whom you speak. My goddess is the White-Eyed Lady, goddess of the dead, the lost, the trapped.:

Chapter 11

Felix

I realized, after a long moment, that I had both hands pressed flat against the tabletop with enough pressure that my fingernails were turning white.

"Felix?" Mildmay said, and he sounded frightened.

I turned my head stiffly to look at him. His green eyes were watching my face intently, and there was none of the hardness I was used to seeing in them. He was frightened, but I realized vertiginously that he was frightened *for me*. No one had been frightened for me since Joline; nobody had cared so much that they . . .

My memory lit for a moment, like a flash of lightning against a brooding summer midnight, a hundred jumbled images of Mildmay watching me with that same mixture of fear and love in his face. And then the darkness closed in again; the past was gone, and the present must be dealt with.

I licked my lips and croaked, "Gideon worships the White-Eyed Lady. The goddess of Nera, and of the labyrinth in Klepsydra."

"Oh," Mildmay said. Then, very quietly, "Fuck."

I had to keep moving, keep responding, keep from breaking down in panic. I asked Gideon, "What does the worship of the White-Eyed Lady entail, exactly?"

:In principle or in practice? I'm not about to murder you both in your beds, if that's what you're worried about.:

"No, I . . . I didn't think . . . I was just . . ." I was babbling. I pressed the heels of my palms against my eyes, took a deep breath, looked at Gideon, and said in a falsely steady voice, "We have had dealings with the White-Eyed Lady. And they have not been pleasant."

:Dealings?: Gideon's eyebrows rose dramatically. :Considering that her worship has been all but extinct for the past several hundred years, I am curious to know what sort of 'dealings' you might have had.:

"When we were in Klepsydra, we—"

"Hang on," Mildmay said, and both Gideon and I jumped. "You asked a question, and I want it answered."

"Gideon says he won't murder us in our beds," I said.

"I'm sure he won't. But that ain't what you asked." After a moment, he added, "I ain't keen on him murdering nobody else, neither."

:I don't want to murder anyone!: Gideon protested.

I relayed, and Mildmay shrugged, looking not entirely convinced. "Then how d'you go about worshipping a goddess of death?"

:It has become a very private religion,: Gideon said after a moment, hesitantly, :although it seems always to have been a mystery cult. The dangers are such—especially in the Bastion—that her devotees almost never meet. We never see each other's faces, and if we ever guess another's identity, we do our best to forget it.:

I repeated what he had said for Mildmay, then asked, "Then why meet at all? Why practice such a dangerous faith?"

Gideon and Mildmay gave me equally impatient looks. Gideon said, :Because we must. Because that is what faith is.:

"But surely you can believe in her without worshipping her? Forgive me, but she does not seem like a goddess worthy of worship."

:You do not understand,: Gideon said resignedly, as if he had expected no better. I felt myself redden.

He took a deep breath, although he did not need it for speech, and said, :When I was fifteen, I wanted to die.:

I repeated his explanation as he gave it, feeling strangely, relievedly

transparent, as if it were Mildmay that Gideon spoke to. Mildmay understood him, I thought, in a way I never would.

:I had been tithed to the Bastion two years before as an oblate, but my
powers had come upon me very rapidly—too rapidly, and I was made a
lieutenant when I was barely fourteen. I was thrust among the Eusebian officers before I had a chance to understand what they were.:

"What were they?" Mildmay asked, his voice unexpectedly gentle.

:You do not trust wizards,: Gideon said, and Mildmay nodded. :The
Eusebians of that generation are the reason I do not blame you. I think—I
pray—that things are better now.:

And yet he had fled, I thought, but I did not say it.

:The details do not matter, and I do not wish to burden you with them.
Suffice it to say, I was desperately unhappy, and the only thing that held me
back from suicide was fear of what would be done to me if someone
guessed my intention before I could carry it through, or if I botched it.

:Now, the White-Eyed Lady is the goddess of suicides. She takes them
as her lovers, uses them, betrays them. It is their nature as much as hers
that makes it so. In the days when she had a proper priesthood—or so the
initiates of her mysteries tell each other—one of her priests' duties was to
mediate between the goddess and those who wished to come to her intem-
perately. It is said there was once a ritual, so that suicides could make of
their deaths a proper gift, could find the peace the Lady promised. But that,
like so much else, has been lost. Now we have only her mystery, and the ritual of initiation that imitates death. In truth, I think that is why the Bastion
turns a blind eye to her worship: for so many of us, that sham death is
enough.:

"Like the valve on a steam boiler," Mildmay said. "You let a little out,
and the whole thing don't blow up in your face."

:Rather, yes.: Gideon smiled, a sudden dazzling sweetness. :Although
your simile is theologically appalling, I find it personally quite apt.:

Mildmay looked down at his hands—flustered, as he always was by
praise. Gideon continued, :Again, the details do not matter. I was initiated
into the White-Eyed Lady's mysteries, and I did not die. My death is hers,
when she chooses to take it.:

Finished, he folded his hands and sat—waiting, I supposed, to discover
whether we would reject or accept what he had said.

After a moment, Mildmay said, clearly struggling with it, "So you ain't—I mean, it ain't about helping other people meet her, whether they want to or not?"

:She is not the God of the Obscured Sun,: Gideon said. We must both have looked dubious, perhaps a little frightened still, for he said, :The God of the Obscured Sun is the god of necromancers. The White-Eyed Lady is the goddess of the dead and dying.:

"I don't think I entirely understand the difference," I said.

Gideon frowned, his hands moving in a frustrated gesture, as if the words he wanted hovered just out of his reach. :The White-Eyed Lady takes the dead into her domain. She neither wishes nor allows their return to this world. Ghosts are those who have lost their way to her—or have been dragged back by the followers of the Obscured Sun, who is both her rival and her ever-rejected suitor.:

I saw Mildmay's flinch as I repeated Gideon's words. "What?"

He shook his head. "Nothing. It just . . . Nothing."

"That was *not* nothing."

"Just something you said once."

"When?"

He mumbled down at his hands, but I caught the word *Nera* clearly enough.

So did Gideon. :Yes. You mentioned a labyrinth beneath Klepsydra, where I did not know any labyrinth existed, and also the city of Nera, which so far as I know has been lost for a thousand years.:

"Oh. Um, yes. There is a labyrinth beneath Klepsydra, which seems to have been sacred to the White-Eyed Lady, and Nera . . . well, I was not myself at the time."

We both looked at Mildmay, who said, "You want *me* to . . . Powers." But when he had collected himself, he told the story well, vividly, and if he was more honest than I would have liked about the spectacle I had made of myself, I supposed it was no more than I deserved for making him tell the story in the first place.

I had the sense, as I had had when he told me about Nera in the Gardens, that there was something he was leaving out, something he did not want to say, but I had no idea of what it might be until Gideon asked, and I relayed, "Do you think the maze worked?"

"Dunno. I can't see ghosts." But his eyes cut away from mine.

"So you're saying you think it was just my hallucination?"

"Not what I said."

"Do you *believe* in ghosts?"

"Well, yeah," he said, as if the answer were so obvious no one should need to ask.

I looked at him, waited until he reluctantly met my eyes. "What aren't you telling me?"

His face colored, and he muttered, "Don't want to upset you."

I wondered if he meant he didn't want to distress me or he didn't want to make me angry. "Just tell me," I said, and tried not to sound impatient. "It could be important."

"Important for *what*?"

"For the problem of the Mirador's dead." Gideon gave me a sharp, skeptical look, but did not interrupt me. "There are parallels between the two situations that could be useful. So out with it. What happened when we made the maze?"

"Fuck," he said. "Okay." Then he stopped, looking at me with a different kind of wariness. "You sure you don't remember it?" and his eyes slid, just slightly, sideways at Gideon.

I understood what he was asking, and I felt for a moment almost physical pain at the loyalty he was showing me, and the completely unexpected sensitivity to something I had never openly told him, but clearly he knew. He knew I was concealing the loss of my memory, and he was willing to help.

I smiled at him. "Let us merely say that I do not imagine my memory of events is at all, ah, reliable." Which was perfectly true, if grossly misleading, and there was appreciation of that in the nod Mildmay gave me.

"Okay," he said. "So, we made the maze and got outside it, and I didn't see nothing, but I could tell you did. And then you . . ." Another pause, and he said slowly, watching my face, "You started for the maze."

I had known this would be unpleasant; I nodded at him to continue.

"I stopped you," he said, "along of how I didn't know what might happen. And you started cussing me out. Said they—the ghosts—they said you could come with 'em if you wanted. And I—"

There was a flash, as quick and bright and painful as lightning searing the sky: pouring rain and a monster pinning me to the ground and voices calling, pleading, promising . . .

"Joline," I said, my voice barely more than breath.

Mildmay's words cut off jaggedly. I realized after a moment that he and Gideon were both staring at me. Mildmay wouldn't ask, of course, but

Gideon would; I had to say something first, had to keep this matter under my control. "They said they could help me find—" But I couldn't think of how to explain Joline. I finally said, inadequately, "Someone I knew as a child," and Mildmay said hastily, as if he were trying to head off further questions, "And after a while you quit fighting me, so I knew the maze had worked and the ghosts were gone. That, um, that was it."

I let my hands grip together beneath the table, welcoming the dull pain of bone struggling against bone, the sharper bite of my rings in the flesh of my fingers. Joline had died more than fifteen years ago; there was no need to allow myself to become overset. I said, "Then we have the testimony of a madman."

:You sound as if you were hoping for something more.:

"It was just an idea," I said and fled gratefully into theory. "I know very little about necromancy, and none of what I know has to do with . . . I believe the term is *laying* a ghost. So I thought, if there was a method that we knew worked—"

:For followers of a particular goddess.:

"Neither Mildmay nor I knew anything about your White-Eyed Lady."

:I mentioned her to you once,: Gideon said. :When I kept you from committing suicide off the Linlowing Bridge, if you recall.:

I had a moment of flat white panic. But he was testing; I saw that particular brightness in his eyes. I said, "Gideon, I know you have high standards, but surely even you cannot expect that someone . . . someone in that situation would be able to understand and remember every word you say. If you tell me you mentioned your goddess, I will believe you, but my own memory . . ." I shrugged, carefully indifferent, and did not let myself appear to watch his reaction. But I could see that he was thwarted, and said, as if this were the point, "Well, let's ask the expert. Mildmay, are there any rituals native to the pantheon of Mélusine that bring rest to the dead?"

"Dunno," he said. "You wanna try that with words for stupid people?"

You aren't stupid. But even if I said it, he would never believe I meant it. "What do people in the Lower City do to lay a ghost?"

"Go to the cade-skiffs. Or the Resurrectionists. Depending on how they died and who you want knowing about it."

"You know perfectly well that's not what I'm asking."

"How can I, when I ain't heard half the conversation y'all been having?" He flinched at his own words and said, "Sorry," to Gideon. "I didn't mean—"

"We have been discussing ways in which to lay the dead. Particularly the dead of the Mirador. Gideon seems to think his goddess's rites won't help." Gideon glared at me, and I glared back; he did not speak.

Mildmay said, "Mostly that stuff's cade-skiff mysteries. Or necromancy, which I ain't into and never have been. But, if you mean that maze we did, ain't that sort of like Heth-Eskaladen?"

I looked at him blankly.

"The curtain-mazes at the Trials. That's what they're for."

"What do you mean, 'That's what they're for'?"

"You walk the maze," Mildmay said patiently. "That's how you get to Hell."

Mildmay

I had to do a lot of explaining before Felix was satisfied, including telling most of the story of Heth-Eskaladen's Trials, with both of them sitting there watching me and Gideon taking notes. Which I got to say I didn't care for.

But I told the story, and Felix sat there and drank it all in like he'd never heard it before.

"Didn't you go to the Trials as a kid?"

He shrugged. "Once or twice," and then him and Gideon got going again, and I followed as best I could from Felix's half—which is to say not hardly at all—but I got enough to figure that Gideon thought Felix's idea was a really bad one, and Felix got his jaw set and that look in his eye like a bad-tempered mule, and I knew Gideon would've had better luck getting him to go to court naked than to let go of this thing he wanted. But it would only piss them both off if I said it, so I didn't.

Finally—sometime after dinner this was, and they'd been going round and round for hours—Gideon stood up, sudden enough to make me jump, bowed to Felix, real stiff-like, bowed to me, and stalked out of the room like an offended cat. When the door had closed behind him, I raised my eyebrows at Felix.

Who had the grace to look embarrassed. "I shouldn't have called him that, should I?"

"I don't even know what all them words mean, and it didn't sound good."

He laughed. "I'll make it up to him later. But just at the moment . . ." His voice seemed to go back on him. He looked away, twisting his rings. "Do you *truly* believe in ghosts?"

"Yeah," I said. "Straight up."

He nodded, still not looking at me, and said, "I need to tell you about something."

"Okay," I said after a moment when he hadn't gone on. "What?"

"Something that happened—something that I *think* happened—when I was mad." His voice got softer and softer all the way along, until at the end he was barely whispering.

"I thought you didn't remember anything from then," I said, trying to be practical because it wouldn't do to have both of us making an opera about it.

"Bits and pieces," he said, pushing his hair back from his face with both hands but still not looking at me. "No, not even that much. Scraps. Four or five sentences chosen at random, each from a different chapter of a very long romance. So I haven't any context. I can't tell you why I was by myself in the lower levels of the Mirador or what I thought I was escaping from, although I know I was escaping from *something*. But I think I met a ghost."

"*Met* a ghost?"

"Yes. I cannot remember . . . it's all warped somehow, but I know he showed me the crypt of the Cordelii."

"Wow," I said. "I mean, um, why?"

"Presumably he was a Cordelius," Felix said. He sounded tired. "And I know he needed me to do something for him."

I waited, along of being pretty sure he wasn't done. He did look at me then, a quick glance and away, and said, "I think he wanted me to lay him."

Another long pause, and I didn't say nothing because I didn't know what the fuck to say. Then Felix said, his words coming faster, "And of course, I couldn't help him at the time, being mad and under interdict, and of course the Virtu's binding on its necromantic foundation hadn't been broken yet. But that isn't true anymore, and I honestly think the maze might work. And if I am not wrong about as many things as Gideon thinks I am, it might solve the entire problem of the Mirador's dead. The only hitch being . . ." He raised his eyebrows at me, like he was inviting me to tell him what the only hitch was—except I saw so many hitches I didn't know where to start.

Felix rolled his eyes. "The only hitch being the location of the Cordelius crypt."

"You mean they don't *know*?"

"It was lost. On purpose, I now suspect."

"I don't get it. Why would you want to lose a crypt?"

"The same reason they chose to lose the knowledge of the Virtu's foundations. Because it was so much more convenient not to know."

"And you want to find it?"

"The more I think about it, the more certain I am that that's where the Virtu's foundation was laid."

"Sorry, what?"

"The foundations for a spell-casting of this nature have to be physically located. Two of the Virtu's three foundations are obviously in the Hall of the Chimeras—the plinth and the oath-taking—but, well, speaking as a Cabaline wizard, if the Cabal was going to use necromancy on the dead of the Mirador for anything, they'd do it in the crypt of the Cordelii. So that's where I need to go."

I still wasn't sure that made sense, but I said, "Okay. So if nobody knows where this crypt is . . ."

"I found it once," Felix said, with a grin that scared the living daylights out of me. "I want to see if I can do it again."

Felix

He came with me.

I had not expected him to, certainly wouldn't have dreamed of asking, but when I said he didn't have to, he just gave me a one-shouldered shrug and said, "You're gonna need somebody to find the way back."

I couldn't argue with that, and I was too selfish to try.

Mildmay didn't even balk when I said we had to go now. I had my arguments marshaled—the fact that there was court in the morning and I would be expected to work with the Virtu in the afternoon, the need to keep secret how close I was skirting to the edge of necromancy, my bone-deep desire to discuss none of this with Mavortian von Heber—and I felt absurdly deflated when none of them was necessary. Mildmay just said, "Okay," and waited for me to lead him where I would.

I wanted to yell at him not to trust me, to take him by the shoulders and shake him until he understood that I was treacherous and fickle and as cruel as a cat playing with a half-dead mouse. But he knew all of that already, and he trusted me anyway.

"To start, we need to go down," I said and led the way to the nearest staircase that would allow us to do so, deliberately ignoring my own knowledge of how hopelessly farcical this idea was. Because there was one truth about the relationship between thaumaturgy and architecture that I did not need Gideon to tell me: the Mirador, a citadel of wizardry for all the long centuries of its existence, had . . . not magic of its own, but something that might be called sensitivity. It spawned coincidences in its halls like maggots from a dead dog—and it occurred to me as we emerged into a narrow corridor, dust-shrouded except for a blurry track down the center, that perhaps the Mirador's coincidences were somehow related to the huphantike, the labyrinth of fortune. There were three places on the floor of the Hall of the Chimeras, each about the size of a gorgon, that were always ice-cold. There was a room along the Stoa Errata—I had forgotten which one, but I could find it again with five minutes' exploration—that smelled of smoke and burning flesh, no matter how many cleansings were performed. Books fell off the shelves of the Fevrier Archive, randomly and without cause. There were other such phenomena, others and others; to list them all would take the length of a night.

And if you went about looking in the right way, in the Mirador you would often find what you sought.

It had been many years since I had done it, as it made Shannon nervous and unhappy when I disappeared into the abandoned levels of the Mirador for hours on end, but I thought I could still remember the trick of it. It was not so different, in its way, from the methods Thamuris and I used to explore the Khloïdanikos.

It involved a good deal of what Thamuris called surrender and what I preferred to call openness. I had not known what this necessary state was before—probably if I had, I would have been unable to achieve it. To anyone taught by Malkar Gennadion, this sort of deliberate vulnerability seemed a suicidally stupid idea. And Malkar had proved how damaging it could be by forcing me open in his destruction of the Virtu. I thought, as Mildmay and I crossed a great pentagonal room with running hounds inlaid in seven different woods as a border around its marquetry floor, that I had more to be grateful to Thamuris for than I had realized. He had taught me that openness had a purpose, that it was an asset, not merely a weakness.

Without him, I doubted I would have understood what the Khloïdanikos showed me.

We moved deeper and deeper into the Mirador, Mildmay, my witch-lights, and I. Mildmay padded silently at my heels—like a familiar in the stories about wizards I had heard as a child, though I'd never met a wizard who had a familiar or had the first idea how one would go about acquiring such a thing.

Simple, I thought bitterly. Just cast the obligation d'âme.

Every time I looked back, Mildmay's eyes were wide and unearthly in the glow of the witchlights, and he was staring around with the unself-conscious wonder of a child. I nearly jumped out of my skin when, after an hour or more, his deep voice said behind me, "That's the Raphenius crest."

We were passing through a ballroom, the floor a vast black and white checkerboard sweep, the plaster on the walls cracked and fallen away in patches to show the unforgiving stone of the Mirador. I followed the direc-tion of Mildmay's pointing finger and saw on a piece of plaster that was cracked and flaking but not yet fallen, a crest of two lions rampant, back to back, the interlaced feathers of their wide white wings like armor along their flanks. I had never seen it before in my life.

"Raphenius?" I said and was pleased it didn't come out in a squeak.

"It would've been them instead of the Cordelii if Claudine Raphenia had just been born Claude. She gave it a good try, though. Which is why you ain't heard of 'em. Paul Cordelius wasn't a nice guy."

"Do tell," I said, and the next slow, winding phase of my exploration was to the accompaniment of Mildmay explaining to me what I eventually realized was the fall of the Ophidian dynasty and the rise of the Cordelian. What astonished me was not so much that Mildmay knew the history—although that was astonishing enough—as that he spoke about the people involved as if he'd known them all personally, as if this was not history to him, but gossip of the sort laundresses traded across their washtubs. I wanted to ask him where he had learned the story of Paul Cordelius's as-cension to the throne of Marathat, but the question would embarrass him, and I was afraid that he would stop talking altogether.

The weight of darkness pressing in on us from all sides was easier to bear with his voice to listen to.

We descended another staircase and another: spiral staircases; staircases barely the width of my shoulders, running inside the walls like mouse trails; broad sweeping staircases; servants' stairs pitched almost as steeply as ladders. We walked through ballrooms, lords' receiving rooms, wizards' workrooms inlaid with symbols I did not know, anterooms and pantries, corridors and stoas and great echoing vaults forested with pillars. All of it abandoned a hundred years ago at least, all of it cold, brooding. Not quite awake enough to be hostile.

Mikkary.

I shivered, thinking that the sensation was not easier to bear for having a name to put to it, and Mildmay interrupted himself in the middle of explaining why the Bercromii had not rallied to the Raphenii's raised standard to say, "Felix? You all right?"

"More or less," I said. "These halls do not welcome us."

"It's that mikkary thing again, ain't it? Because this feels exactly like that fucking maze in Klepsydra."

How many times do you have to learn? I asked myself. Don't underestimate him. "Yes," I said. "This is mikkary. It cannot—" I had to stop, clear my throat. "It cannot harm us. It has not been channeled as the mikkary of the labyrinth was."

"Do all old buildings get like this? I mean, if nobody uses 'em?"

"I don't know," I said. "I know that the problem here, as in Klepsydra, is not merely that the buildings are old, but that they are places where magic was worked. Places *on* which magic was worked. And that makes them . . . different. I think it makes the mikkary stronger."

" 'Cause that's *just* what we need," Mildmay muttered, and made me laugh.

A half staircase and the length of a stoa later, standing at an intersection marked with the points of the compass, I felt it, a jagged sense of déjà vu and broken magic. "There!" I said, and behind me, Mildmay said, "Um, Felix?"

I turned. His face had gone a ghastly color, even allowing for the witchlights. "Did you know y'all got ghouls down here?"

And I remembered, in an entirely different and very visceral way, the death of Sherbourne Foss.

"They ain't noticed us yet, but . . ." And I followed the direction of his stare; far down the corridor to my left, I could just make out dim, scuttling shapes. They hadn't noticed us because they, too, were surrounded by witchlights, which I guessed was the effect of an almost entirely disabled warding spell.

"Come on!" I said, grabbing Mildmay by the wrist and dragging him in the direction of my déjà vu. He followed willingly, only stumbling a little between the slight remaining untrustworthiness of his right leg and his apparent determination not to look away from those faint, moving lights.

"Where we headed?" he said in a voice pitched to carry to my ears and no farther.

"There should be a staircase," I answered in kind. I'd learned that trick as a child, and Joline and I—

I cut that thought off viciously.

Then my witchlights, skittering and spinning, illuminated a pair of marble columns, an arch of roses. "That's it," I said, and Mildmay moaned behind me, "Oh shit they spotted us." The next second, his hard, fierce weight knocked me off my feet and, for a moment, entirely clear of the floor. Then we were rolling, blunt edges and hard flatness, down the stairs, a tangle of limbs, and Mildmay was dragging me, one hand on my wrist and one painfully in my hair. White marble and a black iron threshold. He let go of me with a shove and I skidded on cold stone, and at the same time heard the great rasping groan of the door swinging shut.

And the next second something hit it from the other side, hard and with a terrible hungry scrabbling as of claws.

"Fuck," Mildmay said, a half-breathless exhalation.

I propped myself up on one elbow to look at him. He was leaning against the door, his forearms braced and his head resting against his hands. From the other side of the door, the scratching continued, interspersed with the thud of bodies throwing themselves against its blessedly unyielding mass.

"Are you all right?" I said.

"You ever seen anybody bit by a ghoul?"

"No, of course not. The Mirador doesn't—"

"Believe in 'em," he finished for me. "Yeah, I know. Well, I saw what was left of Rory Salpêtre after the ghouls got done with him, and I almost got bit once myself. If I'd known there were ghouls down here, I wouldn't've come, and I wouldn't've let you come, neither."

I didn't think I'd ever heard him say so many words at one time when he wasn't telling a story, and I bit back my reflexive response: *you couldn't have stopped me.* Instead, more reasonably, I said, "I didn't know either. Do you think they'll be able to get in?"

He straightened away from the door. "Nah. This fucker's solid. And . . ." He broke off, and I had just enough of his profile to see his frown. Then he said thoughtfully, "Well, fuck me sideways," and I heard the unmistakable sound of bolts being thrown, one at the top of the door, one—with an awkward stoop—at the bottom.

"Bolts?" I said stupidly. "On the *inside* of the door?"

"Yeah." He extended a hand, and I let him brace me to my feet. "Guess they didn't want nobody crashing their funerals."

I tried not to laugh, but it was a lost cause. We ended up leaning against the tomb of Paul Cordelius in an act of the grossest lèse-majesté, both of us giggling and gasping for breath, more giddy than actually amused.

The ghouls continued to paw at the door.

Finally, Mildmay said, "I hope you've got some bright idea for getting us out of here. 'Cause I'm guessing there ain't no back door."

"If what I'm trying to do works, we won't need to worry about it."

"And if it don't?"

"Doesn't. And let's not worry about that until we have to."

"Okay." And then he raised one eyebrow at me. "What do I do to help?"

Mildmay

I got to admit, I love making Felix's jaw drop.

And I guess he must've been expecting me to argue with him or something, because that sure did it.

He just stared at me for the longest time, like I'd, I don't know, told him I was going to go set up as a portrait painter or something, and then he kind of shook himself and said, "It would help greatly if we could find the focal point of the original foundation. I know you can't sense that sort of thing, but will you stay with me while I search?" He gave me a one-sided, not very happy smile. "I find my nerves are a little bit on edge."

"Sure," I said. "I mean, me, too. Where d'you want to start?"

"My first guess would have been the tomb of Paul Cordelius," he said, laying a hand on the tomb we were standing next to. "Since it's here so conveniently by the door. But there's nothing here. My next guess would be John Cordelius, but I can't imagine . . ." His voice kind of died in his throat, and he put one hand up to his head. It should've looked like a pantomime actress making fun of Madeleine Scott or Susan Dravanya, but it didn't.

"What is it?" I said.

He gave me a look that was either a snarl or a smile, I couldn't tell which, his eyes glittering in the witchlight in a way that spooked me the fuck out. "Let's call it a hunch," he said and took off down the line of tombs, muttering their names as he went: "Paul, Matthias, Sebastian, Edmund, Laurence, Charles . . . Claudius . . . Jasper . . . John. Damn them. I *knew* it. *Damn* them."

"What?"

"It's right here," he said, and that look was a snarl, no two ways about it. Both hands were gripping the edges of the tomb like he was trying to break it in half.

"*What* is?"

"John Cordelius," he said, glaring at me like he thought I was going to try and deny it, "last king of Marathat, was killed—executed—in a revolution that not merely brought his dissatisfied cousin Michael Teverius to power, not merely abolished the kingship, but also entirely exterminated the Cordelian line, since Queen Alix Cordelia and the infant prince Daniel Cordelius were both executed—or murdered, if you prefer—along with John. Why, then, *why* would anyone go to the trouble of interring him in the Cordelius vault, a foolishly sentimental gesture that would certainly get you hanged for treason if you were caught? *Why?*"

"Dunno," I said, although I was beginning to have a nasty feeling like maybe I did.

"Because necromancy works most strongly upon the newly dead. And most enduringly upon those who died by violence."

My fingers were making the sign to ward off hexes before I could stop them. "Powers and saints. So you mean—"

"There's something rather grimly appropriate about the symbolism—which may help to explain the Virtu's legendary stability. The Cabal quite literally built their working on John Cordelius's dead body."

We stared at each other for a long time, listening to the ghouls thump and scrabble against the door. Finally, I said, "So what do we do to break it?"

And Felix said, "We draw a maze."

⚡

He had chalk in his pockets, so he took one stick and I took another, and we laid out a maze around the tombs of the Cordelian kings and their wives and their children.

It wasn't nice work, in case you were wondering, and the sound of the ghouls trying to break the door down didn't help. Felix asked once, almost whispering, "If this doesn't work, will they give up? Eventually?"

"Nope," I said, and I was whispering, too, although there wasn't no reason to. "They ain't smart enough."

"Fantastic," Felix said with a shudder, and we kept drawing.

When the maze was done—and I don't suppose I need to mention how hard I was trying to keep from thinking how much the lines of red chalk looked like old faded bloodstains—it covered most of the floor space in the crypt, except for a piece right by the door that Felix had told me to leave clear. John Cordelius's tomb was the heart, which made things pretty badly off center, but we'd worked it out okay.

We were both standing in the clear space by the door. I gave Felix back the chalk, and he dropped it in his pocket without seeming to notice. He was frowning at the crypt, sort of generally, and then he turned and frowned at me, but not like I'd done something wrong. Then he got down on his knees and drew a diamond around me, scribbling a symbol at each point.

"What . . . ?"

"That *should* keep you safe," he said, scrambling up and dusting off his trousers. "And if it doesn't, I apologize in advance."

"Wait—what about you?"

"I have to walk the maze."

"*What?*" It came out almost in a sort of shriek, and I lowered my voice. "Are you absolutely *batfuck*?"

"You told me the story yourself," he said, not loud or angry, and I knew I didn't have a hope of changing his mind. "At the Trials, when you walk the curtain-mazes, what are you doing?"

I didn't want to answer, but it wasn't like I could pretend I didn't know what he was talking about. You and your big fucking mouth, Milly-Fox. "Finding the way so the dead can follow."

"Exactly."

"But them ghosts in Nera—"

"Were, as Gideon was at such pains to point out, followers of a different religion. These are the dead of the Mirador, and they need a psychopomp."

"A what?"

"A guide. Someone to find the way."

"You."

"Yes. Stay within the diamond. Please. I don't want you hurt."

Powers, he was a manipulative bastard. Because of course I went all
blotchy red and said, "Okay, I promise," and he got what he wanted just
like always.

"Good. Wish me luck?" And then he gave me this twisted, nervous little smile, and I realized he was scared half out of his mind. Remembered
that he might *sound* like he knew what he was doing, but it was all just
guesswork and old stories.

I had to clear my throat twice before I could get the word out, but I
said, "Luck."

He nodded, kind of choppy, then turned and started to walk the maze.

Kethe, I hated standing there watching him and not being able to do
nothing. He didn't go fast. Good, steady pace, and his head up, and I knew
he was trying to give the thing some dignity, for all these dead people who'd
been stuck here for almost four Great Septads by what the Cabal had done.
And I loved him for it.

He reached the heart of the maze we'd drawn, poor greedy stupid John
Cordelius's tomb, and he got his chalk out and started marking symbols
around and on top of it. He was muttering under his breath, but I couldn't
make out the words, and I wasn't sure it mattered.

I can't feel magic, but I knew when Felix's spell took, all the same. The
ghouls quit beating themselves against the door.

There was a long silence, heavy and thick, and me and Felix staring at
each other with our eyes as big as bell-wheels. And then a voice, a woman's
voice, low and moaning, and Kethe my skin was goosefleshing so bad it felt
like it was trying to crawl right off my body, "Please. Let us in. Let us walk
the maze."

"Can . . ." Felix took a deep breath. "Can you open the door?"

I started toward it, then stopped myself. "Not without leaving the diamond. And, I mean, I will, but you said—"

"No," Felix said, his voice tight and harsh.

"Please," the dead woman said, and I could hear other voices behind
her, mumbling and moaning, "please let us. Please."

I stayed where I was, 'cause Felix had told me to. He reached toward
the door with one hand. His eyes were wide, and I could see sweat beading
at his hairline and on his upper lip.

And I heard it when the top bolt on the door slid back.

I was praying, a kind of panicked babbling in my head that didn't amount to much more than the ghouls' *please please please*. Please let this work. Please let this be the right thing to do.

The second bolt went back, and now Felix was leaning on John Cordelius's tomb, and I could see his hand shaking. "Please," sobbed the dead people, and there was the heavy clank of the latch, and the door shuddered open the tiniest fraction of an inch.

I had to force myself to take a choked little breath that hurt like fuck, and then another, and Felix was kind of hanging on John Cordelius's tomb like otherwise he'd be sprawled all over the floor, and the door swung open, first just an inch and then it *slammed* into the wall, and I had one moment where I thought, perfectly clear, This is it, we're fucked. And then the ghouls were in the crypt.

They weren't even looking at me. As far as they were concerned, I might have been so much marble and iron. And they didn't head straight for Felix to rip his guts out, neither. They were all about the maze.

I stood there and reminded myself to keep breathing, and the ghouls walked the maze. And I'm pretty sure they weren't the only ones walking it. They were just the only ones I could see. It kept getting colder and colder in the crypt, that much I know.

The ghouls didn't move like ghouls anymore. They still looked like ghouls, all withered and black and with the crazy red eyes, and powers and saints they still *smelled* like ghouls. But they moved like they were alive again. Like they remembered who they'd been.

It didn't take long. Felix moved so he had the tomb between him and the ghouls when they came into the heart of the maze. I didn't blame him, but it turned out it didn't matter. Because the ghouls didn't look at him any more than they'd looked at me. They just reached for John Cordelius's tomb, and when they touched it—I mean, the *second* they laid a finger on it—they kind of crumbled and fell apart into dust. I don't know how many of them there were. Felix said later he thought there were only twenty or so, and it just seemed like more. And like me, he thought there were a bunch of dead people besides the ghouls using the maze.

After a while, I noticed it was getting warmer again, and then that my breathing had quit sounding so much like I was carrying something too heavy for me. And then the last ghoul touched John Cordelius's tomb and was gone.

Felix kind of staggered sideways, and I almost forgot and stepped out of the diamond to go to him. But I didn't. I stayed where I was and called, "You okay?"

"Yes," he said, although he didn't sound sure about it. "I think it worked."

"Well, yeah."

"No. I mean the necromantic foundation. I think it's truly gone. I think this insane idea really *worked*."

He sounded pretty punchy. I said, "Hey. Can I get out of this diamond now?"

"Wait a moment. I have to perform the dispersal."

So I waited, and he did his hocus-stuff. I knew he was done when all the chalk lines disappeared.

He pushed his hair back from his face and said, "All right. Do you think you can find your way back?"

"Watch me," I said, and made him laugh.

Chapter 12

Felix

Court the next morning was rendered hideous by Stephen's saying, almost the instant the necessary business of ritual was out of the way, "Felix, I've been told by several people that you did something to the Mirador last night. Would you mind explaining?"

I managed to keep myself from answering honestly, *Yes.* What sleep I had gotten the night before had been restless and patchy, plagued, not surprisingly, by nightmares in which I was trying to reach the Khloïdanikos through the labyrinth of Klepsydra, and was prevented, first by ghouls, and then, when I had at last eluded them in the oldest and darkest corners of the labyrinth—which was somehow also the Mirador—by the Sim running black and cruel across my path. I said, "Were your wizards not able to inform you, my lord?" earning myself a black look from Vicky as well as Stephen.

"It's *your* explanation I'm interested in."

The temptation to tell the truth—the *exact* truth—was almost physical, like something stuck in my throat. But the envoy from Vusantine stood on the dais, his eyes sharp and cold and very watchful, and any truth I gave to court and Curia, I gave also to the Coeurterre.

And thus I shrugged and said negligently, "Just tidying up a few loose ends."

"That's an interesting way of putting it. You seem to have entirely rid the Mirador of ghouls."

"Oh. I'm sorry. Did you want to keep them?"

Baiting Stephen had once been my favorite hobby. And even though I no longer enjoyed it as I once had, there was a certain bitter satisfaction in seeing I hadn't lost my touch. He quite visibly repressed his first response—and possibly his second—and said, "What I *want* is for you to tell me what you did."

"Entirely rid the Mirador of ghouls." And I smiled at him brightly to hide my wince as Mildmay kicked my ankle.

It hung in the balance for a moment; then Stephen snorted and said, "All right. I'll leave it to your colleagues to get the truth out of you." And turned his attention to the next item in the day's docket.

I did in fact have to endure a rather unpleasant half hour with Giancarlo, but ironically, because he was a wizard and understood what had caused the problem—if ghouls might be so lightly described—it was easier than it would have been with Stephen to avoid deeper questions, the answers to which would only cause pain and distress. There was no need to burden the Curia with the truth, and I reminded myself that I wanted to prove myself better than they thought me, not indulge in an unending succession of petty acts of revenge. I told Giancarlo it was necessary work before mending the Virtu, and made up some persiflage about old and disrupted magic interfering with the patterns my Fressandran colleague was looking for. Giancarlo leapt at the bait and lost sight of the ghouls entirely in bombarding me with questions about Fressandran theory and praxis in general and Mavortian von Heber's probable intentions in particular. I lied extravagantly when I could not answer with the truth, and Giancarlo finally let me go—mollified, if not actually satisfied, by my explanations.

I was left in peace for several days thereafter to do the work I had been appointed. Wizards and courtiers alike skirted me as widely as if the broken state of the Virtu might be contagious; Stephen glowered, but did not speak. Mavortian, like any wizard worth the name, would let personal considerations go in the pursuit of a conundrum; Gideon, too, threw himself willingly into research among the Mirador's scattered libraries, although we had had no personal exchanges since I had called him a reactionary close-minded intellectual coward. He would probably have forgiven me if my attempt to lay the Mirador's dead had failed, but it is hard to be generous when events have conspired to prove an unflattering estimation of one's character to be, even partially, correct. Mildmay stayed at my side, unquestioning, uncomplaining, as if he'd been born to it.

My dreams continued to harp tiresomely on ghouls and the Sim and the labyrinth of Klepsydra, but nightmares were nothing new or surprising.

It was too good to last, and, of course, it didn't.

The afternoon of our fifth day of work, we were afflicted with visitors. Mortimer Clef, the envoy from Vusantine, wished to see what progress we were making, and Stephen had been prompted by some malicious urge to deputize Shannon to accompany him.

Even so, at first it wasn't too bad. Mortimer Clef seemed as willing to answer questions as to ask them, and for an annemer, he had a remarkable grasp of thaumaturgy and its theory. He was able to satisfy my curiosity about the work that had been done in Hermione and what part the wizards of the Coeurterre had played in repairing and rebuilding the magical defenses of the Mirador. I imagined he could also have told me a good deal about the part the High King's treasury had played in repairing the physical structure if I had been inclined to ask, which I was not.

But then he desired to speak to Mavortian, and I was left standing face-to-face with Shannon Teverius.

It would have been a lie to say I did not want him. I wanted him as desperately as I ever had, wanted that fragile gold and alabaster beauty to be mine. What I did not want were the memories, of my cruelty, of his. I remembered striking him, so vividly it might have happened yesterday, but I also remembered, as one remembers things dreamed in a fever, flinching from his words, from the vicious triumph in his voice.

We had hurt each other, and the weight of that pain was simply more than I was willing to take up again.

"Good afternoon, my lord," I said, voice pleasant, face neutral.

"*You're* awfully formal," he said, and my heart sank. "Trying to keep your distance? Afraid I might bear tales to your new light of love?"

Of all the things that worried me, that surely was not on the list. I could not imagine Shannon, whose sheltered life had left him deeply uncomfortable with deformity, with incapacity, talking to Gideon, and even if he did, Gideon was far too canny to listen.

He must have seen in my face that his shot was wide of the mark, for he said, "But then, your standards aren't as exacting as they used to be, are they, darling?" His imitation of me was devastatingly accurate; I had to fight to hide my wince. "Honestly, Felix, even for you, isn't this a bit much? Slumming is one thing—we all do it, powers know—but *incest*? One would think you were living in the days of the Puppet Kings."

It took me a moment to realize what he was implying, and then all my resolution, my calm, my self-control went up in a scouring white blaze of fury—all the worse for the fact that it was by no wish of mine that Shannon's allegations were false.

"Truly," I said, "you are your mother's son, aren't you?"

Shannon went stark white. His mother, Gloria Aestia—the only annemer ever burned at the stake for treason—was more than a sore spot with him; she was a raw, still-bleeding wound. The Lower City had called her the Golden Bitch, and she had earned that soubriquet seven times over. Legally, Shannon had no connection with the House of Aestius, as if Gloria Aestia had never existed, but the fact that he was as uncannily like his mother as I was like mine meant that she could never be entirely forgotten. She was a byword for faithlessness and slander, and I added before Shannon could find his voice, "But then, there's never been any doubt of *that*."

"You're a fine one to talk. How many pretty boys did you leave pining on your way across the Empire?"

"How long did you wait," I countered, "before you found someone else to warm your bed? A week? Two?"

"What's the matter, Felix?" Shannon hissed. "Jealous? Won't your little gutter rat—what's the appropriate expression?—*put out*?"

"He is *not*—" And I realized that my voice had risen, that the echoes were catching and multiplying in the darkness of the vault above us, that Mavortian, Bernard, Mildmay, and Mortimer Clef were all staring at me as if I had gone mad.

An unfortunate comparison.

It was a struggle to lower my voice. "Whatever it is you wish to say, my lord, say it and have done."

"I don't know that I wished to say anything at all," Shannon said, with the smile I had once found charming, and sauntered away to join the envoy from Vusantine.

I stood a moment, feeling my nails bite into my palms, and then started for the doors. I waved Mildmay away savagely when he started to follow me, and said, "Don't come after me," using the obligation d'âme without subtlety. I felt him stop, felt him run into my words as if into a wall, and I was glad of it.

I walked fast, head down, paying no attention to my surroundings, seeking only to outdistance the black snarling beast in my chest. A futile endeavor, and I knew it, but I did not want to pick a vicious fight with Mildmay, and that was the only other option I saw.

I looked up sometime later, out of a dark haze, and discovered that my feet had led me to the Mortisgate, to the Arcane—where I had always gone when the black fury in me was more than I could allow the Mirador to see. I shivered at the memory of some of the things I'd done, but kept my head up as I strode through the Mortisgate, not acknowledging the guards on duty. Once the men stationed there might have been my friends; at the least, I would have been able to greet them by name. But now the uniform of the Protectorate Guard made me think only of monsters with the heads of owls.

The guards, for their part, made no attempt to catch my eye.

I walked through the Arcane as I had walked through the Mirador, without heeding my path or my whereabouts. No one in Mélusine was foolish enough to interfere with a wizard emblazoned with the Mirador's tattoos, and if I did become lost, a gorgon would serve to hire a child to lead me back to the Mortisgate. In truth, a handful of centimes would serve that purpose, but it did me no harm to pay generously.

I walked—not thinking, for in this state my thoughts would be only malevolent, incendiary—and did not wake to my surroundings until the stench of the Sim was strong enough to make me cough. And then I did not need to look to know where I was, although this was a part of the Arcane I had always been careful to avoid.

Keeper had had friends here.

Once, in ages long past, before the Arcane was the Arcane, this must have been conceived of as a pleasure walk, like the Queen Madeleine Garden among the roofs of the Mirador. I could not myself imagine *wanting* to walk along the Sim, but the evidence was all around me in the carved columns and the checkerboard stonework of the floor. There were the remains, too, of a wrought-iron fence, although it was a patchwork thing now: three different patterns of ironwork; a stretch of what must once have been a banister in a noble's town house, the posts sawn off, the flourish of the newel sticking up foolishly and obscenely; a short length of masonry; bits of picket fence; even a section of what looked to me like woven bamboo. On the other side, forty feet straight down, the Sim ran swift and black and cold as death.

There was a bar on the inner side of the colonnade now, the Griffin and Pegasus, and the scene its sign depicted, a cruel mockery of the bourgeois and nobles who favored the card game, was crude enough to make me blush; I knew the sorts of people who would sit at its tables, knew the sorts of services you could buy if you knew whom to ask and what to say to them.

I thought, with horrible clarity, I could buy phoenix here. The heavy, sweet weight of it would keep me from thinking; that, after all, was why the procurers of the Lower City loved it, why Malkar had never tried to cure me of my addiction.

And for a moment, it seemed like a good idea.

Then I recoiled, so violently that I actually staggered sideways, catching myself against the clammy iron of the fence. And I was looking down at the dark, rushing water, at the tiny glints, like drowning stars, that were the reflections of the torches that stood on poles at intervals along the fence. My hands clamped against the iron railing hard enough to hurt, and I wrenched my head up.

I stared across the river, squinting hard, trying to make out the opposite bank. And at the same time I caught up with myself enough to wonder what I was trying to see, when all that would be over there were smugglers' caches and businesses even more dubious than the Griffin and Pegasus, I realized that I was looking for the white flowers of perseïdes, for the Khloïdanikos, and I remembered my nightmares.

And I wondered if the Arcane partook enough of the nature of the Mirador that it was a mistake to assume anything was coincidence.

I took a deep, unwilling breath, the bitter metal scent of the Sim biting at my nostrils. First ghouls, and then the Sim, keeping me from something I wanted. First ghouls, and then the Sim. First necromancy, and then . . .

I might have screamed. If I did, it was a thin noise, inaudible over the river. My hands were cramping tighter and tighter, and I thought for a moment I was going to vomit.

The Mirador is a labyrinth.

It was so clear, so terribly clear. That was what my dreams were trying to tell me: the Mirador was a labyrinth with the Sim at its heart, just like the labyrinth of Klepsydra. Or, to turn it around—and I was laughing now, tiny hysterical shrieks under my breath—the Sim was the heart of the Mirador.

Or to put it still another way, the Sim was the *foundation* of the Mirador, and I knew how to mend the Virtu, and I would have given anything not to have that knowledge.

I leaned over the railing, half-sick with terror and inevitability, and swore, all the worst words I knew, all the words Malkar had taught me never to say, never even to think, a whispered river of invective and filth, like the river which, unheeding, poured itself through the rock and darkness beneath my feet.

Mildmay

When Felix came in, he looked like sixty-nine different kinds of death.

Me and Gideon were playing Long Tiffany—because what the fuck else did we have to do?—but we both put our cards down when we saw him.

"You're here," he said to Gideon. "Good. I need your help."

Gideon's eyebrows went up, and he must have said something pretty snarky, because Felix said, "Don't start," and he sounded so tired, so *beat,* that Gideon's face softened and he stood up.

"Thank you," Felix said. "Hydromancy. Anything you can find about it."

This time Gideon's eyebrows practically hit his hairline.

"I know," Felix said. "Believe me, I know. But . . ." He shook his head, like a bear that's been in the baiting-pits a long time, trying to shake the flies away from where it's bleeding. "I figured it out. I know how to mend the Virtu, but it all depends on whether I can cast a foundation on the Sim and make it stick."

I didn't need to hear Gideon to know what he said. It was all over his face. And I guessed that meant that knowing about magic didn't make Felix's idea sound any less crazy.

"It will work," Felix said. "If I can figure out how to do it."

Gideon said something. Felix laughed. When he pushed his hair off his face, I could see his hands shaking. "Then I suppose I'll die trying."

☆

And of course the next afternoon, Felix had to have the whole conversation all over again. Mavortian was still pissed at him for undoing the spell on John Cordelius's tomb without asking first, and this new thing didn't help at all. Mavortian said it was crazy, and had a list of reasons as long as your arm, and Felix just stood there and heard him out and then said, through his teeth, "Yes, but will it work?"

Mavortian said, "Did you hear me?" and I couldn't stand it no more and said, "Just give the fuck up already."

"I beg your pardon?" Felix said and gave me the mother of all nasty looks.

"Not you. Him. He ain't never going to get you where he wants you, and I'm sick to death of listening to him try."

Felix looked from me to Mavortian and back at me again. "And where is it he wants me?"

"Under his thumb."

"Ah," Felix said and gave Mavortian a thin little smile. "He's right. I don't follow orders well. And in any event, I will do this with or without your help. I would merely *prefer* it to be with."

Mavortian had gone red, and Bernard was giving me this look like I was dead the next time he had a moment to spare. But I'll give Mavortian von Heber this much: he bounced back quick. He said, "You're far more likely to bring the Mirador down around your ears, but, no, I can see no reason in theory why it *couldn't* work."

"And I thank you for your vote of confidence," Felix said. "Now, if you please, let us get to work."

I thought they'd been working before, but not the way Felix saw it. I don't think he slept four hours a night for the next half decad. Him and Mavortian spent hours in the Hall of the Chimeras, and he made them light the candles for him so he wouldn't have to bother with witchlights. And then he'd come back and spend hours with Gideon and piles of books that I swear got bigger every time I turned around.

He gave me the maps.

"They aren't complete, and they probably aren't accurate," he told me, "and if they aren't helpful, for goodness' sake don't say so, since Stephen seems to value them rather more than he would his firstborn child if he had one. But I need you to find me a way to get down to the Sim as near to directly beneath the Hall of the Chimeras as you possibly can—if it's possible at all. I'm afraid it may not be." And he gave me a kind of distracted smile.

Powers, I was just so glad there was something I could do to help, I didn't care *how* hard it was. And I knew about the city and the Sim. There'd be a way.

It was a real bitch of a job, though. Because it wasn't just that the maps weren't complete, it was that there was five different sets of them, plus a bunch of single maps that didn't match up with anything else, and they'd all been drawn by different people at different times for different reasons, and I swear some of them were drawn by spiders who'd taken a bad hit of rose-blood. I ended up a lot of the time, when Felix and them were in the Hall of the Chimeras doing hocus-stuff, wandering around in the lower levels of the Mirador and scaring the daylights out of the maids. But when I got up the nerve to ask them what they knew about the Mirador, they answered me perfectly polite, and told me who else to ask, and even found out some answers for me. And I spent a long afternoon with Master Architrave and *his* maps, which weren't at all like Lord Stephen's maps along of how the maps Master Architrave had were the ones drawn by people who were actually trying to figure out how to get from one place to another without getting lost six times along the way.

And I found out where the flashies' lights of love hung out, and where the servants slept, and the chunk of rooms they'd given over to the musicians. That was one of those weird little pockets where two different buildings had rammed up against each other—in a sort of historical sense, I mean, not for real. It was called the Mesmerine, and it was a good place to keep the musicians out of everybody else's hair.

And of course, I spent two hours there, didn't see a soul, turned to leave, and came face-to-face with Hugo Chandler. He wasn't no happier about it than I was. Went bright red, made a noise like a sheep, and started stammering.

"What?" I said.

Hugo stammered and made noises like a sheep some more.

"*What?*"

"Is it true you're Felix Harrowgate's—"

"Brother? Yeah."

"Lover," Hugo said, although the end of the word pretty much got lost in the sort of noise a sheep would make if it found out it'd just said something rude to a wolf.

I tell you, he was lucky I didn't fall down dead on the spot and leave him to explain it to Felix. I said, "No! Fuck! Where the fuck did you hear that?"

"I, um, everybody's saying it." And he mumbled something I couldn't follow. But I heard the word "lord" all right.

"Who?" I said, and only realized when Hugo backed up that I'd started to move in on him.

Hugo shut his eyes. "Lord Shannon. He keeps asking for the 'Lai of Mad Elinor.' "

Not very fucking subtle. But I remembered that fight him and Felix had had in the Hall of the Chimeras, and I had a sick feeling I knew what it'd been about. Who, I mean. "It's not true," I said, and yeah, I was up in Hugo's face about it, but powers and saints, I remembered standing in the river under Klepsydra, and I remembered that kiss in Farflung, and Kethe, it was just too close to being true to be funny. "Not. Fucking. True."

"Okay, Mildmay. I believe you. Really." And I couldn't tell if he did, or if he just wanted to get away from me, but it wasn't like there was anything I could do about it either way. So I stepped back, because it wasn't Hugo's fault after all, and he sort of squeaked, "Sorry!" and bailed. And I stood there and didn't say none of the things I was thinking out loud, because I didn't want to scare the musicians.

I didn't mean to say nothing about it to Felix, either. I didn't want to talk about it, and I was pretty sure he didn't want to talk about it, and anyway he already knew what Lord Shannon thought. But I came through the door, and he looked up from his books and said, "What's wrong?" and the simple stupid fact that he sounded like he cared made me blurt it out like I didn't have no more sense than a little woolly lamb myself.

"I know what you and Lord Shannon were fighting about."

"Oh," he said. He'd gone very still. "Damn. Someone told you."

"Kind of on accident," I said, almost like I was apologizing for it, and how fucking stupid is that?

"How does someone *accidentally* . . . No. Never mind." He gave me a look, kind of half-exasperated and half-helpless. "I suppose I must admit it was foolish to imagine I could keep you from finding out." Like I'd done it on purpose or something. He rested his face in his hands for a moment, and I really did feel like shit about it, because, powers and saints, didn't he have enough in front of him already?

You and your big fucking mouth, Milly-Fox.

"I'm sorry," I said, but he waved it off without raising his head.

"You have nothing to be sorry for. None of this petty, sordid mess is your fault. Shannon knows me too damnably well."

I didn't want to talk about it. Kethe bless my stupid head, did I not want to talk about it. I said, "You wish it was true, don't you?"

His head came up, spooky eyes wide. Last thing in the world he'd expected me to say. I was kind of surprised myself. I stood there and watched him think about lying to me, watched him decide not to. I hoped, kind of sideways on to anything else, that he didn't fancy himself a cardplayer, because he'd get skinned alive, a face like that.

He said, "Yes, I suppose I do."

My heart was slamming against my ribs like it wanted out, and my mouth had gone dry as cotton. "Ain't it incest?" I asked, because I needed to hear what he'd say.

He raised an eyebrow at me. "Afraid I'll get you pregnant?"

"Oh, fuck you," I said and winced, but he didn't jump on it.

"Yes," he said. "It would be incest. That's what makes it such good gossip."

Neither of us said anything for a minute. He was watching me like right then I was the only thing that mattered. Only thing ever.

"Um," I said. "What d'you want me to say?"

"What you think," he said. He sounded tired. "That's all I ever want. It bothers you, doesn't it?"

"Which part?" I said, and I was so relieved when he laughed that I laughed with him.

But he quit laughing pretty quick. "The fact that it's incest, for a start."

"Don't it bother you?"

He shrugged, and something about it made me remember he'd been a Pharaohlight whore before he'd finished his second septad. "I wouldn't let it stand in my way, no."

"Powers," I said, real quiet along of not having any breath to get some sound behind it. My shoulder hit the door, which was the first I realized I'd been backing away from him. "I ain't molly."

"I know that," he said.

Sacred fuck, I couldn't breathe. I was pressed up against the door like it was going to save me, and part of me wanted to bail, just bolt out of the room like a racing dog. But I couldn't run away. Couldn't do that to him.

"Look," he said, like now it was getting hard for him to get words out.

"I'm not going to rape you. I don't deny that I desire you. I'll even admit that I think I could make it good for you. But you don't want to. And therefore, I will not. I am not Porphyria Levant." A pause while he heaved in a breath. "Now tell me truthfully. Do I disgust you?"

"No," I said, pure reflex. "You scare the shit out of me, but that ain't the same thing."

He smiled, and I thought he meant it. "No, I suppose it isn't."

Felix

I put it off as long as I could. Even after Mildmay told me he thought he could find the place I needed, even after Mavortian had grudgingly said that the work we'd done on repatterning the Virtu ought to hold, I kept seeking reasons, excuses, the flimsiest and frailest of rationalizations—anything to keep away the inevitable.

And no one said anything to me. I was sure they could see my reluctance, and Mildmay at least knew of my fear, but not even Mavortian demanded to know the reason for my delay. And I knew why. Neither Mavortian nor Gideon believed it would work.

The knowledge was like lead, to add to the ice of my helpless, irrational terror. And I could not bring myself to open the subject, to ask if they had reasons beyond the fact that it had never been done before—to ask for their help. Not just their assistance, but their support. I could not do it; I could not beg.

My dreams got steadily worse, and that first nightmare became a grim prophecy: I could not concentrate, awake, asleep, or in between, and thus I could not find the Khloïdanikos. All I could find was the Sim.

I knew I had to break this paralysis, and yet I did not know how. I had always dealt with my terror of the Sim by staying away from it; with that strategy denied me, I was simply at a loss.

And thus I blurted at Mildmay one evening, when I should have said good night, "What are you afraid of?"

"Sorry?" He turned, eyebrows rising, hand frozen in the act of opening his bedroom door.

I hadn't meant to sound so accusing, especially in the wake of that jagged, dreadful conversation when he had admitted he was afraid of me. "I mean, what things frighten you? And how do you . . . how do you deal with it?"

"Dunno," he said, predictably. It was his first line of defense. But I waited, and he seemed to decide I was serious, for he came back toward the table where I sat surrounded by books.

"Don't like ghouls much," he said, and got a smile out of me. "Afraid of a lot of things, I guess. Most people are. And you deal with it the best way you can." He hesitated, those green eyes watching my face as if what he truly feared was that I would bite him. "D'you want to talk about it?"

I supposed I had been rather transparent. "No," I said, "but maybe it would help."

He nodded; then, still watching me, he pulled out a chair and sat down. And waited—no fidgeting, no impatience, and I had no idea what was happening behind those watchful, beautiful green eyes, though at least I'd disabused myself of the notion that nothing was happening at all. He would wait as long as I needed him to, and he would still be here when I was ready to speak.

Something in that realization, some shame, some comfort, acted as a spur. I opened my mouth and heard myself say, "I grew up beside the Sim—on top of it, really."

Mildmay said nothing, but I could see that he was listening; that pin-scratch frown was already between his eyebrows, and I thought he knew he wasn't going to like what he heard.

"My keeper," and saying those words was still hard, after all the years of not saying them, of denying they were there to be said, "he—well, I don't know if he owned them or not, to tell you the truth, but he used the Paladin Warehouses, in Simside."

"I been there," Mildmay said grimly.

"Then you know about the basement."

"That ain't a basement at all, yeah."

It seemed unfair that this should get harder as it went along. "You've seen my back." Not a question, since I knew he had: an awkward moment in a wretched hotel in the middle of the Grasslands, and why I should have forgotten so much and yet have to remember *that* . . . I'd lied to him then, but I'd told the truth later. "And I told you that was Keeper's second-worst punishment."

"You said he'd hold you under."

I nodded once, convulsively. "But I don't think I . . . do you know how many of us he drowned?"

Mildmay shook his head, his eyes never leaving my face.

"Neither do I," I said, and bit the inside of my lip hard against a sob. Against remembering.

"Kethe," Mildmay said softly, and I knew he understood—or was starting to.

"I don't know how many times I earned the river," I said, to my hands now, staring at the rings and tattoos that reminded me I had escaped Keeper, that I wasn't that weeping, terrified little boy any longer. "But I know I *almost* drowned five times between the time I was six and the Fire when I was eleven. When Keeper died." I could still remember the way the river tasted when it rushed in, filling nose and mouth, throat and lungs and stomach. And I remembered how much worse it tasted afterward, as I lay on the bank, coughing and vomiting and sobbing, and none of the other children daring even to offer comfort. "And . . . he made us all watch, you know. Whatever the punishment was. If it was the river, we all had to go down there and stand and *watch*. I watched him drown Ursy. And Rhais. And Belinda. We all did. We stood there and watched him murder our friends, and we didn't do *anything*."

"You were little kids."

"If we'd all rushed him at once," I said. "We could have pushed him in. Big as he was. And he couldn't swim, either. *We could have stopped him*."

"You were little kids," Mildmay said again, even more gently. "And you were scared to death of him."

"I still am."

I looked up then, in the silence; Mildmay was watching me, eyes anxious. He'd been a kept-thief, too, and in that moment I saw the child he had been, just as he probably saw the child I had been. "That's what I'm afraid of," I said. "The river is just the river. If I fall in, I'll drown. But it won't . . ." I managed a laugh, although it was shaky and unconvincing. "It won't reach up and drag me in. I know that. But I . . . I'm afraid of *him*."

"You told me he's dead."

"He is. He died in the Fire, in the Rue Orphée." I stopped, dragged a breath in through my tight and aching throat. "Just like Joline."

"Your friend," he said, and it astonished me that that brusque, slurred, drawling voice could be so kind.

"We told each other stories where we were brother and sister. And they always felt like they were true." I forced myself to meet his eyes, forced myself to drag in another breath. "You remind me of her."

For a moment, there was no jade hardness in his eyes at all. Then he looked away and said, "I do my best."

"If . . . if I did fall in the river . . ."

"I'd jump in after you. Done it before."

And he had. When I thought of the river beneath Klepsydra, I mostly thought of that moment of scalding humiliation when I had betrayed my desire to him. But it was true. I had fallen in, and he had come after me. And saved me.

And somehow that helped. Remembering that one time at least I had come out of the river before Keeper let me up. Quickly, while I still had this momentary bravery, I said, "Tomorrow, then. After court."

"Tomorrow?"

"I can't put it off any longer. I shouldn't have put it off this long."

He thought about that. "Okay. And if you fall in, I'll be right behind you."

I smiled at him and thought, although I could not bring myself to say: I love you, too.

✂

Mildmay had sensibly chosen not to explore the uninhabited depths of the Mirador alone, so he, too, walked our path for the first time. The Mirador is a labyrinth, I thought again and shuddered, a hard spasm that made Gideon look at me anxiously, although he said nothing. I knew that he was wary of intruding and that I would have to reach out to him first, but I felt flayed and brittle with what I was about to attempt; I could not let my defenses down now.

We descended through dust and cobwebs, past the tiny bones of mice caught and slain by long-ago cats. Mildmay carried no map with him, but it was clear he did not need one. He solved this labyrinth as easily as he had solved the one in Klepsydra.

And the deeper we descended, the stronger the smell of the river became. I saw water damage on the paneling of the walls; brackish silt gritted the floor beneath my feet. I wondered how often the Sim flooded these halls, with no one to notice or care as they drowned. I realized that the noise at the edge of my consciousness was the voice of the river, not the full-throated roar I had been expecting, but a more delicate sound, the noise of a thousand tiny streams braided together. To distract myself from it, I said, "How long has it been, do you think, since these levels were used?"

"Dunno," Mildmay said, "but this is old shit. I mean, Thestonarius old." And the Thestonarii were the kings and queens who had built Mélusine's walls.

"Are we even *on* the maps any longer?"

"Nope," Mildmay said cheerfully.

"You mean we're lost," Bernard said from behind me. He was supporting his brother—carrying him when the going became too treacherous—and I supposed he had reason to be ill-tempered, although I did not like his tone.

"Nope," Mildmay said again, just as cheerfully. "This is like some pieces of the Arcane. I got the hang of it."

"I wish I found that comforting," Mavortian said.

"You should," I said. "He knows what he's doing."

"If you say so," Mavortian said, and I bit my tongue against an intemperate reply. Quarreling with Mavortian would serve no purpose, and Mildmay would not thank me.

The sound of water was growing clearer, the scent and feeling of it in the air stronger, heavier. "Down here," Mildmay said, and led us down a narrow spiral staircase; in the light of lanterns and witchlights, the carvings of water lilies and koi along the walls almost seemed to move.

At the bottom, I instinctively cast for more light, feeling the size of the darkness that met us. We all stared for a moment, unable to take in what we saw.

Mildmay said, "Sacred bleeding fuck," mostly under his breath, a genuine expression of awe.

Gideon said, :I thought she was not worshipped this far west, but—:

:I know,: I said, answering in kind because I did not care to have Mavortian hear. :I can see it.:

It was not a temple, as in Huakinthe, nor a great cathedral, as in Klepsydra. I wondered if the labyrinth in Nera might once have been like this, and knew that, whether it had or whether it had been completely different, the ancient Troians had destroyed without bothering first to understand. *They worshipped abominations,* Themistokles had said, and if they had worshipped the God of the Obscured Sun, that was certainly true.

But still . . . even in the darkness and decay, even through my own fear and desire for flight, I could see what had been here. It was the obverse face of the labyrinth in Klepsydra, a reminder that the White-Eyed Lady could also be kind.

Someone had made of the Sim a water garden, laid out in the twining, spiraling knots of a maze, and all these centuries later, it still ran obediently in its channels, still sang as the maze's designers had wished. I hated it, and yet I could not deny its beauty, could not deny that what they had done was a work of reverence and honor.

Mavortian said, "I would be quite surprised to discover that the Virtu is not directly above the center of this maze."

"Heart," Mildmay said, and I nodded at him in appreciation of the distinction. Mavortian ignored him.

"Thaumaturgical architecture is a very odd discipline, but I think I am beginning to grasp its principles. Shall we go find out if I am wrong?"

:Architectural thaumaturgy,: Gideon said, crossly pedantic.

There was nothing I wanted less than to find the heart of that maze, to stand and try to work magic while surrounded by the Sim. Be grateful, I said to myself. You could have found yourself trying to work magic while standing *in* the Sim. Small favors, as Mildmay sometimes said. I smiled at Mavortian and agreed, "No time like the present."

✻

The maze beneath the Mirador—if "beneath" was the correct term when it had once been part of the Mirador as the Hall of the Chimeras was now—was not difficult; it was not meant to be. :It's quite like that hedge maze in Hermione,: Gideon said, :only here we can each serve as our own observation tower.:

I made some noncommittal agreement, and would have even if I had remembered what he was talking about. The farther into the maze we penetrated, the sharper my memories of Keeper became. I was flinching from the expectation of hearing his voice over the gentle music of the water maze.

I'd learned to fellate a man when I was eight years old. Two of the five times I'd come close enough to drowning to feel death—to feel, I realized, the White-Eyed Lady's cold kiss—had been for refusing. Or trying to.

One of the five had been for doing it too well, to the wrong man.

Keeper had taught me I was a whore. He had taught me I was beautiful, too, by the way he looked at me. He'd taught me how to use what I was to get what I wanted, even when all I wanted was not to be hurt anymore. He'd taught me how not to gag on an erect penis, taught me how to swallow semen and say thank you for it.

He'd taught me how to die.

And he'd taught me how to fear, taught me so well that all these years later, I was still afraid.

If you fall in, I reminded myself, Mildmay will come in after you. But it wasn't the river I was afraid of, and I wasn't sure Mildmay could save me.

I wasn't sure anyone could save me. Keeper had taught me I could not save myself. Malkar had hammered that lesson home. And if it needed an object lesson, the shards of the Virtu hundreds of feet above us would do nicely.

But I kept following Mildmay, my hands knotted into fists and my teeth digging into my lower lip. Not screaming, not running. Continuing into the water and darkness in the arrogant and misguided belief that I could for once in my life do something right.

And if I was wrong . . . none of us would survive to explain, and it was quite possible that no one in the Mirador would survive to care. Water-working was chancy at best—though not as straightforwardly suicidal as wood—and working at this scale meant that even the tiniest of mistakes would be magnified.

It was the only solution I had, I reminded myself, and I had learned enough from observing Mavortian to be able to feel the necessity of doing *something*. If we simply dismantled the Virtu entirely, the Mirador's magic would fall apart, the Cabaline school would dissolve—maybe not this month, or this year, but soon. Or would simply not be strong enough to withstand another assault. The Virtu, and the oaths sworn on it, and the tradition it represented, were what held us together, and we needed that. But unless the Virtu was restored, able to resume its function as a power-channeler, to find all the voices of its fugue again, the magic of the Mirador would be dragged continually askew, warped by the brokenness at its center. Again, weakness led to vulnerability, and vulnerability was what the Bastion was waiting for. Waiting for the moment when they could conquer: burn the city, raze the Mirador, put to death every Cabaline wizard who did not flee swiftly enough. They had not attacked yet presumably because Stephen had had the wits to call in the Coeurterre, and the High King of Tibernia behind them, but the Coeurterre would not stay forever. Stephen would not permit it; Marathat was not a vassal state of Tibernia any more than it was a duchy of Kekropia, and the balance between the two was one that the Lords Protector had been maintaining for the nearly two hundred years of the Teverian dynasty. And Stephen had to be aware of how close that balance was to slipping. It was no wonder he had agreed to my reckless gamble.

We reached the heart of the maze, a broad disk carved and channeled into a mandala of water—itself a symbol of balance, and I wondered if I dared believe in omens sufficiently to take that as a good one.

"Yes," Mavortian said. He was standing in the center of the mandala, craning awkwardly on his canes to look up at the ceiling, his witchlights strung out in a vertical line like beads. "Directly above us. I still think you're insane, but there's a possibility this will work."

"It will work," I said, with more confidence than I felt, and joined him at the center of the mandala. The water was only an inch deep, and I could feel the symmetry of the maze converging on this place. I could also feel a faint echo of the Virtu, like a faraway jangle of untuned violins.

"Maybe if they had known this was here, they wouldn't have . . ."

"You said it yourself," Mavortian said. "They were trained necromancers. They wouldn't have taken a risk like this."

"I suppose not." I sighed, looking down at the dark water with a grimace. "I'd better take my boots off."

Boots and stockings, given to Mildmay to hold. The water was cold, the current tugging gently at my toes as I planted my feet. I clenched my teeth until the urge to scream ebbed a little, then said, "It would help if each of you would stand at one of the compass points." I caught the anxiety in Mildmay's look and said, "As placeholders to help guide me. Nothing more." He nodded, although the tension did not dissipate from his shoulders. I directed him to the south, Gideon to the east, Mavortian to the north, and Bernard gave me a grudging half nod and took west.

I stood facing Mavortian, feeling oddly reassured by having Mildmay behind me. Mavortian said quietly, with no trace of his usual bite, "You don't have to do this."

"I do," I said. "You know what I need from you?"

"Yes." He banished his witchlights.

"Good."

I shut my eyes for a moment, wishing the smell of the Sim was not thick enough in the air to taste, and banished my own.

We still had light; Mildmay was holding a lantern, and—I reminded myself as my nails bit into my palms—either I or Mavortian or Gideon could summon witchlights anytime we chose. And the water was still no more than an inch deep, the current still no more than a very gentle pull. This was not the labyrinth beneath Klepsydra. For all its age and long desertion, for all that it was a place meant for the White-Eyed Lady, there was no mikkary here, no old hatred running in the lines of the maze. And that, more than anything, made me hope that this casting would work, that the third foundation would hold.

We had straightened the Virtu's twisted magic, Mavortian and I, working from the patterns he and his cards found as a dowsing rod finds water. I could feel the Virtu now, from where I stood, feel the way it pulled against its two anchors, the Rock and the Dog. Mavortian took out his cards, ran them through his hands, pulled out, one at a time, the Rock, the Dog, the River; he put the other cards back, held the Rock and the Dog in his left hand, raised the River in his right. I reached into the pattern we had made, found the place where the third anchor belonged, gave it that card of the Sibylline.

That was the easy part; even broken and twisted, the Virtu was responsive, willing. But the card was only a placeholder, as the men standing at the points of the compass around me were placeholders, to keep me grounded in this place. This place and no other. As a placeholder, the symbol of the River wouldn't stand for very long; the Virtu's anchors had to be thaumaturgically stable, like stone, or constantly renewed, like the Cabaline oaths. Or constantly moving, unstable, shifting, changing, but undying, like the black river that was Mélusine's blood.

I had to show the Virtu that the Sim was the River, that the symbol I had given it as an anchor represented this flowing darkness, this cruelty and strength. This river and no other. But to do that, I had to work the Sim into the pattern. And that meant . . .

I forced myself to keep breathing deeply, forced myself to be aware of Mildmay, Gideon, Mavortian, Bernard. I forced myself to feel the water against my feet. I knelt and did not allow myself to wince as the water soaked into my trousers. I sat back on my heels to find my balance; then carefully, slowly, I reached down, both hands, and laid my palms flat against the stone. I looked up. Mavortian was still holding the River face out in his left hand. I could feel the pattern of the Virtu's magic pulling to the card and then pulling away again.

I took a breath, held it a seven count, let it out again. And began to work the river.

It was like drowning again. Only this time, it was my own hands holding me under. I remembered not to struggle. I let the force of the river take me.

Though they had never said so, I knew Mavortian and Gideon had expected me to fight the Sim, to control it. That was how most wizards thought, Cabalines and Eusebians, Fressandrans with their strong divination. But I had learned from Thamuris and the Khloïdanikos. I could not control the Sim; I could only kill myself trying. But I could open myself to the river, surrender to the river.

I could drown. I could drown in an inch of water, and they would find no water in my lungs.

That will happen if you panic, I said fiercely to myself. Remember where you are. I could not lift my head, could not tear my gaze away from my hands, from the distorted underwater gleam of the garnets in my rings. But I could feel Mildmay behind me, the obligation d'âme like a rope between us, a rope woven of iron and silver, the heat of breath and the salt of skin. He won't let you drown, I said to the screaming, sobbing child locked in the cage of my ribs, and my magic gathered and reached into the heart of the river.

It was the surrender that was hard, not the magic. The pattern was there in the thaumaturgy, just like the pattern of channels that made the water maze. The river flowed into it, into the course Mavortian and I had laid. I watched it twine around the other two foundations, felt a hesitation, a shudder, and for a vivid moment saw them braided together, black and silver-gray and scarlet, river, rock, and blood.

And then I was on my knees in the water, starting to shiver with cold.

The Virtu was still unawakened, still dark.

But the third foundation was set.

Chapter 13

Mildmay

I woke up—some dream about trying to drag chests out of the Sim before the water got into them, and sometimes I'd look at the chest and it'd be a little kid instead—and Felix was in the doorway, holding a lantern.

He looked like shit, to be perfectly frank. He said, "Let's finish this now."

"Finish . . . oh. *Now?*"

"Now," he said.

I sat up. "You sure? I mean, ain't you done enough today?"

"Now," he said again, and powers, I was scared to argue with him.

"Okay, give me a second."

I ran both hands hard up my face, dragged on yesterday's trousers and shirt, was looking around for socks when he said, "You won't need your boots." I saw he was barefoot, wearing just a nightshirt and his beautiful quilted dressing gown.

"Felix? You, um, wanna put some clothes on?"

"This won't take long," he said, and there I was again, scared to argue with him. I wasn't scared of what he would do to me, exactly. More scared of what he might do to himself. That was how bad he looked.

So I followed him, and let me tell you, wandering around the Mirador at night is not the way to find a good time. Felix didn't seem to notice anything, but, Kethe, I felt it. Didn't know what it was, mind, but I felt it all right. Felt it in every separate bone of my spine, and ended up walking about as close to Felix as I thought he'd let me, spooked right straight out of my skin.

He didn't go round to the big bronze doors of the Hall of the Chimeras. Instead, he took a way I hadn't known about before, and we came out through the door that Lord Stephen used. And, no, I wasn't happy about that, neither. But I did figure it was the least of my worries.

"Shouldn't you at least have Mavortian with you?" I said. "Or Gideon? Or *somebody*?"

He stopped right by the big stone pillar the Virtu sat on. It was the right shape again—him and Mavortian had done that, got it back to being a globe instead of an ugly set of teeth. Felix said, "You're all the help I need," and his witchlights were all around his head like a crown, and the way they made his eyes shine was nothing I ever want to see again.

"Me? But I'm, I mean, I'll do anything I can, but—"

"It isn't a matter of magic," he said. "I have *that*. I need . . ." He stopped, seemed to look at me properly for the first time that night. "If you are willing to help me, that is."

"You don't need to ask that."

"I know. But I'm asking anyway." He smiled at me, a real smile and meant for me. "Will you help?"

" 'Course. Tell me what to do."

"I need your strength," he said. "I felt it earlier, through the obligation d'âme. And I wouldn't want to try this with another wizard. I might inadvertently do to them what Malkar did to me."

"Oh." After a second I got the part he wasn't saying. Whatever exactly it was—and I didn't want to understand it better than I did—he couldn't do it to me. I'm annemer. Nothing for him to take, whether he wanted to or not. My voice was pretty steady when I said, "Okay. Tell me what to do."

"Give me your hands," he said. "And don't let go, no matter what happens."

I would've felt better about the whole thing if that hadn't been an echo of what Thamuris had said to me when he was doing his pythian casting, and, fuck, Felix didn't look much better than Thamuris had, even figuring for the consumption and all. But he trusted me, and I knew for him to ask for help meant he needed it, and not in no half-assed way, neither. And I was still scared of what might happen to him if he couldn't do this. He looked like he was about half a step from completely losing his shit.

"Okay," I said.

I put my hands out, palms up. He took them, held them a moment, his hands warm when I'd expected them to be icy. He said, "Thank you," very quietly, and then locked his grip around my wrists. Not sure if it was right or wrong, I did the same, and he nodded.

"Don't let go until I tell you it's all right," he said, and then his hands clamped down and he was gone from behind his eyes.

The bands on his rings bit like double-jointed alligators. I couldn't help the way my breath hissed in, but I'm pretty sure Felix didn't notice, and I didn't flinch or try and pull away, and that's what counts.

I wish I knew the first thing about what he was doing, so I could explain it right. But I don't. I couldn't even tell anything was happening, except for the grip he had on my wrists, and after a while I started getting a headache. Not much at first, but it kept getting worse and worse until it was like some fucker had gotten an ice pick and was jabbing it between my eyeball and the bone behind my eyebrow, right in time with my heartbeat. I tightened my hold on Felix's wrists so I didn't do something stupid, and just hung on. It was all I could do, all he'd told me about. I kept my gaze down, on our hands, because I couldn't stand looking at his face with nobody in it, and a second after I felt something wet on my upper lip—right side, same as that fucking ice pick—I saw the blood land, bright red, on the joint of my thumb.

I hoped like fuck there wasn't a connection, but you know, I wasn't doing real good convincing myself. Come on, Felix, I thought. Hurry it the fuck up already.

Nothing happened for a while, and I watched blood drip from my nose onto my hand. Then Felix's fingers clamped down even harder, and, powers and saints, I'd been seriously underestimating how strong he was. I could feel his rings all the way to the bone. He yelled something, and it might've been a language I don't know, or no language at all, and then, Kethe, like a body blow, the Virtu lit up.

Bright blue everywhere. Bright fucking blue. I made some kind of a noise, I think, but I couldn't even hear myself. It was too fucking blue. I had just enough time to wonder if it had struck me blind and this fucking blue was all I was going to see for the rest of my life, before it started backing off again, and I could tell that me and Felix were still standing on the dais just like we had been, with our hands locked together and his rings digging into my wrists and blood dripping down my face.

He said, "There," in this nice normal voice, like nothing weird had been happening at all. "You can let go now." I looked up and was just in time to see his eyes roll back in his head.

He went down like he'd taken a sledgehammer between the eyes. I managed to catch him, but he was so much taller than me that there wasn't much more I could do than just slow him down so he wouldn't hurt himself. And then I found a handkerchief in my trousers pocket and sat down under the Virtu to try and get my damn nose to stop bleeding before I dragged the dead weight of my brother back to his bed.

Felix

The first thing I heard when I woke up was Mildmay and Bernard shouting at each other. My immediate impulse was to bury my head under the pillows and go back to sleep, but I rolled over to look at the clock, and half a second later was out of bed, standing in the doorway, demanding, "What were you thinking to let me sleep this late?"

Mildmay turned. Bernard glared at me. Mavortian, in my favorite chair, did the same.

"Well for one thing," Mildmay said in his slow drawl, "I didn't think I'd be able to wake you up."

"What do you mean? I never . . ." My voice trailed off as I took in his appearance. Neat as ever, but he was haggard, the lines too strongly marked around his mouth, eyes bloodshot, especially the right one. "What happened to you?"

"From what little he's said," Mavortian put in, "I gather *you* did."

"I . . ."

"What's the last thing you remember?"

"We cast the foundation on the Sim," I said. "Came back, had a well-deserved dinner, and . . ." I felt my eyes widen, felt one hand go up to my mouth in a pantomime-cliché gesture of distress. "I didn't."

"Look," Mildmay said. "I been telling them. It's no big deal. I said yes." He sounded exasperated, but the shadows under his eyes, the lack of color in his face . . .

"How badly did I hurt you?"

"You didn't."

"Those bruises on your wrists say otherwise," Bernard said.

Mildmay gave him a venomous glare, but I said, "Show me."

"Felix, it don't—"

"Yes, it does. *Show me.*"

I didn't use the obligation d'âme, although we both knew I could have. He sighed, shrugged off his coat, and removed his left cuff link. He pushed his sleeve back and held his arm out.

My breath caught. Livid purple and yellow bruises in an uneven ring around his wrist. I took his hand, turned it over gently; the soft skin of his inner wrist was even worse, with scabbed-over tears like the marks of tiny, vicious teeth. "*I* did that?"

"You didn't mean to. And I ain't mad, so it don't matter. Okay?"

I let go of him and turned away. "What an abysmally, *damnably* stupid thing to do."

"At least you admit it," Mavortian said.

"He didn't do no better for himself," Mildmay said. "You been sitting here same as me the past two days, so it ain't like you don't know that."

I doubted Mavortian had caught one word in five, but something else took precedence. "Did you say *two days*?"

"Two days," Mavortian said, not pleasantly. "Well over forty-eight hours."

I looked at Mildmay, who shrugged. "I went in and checked you were breathing a couple times. I couldn't make you wake up, and I didn't think you'd want anybody knowing. Couldn't keep *them* out"—with an eloquent jerk of his head toward Mavortian and Bernard—"but I told everybody else you were resting and didn't want visitors."

"Everybody else?"

He pointed at the table. "Can't keep people from noticing you fixed the Virtu, neither."

Letters on every color of paper imaginable swamped one end of the table. "Goodness," I said and moved past Mildmay to open the first one.

"A singularly inappropriate word," Mavortian said, "when what you did is the rankest kind of . . ."

I let him harangue me, since it was clear I could not stop him, but I did not listen. I had heard the same, over and over again, from Giancarlo and Victoria, from Vida and Thaddeus and all those other wizards who'd thought they had the right to tell me what to do. Though not from Malkar, who had had his own methods of making his displeasure felt. I continued opening letters, one after another, congratulations from wizards, and annemer courtiers, a stiffly polite little note from the envoys of the Coeurterre, a letter from Stephen so charmingly begrudging that I thought I should have it framed, a letter from Master Architrave "on behalf of the domestic staff of the Vielle Roche." An announcement of a soirée to be held in honor and celebration.

"What's the date?" I said without looking up.

"Knew you'd ask that," Mildmay said, sounding almost pleased with himself. "So I got Rollo to give it in the flash calendar. Dai twenty-sixth."

"That's tonight, then."

"Have you heard a word I said?" Mavortian demanded.

I gave him a perfectly insincere smile. "Of course." And gave his words back to him verbatim, a trick I'd learned in self-defense as Malkar's creature, although it was far more satisfying as an offensive weapon. I continued opening letters as I recited, checking off names against the mental lists I had of allies and enemies. My lists of course were woefully out-of-date, but there was interest and information still in how these letters matched up with where I thought I stood.

And then I opened a heavy cream paper, sealed with blood-red wax, and an enclosure fell out. I picked it up, glanced at it, and dropped it, my fingers suddenly nerveless and my voice charred to ashes in my throat.

"Felix?" Mavortian said.

"What's wrong?" Mildmay came around the table, though he did not quite reach to touch me.

"Malkar," I croaked.

"Fuck," Mildmay said. "Here. Chair."

I sat down heavily; it was only barely not an uncontrolled fall. I told myself it was ridiculous, childish, to be this badly affected by the mere sight of his handwriting, but I could do nothing about my shaking hands or the way I was having to fight to keep my breath from shortening.

"Food," Mildmay said. "Powers, I'm an idiot. Be right back."

He left, and Mavortian struggled to his feet. "He's very protective of you, you know. Charming, if rather misguided. I imagine you find it very useful."

"I don't . . ."

"And Malkar Gennadion. I admit I've become quite curious . . ." He'd reached the table and picked up the letter. My instincts screaming, I was already standing up to reach for it when I realized his voice had died just as mine had, the color draining from his face.

"Mavortian?" Bernard, and I thought that if anyone should know about being the object of protectiveness, misguided or otherwise, it was Mavortian.

Mavortian ignored Bernard completely. He looked at me, eyes blazing in his pale face. "Do you know whose handwriting this is?"

"Of course," I said. "I told you—"

"Beaumont Livy's."

We were still staring at each other, trying to make sense of it, when Mildmay returned.

He stopped just inside the room, his gaze going from my face to Mavortian's, wary as a fox inspecting a trap. "What's going on?"

"We've made a very interesting discovery," Mavortian said, "and found the answer to a riddle that has been plaguing me for a very long time."

Mildmay looked at me. I said, "It seems that Malkar Gennadion and Beaumont Livy are one and the same."

"What? *Your* Beaumont Livy?"

"His handwriting is distinctive," Mavortian said.

Mildmay was silent; I saw him exchange a glance with Bernard that I could not interpret. Finally, he said, "So what're you gonna do?"

"Well," I said, "the first step must be to find out what Malkar feels he has to say to me." I held out my hand for the letter, and Mavortian yielded it.

I knew Malkar too well to make the mistake of reading his letter out loud. After the first two words, I got up and moved over to the fireplace so that I could burn it as soon as I finished reading.

My darling foolish child—
Vey has brought me word of your latest exploit and promises she will enclose these few words of mine in the congratulatory letter she herself intends to send.
I am very proud of you, my darling, and cannot help feeling it is a pity your most heroic and truly astonishing efforts will be in vain. I feel this so strongly, in fact, that I am going to give you a chance to salvage something from the wreckage.

*I can almost see you frown as you struggle to understand me.
I will be clear, for I know you will not share these words with
anyone.*

    *I have entered into an agreement with Vey Coruscant—who
I believe is known in Mélusine by the charming soubriquet of
Queen Blood—to assassinate Stephen Teverius as Brinvillier
Strych assassinated his grandmother. Vey was Strych's last,
dearest, and greatest pupil, and helped him as she will help me.
Trust me, my darling, we will succeed.*

    *I should regret it if you were to be destroyed with the rest.
There is time yet—even with Vey's knowledge and advice, it is a
tricky matter—so consider your options carefully. But do not
consider for too long.*

    If you wish to find me, dearest, you know where to look.

He had not signed it, but he did not need to. As Mavortian had said,
Malkar's handwriting was unmistakable, and even if he had hired a scribe,
I would have known the letter was his. Every word reeked of him.

I crumpled the letter viciously, but did not throw it in the fire as I had
intended and passionately desired. It was proof of Malkar's plans; it might
be necessary to allow other people to read it. The thought was enough to
make me feel withered and ill.

First things first, I said to myself grimly. And the first thing was to see
what Malkar's new confederate had written. I wondered if she'd read
Malkar's letter before she sent it, and knew she had. It was what I would
have done.

I straightened and refolded Malkar's letter, put it in the inner pocket of
my waistcoat. Then I went back to the table and picked up the second letter. I recognized the name. I had grown up hearing the stories about Queen
Blood—a fact that Malkar had no doubt guessed and was delighted by. And
the Curia had periodically agreed that something had to be done about Vey
Coruscant, although nothing ever was.

Her handwriting was small, slanting, with extravagant tails to the g's
and y's. Clerk's hand, with the idiosyncracies of someone whose living did
not depend on her script:

*To Lord Felix Harrowgate of the Mirador, late of Pharaohlight
and Arabel, greetings.*

*I understand now why Lord Malkar speaks so highly of
you. Your accomplishment is marvelous enough that I am sure
it did not even grow in the telling as it traveled from the
Mirador to the Lower City. Indeed, it must have shrunk, for
one part of your great feat I have not heard mentioned at all.
Perhaps the Mirador does not like it spoken of, that their
prodigal child has been dabbling in necromancy. Certainly, it
would be an embarrassment to them were it to become common
knowledge.*

*I, on the other hand, am intrigued—indeed, quite eager to test
your strength against my own. We would, of course, wish to do
such a thing quietly, so I propose that you meet me at sunrise,
Dai 27, 2281 AUC, in Adrian's Park, where we may discuss the
matter quite undisturbed.*

*If you do not feel it necessary to meet me, I shall of course
understand, and will have no qualms about pursuing my inquiries
through more public channels.*

Yours most respectfully,
Vey Coruscant

I put Vey's letter down carefully, as if it might break, or bite me, and
said, "Blackmail."

"You're going to have to give us more information if you hope for a
useful response," Mavortian said.

"I don't." But I could not contemplate "the matter," as Vey had so tact-
fully phrased it, in silence. I said, "Malkar plans to assassinate Stephen, and
Vey Coruscant has challenged me to a duel."

I looked up as I said it, and was gratified by their reactions. Bernard
looked merely irritated and anxious, but Mildmay went white as bone, and
Mavortian said something in Norvenan I recognized as a curse. After a moment he asked, "What are you going to do?"

"I don't know. Fight a duel, I suppose." The Mirador had outlawed duelling in the Protectorate of Helen, but no one had ever gotten around to
patching that loophole in the oaths and wards. And I knew how to use it.
Malkar had been very interested in the loopholes in the Mirador's wards,
and with hindsight, I now knew why.

"You can't!" Mildmay burst out at the same time Mavortian said, "Don't be ridiculous."

"But I don't see what else I can do. I can't have her going to Stephen saying I was using necromancy in the Cordelius crypt."

"Yes, but fighting a duel with her isn't the answer. And, besides, isn't it more important to deal with the assassination plans?"

"I've got time to worry about that. She wants me to meet her tomorrow morning."

"So tell Lord Stephen tonight," Mildmay said, so vehemently that we all turned to stare at him. His face reddened, and he looked down at his hands, muttering, "You don't want to fuck with Vey Coruscant."

"Do you seriously imagine I can't defeat her?"

"Ain't that," Mildmay started, but Mavortian was already saying, "Perhaps it would help if you told me who Vey Coruscant is."

"A blood-wizard. Very powerful. According to Malkar, Brinvillier Strych's last pupil. Malkar's taken up with her in hopes of repeating Strych's assassination of Jane Teveria."

Mavortian tilted his head, blue eyes bright. "So Maselle Coruscant is essential to Livy's—I beg your pardon, I mean Messire Gennadion—Messire Gennadion's plans?"

"His letter certainly carries that implication." I felt my mouth twist, had to resist the urge to get Malkar's letter out again and tear it into shreds. "Trying to make me jealous."

"Interesting," Mavortian said. "And this duel. Is *that* part of Messire Gennadion's plans?

"No," I said slowly, thinking it through. "Malkar's plan seems to be for me to betray the Mirador and join him."

"And yet Maselle Coruscant wishes to kill you."

"Jealous," I said. "Malkar always sets his disciples at each other's throats."

"Ah," Mavortian said, as if he was matching that up against some experience of his own. "Do you think she *can* kill you?"

"Unlikely," I said. "Even if—"

"Thought you weren't gonna commit heresy no more," Mildmay said scathingly.

I flinched. Mavortian said, "*Is* it heresy for you to kill a blood-wizard in a duel?"

"Petty heresy. Duelling is petty heresy. Not gross heresy like killing another Cabaline or practicing necromancy. But it *is* heresy, and I . . ." I swallowed hard and said, my voice ridiculously small, "I'm not sure I could do it anyway."

"Then don't," Mildmay said.

"And have Stephen find out about the gross heresy I *did* commit?"

"No, he's right," Mavortian said. "You shouldn't meet her. But that doesn't mean she can't be dealt with."

"Beg pardon?"

"Clearly, from what you've said, removing Maselle Coruscant from the playing field will greatly inconvenience Messire Gennadion."

"But you just said—"

He continued over me: "If Maselle Coruscant wishes to meet you tomorrow morning, I believe we must move tonight. And since she expects a wizard, I suggest we send an annemer." And he turned his brilliant gaze on Mildmay.

"No," Mildmay said. "No fucking way."

"But it's perfect," I said. With Vey Coruscant gone, Malkar would not be able to assassinate Stephen. With Vey Coruscant gone, I might not have to tell Stephen about any of this. The thought was a giddy relief. "You've killed a wizard before."

"I didn't—"

"Of course you did. You admitted it to the entire Mirador. You can hardly try to deny it now."

"It won't do you no good."

"What do you mean by that?" Mavortian said.

"If she knows about the Cordelius crypt," Mildmay said, to me, as if Mavortian didn't even exist, "then she ain't the only one. I get that you don't want Lord Stephen to know, but he's gonna find out anyway."

"And what about Malkar's plans?"

"Tell him that, too! He's the Lord Protector—it's his *job*!"

"Do you have any idea what Stephen will do to me?"

"He's gonna find out anyway," Mildmay said again, mulishly.

"Yes, most likely," Mavortian said. "But there is a great difference between bringing news of a planned assassination, which one has received from a dubious and compromising source, and bringing news that one has *prevented* a planned assassination. Preferably with Messire Gennadion's head as evidence." His smile was feral, bloodthirsty, and I smiled back.

"Are y'all listening to yourselves?" Mildmay said. His voice had gone up, and he reached across the table to grip my forearm. "Felix, please. Can't you see how crazy this is?"

"The combined power of the entire Curia, with the Mirador behind them, wasn't enough to save Jane Teveria," I said, freeing myself from his hand. He let me.

"And do you imagine you could even *get* that kind of unanimity?" Mavortian said. "Especially with the emissaries of the Coeurterre in the equation?"

I hadn't thought of that. "Stephen won't even listen to me," I said. "Not until he's actually alight and burning, and by then it will be too late."

Mildmay must have looked at Bernard, for Bernard said, "I'm not getting in his way." It wasn't clear if he meant me or his brother, and it hardly mattered.

I said to Mildmay, "You've done it before."

"That don't mean I want to do it again."

"It's the best way. And we do have to move tonight."

"So move to Lord Stephen," Mildmay said between his teeth.

"And what's Stephen going to do? You know as well as I do the Mirador won't touch Vey Coruscant."

He opened his mouth to argue, realized I was right, and closed it again. And was staring at me, frustrated and searching for words, when there was a knock on the door.

Mildmay answered it. "Yeah, he's awake," he said. "Maybe you can talk him out of it." He stood aside and let Gideon in.

"Splendid," Mavortian said and smiled. "Messire Thraxios's wisdom having proved so helpful in the past."

Gideon looked from Mildmay to Mavortian to me, his eyebrows going up. I explained the situation briefly; it was not getting more pleasant with practice. Gideon agreed with Mildmay, as Mavortian and I had both known he would, but he could not offer any reasons better than those Mildmay had already tried. And he could not argue that Malkar and Vey did not need to be stopped.

:Felix,: he said finally, :may I speak to you alone?:

"It seems entirely unnecessary," I said. "We are agreed that we must act, and I have chosen a course of action."

"I won't do it."

I stared at Mildmay. He flinched and looked down, but said, "I told you the next time you wanted me to kill somebody, you'd better pay me for it. And I'm telling you now, you can't pay me enough. Can't nobody pay me enough."

"We need her dead," I said, trying to keep the frustration out of my voice, trying to make him understand.

"You *need* to talk to Lord Stephen."

"No," I said, remembering years of hatred, of bitter quarrels, the two of us fighting over Shannon like two coyotes over a bone. "Mildmay, please. I need you to do this for me."

"No." Flat, hard, like a slap across the face.

"No?"

"I won't do it."

"But that's where you're wrong," I said. "You will do it."

His head came up. "You wouldn't."

"I most certainly would."

He set his jaw. "Then you'll have to."

He had called my bluff, but I wasn't bluffing.

"Can you find Vey Coruscant?" I said.

"Felix, can't you see what—"

"Can you find her? And don't lie." The obligation d'âme could be a weapon, and I was furious enough to use it.

His face had gone white. "Yeah."

"Do you know how to kill a blood-wizard?"

And with the obligation d'âme on him, he said, "Yeah."

"Then you will do as I tell you. You will find and kill Vey Coruscant tonight."

He smiled at me. I had never seen him try to smile before, and the twisted mask it made of his face would have been ghastly enough without the venom behind it. "You're gonna have to give me permission to go to the Lower City first."

I had forgotten I had forbidden it to him. "Yes," I snarled. "You have permission. Just go. All of you! Out!"

They left, even Gideon having the sense not to try to linger. My fury drained away, and I felt clear, resolved. Vey Coruscant would die tonight; Malkar would be infuriated, a wounded lion, easier to track and kill. And I had a soirée to prepare for.

Mildmay

He'd told me to go, and I had to go.

He'd told me to kill Vey Coruscant, and I had to kill Vey Coruscant.

But I didn't have to do it right away.

Okay, I know it was stupid and childish and not even worth it, and I know I was the one wanted the binding-by-forms in the first place. So it's my own fault. But I'd trusted him. That was the really stupid thing. I'd trusted him not to pull this sort of shit on me, and now I couldn't even figure out why. Why I'd thought he wouldn't walk all over me the second I was in the way of something he wanted.

I went to Mehitabel because I wouldn't have to explain it to her. She knew about the obligation d'âme. Fuck, she knew about Felix. She knew what he was and what I was. And the worst I had to worry about was her saying *I told you so.*

I didn't even stop to think she might not be there, and I don't know what I would've done if she hadn't been. But she was. Her door was open, with candlelight like a beacon, and when I looked in, I saw she'd got four or five candelabra crammed in around her vanity, to give her really good light to look at herself by.

She was dressing for the soirée, and I wasn't even surprised she'd gotten herself an invitation. She was the sort of lady who mostly did get what she wanted.

She saw me in the mirror, turned, started to get up, but kind of stuck halfway. "What *happened?*"

I looked at my own reflection and saw what she meant. Powers, I looked like I'd been dead three days and it hadn't been no nice death, either. "I won't keep you," I said. "I just wanted to . . ."

Well, what did you want to do, Milly-Fox? Do you even know?

"Mildmay." She got her dress, yards and yards of this gorgeous indigo crushed velvet, free of the little vanity stool, and came over to me. She was beautiful. I don't know how she did it, because, I mean, I knew what she looked like, I knew her sallow skin and the way her upper lip overhung her lower, and I knew what she was, and all the same—Kethe. She was so beautiful it hurt.

"Mildmay," she said again, kind of gentle, like she was afraid I was going to spook and run. "What is it?"

"I wanted to say good-bye," I said.

"Good-bye? Where are you going?"

Deep breath, and the words still kind of stuck, like there was rust and sand in the gears. "Felix is sending me to murder Vey Coruscant."

Her eyebrows went up, and I saw the sharp teacher-lady in her face, the one I'd met in Klepsydra. "I'll assume he has a good reason for it. Who's Vey Coruscant?"

"She's a blood-witch. And she's in with Felix's old master, the one who drove him crazy, and it turns out he's the same guy that Mavortian's been after all this time, and fuck, I think they're *both* crazy now, if you really want to know."

"Slow down," she said. "Come on—*sit* down. Tell it the right way round and from the beginning."

"Can't," I said. "I got to go. He, um."

The way she frowned should have been funny. I mean, here she was, beautiful lady, with the dress and the maquillage and her hair up and everything, and with her big eyes and soft little mouth that made her look like she'd *maybe* finished her second septad, and that scowl should have looked plain ridiculous. It didn't. She said, "He used the whatsit, didn't he?"

"The obligation d'âme," I said. "Yeah. He, um. He kind of did."

"That *asshole*. You wait here. I'll go—"

"No!" My hand was clamped around her wrist before either of us realized I'd meant to move. "You can't. I mean—you *can,* but it won't change his mind. And it'll just make him pissed off at me. More pissed off, I mean. And I can't . . ."

But I couldn't find the end of that sentence, either.

She said, "You're hurting me."

I let her go like she'd caught fire. "Oh, powers, sorry! I'm really sorry. I didn't mean—"

"I know you didn't. I won't do anything you don't want me to. But if you're coming to say good-bye, does that mean you think you won't succeed?"

"I've got a bad feeling about it," I said. "I get 'em sometimes, and I got one now."

"What kind of bad feeling?"

I shrugged. "Just . . . it's gonna go wrong. That's all."

"Did you tell Felix?"

"He didn't give me the chance."

"Are you sure you don't want me to talk to him?"

"It's really nice of you. But, no. I swear to you, it won't help. I'll just be extra careful, is all."

"Do you think that'll be good enough?"

"No. But it's all I can do."

"Mildmay." I looked at her. She put one hand very gently on my shoulder and leaned in to kiss me on the mouth.

"What was that for?"

"Luck," she said. And she smiled at me like nobody had smiled at me in I didn't even know how long.

"Um, thanks," I said, and, powers, I was blushing. I backed up a step, couldn't think of anything to say. "Thanks. I, um. I mean . . ." But, Kethe, whatever I meant, I couldn't say it. I said, "Thanks," again, like a half-wit dog, and then just turned and went.

Off to kill Vey fucking Coruscant, may all the powers and saints preserve me.

Felix

If I tried, I could remember the last time I had been in the Hall of the Chimeras for a soirée: the night I went to Malkar, the night I hit Shannon, the night Robert told the Mirador what I was.

I did not try.

In truth, I did not have time for morbid reflections on the past. It had been left carefully unclear whether the soirée was being held in my honor or the Virtu's, but it was not a secret that I was the person who had mended what was broken, and I was all but besieged with well-wishers, sycophants, wizards and courtiers jockeying for interest. Mavortian was similarly occupied, and I was glad of it. I did not want to think about Malkar tonight. There would be time enough for that tomorrow.

I talked and drank and danced. Shannon and I were scrupulously polite to each other; Vicky gave me a cold, formal nod. Every time I turned around, it seemed that Stephen was glowering at me, but having given his official speech, he did not approach me. The Virtu, blue and beautiful and serene, presided like a bride.

I talked to Thaddeus de Lalage, still uncertain whether I counted him as friend or foe. He seemed equally uncertain of me; our conversation was stilted with caution and mostly about politics. He did not mention Gideon, nor did I.

I saw Mehitabel Parr once, in the glittering, swirling crowd, and she looked straight through me as if I didn't exist. It was her prerogative, and I hardly cared—certainly not enough to try to find out what it was I had done this time to invite her wrath.

Gideon was not there at all.

I talked to wizards I knew, wizards I didn't know; made polite conversation with one of the painstaking junior envoys from the Coeurterre; danced with noblemen's wives and lovers and daughters; in two cases danced with the daughters' lovers. I was standing by the bust of an early Ophidian king, drinking lemonade and flirting absentmindedly with Edgar St. Rose, who knew better than to take anything I said seriously, when I felt the hairs on the back of my neck stand up. I didn't turn, but leaned closer to Edgar and said, "Who's staring at me?"

Edgar was a veteran of Cabaline politics; he glanced around without seeming to, then grimaced expressively and said, "Robert."

"Oh, marvelous. Does it look like he's going to come over here?"

"Yes. In fact, here he comes, and if you don't mind, I think here I go."

"I don't blame you," I said. Edgar ducked into the crowd; I sighed and shifted my weight, and managed to time it so that I turned just as Robert opened his mouth to demand my attention. Anything to wrong-foot him.

He recovered swiftly, with an entirely insincere bow, and said, "Lord Felix. You are much to be congratulated."

"Thank you, Lord Robert."

He gave me a sly look. "Do you find yourself quite recovered from your, ah, 'indisposition'?"

"I beg your pardon?"

He widened his eyes at me in that mock-innocent way of his I particularly loathed. "We were all very worried about you, you know. Especially after you disappeared from Hermione like that. Brother Orphelin was most anxious."

"You're babbling." I wanted only to get rid of him, to end this conversation before anything regrettable happened. But his head jerked back; his eyes widened, then narrowed in an expression I was all too familiar with: I had just given Robert the gift of ammunition.

"Am I?" He smiled, slow and wide. "Have you *forgotten* your stay in St. Crellifer's? They will be most disappointed to learn of your ingratitude."

"I don't have time for this," I said and left him there, desperate to disengage before he could mire me further.

St. Crellifer's.

The madhouse.

A year of my life I did not remember.

Although the Hall of the Chimeras was stuffy and overwarm around me, I found that I was shivering.

Mildmay

I could find Vey Coruscant all right. Not that I'd ever been crazy enough to want to, but I knew where her house was. When I was a kid, we'd used to dare each other to go over to Dassament and walk along Sonnet Street—on the other side of the street from her house. We were stupid kids, but we weren't, you know, suicidal.

And if she wasn't there, there'd be somebody who could tell me where to look. Whether they wanted to or not.

I'd done this sort of thing for a living. And I'd been good at it. And the fact that I didn't want to be doing it now, and I had that terrible crawling feeling that it was all fucked in ribbons, well, in a weird way, it helped. Because it made it fucking easy to just concentrate on getting the job done.

I could remember feeling like this a lot, the last half indiction or so I was with Keeper.

And, you know, I think the worst thing was that I knew what to do. I didn't have to think about it. Didn't need to plan or ask questions or nothing. It was just there, all them ugly facts, just waiting for me to pick 'em up again.

You want to kill a hocus, you got to take 'em by surprise. Miriam had told me that, when she sent me to kill Cerberus Cresset. 'Cause where hocuses are different from annemer ain't in their bodies, in their flesh and blood and the way they breathe. It's somewhere else, and I don't know if you call it mind or soul or spirit or what, but it ain't the body. Body's just as vulnerable as anybody else's. Now the Mirador tries to get around that with all their oaths and warding spells and the fucking curse that had crippled me, but blood-witches don't have that kind of thing. Most people would agree as how they don't need it. Most people aren't stupid enough to go and fuck with a blood-witch, but here I was anyway.

So you got to take a hocus by surprise, to kill them. You got to be fast, and you don't want to give them time to say nothing. Not even a word, Miriam said, so I'd gone straight for Cerberus Cresset's heart, and nailed it, too. And he hadn't made so much as a squeak. But blood-witches—and my friend Zephyr had told me this, because he was worried about me and the shit I was getting into, and Kethe he'd been right and I only wished I could tell him so—you also got to watch out that nobody starts bleeding. Not you and not them. Because they're called blood-witches for a reason, and it ain't for the poetry of it.

Knives are right out.

First job I ever did, I garotted a guy. What goes around fucking well comes around, Milly-Fox. And I'd kited a scarf from Mehitabel's room.

I could get it done.

I got into Dassament through the Arcane. It was better than going through the streets, although I didn't think anybody in the Arcane was going to like me anymore. People in the Arcane don't make eye contact, and they don't look you in the face, and I'd hidden my hair under Mehitabel's scarf, and I figured I probably had about enough leeway to get me where I was trying to go. Never mind about getting back. Most of me didn't think I was going to last long enough to worry about it.

I went the back ways, down on the levels where nobody much goes. Because even when a job's going to be bad, you don't need to be stupid about it. Came up the Thimblespring Spiral, dark and dank, with the iron of the banister rusty and wet under my hand, and out into the old Clockmakers' Guild that ain't been used—at least, not by clockmakers—since sometime back in the reign of Mark Ophidius. The Nemesis Clock was pretty much the end of that guild, and clockmakers now call themselves horologers and have a nice shiny new guildhall over in Sunslave.

I didn't go out the front door. Went up to the roof—nobody ran Dassament's roofs along of not wanting to fuck with Queen Blood, and, Kethe, what the fuck am I doing here?

But I didn't even think about turning back, even though I wanted to so bad I could taste it. I knew I couldn't do it. Even if I tried, the obligation d'âme wouldn't let me. I could feel it, like an iron plate at my back, pushing me forward. Fighting it wouldn't do me no good, and it'd just fuck up my concentration. Which I needed for other things, thank you very fucking much.

Along the roofs, tenements and warehouses and the big ugly wart of the Vespers Manufactory, where most of the girls who didn't die in Lornless's over in Dragonteeth came to die instead. I went down the fire escape of the Pinchbeck, a gambling hell that'd been running longer than I'd been alive, cut across two alleys and a courtyard, and there I was on Sonnet Street, with Vey's big ugly house looking like it was about to fall down and smash us all flat.

There was this fad, two, three Great Septads ago, for houses built like the Mirador, big high walls and no windows fronting the street. Great for a blood-witch, I reckon. Lousy for a cat burglar. I looped the block. Vey's house was the middle third of the block, from Sonnet Street on one side to the Boul'Neige on the other. And I wasn't real surprised to see that the rest of the buildings on the block were vacant. Who'd want Queen Blood as their neighbor?

So it was easy to get into one of them buildings, get up to the roof— give or take a couple nasty minutes with some rotted treads on the stairs— and vault across to Vey Coruscant's roof. My bad leg didn't like the landing, but it held up okay.

You just don't find buildings in the Lower City without a door onto the roof. Vey'd bothered to put in a decent lock, but a good hard kick just under the plate was enough to break it. I wasn't feeling subtle, and it wasn't like they weren't going to know I'd been here.

The stairwell was a weird sort of tower thing—I guess trying to imitate all the Mirador's towers—and had stairs going up as well as down. I checked up first, but there was nothing there but a skylight and an astrologer's glass, so I went down.

Top floor was storage and stuff, dusty and closed off and not where you'd hang out if you had better choices. Next floor down was servants' rooms—no joy there, either. Then things started looking better. Carpet and nice furniture and paintings and shit. I found a room I was pretty sure was Vey's dressing room. Seriously flash ladies' clothes, and some of the stuff in the back of the armoire had these stains around the cuffs, and even though I wanted to, I couldn't pretend I didn't know what they were.

And I was just wondering what my next move was when I heard the door to the hall start to open.

Which meant my next move was straight into the armoire. I tugged the door to behind me and heard the rustle of a lady's dress against the carpet as somebody came into the room.

Sloppy, Milly-Fox. Very sloppy, and if you end up dead for it, don't come crying to me.

But it had to be Vey Coruscant, because even flash ladies' maids didn't wear floor-length skirts. Unless, of course, it was Vey's light of love or niece or something, and while if she was either of those things, she probably wasn't no nice person, that didn't mean I wanted to murder her on accident. And I didn't know what Vey Coruscant looked like, having gone pretty far out of my way to be sure the lady and me were never eye to eye.

Closest I'd ever been to her before, it was pitch-dark and raining in the Boneprince.

And then she called, "Go ahead and make yourself comfortable. I'll only be a moment." I heard footsteps in the hall, moving away, but, Kethe, I didn't care. I had a cold sweat starting in my armpits, because oh fuck oh saints and powers and Kethe patron of thieves and secrets, I knew that voice.

It was Vey Coruscant, all right.

That was when she opened the armoire, and I was moving, cold and clear and like I had a diagram to follow. I had the scarf that'd been covering my head, and it was looped around Vey's neck with the knot tightening before she even knew I was there. Her mouth came open, but she never had a chance. I'm no hocus, but I can move fast enough to beat one. We hit the floor hard, me on top, and I got my knees braced to pin her arms, set my wrists, and pulled.

Strangling is a fucking ugly way to die. She'd been pretty, Vey Coruscant, with light brown hair and hazel-green eyes, not looking a day past her third septad. Blood-witches can do that. It's in all the stories, though I've never wanted to ask exactly how they go about it. She thrashed under me, and her light brown hair came loose from its pins as her face turned blue, then purple, and her hazel-green eyes bugged out of their sockets. She didn't make a noise, though, not loud enough for anybody but me to hear.

And then she was dead.

I unknotted the scarf, tried to smooth it, although I knew it was useless, and why the fuck was I bothering? I could get it ironed, back in the Mirador. Give it back to Mehitabel. Maybe she wouldn't've noticed it was gone, and I wouldn't have to tell her what I'd done with it.

Get up and go, Milly-Fox, said that voice in my head, and I stuffed the scarf in my pocket and started to get to my feet—and what the *fuck* had I done to my bad leg?—and then I realized there was a shadow in the doorway.

I was up, my heart slamming in my chest, and staring at this guy. He was big, taller than me and bulky, with dark red-brown hair queued back like a flashie, and light brown eyes that looked as clever and fake as glass.

"Gracious," he said mildly, like there wasn't a dead body on the floor and it wasn't somebody he knew. "*You* weren't the tiger I was expecting to catch."

I couldn't move. It was like them shiny eyes had me pinned, same way I'd pinned Vey Coruscant. He stepped into the room, closing the door behind him, and then reached out, like I was so much fucking statuary, caught my chin in one hand and tilted my head. He had rings on his big broad ugly hands, but no tattoos.

"How intriguing," he said. And I couldn't stop him, couldn't move, couldn't even fucking fall down and die. "How *very* intriguing. And this may serve even better than my original plan. Certainly, you have rid me very tidily of one obstacle."

He nudged Vey's body with one foot. "She was a clever child, but a faithless one. That much I will grant Felix. He has tried to rebel against me, oh, many times, but he has never *betrayed* me. Of course, I was a far stricter master to him than I ever was to Vey. Truly, discipline *is* good for the spirit." He smiled like a dog snarling, I guess at the look on my face. "I see you've realized my secret. You must be smarter than you look—although that wouldn't be difficult." His voice had dropped down into a purr, and I hated it and recognized it because I'd heard it in Felix's voice a thousand times. "But, please, I must not neglect my manners. Allow me to introduce myself." The smile widened, and I wanted to look away but I couldn't fucking *move*. "I am Malkar Gennadion. Otherwise and formerly known as Brinvillier Strych."

Chapter 14

Felix

It was the nightmare again—the dark room, the table with straps, the heart of the maze, the heart of the monster—and I was almost glad to be woken by someone pounding at the outer door of my suite as if they meant to break it open with their bare hands.

A woman's voice, carrying well, "Felix! Goddamn you, I know you're in there! *Felix!*" Mehitabel Parr's voice.

I remembered she had been furious with me at the soirée the night before. I still didn't know what I'd done, but it looked rather as if I was going to find out.

I crawled out of bed, groping for my dressing gown. She was still hammering, and I wondered why Mildmay hadn't opened the door. He wasn't a heavy sleeper to begin with, and—

For a moment, everything seemed to stop. My mind, my breath, the heart in my chest, the blood in my veins.

Mildmay hadn't come back. I had sent him to murder Vey Coruscant,

Queen Blood, the greatest, and possibly only, blood-wizard now living. He hadn't returned, and I wondered dizzily why I'd thought he would, why I'd thought my annemer brother would be able to defeat the queen of blood, the queen of stolen bones and graveyard earth.

I had promised not to rape him, and what a lie that had turned out to be.

I was lurching like a drunk by the time I reached the door. I threw it open and said to Mehitabel Parr, "He's dead, isn't he?" Dead, and my fault. Dead, and I killed him.

"No," she said, startled. "Well, he might be by now."

I realized there was someone with her, someone I didn't know. A man, short and slight, wearing a long black coat and holding a broad-brimmed soft black hat in both hands. I recognized the traditional clothes of a cade-skiff, and looked back at Mehitabel in confusion. If he wasn't dead, why was a cade-skiff here?

"This gentleman has some information for you," she said. "May we come in?"

I stood aside obediently, shut the door behind them. "Why are you here?" I said to Mehitabel and realized a moment later how rude that sounded. "I didn't mean . . . but—"

"Let's take the story in order," she said. "Starting with Cardenio's information."

"Cardenio?"

The cade-skiff blushed bright carnation pink and mumbled, "Yes, your lordship." Mousy, unremarkable face, accent thick enough to butter bread—Mildmay's friend.

"Sit down," I said, my voice thin and utterly hollow to my own ears. "Please. And tell me what news you have brought."

He sat, almost swallowed by the armchair. I took the other, and Mehitabel dragged over a chair from the table. I saw Cardenio's fingers tighten on his hat, but his voice was level and clear when he said, "I got a visitor this morning told me they saw Mildmay being taken out of the city by a hoc—by a wizard who smelled like bad magic. And when I came out of the morgue my master told me Vey Coruscant had been murdered."

"Wait," I said. "Someone came to you *in the morgue*?"

"Yes," he said and met my eyes when he said it. "Out of the river, actually."

A headache was starting to throb in my temples. "Wait," I said. "Stop. Can we take this one fact at a time? Vey Coruscant is dead."

"Murdered," said the cade-skiff. "Strangled. I saw the body. I only know one man in Mélusine who could have done it, and that's Mildmay."

"And he's left town?"

"Been taken," Cardenio corrected me. "Out through the Seventh Gate."

"The river."

"Yes."

"But if Vey Coruscant is dead, then who . . . ?"

"I believe," Mehitabel said waspishly, "the gentleman's name is Malkar Gennadion."

🙦

I got the story from Cardenio question by question, patient answer by patient answer. I had already slept through court for the fourth day in a row; we were not interrupted. I could not let myself think beyond the next question, the next answer. Could not let myself think about what I had done.

Around the eleventh hour of the night (Cardenio said, and I mentally converted to about five o'clock in the morning), he had been roused by a confrère of his, the journeyman who had night duty in the cade-skiffs' morgue beneath their guildhall; Cardenio did not tell me what night duty entailed, and I did not ask. This cade-skiff told him that someone wanted to see him, and refused to say anything more beyond the fact that he didn't think they should be kept waiting. Cardenio had dragged some clothes on and accompanied his colleague down to the morgue.

From Cardenio's manner, I gathered that this was not the first strange request he had met with since joining the guild.

What was waiting for him was a monster. He described it as best he could, and I gained an impression of a creature like the mermaids of folk-tales, only not a half-human maiden, whether benign or malevolent, but a scaled thing, with a human torso and arms but a tail like a sea serpent, and great pale eyes like nothing, Cardenio said, he had ever seen before. But what really took him aback was when it spoke to him, calling him by name.

It demanded to know if he was Cardenio, and if he was a friend of Mildmay's. He said yes, to both—"I ain't seen him in a long time, but if we ain't friends, it's on his side, not mine." His eyes met mine, not defiantly, but steadily, and I said before I could stop myself, "You're the only person I've ever heard him call a friend."

He said shyly, "I'm glad," before continuing his story.

The monster identified itself as the Kalliphorne. To Cardenio, that name had evidently meant something. To me, it meant nothing. He had to explain about St. Kirban's flooded vaults, the nature of the traffic through them, the man who controlled them, and just how he kept that control. As a cade-skiff, Cardenio had seen what Phoskis Terrapin's watchdog could do; he had never doubted that the creature existed—as many in the Lower City apparently did—and he had no hesitation in believing it.

It told him Mildmay had spoken of him as someone who could be trusted, though it did not explain how it came to be on speaking terms with my brother, and it told him what it had seen and smelled that night: a man reeking of bad magic and Mildmay in his company. "It said there was something wrong with him. Like he couldn't see where he was going."

Or hear anything but Malkar's voice in his head, most likely, I thought, remembering the times Malkar had done that to me. My heart was thudding nauseously in my chest, the feeling too raw to be described as anything as clean as guilt.

I should have known, a thought so heavy, so massive, that I could barely breathe around it, could barely keep my shoulders straight, my face composed. *I should have known.*

Mercifully, although it was not a mercy I deserved, there was not much more to the story. The Kalliphorne had followed the boat at a careful distance until the current carried it out of Mélusine. Then the monster, with a concern and effort that were surely the opposite of monstrous, swam back to the cade-skiffs' guildhall to find Cardenio. And Cardenio, having discharged his portion of the cade-skiffs' duty to the remains of Vey Coruscant, had gone to Britomart and indebted himself to Mildmay's former keeper for a way into the Mirador.

"But you're a cade-skiff," I protested. "You could have come openly."

"I couldn't have gotten to you without stating my business, and the Kalliphorne begged me not to tell anyone except the people who could help him." He frowned. "Mr. Terrapin must have some sort of hold on it."

"But to go to Mildmay's keeper—!"

"Madame Kolkhis has connections," he said, with a pragmatic ruthlessness that sat oddly with his nondescript face and gentle eyes. "She gave me a letter of introduction to a musician named Hugo Chandler, and he brought me to Miss Parr—"

"Who brought him to you," Mehitabel finished. "Sometimes clandestinely *is* the best way to get things done."

"Oh, and Madame Kolkhis gave me this to give to you." He handed me a sealed paper, which I held, feeling as if it was poisoning me through the skin of my hands.

There was a pause, an awkward stillness. Cardenio said, "Lord Felix, what are you going to do?"

"I don't know," I said, and to Cardenio's frown, Mehitabel's incredulity, I could only say again, helplessly, "I don't know."

To get away from their eyes, I opened the letter from Mildmay's keeper:

> *Cardenio Richey tells me that Mildmay the Fox is in trouble, and*
> *that it is serious, although he will not tell me what the trouble is.*
> *Although I am fond of all my children, I have loved few of them*
> *as I loved Mildmay. If there is anything I can do to help him, a*
> *message to the Stag and Candles in Britomart will find me.*

Like Malkar, Mildmay's keeper did not sign her correspondence.

I said, bewildered, "She says she will help him if there is any way she can. But I thought . . . I thought she hated him?" It twisted into a question, and I looked at Cardenio.

"*Hated* him? No, m'lord. Not Madame Kolkhis. We reckon she'd do just about anything to get him back."

"He doesn't speak of her with any fondness." When he spoke of her at all.

Cardenio grimaced. "I don't know how he feels, m'lord. You never do, with him. But she was crazy about him. Nearly scared her kids to death, the fit she pitched when he left her."

"Wait," I said, feeling bludgeoned again and terribly stupid. " 'Crazy about him'—are you saying they were involved *romantically*?"

"They were lovers for indictions," Cardenio said. "After he . . . you know, after his face."

"When he was *fourteen*?" My voice had risen, and part of me wondered cynically—considering what I'd been doing when I was fourteen— why I was so shocked.

Cardenio blinked at me in alarm. "I thought you said he talked about her."

"He didn't mention that part."

"Oh. Well, I guess he wouldn't. I know she hurt him, but he'd never talk about that, either."

"Of course he wouldn't." I shook myself. At the moment, Mildmay's past, and what he had or had not told me about it, did not matter. "When Kolkhis says she will help," I said carefully to Cardenio, "can I trust her?"

"Dunno what she can do, but yeah. She keeps her word."

"Would we could all say as much," Mehitabel said; I managed not to flinch.

"I'll help, too, m'lord, if there's any way I can," Cardenio said, getting up. "Just send to the Fishmarket—they'll know how to find me. But I got to go. There's, um. Well, with Madame Coruscant dead, there's stuff we've got to do."

"I can imagine," I said. "Thank you."

He bowed to both of us and left. I wondered for a moment if I should have summoned someone to show him the way, but then remembered he was a cade-skiff. He could take care of himself.

Mehitabel stood up, shook her skirts out sharply. "Nothing I say to you will have the slightest effect, so I'm not going to bother."

The door closed decisively behind her, leaving me alone with myself. She was right; nothing she could have said could have hurt as much as that.

🙼

I managed to avoid Mavortian for four days, largely by the simple expedient of never being in my rooms. I did not want to talk to him, did not want to look at him. I did not want to see my own evil reflecting at me from his eyes. And I did not want to face how successfully he had manipulated me, how witlessly I had danced to his tune. I sent a note, brief, impersonal, detailing the facts of Vey Coruscant's death, Mildmay's capture, and Malkar's flight, and then did my best to forget that Mavortian von Heber even existed.

But he ran me to earth in the end—or had Bernard run me to earth, which was very much the same thing. I had been working in the Fevrier Archive, searching for some way that I could use the obligation d'âme to find Mildmay, when a shadow fell across my notes and Bernard said, "*There* you are."

I put down my pen. "Yes," I said. "Here I am."

"He wants to talk to you."

"I'm not surprised." I looked up at him; I hadn't been sleeping more than two or three hours at a time, and I saw him with the clarity of exhaustion: the gray in his mustaches, the frown line worn between his eyebrows. "What do *you* think of all this?"

"Me?" He was visibly taken aback.

"You're neither an automaton nor a beast of burden, regardless of how Mavortian treats you. You *must* have opinions."

"You're a fine one to talk," he muttered.

"About having opinions?"

"About treating somebody like a beast of burden."

"You think that's how I treat Mildmay?"

He snorted. "There's no *think* about it. I've watched you. And I've watched him. Powers know, I don't like him, but you want my *opinion,* my *opinion* is, I wouldn't wish you on my worst enemy."

"Thank you for your candor," I said. I wanted it to be bitter, venomous, and was horrified at how tired I sounded, how sick. I had no right to pity, had no right to sound as if I pitied myself. I shut my eyes for a moment, took a deep breath. "But truly, I want to know. What do you think of your brother's grand scheme of vengeance?"

"Half brother," Bernard said, and there was all the bitter venom I hadn't been able to put into my own words. "I don't think anything. That's not what he pays me for."

"He pays you?"

"I'm the hired help, like my mother. And that's as far as I go. Now, come on. He wants to talk to you, and it's my job to be sure he gets what he wants."

I could have refused him; we both knew he couldn't actually force me. But I was too tired to continue to fight against the inevitable. I was a monster; denying that fact would not change it.

"All right," I said, gathered up my pen and quire of notes, and accompanied Bernard silently back to the Filigree Corridor, where he and Mavortian had been housed.

Mavortian was laying out his cards by witchlight, his engraved silver focus pressed between the hollow of his thumb and the deck.

"Bernard found me," I said. "What did you want to say?"

"We need to decide what our next move is going to be," he said, without taking his attention away from the cards.

"Our next move?"

"Now that Messire Gennadion has been driven out into the open, we must decide how we are going to confront him."

" 'Driven out into the open'? Is *that* what we did?"

The look he gave me was just barely short of rolling his eyes. "I regret as much as you do Mildmay's bad luck—"

"Somehow I doubt that."

"*But,*" he continued over me, "we cannot change what has happened. Therefore, it only makes sense to consider how we may best turn it to our advantage."

"We *have* no advantage."

"Maselle Coruscant is dead."

"And if you think that isn't exactly what Malkar wanted, you're even more stupid than I am." Mavortian frowned at me, and I continued, "He intended me to get rid of Vey for him. He probably drafted that letter she sent. He was *there*, Mavortian. If he hadn't wanted her dead, she wouldn't be."

"You talk about him as if he were a god. He's as fallible as any of us."

I hesitated on the brink of arguing, but I knew I would not be able to make Mavortian understand. It was quintessentially Malkar—as I *had* told Mavortian, listening to my own words no more than he had—to pit one follower against another, telling each a different lie, and now that I had had time—more than enough time, long, cold hours of the Mirador's sleepless darkness—to think the thing through, the story about emulating Brinvillier Strych was thin. Malkar did not follow in other wizards' footsteps, and I wondered what his real use for Vey Coruscant had been. Clearly, whatever it was, it had been of limited duration.

Instead of any of that, I said, "Regardless, we don't know where Malkar is, we don't know what he's planning, and he has a hostage. Where, exactly, do you see our advantage?"

He scowled. "I had not expected that you would run craven."

"And I hadn't realized you were a madman. So I'd say we're even."

He opened his mouth, but I cut him off. "I don't want anything more to do with your revenge, or with you, and I should greatly prefer it if we never spoke to each other again." I turned to go, turned back to say, "*Don't* send him after me."

I left then, and although Mavortian shouted, "Felix! Damn you, come back here!" he did not send Bernard.

🙚

Court was a penance. No one knew, of course, that it was my doing Vey Coruscant was dead, and my feeble explanations of Mildmay's absence were accepted—because no one cared. They were grateful an embarrassment had been removed, and not at all concerned about what I had done to remove it. They wouldn't have cared if I'd killed and eaten him; they probably wouldn't even have been shocked. I saw the truth in every face I looked at; I was a monster, and no one expected anything better of me.

It was on the sixth morning since I had woken to the realization of my own terrible, arrogant stupidity that I left the Hall of the Chimeras alone, chin up, avoiding eye contact, and heard Robert of Hermione's voice calling, "Lord Felix!"

I knew better than to pretend I had not heard Robert; he would only follow me. I stopped, waited. Did not turn, and was gratified by the hint of annoyance in Robert's voice when he said, "Good morning, Lord Felix."

Then I turned. And smiled and said, "Good morning, Lord Robert," as if there were no hostility between us at all.

Anything to disconcert him.

It did not faze him for long; he smiled in return, the wide unpleasant smile that I had hated for years. "Dear me, you look dreadful."

"I *beg* your pardon?"

"I really begin to wonder if Giancarlo is right to be so sanguine about your stability."

"I am perfectly stable." *As stable and resolute as an aspic,* Malkar's voice said mockingly in my memory. I did not flinch.

Robert raised his eyebrows in a parody of polite skepticism, but something else had caught my attention. "When were you talking to *Giancarlo* about my stability?"

"I was worried," he said, as if that were any sort of an explanation. "You don't look like you've slept more than five hours in the past week. Have you?"

"It is no business of yours."

"Considering what you're capable of, that's a remarkably naïve thing to say. Would you say the same to your friend Sherbourne Foss?"

"You are not Sherbourne. Nor are you my friend."

"That won't save me if you run amok again."

"I did not—!" I bit the inside of my lower lip, let my nails dig just a fraction harder into my palms before I relaxed my hands. "What do you want, Robert?"

"I told you. I'm worried about you."

"Your concern gratifies me. What do you *want*?"

"I want you to come to St. Crellifer's with me."

I stared at him for a full five seconds before I could find anything to say, and even then it was an inelegant, *"What?"*

"The monks there have a great deal of experience with illnesses such as yours. They may be able to help."

"I am not insane," I said through my teeth.

"Then you lose nothing by a visit except an hour or two of your time."

"And if I refuse, you'll go to Giancarlo and tell him I'm being unreasonable."

His smile widened. "It would be nothing but the truth. This is not a great deal to ask."

I eyed him, wishing—and not for the first time—that murder were a viable alternative. "It is ridiculous."

"You may find it so, but I assure you there are many in the Mirador who would not."

It was a threat, and we both knew it. And although I did not think Robert could get me reconfined to St. Crellifer's as he clearly wished to, he could create a nearly infinite series of blocks and impediments, eroding time away from me one frustrating minute after another. And that probably *would* drive me mad.

"Very well," I said levelly—an elaborate pretense of nonchalance would gratify Robert nearly as much as spitting rage.

Robert smiled, poison-bright, and said, "I knew you'd see reason eventually."

🙟

The trip to St. Crellifer's was made in stony, frozen silence. The first thing either Robert or I said was when I told the hansom driver to wait, adding pointedly in Robert's direction, "This won't take long."

I had seen the madhouse before, driven past its high wall with Shannon on some junket of pleasure or another. But I had never . . .

Only, of course, I *had*.

Seething, I followed Robert across the courtyard, up the grim gray steps. The door swung open as we approached, and I knew that the denizens of St. Crellifer's had been waiting for us. The porter, a ghastly, gnarled, yellow-toothed creature, bowed us in, fawning at Robert, saying something about the warder being very pleased.

And the smell hit me like the stroke of a hammer against my breastbone.

It was foul enough on its own—sweat and rot and fear, urine and excrement and death—but what was worse was that I *remembered* it. It was the memory I choked on, not the stench itself; my muscles twisted in a violent shudder, and I found my hands knotted in my hair as if I were trying to keep my skull from flying apart.

"Felix?" Robert said, his tone a parody of concern. "Are you all right?"

I forced my hands away from my head, forced my spine to straighten, gave Robert a smile that was close kin to one of Mildmay's snarls. "Fine," I said. "I merely find the . . . atmosphere . . . a bit oppressive."

Before he could decide how to respond, a cold, colorless voice said, "Lord Robert, Lord Felix. Welcome back to St. Crellifer's."

I turned. A small, spare, balding man, dressed in the habit of a monk of St. Gailan. Cold eyes, a cold, composed face. There was no irony, either in his voice or in his face; he was clearly one of those men for whom the concept was alien and incomprehensible.

"Brother Lilburn," Robert said, smiling widely. "You remember Brother Lilburn, don't you, Felix?"

But there was nothing familiar about the monk—nothing I wanted to be familiar, either.

"Perhaps you don't," Robert said; I could hear the smirk in his voice without needing to see his face. "Brother Lilburn remembers you, though, from your stay at St. Crellifer's. Right, Lilburn?"

"Yes, my lord," the monk said in a cold, flat voice. I knew that he was telling the truth—that nothing Robert had to offer could have induced him to lie. And a hysterical voice in the back of my mind whispered, He's still dead.

It made no sense, but at the same time it made all the sense in the world.

"You see why I am concerned," Robert said loudly, carefully, like a man reciting from a script.

"Yes, my lord," the monk said in his cold, colorless—dead—voice. His gaze had me pinned; I didn't remember him, and I didn't want to, but he terrified me all the same. "I'm sure the warder will wish to speak to you both. This way, please."

I wanted to bolt—to turn like a fox doubling back under the noses of the hounds and run—but I couldn't. I followed Brother Lilburn, and the obedience was familiar even if the man was not.

The Hospice of St. Crellifer's had once been a nobleman's town house; I could see its history in the sweep of the staircases, the lovely arches of the doorways. But it was dark and fetid now, and instead of the sounds of a hired orchestra or the murmur of gossiping ladies, I heard screams from some distant part of the building, screams of such grief and rage that they scarcely seemed human.

"Jeanne-Chatte's at it again," a voice said near my feet, the right side, and I had been focused on Brother Lilburn, not on my surroundings. "Noisy bitch."

To say that I jumped would be a gross understatement. I shied sideways, as violently as a spooked horse, slammed up against the wall hard enough that I was momentarily breathless. And the thing that I had taken for a clot of shadows or a pile of discarded bedding—or a ghost, a voice whispered in the back of my mind—raised its head, its eyes nearly as wide as my own. "Beg pardon, sir. I thought you were—"

One hand went up to its mouth. It was a young man, I saw, skinny, dark, dressed in ragged layers of cloth washed to colorlessness. "But you *are* Felix!" it—he—said. "What—"

"Wallie." Brother Lilburn's voice, cold and flat and hard as iron. The madman and I both flinched. "You have work to be doing, and it does not involve bothering visitors."

"Yes, Brother Lilburn," the madman said, lowering his head. He was scrubbing the flagstones, I saw, a bucket of the Sim's dark water at his side.

Brother Lilburn watched him a moment, expressionless. "Better," he said, and gestured to Robert and me to resume walking.

It was all I could do not to stumble as I followed in his wake. My hands were starting to shake, and I laced them together tightly for a moment, feeling the cold weight of my rings, before letting them fall back to my sides as if I were unconcerned. Desperately, selfishly, I wished Mildmay were here. With him on my right, I wouldn't have had to worry about what might be lurking where I could not see it.

And if Mildmay were here, it would have been because I had not betrayed him.

I swallowed hard and climbed a seeming infinity of stairs behind Robert's boots and Brother Lilburn's flat sandals. Then Brother Lilburn stopped, opened a door, said, "In here," with no more inflection or interest than he had said, *Welcome back to St. Crellifer's.*

The room was circular, the plaster yellowed, cracking. The man rising from behind the desk was monstrous, surely the biggest man I had ever seen in my life.

"Robert!" he said. "Felix! How lovely to see you again!" And in his voice was all the irony Brother Lilburn had not used.

My heart was slamming itself against my ribs like a bird trying to escape a windowless room. This man, I knew; this man was the monster of my nightmares, the monster whose heart was the table fitted with straps in that dark, dank room . . .

. . . which lay beneath St. Crellifer's.

I knew it, as surely as I knew the magic coiled about my bones and beating heart.

I lost several moments to a wild, bleeding kaleidoscope, a cyclone of glass, and when the dust settled, and the pieces lay in a quiet mosaic, shards of memory connected now by understanding, I knew things, too many things, and I wanted to scream like the madwoman Jeanne-Chatte.

I remembered her, too.

I was leaning with one hand braced against the tacky, sweating plaster of the wall, Robert and Brother Orphelin staring at me like a pair of coyotes watching a lost buffalo calf. Robert opened his mouth to say something—no doubt along the lines of, *He's clearly unstable, don't you agree?* as if there were a wizard in the entire Mirador who could claim more than a passing acquaintance with "stable" to begin with.

I cut him off. "What did you think you were doing?" I straightened away from the wall, dusted my hands against the legs of my trousers, smiled at him pleasantly.

"I beg your pardon?"

"Last year, Robert, in the basement of this very building. I'm sure you remember. What *did* you think you were doing?"

Robert's face turned very nearly the color of the walls. "Felix, I . . . I don't know what you're talking about."

"You'll have to do better than that," I said. "Or perhaps Brother Orphelin can explain."

The warder wasn't monstrous anymore, just a grotesque, petty creature as trapped in this madhouse as his charges were. Still dangerous, and I was not fool enough to forget it, but not the all-powerful malevolence of my memories. He could not hurt me unless I gave him the power to do so, and the wariness of his tiny stone-chip eyes indicated that he knew I was not about to do any such thing. He made a broad, helpless gesture and said, "I am annemer and know nothing of these matters. If Lord Robert told me he was trying to cure you, I would believe him."

I could not help admiring the deft coupling of that total disavowal of responsibility with a suggestion to Robert of how to defend himself. "*You* might," I said, and there was satisfaction in being able to load my voice with contempt, "but I wouldn't. Well, Robert?"

"You can't prove anything," Robert said. "You can make as big a stink as you want, but you can't prove anything, and you know Stephen won't believe you. And if you think I care what *you* say, you are very much mistaken."

The things I wanted to say in response crowded my mind, and even with Brother Orphelin listening greedily I might have said them. It would have been a relief, a terrible, glorious relief, to express some of the fury that had been building for days—fury at Malkar, fury at Mavortian, fury above all at myself and my stupidity and my pride.

But it would also have been a waste of time.

Perhaps my researches were also a waste of time, but even if they were, at least I was *trying*. I didn't believe in redemption, or atonement; if anything existed beyond this frail and sordid mortal life, I knew I was damned. Knew, and no longer cared. I couldn't make right what I had done wrong. But that did not exempt me from dealing with the consequences of my stupid, evil, selfish behavior. And that responsibility, even if it was futile, was more important than anything else. And especially more important than Robert of Hermione.

"Then we'll call this a draw then, darling, shall we?" I smiled at him and Brother Orphelin, beautifully but insincerely, said, "I'm sure you two have lots to talk about," and turned on my heel and left. Not running, my head up and my face composed, nothing in my bearing to indicate the horror I felt, horror and revulsion and pity for the men and women trapped here by their own minds.

The hansom driver wasn't inclined to argue with me when I told him we were leaving.

☙

By the time I returned to the Mirador, my head was throbbing with the tangle of half-understood memories St. Crellifer's had uncovered. I was still missing more than I had recovered, but I had a framework now. I knew what had happened to me.

I paused just inside the Harriers' Gate. The impulse to return to my suite, to hide like a hurt animal and lick my wounds, was painfully strong, but there was something I needed more. Robert had said I couldn't prove anything, and I needed to know if that was true.

And I remembered enough now to know that the person who could tell me was Thaddeus de Lalage.

We had been friends. Thaddeus seemed still to think of me as a friend, and although I no longer trusted him, for reasons that remained murky, I owed him a meeting. He had gotten me out of St. Crellifer's.

And what, pray tell, do you owe Mildmay?

An hour, I bargained with myself. An hour and I could put this whole business out of my head, one way or another. And the ugly truth was that an hour wasn't going to make any difference. It wasn't as if I were close to an answer to anything.

Finding Thaddeus was not difficult. The Mirador was resistant to change; just as no one had taken my suite or my workroom, even when there had seemed no chance of my returning, so Thaddeus's workroom had been left undisturbed for the five years he had been in Aurelias, and as I had expected, he was there, working on another of his infinite permutations to the same complex of light spells. It was important theoretical work—as Thaddeus would remind anyone unwise enough to comment—but it was monumentally boring. Thaddeus claimed it wasn't; I thought, remembering something Gideon had said, that that was another thing Thaddeus had talked himself into believing. I could see no other way that he could have borne it.

He left his door open while he was working, and I stood in the doorway watching him for almost a minute before he noticed me. I was grateful for the chance to observe him, to ground myself against the bewildering array of things I felt about him.

Thaddeus had been one of the first friends I made when I was trying to break free of Malkar. With his experience in the Bastion, he understood better than any orthodox Cabaline how Malkar had treated me—although

I had never told Thaddeus more than fragments of the truth. I had sworn him to secrecy, so terrified of Malkar I could barely breathe, and whatever else might have happened between us, he had never broken that promise. He was honorable to the point of rigidity, incapable of seeing the world in other than black-and-white.

He had rescued me from St. Crellifer's, and after that . . . I could remember that he had been angry at me, could remember that I had been afraid of him, but the whys and wherefores were gone. There had been a monster, but I did not know what that monster had been. From the vantage point of sanity, of distance, I thought I could fall back on a simple summation: I had been insane—defenseless and hurt—and he had bullied me.

I could even understand why—I knew Thaddeus well enough for that. In his simple black-and-white world, one identified problems and solved them. And when one had solved them, they *stayed* solved. I had been a problem, and he had solved me. He had gotten me out of St. Crellifer's, convinced the Curia to remove Malkar's compulsion. And I had not had the decency to stay solved. There was no room for me in Thaddeus's cosmology, and so he had been impatient, angry. He had hit me, I remembered, a sudden sense memory almost enough to make me wince.

He had hit me, and I would not have thought it of him, and that was ultimately the cause of my confusion about him. I knew Thaddeus was intolerant, close-minded, rigid in his thinking, but I had never thought he would be a bully.

He saw me then, out of the corner of his eye, and swung round. "Good God, Felix, what are you doing? Trying to give me a coronary?"

"I wanted to talk to you," I said.

"Did you? Have you finally seen the truth about Gideon? I understand how charming he can be, how plausible, but you—"

"What are you babbling about?" I said, cutting him off sharply. "More of your nonsense about spies and cultists?"

"It is not nonsense," he said, putting down the double compass and a handful of amber beads. "It is the truth."

"Was the truth."

He snorted. "Do you think leopards can change their spots, then? Wash them away?"

"I think Gideon is not a leopard."

"You and your willful blindness. I thank God you're off the Curia, you know."

"Have you been spreading poison? I thought that was better left to people like Robert and Agnes."

"I'm telling the truth. The Curia shouldn't make any decisions about him without knowing what he is."

"Decisions?"

"He's already petitioning," Thaddeus said, scowling blackly at me. "As if they'd be fool enough to let him take our oaths."

"They let you," I said.

"I am not a spy!"

"Neither is Gideon."

"You'll believe anything a man tells you when he's buried in your ass, won't you?"

I recoiled physically, as much from the uncharacteristic vulgarity as from the contempt in his voice. I had always known Thaddeus regarded the ganumedes with suspicion, believing them weak, effeminate, perverted. But I hadn't thought he saw me that way, had thought . . .

I'd thought I was an exception to his rule, and that had been stupid. Willfully blind, as he had said. And looking at him, anger and disgust on his face, I realized what had happened, why he had been angry in Hermione. Why he had hit me.

Madness was weakness; weakness was what one expected of a moll. He'd thought I was an exception to his rule, as well, and if there was one thing in the world Thaddeus de Lalage hated, it was being proved wrong.

I felt sick, almost to the point of literally vomiting on Thaddeus's workroom floor. Sick of Thaddeus, sick of myself. "If that's what you think," I said, "I won't keep you." I did not run, although I wanted to; some absurd remnant of pride insisted that I not let Thaddeus hear my bootheels clattering as if I were fleeing from him.

Now, more than ever, I wanted to retreat, to hide. Thaddeus had answered my question before I'd managed to ask it: he would be all too glad to tell anyone who asked that I was unstable—to use Robert's word—and not to be heeded. *Are you satisfied?* I asked myself savagely. *How many more blows will it take to kill your vanity?*

An imponderable, like the number of angels who could dance on the point of a needle. And unimportant. For if Thaddeus's tongue had been busy while I had been hiding, craven, from my own culpability, then the person I needed to worry about now was not myself, but Gideon.

He was not in the room he had been given, and I only very briefly contemplated the idea of asking Mehitabel if she knew where he was. Whether she knew or not, I would be pressing my luck to try to convince her to tell me.

But where could he go? The Mirador was not kind to strangers, and as far as I knew, he had no friends here. Where would he go, if his room was not a haven?

Thaddeus probably came preaching at him. It was the worst of Thaddeus; he so passionately believed in his own rectitude that he could not leave other people alone in their wrongdoing. I couldn't imagine what he thought he wanted to persuade Gideon to do—return to the Bastion? confess himself a spy in front of court and Curia? commit a quick and gentlemanly suicide?—but I knew he wouldn't let it rest. It was how he'd gotten me out of St. Crellifer's, after all.

I knew where I would have gone—where I *had* gone, in years past, to get away from Robert or Roseanna Aemoria, even sometimes from Thaddeus himself—and in a whimsy born of defeat, I found the nearest staircase to the battlements and climbed it.

Gideon was there, small, shabby, tired—looking not out over the city as I always did, but back at the roofs of the Mirador, at the fire-savaged remains of their gaudy, brassy beauty. He did not look surprised to see me. Neither did he look pleased.

"Gideon," I said. I tried to remember the last time I'd seen him, and then wished I hadn't. I'd thrown him out of my room, along with the others, when I was making my insane, malevolent, stupid decision about Vey Coruscant. He hadn't spoken to me since.

:Felix,: he said. A small, meticulously polite nod of the head.

I did not approach him, knowing he would only move away. "I, ah, I just talked to Thaddeus." Gideon waited, one eyebrow rising, and I said lamely, "Is he causing you very much trouble?"

Gideon's laugh was bitter mockery. :Your concern is touching, if hypocritical.:

"I have never thought—or said—that you were a spy for the Bastion."

:You wouldn't care if I were. Unless I threatened you, and then I imagine you would be quick enough to dispose of me. Or until you get bored. Will it amuse you, Felix, to throw me to the wolves?:

"I wouldn't—"

:Of course you would,: he said wearily. :You haven't hesitated to lie to me. I'm not about to expect you to keep faith.:

"Have I been lying to you?" I said, trying for lightness.

There was open contempt in the look he gave me.

I turned away quickly, making my own survey of the damaged roofs.

:You have been allowing me to believe something that is manifestly untrue. Do you remember anything of the time we spent in each other's company last year?:

He knew. I knew he knew, and yet I could not keep from defending myself. "We've talked before about what is and is not reasonable to expect me to—"

:By the Seven Saints of Hellebore, I am tired of this.: He came around in front of me, met my eyes fiercely. :Suppose you try telling me the truth. If you have even the faintest idea of what that word means, which I doubt.:

I flinched back, but his hand shot out and caught my wrist. :*What do you remember?*:

"Being afraid!" The words burst out now, like water pent up too long behind a dam. "Being in pain and alone and there were monsters everywhere." I wrenched free of him. "Mildmay helped me, and I guess I've shown him what a stupid idea that was. Now I'm one of the monsters, so why don't you just fuck off?"

We were both frozen, both of us hearing, not merely the obscenity, but more than that: the shift in my vowels, the nasal stridency suddenly in my voice. I took a deep breath, then another. Realized they weren't helping and leaned against the battlements, burying my face in my hands. "Maybe Robert was right."

:Robert of Hermione? I doubt it.: Gideon's voice was dry again, dispassionate. He touched my shoulder, and although I did not want to, I looked up. :Felix. I do not want to 'fuck off.' Unless you truly do not wish my . . . : He hesitated, visibly searching for a word. :Companionship.:

"I don't deserve your companionship, and you know that as well as I do."

:None of us get what we deserve,: he said, and I flinched.

A silence, fishhooks and shards of glass. I said, "You want to stay?"

:I do.:

"Even though . . ."

:Even though. I don't expect you to be other than you are.:

I swallowed hard against the lump in my throat. "You're a fool, you know that?"

:Yes. I know.: Gideon's fingers brushed gently against the dampness on my cheekbone. :Felix, come to bed with me. We can talk later.:

I nodded, mutely grateful, and followed him down the stairs; then, for he did not know the corridors, I led him to my suite. I closed and locked the door behind us; he stood in the center of the room and watched me, his eyes dark and bright and deep enough to drown in.

:Felix. Come here.:

I went to him, bent my head obediently to be kissed. His hands came up, one cupping my jaw, the other clenching in my hair, holding me still.

My heart kicked against my ribs, but I knew now where this fear came from. It had nothing to do with Gideon, as it had had nothing to do with Ingvard. It didn't even have very much to do with Malkar, although all my sexual responses were influenced by Malkar, and I knew it. No, this fear belonged to the basements of St. Crellifer's, to a table with leather straps, where I had been held down and . . .

:Felix?:

I did not answer him with words, merely moved closer against him. I could do this; if Gideon wanted to be in control, I could let him.

We made our way to the bedroom, and there he pushed me flat on my back on the bed and kissed me hard, biting, his hands catching my wrists and pinning them down.

And I couldn't do it.

I knew what was wrong, knew why I was panicking, and I still couldn't control it. I was ashamed of myself, even as I was shoving against Gideon, humiliated and infuriated even as I flung myself off the bed, mortified beyond bearing as I came up flat against the wall.

:If you didn't like what I was doing,: Gideon said, mild and deliberate with his own fury, :you could have just said so.:

"I'm sorry," I said, and I was gasping for breath, fighting to keep from bursting into tears like a child. "I'm so sorry."

:Felix?:

The last thing in the world I'd wanted: Gideon's undivided attention. I would have preferred to have him angry, if only I had been sufficiently in control of myself to provoke him.

:What's wrong?: Gideon said, getting up and approaching me cautiously, as if I were a wild animal . . . or a frightened child, and I hated the comparison but could not deny its truth. :Did I hurt you?:

The noise I made was half laugh, half sob. I'd been earning favor from tarquins before I turned twelve, and while pain was not exactly, usually, arousing, nothing Gideon could or would do to me would even be enough to make me wince. I shook my head, not wanting to trust my voice, and he said, :What, then?:

"I . . ." But my voice wouldn't work, all breath and tears. :I can't.:

:Can't what?:

:Just . . . I *can't.*:

:You haven't had this problem before,: he said dryly. :Does power truly mean that much to you?:

I felt as if he'd hit me. I stared at him, my jaw going slack and my eyes widening. He colored a little and said, :That *is* what all of this is about, isn't it?:

I couldn't answer him, and his lips twitched in a grin. :Did you think I hadn't noticed? You're a manipulative bastard, and you can't stand not having things your way. I know that. I just thought . . . : He sighed, and he looked so tired, so defeated, that I finally found my voice.

"It isn't that, I promise. That is, you're right. I *do* like controlling things. But it isn't . . . it's not that I can't . . . that I won't . . . Oh *damn.*"

Cautiously, slowly, he reached out, took my hands. His hands were square, sturdy, shorter-fingered than mine but broader across the palm; his grip was firm and warm and somehow comforting. :Come sit down,: he said, :and tell me what's wrong.:

I let him tug me back to the bed, sat down next to him, stared at our clasped hands, mine all pale skin and gaudy ink, his darker, unmarked. :Felix,: he said gently, sternly, and I knew he was not going to allow me to escape.

"When I was . . ." My throat seemed to close; I had to swallow hard, twice, before I could continue. "When I was not myself, in the madhouse, something . . . something happened to me."

His fingers tightened slightly. :Were you raped?:

He startled me into looking up. "No, not that. That wouldn't . . . never mind. Someone thought they would turn what Malkar had done to me to their own advantage. They tied me down"—and I removed my hands from Gideon's, indicating where the straps had gone—"so I couldn't move, I couldn't even turn my head, and then they . . ." I pressed the heels of my palms against my eyes, refusing to cry.

:You *were* raped,: he said. :Just not physically.:

"I suppose," I said, heaved in one painful, shaky breath, and then another.

:Was Robert successful?:

"I didn't—"

:You didn't need to.:

"Oh. I . . . I don't remember that part very clearly, but I don't think so. He brought me back here, I think?" I couldn't help it being a question, even though I knew it was nonsense to look at Gideon for the answers. "He did. And he tried . . ."

:He tried to use you to mend the Virtu,: Gideon said. :Thaddeus quite forgot he hated me in raving about that.:

"Thaddeus was *there*?"

:No. But he heard about it. Surely, I don't need to tell you how gossip travels in this place.:

"No," I said, "no, you don't." And then something else occurred to me. "Why wasn't Robert burned for heresy on the spot?"

:How should I know?: But his dismissive shrug was not entirely convincing, and I only had to wait a few moments before he said, :They were desperate and frightened, circumstances that can cause the strongest theology to wobble, and I understand that Robert was quite convinced it would work.:

"And?"

:And you were a traitor, heretic, madman, and according to the reports from St. Crellifer's, no better than a beast.:

"Not worth burning anyone over."

:They believed you had broken the Virtu yourself,: he said, almost gently.

"I'm not saying I didn't deserve what I got. I just—"

:Then you should be.:

I had been staring at my hands, running my fingers over and around my rings. I looked up at Gideon, shocked. "*You* say that? You know what I am."

:Whatever you are, or aren't, you did not deserve what happened to you.: He leaned forward, kissed me gently. :I understand why you don't want to be dominated in bed, but can we . . . ?: He was blushing again.

"Try for equality?"

He nodded, almost shyly.

"I would like that," I said, and his smile was beautiful enough to make me believe it might work.

Chapter 15

Felix

In my dream, I am in a vast vaulted room, a room the size of the Hall of the Chimeras, but abandoned, desolate. There are the remains of a mosaic beneath my feet, but in such a fragmentary condition that I cannot tell what the subject matter might once have been; there are only scattered spots of color, blue and green, gold and red. It is the most miserably forsaken room I have ever seen. There is a single light, a cold, hard, pitiless white witchlight that hangs like a tiny, unnatural sun beneath the vault; around me, under my feet and over my head, pressing in against my body, I can hear a slow pulse, a throbbing mechanical heartbeat, the relentless ticking of a clock so vast it could cast a shadow against the stars.

Someone is shoved into the illuminated circle cast by the witchlight. A man, naked, his hands manacled together behind his back, a collar around his neck, and a leash stretching back into the shadows. He goes down on one knee, and I see whip weals scrawling their cruelty across his back. He struggles to his feet again; he almost falls when his right leg buckles beneath his weight, but he saves himself, an effort of raw strength that it hurts to witness. I want to go to him, to help, but I cannot. His head is down, his face obscured by his long, tangled hair, but I can see bruises on his chest and stomach, more welts marking his thighs. He is shivering, although whether with cold or fear I do not know.

I don't hear the voice that shouts at him, but I know what it says: Raise your head! It shouts it over and over again until he does, bludgeoned into obedience with sound. His face is horribly bruised as well; a scar slashing across the left side of his face stands out stark and livid. One eye is swollen shut; the other is wide and green and not quite sane.

The voice shouts again. It wants him to say something, to send a message to his loving brother. For a moment, he seems unable to respond, unable to form words, and then he is shouting, a single word over and over and over until the leash jerks, dragging him back into the shadows, dragging him into silence. I wake with the word "Strych" ringing in my ears.

ॐ

I woke tangled in the sheets, my breath coming in hard, painful gasps.

:Felix?: Gideon, sitting up next to me, his eyes dark with worry in the shine of his witchlights.

I couldn't say anything. Couldn't stop shaking. Couldn't stop the horrible noises I was making. Gideon put his arms around me, and I let him, even leaned against him, grateful for the warmth, for the quiet, natural sound of his heartbeat. And after a while, I had some shreds of control again, some vestiges of my rational self, and I told him what I had dreamed, start to finish.

And he sat and held me and listened, and when I was done, said, :I remember that you are prone to true-dreaming.:

"This wasn't a dream," I said. "It was a sending. Malkar's good at them. But I'm sure he didn't believe Mildmay would have the wits to turn it against him."

:You think that wasn't—:

"If Malkar had wanted me to know he was Brinvillier Strych, he had all the time and opportunity in the world to tell me. I wish Mildmay hadn't done it, though."

:But at least now you know what you're up against.:

"I already knew that. Just because he's also Strych doesn't mean he's not Malkar."

:Ah. I see your point.:

"Yes." But even in the midst of the horror and guilt and grief that had my heart pounding like a lead pendulum against my ribs, simply knowing that Mildmay was not dead, that it was not too late, was a thin, cold mercy, something at last that I could hold to. And as I thought about the dream, thought about the details around the image Malkar had orchestrated, I realized I had something else.

"I know where he is," I said.

:You what?:

"I know where he is. I know where that room is. I know what that *sound* is."

:Felix?:

"He's in the Bastion." Saying it out loud made it horrifyingly real. Gideon's grip on me tightened, as if in protest.

:How can you be sure?:

I couldn't smile at him, couldn't be reassuring. "Because the Titan Clock of the Bastion is still running."

ᔓᔕ

The Titan Clocks were ancient, dating back to the days when the Mirador and the Bastion had been fortresses in the service of the same emperor. Juggernaut was the Bastion's clock; Nemesis had been the Mirador's. And there had been others, although their names and locations were now lost.

Five hundred years ago, the Nemesis Clock had been dismantled, ripped out of its matrix of stairs and hallways, and destroyed. Accounts differed as to the cause, most wizards preferring to blame the Clockmakers' Guild—which had certainly borne the brunt of the city's fear and anger—without ever explaining exactly how a group of annemer craftsmen, some of them only semiliterate, could have done *anything* to affect a Titan Clock. Annemer accounts were much simpler. They said the clock was haunted.

Titan Clocks were made with iron and gold and human bone; they did not break, and they did not fail. Haunting was not at all unlikely, and certainly the Nemesis Clock must have been saturated in mikkary.

Nemesis was no more; the only Titan Clock remaining was the Bastion's Juggernaut. And I knew the ticking of Juggernaut had been the sound underlying Malkar's sending.

:But how can he be in the Bastion?: Gideon said.

I shrugged. "It is where he said he was going, all those months ago.

I think the more important question is how I'm going to get into the Bastion to find him."

:To *find* him? Are you *mad*?:

"I have to get Mildmay away from him. I know what Malkar's terms will be, when he gets around to sending them, and I can't accept them. I can't . . . If it were *just* me, if I were annemer, I'd trade myself for Mildmay in a heartbeat—if I thought Malkar could be trusted to honor his bargain. But it isn't just me. I can't let him have the use of my power again."

:It's a pity you didn't think of some of this sooner.:

"Yes, it is. But I can't do anything about that. I can only deal with the situation as it is, no matter how much I wish my own selfish stupidity hadn't caused it."

:I am sorry. That was unfair. And you do not bear sole responsibility, you know.:

"If you think that makes things any better, you are sadly mistaken. But it does remind me—I need you to tell me what Mavortian did to you."

:Why?: Gideon said warily.

I couldn't help sighing. "Because I can't do this alone."

:I—:

"You can't go."

:I most certainly can.:

"They will recognize you. And once that happens, you're doomed, I'm doomed, Mildmay's doomed. And most likely the Mirador is doomed as well."

He glared at me, but he couldn't deny that what I said was true.

"I can't go to the Curia," I said, painfully spelling it out for both of us, "because they won't believe me. And if they do, they won't trust me. Especially since I didn't tell them about Malkar and Vey in the first place." I bared my teeth at him, not in a smile. "A course of action I regret."

:But you have friends. Surely—:

"Who would you suggest?," I said, vicious with my fear for Mildmay. "Thaddeus?"

:No,: Gideon said. :*Not* Thaddeus.:

"And my other friends . . . I was mad, and then I was gone, and now that I'm back, they don't quite know what to do with me. I can't ask it of them. Not now. And that leaves Mavortian."

:Yes,: Gideon said, his mouth thinning. :Mavortian.:

"And thus I need you to tell me what he did."

:You admit you don't remember?:

"Yes, damn it. Is that what you need to hear?. I don't remember what Mavortian von Heber did to you."

:Very well,: Gideon said. :The short version is that he blackmailed me. The longer version is that, if it were not for him, I would still have my tongue.:

"Oh," I said, almost voicelessly.

:You had had a dream,: he said, dispassionate now, as if recounting the events of a romance he had read. :You couldn't explain it, but you said you had to go east. Across Kekropia. And Mildmay said he would go with you. You weren't coherent enough to be argued with, and nothing I could say, or Mavortian could say, would budge Mildmay in the slightest. He said he'd promised you, and as far as he was concerned, that was that.:

"Is there a way to tell this story that doesn't increase my feelings of guilt?"

:Probably not. Once Mavortian realized he couldn't change Mildmay's mind, he decided we would *all* go.:

"Why in the world . . . ?"

:Beaumont Livy. You were his key to Beaumont Livy, and he wasn't about to let you out of his sight. He insisted I come, too, although I am not in retrospect certain whether it was for his stated reason—to protect you from being detected by the Bastion's warding spells—or merely because he did not trust me not to betray you. And when I said I would not go, for I thought then and think now that it was an insane and suicidal thing to do, he blackmailed me by threatening to have Bernard take me to the nearest town and tell them I was a Eusebian. And as he very kindly pointed out, once we were in Kekropia, it would be even easier to denounce me to the Eusebians as an apostate.:

:I didn't know,: I said, mind to mind, desperately. :I swear to you, I didn't remember. I still don't.:

:I know that. I knew it during that horrible argument. If you'd remembered—:

"If I'd remembered, I wouldn't have been talking to Mavortian von Heber at all."

Gideon made no answer, one eyebrow rising in eloquent skepticism. I blushed and was unable to meet his eyes.

After a moment, he took pity on me and said, :Be that as it may, the question, as you said, is what you are going to do now. Do you still think Messire von Heber a suitable ally?:

He expected me to say no. I wanted to say no. But the sending was still raw and vivid in my head: the welts on Mildmay's back and thighs, the swollen mess of the left side of his face, the dried blood around his nose and mouth. The way he shivered. "I'm afraid it's hard to think of anyone *more* suitable." I felt Gideon stiffen and said, almost apologetically, "We want the same thing."

:You want Malkar Gennadion to die horribly? To the exclusion of all other desires?:

"I didn't say we wanted it in the same way. But—"

:You needn't go on. I understand. But do you really think this is the way to help your brother?:

"If nothing else, Mavortian will distract Malkar. Even if he isn't successful. Malkar loves to gloat." I couldn't hide the shudder that wrenched through me, and Gideon's arms tightened comfortingly.

He said, :Your ruthlessness, in this instance, actually pleases me. But you have to have someone who knows the Bastion. It's every bit as labyrinthine as the Mirador.:

The word struck an echo in my mind. I remembered sitting with Mehitabel in the labyrinth beneath Klepsydra, remembered her saying, *I worked in the Bastion for a time.*

"I have someone who knows the Bastion," I said. "And I think she'll be happy to help."

☙

"You must be mad," said Mehitabel Parr.

"Mehitabel—"

"No!" She had risen to pace somewhere in the middle of my explanation, and now she whirled to face me. "Look. I'm as sorry as anyone about Mildmay, and I'm glad you want to help him. I really am. But what you're asking . . ."

"Would you prefer I took Gideon? He's already volunteered."

"Oh, God, no." From her expression, she knew what the Bastion did to wizards who tried to run.

"Mehitabel, I need someone who knows the Bastion. Someone I trust. Someone who can get Mildmay out, even if everything else goes wrong."

"And you think I'm that person?"

"Yes," I said, with perfect truthfulness.

"Damn you," she said and started pacing again.

I waited; there was nothing more I could say, nothing she did not already know. I had described the sending as graphically as I could bear to.

She said, "I have spent the past three years doing everything in my power to get *out* of Kekropia. And now you want me to walk back *in*?"

"I want to save my brother," I said.

And when Mehitabel began cursing in a bastard argot of Kekropian and Midlander, I knew that she would help.

ᔓᔍ

Mavortian was easier, if even more degrading to my pride. He had the tact—or perhaps the wisdom—not to gloat over me, and the only questions he asked were sensible ones about logistics and plans.

We had several problems facing us before we even confronted Malkar. I had to invent an acceptable reason to absent myself from the Mirador for two weeks or more, and then we had to find a way to leave Mélusine unobserved, since anyone who knew I was heading east would instantly assume they knew where I was going—about which, admittedly, they would not be wrong—and why. And I did not think anyone would listen to my explanations. Then we had to get across the border into Kekropia. And once we reached Lamia, assuming we were arrested by neither Protectorate Guards nor Imperial dragoons along the way, we had to get into the Bastion, again without being observed. And *then* we could worry about Malkar and Mildmay and getting out again.

Mehitabel said that if her information was still good, she could get us from Lamia into the Bastion—although she warned me to bring all the gold I could lay my hands on. In an odd way, it was comforting to have evidence that Lamia was as corrupt as Mélusine.

After some careful thought, I went to Giancarlo and said, truthfully, that I was feeling the strain of my exertions in mending the Virtu and, also truthfully, that I did not find the atmosphere of the Mirador conducive to recovery. I mentioned neither Robert nor Shannon by name, nor did Giancarlo, but he agreed with me that the Mirador was not a restful place and suggested I should go south to St. Millefleur to recuperate. He even advanced me generous traveling expenses out of my stipend without my having to say a word. I answered my guilt at deceiving him with the memory of Malkar's sending and turned my attention to the next task.

My thoughts kept returning to the letter from Mildmay's keeper. She had said she would help Mildmay if she could, and I remembered Mildmay mentioning, in an offhand way, having done work with smugglers as a teenager. Was it so very unreasonable to put those two things together?

At the least, I decided, as we neared the midpoint of the second week that Malkar had had Mildmay in his power, I could ask her. I knew how things worked in the Lower City. If Kolkhis herself could not help me, she would know someone who could. And I could pay for any help provided.

I did not want to write her a letter, for anything put in writing was potential ammunition against me later—assuming there was a later, and I was going to assume that until every other option had been taken away from me. Therefore, I went to Mavortian and asked to borrow Bernard.

"What in the world for?"

"I need to go into the Lower City, to speak to someone about . . . well, let's say arrangements and leave it at that."

"And you need Bernard for this?"

"A Cabaline wizard alone in the Lower City sends entirely different signals than one who's brought a bodyguard. I don't want anyone to get confused."

"Ah," said Mavortian. "What singularly unpleasant vistas that opens to the imagination. Then, yes, by all means, take Bernard."

And Bernard rolled his eyes but didn't complain. We did not need to like or respect each other as long as he continued to do what Mavortian told him, and whatever the bargain was between them, he showed no signs of breaking it.

We took a hansom to Britomart, although the driver was not happy about admitting he knew the Stag and Candles, or how to get there, or that there was a district of Mélusine called Britomart at all. We had, however, come out of the Mirador, and I let him get a good look at my tattoos and an even better look at the septagorgon I was offering, and he acquiesced. Bernard and I said nothing to each other all the way there.

The Stag and Candles was higher-class than I had expected; floor and bar alike gleamed with polish, and the thin, ferret-faced bartender sent a girl around to scrub the tables once an hour or so. Although exquisitely polite, he was even less happy than the cabdriver about admitting he could help with what I wanted. But his eyes kept skittering back to my tattoos, and he finally gave in and bellowed, "Hey, Hob!"

A gangly teenage boy emerged from the back, drying his hands on his pants as he came.

The bartender gave him a sour look. "Run to your *other* boss, and tell her there's a gentleman here wants to talk to her."

"Right," Hob said, and then his eyes reached my face. His jaw dropped, and I thought for a moment he might faint.

"No, I'm not him," I said. "But go tell Madame Kolkhis I need to see her."

"Yes, sir," the boy said, then caught sight of my rings and turned even paler. "My lord. I'll . . . I'll be quick, my lord!" He dashed off, all awkward knees and elbows, but moving fast.

I bought a bourbon for myself and a beer for Bernard, overpaying fairly lavishly, and we retired to a corner table to wait. And continued to say nothing to each other.

We waited half an hour, at my best guess, before the gangly boy returned. He gave our table a nervous, sidelong look, and vanished into the back again. Two minutes later, the door opened.

She was tall, slender, lithe. She wore her hair in smooth black coils around the perfect oval of her face, and her eyes were pale gray, the color of fog. She wore the clothes of a lady with neither apology nor discomfort, dark purple poplin trimmed with black lace, high-necked and formfitting with a great swag of bustle behind. She saw us and made her way across the room without hesitation. She sat down, managing her skirts with the absent dexterity of one who did so daily, gave me a flat, level look. "Is it true you're sleeping with him?"

Bernard choked on his beer.

I had expected some form of attack. I said, "No."

"How about the obligation d'âme? Did you cast that on him?" She had made no effort to lose her accent, although her grammar and phrasing, like her clothes, were those of a lady.

"Yes. At his request."

She said nothing, but I could feel her disbelief. I wanted this conversation to end, wanted to get away from this woman who seemed to represent my past as much as my brother's. "You said you would help Mildmay if you could," I said, forcing my eyes to stay steady against hers. "I have found a way that you can."

"Tell me."

"I need passage for four people on one of the, er, unofficial caravans that run from here to Lamia."

"To Lamia?"

"He's in the Bastion."

"Wizards," she said with loathing. "See it in a crystal ball?"

"Something like that. I assure you, I wouldn't go anywhere near the Bastion if I didn't know for a fact my brother is there."

"Your . . . brother."

"Is the family resemblance not strong enough for you?"

"Oh, I believe you're brothers. I just find the fraternal concern a little overdone."

"And what is *that* supposed to mean?"

Her smile made my blood run cold. "Leaving aside the indictions when he could have used a brother and you were . . . somewhere else, I didn't raise him to be stupid. If he went after Vey Coruscant when and how he did, it was someone else's idea. At a guess, yours."

"And sending him after Cerberus Cresset was a stroke of genius?"

"He got out again."

"With a curse on him that nearly killed him!" After a moment, I was able to straighten the fury and tension out of my fingers. "That is neither here nor there. If I have made mistakes, I am trying to rectify them. Will you do as I ask?"

"It depends," she said and smiled, an ugly smile, cruel and thin.

"Depends on what?"

"On what you're willing to do for me in return."

For one ghastly moment, I thought she was propositioning me, but she continued: "The Mirador confiscated certain of Vey Coruscant's personal effects, including something that I want."

"Something that *you* want?"

"Yes," she said, unperturbed. "For a client."

"And what is this object?"

"A book."

At once, I understood why she wanted my help. The Mirador did not confiscate books so much as absorb them; no outsider had a chance of success, even knowing exactly what they were looking for. "Which book?"

"It is a Midlander book—" She produced a piece of paper from a hidden pocket, consulting it with a slight frown. For a moment I was convinced she was going to say *The Doctrine of Labyrinths*, and bit my lip against a hysterical shriek of laughter. "Artemisia de Charon's *Principia*—"

"Principia Caeli," I finished in relief. "Yes, I know it. It's not exactly an uncommon book. It's not even heretical."

"My client wants Madame Coruscant's copy, and no other. And I am assured the book is identifiable as such."

"And you want me to fetch it for you?"

"Not the word I would have chosen, and I certainly wouldn't insist you deliver it in person. But if you want my help getting out of Mélusine unobserved, that is my price."

"I shouldn't have expected you to do it out of the goodness of your heart," I said, choosing my inflection carefully to suggest that both *goodness* and *heart* were words I did not expect her to know.

"No, you expected me to do it for your brother's pretty green eyes. But that isn't how things work. You send your bruiser with the book, and I'll see what I can do. He can leave it with Byron at the bar." She stood and turned on her heel in one smooth motion, and was gone with barely a ripple through the crowded tavern.

Now I know where Mildmay learned to move like that, I thought stupidly; I was aware of something leaving the room with her, something like the oppressive miasmas that brought fevers to the Lower City in summer.

Bernard said thoughtfully, "That woman could have your balls off before you even knew she had a knife."

༂༂

De Charon's *Principia Caeli* was a book on weather-working, the sort that most wizards referred to as a "classic in the field" without ever having bothered actually to read it. I *had* read it; it was dull, methodical, and utterly harmless. Even Vey Coruscant's marginalia seemed unlikely in the extreme to change that, and it was not as if the Mirador did not have a half dozen copies already.

I was rationalizing, I admitted to myself that night as I opened the door to the Archive of Cinders, having left Gideon asleep in my bed, frowning slightly as if he sought for a lost earring in his dreams and could not find it. But whether I rationalized my actions or not made no difference. I did not know any other way to make contact with someone who could bypass Mélusine's ever-guarded gates, and the problem with knowing that Mildmay was alive was knowing that he might not stay that way for long.

The Archive of Cinders was not the only place confiscated books were stored—the Archive of the Chamberlain and the Archive of Brocades were also used for that purpose—but the Archive of Cinders was the most likely place to find a book that had interest only by association. I had to drag a chair over to reach the top shelves, for the Archive of Cinders was far taller than it was wide, lending credence to the story that it had gotten its name from having once been a chimney, but up there, on a quite recently dusted shelf, I found what I was looking for.

It was an octavo volume, bound in dark red leather, embossed and gilded, more suited to a nobleman's library than a blood-wizard's. But I thumbed through it quickly—my witchlights providing enough light to see, although I would not have wanted to try to read without a good branch of candles—and observed writing in the margins with the same distinctive looping tails I had observed in Vey Coruscant's letter to me. And on the back flyleaf I found her seal, impressed without wax. As Kolkhis had said, it was unmistakable, and I slammed the book closed with a shiver.

Regardless of what Kolkhis's client wanted the book for, I was not sorry that it would not be in the Mirador, would not be adding its mite to the weight of mikkary we all lived under.

⚜

Although I would not have been surprised if she had betrayed me, Kolkhis was as good as her word. The smuggler's name was Theodore d'Erda; I did not ask what he and his cousins and their patient oxen were taking to Lamia, and he in return did not ask about our plans and did not so much as raise an eyebrow at our patently false names. I had expected smugglers to be a rough and vulgar lot, but d'Erda and his cousins were perfectly polite.

The journey was torture, and knowing I deserved it did not make it easier to bear. After three nights of patchy sleep and horrific dreams, afraid to resort to methods of gaining deeper sleep lest it should disrupt the spells of concealment Gideon had taught me—I decided that I no longer had enough pride to worry about, and went to Mavortian.

"Teach me the cards," I said.

He gave me a look of polite incredulity and said, "I beg your pardon."

I sat down opposite him. "I am going mad by inches. And since there is nothing I can do, and no way on earth to make these damnable oxen walk faster . . . teach me the cards."

"Very well. Now?"

"Please," I said. "Now."

Mildmay

Small room. Stone walls. No windows.

Ironbound door. Hinges on the outside. Keyhole you could drive a coach and four through.

One lamp wired into a bracket on the wall.

Fucking clock. Fucking binding-by-forms, like a guy yanking on a leash.

Two cots, sagging mattresses, threadbare dirty blankets. Better than nothing.

Two men, one tall and skinny, the other older and fat. Both with the tattoos. The skinny one wears spectacles, all held together with bits of wire. The fat one—well, he don't look too good. Gray-faced, and he breathes like a bunch of carnival rattles being shaken in a bag. He ain't a threat, and the skinny one don't have but three whole fingers on both hands put together. So he ain't a threat either.

That's good.

They talk a lot. Skinny one's named Simon, fat one's Rinaldo. They been prisoners here a long time, long enough that the guards talk to them, give them all the good gossip. Guards are annemer. Don't matter as long as they don't let the hocuses out the door. Magic don't work in here.

The hocuses do their best to help, but there ain't much they can do. Wait for the bruises to fade and the cuts to heal. No bones broken. Small favors.

"Stop pacing," Simon says. "Rest. You'll never heal if you don't rest."

Rinaldo says, "Obviously, he can't."

"You could sit on him."

"I doubt I'd survive the attempt." Rinaldo don't miss much.

"But *why?*" He sounds like he really wants to know. "*Why* can't you rest?"

"At a guess," Rinaldo says, "egregiously unfinished business with someone on the other side of that door." They're both quiet a minute, then Rinaldo says, "Whoever he is, I'm not going to stay up nights praying for him."

He's sure as fuck right about that.

Felix

The Bastion loomed over us for three days, gradually eating more and more of the horizon, before we reached the outskirts of the "city" of Lamia, where we parted from Theodore d'Erda and his cousins and their unmentioned cargo.

Lamia had been a true city once, a sister to Mélusine, but one of the early Eusebian generals, declaring it to be nothing but a breeding ground for sedition and disease, had put the entire city to the torch.

It had grown back, of course, like the many-headed Hudra of Kekropian legend, but only as a tent city, something the generals could pretend was ephemeral, even if some of those tents—loosely so-called—had been standing longer than the oldest wizard of the Bastion had been alive. Certainly the population was in constant flux—merchants and smugglers and craftsmen and prostitutes—but I suspected Lamia remained a breeding ground for all sorts of things, in this incarnation just as much as in the last.

When we left the d'Erdas, Mehitabel rather grimly took over. I was certain within five minutes that I had done the right thing in convincing her to come. We had entered Lamia, as we had left Mélusine, in the dead of night, but Mehitabel led us directly to a sprawling canvas-sided hotel where the night clerk asked not a single question beyond how many rooms we wanted.

We went to our rooms through a confusing tangle of tent flaps and ropes, Mavortian and Bernard in one, Mehitabel and me directly adjacent. Mehitabel put down her valise, said, "All right, sunshine. Here we are in Lamia, just like you wanted. I'm going to go find out just how out of date my information is, and I suggest you and your coconspirators give some thought to what you're going to do now."

"Mehitabel."

She stopped and turned to face me, her spectacle lenses glinting in the lanternlight. She said nothing, simply waited as she must have waited for Delila or Angora to come up with the right answer.

"I told Mildmay not to trust me," I said at last.

"I wish he'd listened to you," she said, and was gone.

$$\mathfrak{H}$$

What we did, for most of that day, was read the cards.

Our success depended on so many factors that it seemed almost ridiculous to plan in any greater detail than agreeing that we had to get into the Bastion, find and rescue Mildmay—and although I had expected him to, Mavortian did not argue about that being our first priority—find and kill Malkar, and get out. Mavortian seemed confident, now that he knew Malkar's true identity as Brinvillier Strych, that he could use his silver focus to find him. "It is, after all," he said with a thin smile, "what it is *for*."

But the rest of our plans seemed to depend almost entirely on Mehitabel. According to the research I had done, I should have been able to find Mildmay using the obligation d'âme, but although I had learned to feel him consciously, the feeling refused to localize. The only certainty I had was that he was not dead, and while that was a comfort, it was not terribly helpful.

Thus, we read the cards, looking for the patterns, the ways the future might unfold in front of us. Mavortian had been surprised at how quickly I had learned the dance of significances through major and minor arcana; I had wondered with irritation how he imagined I had earned my tattoos, if he had so poor an opinion of my intelligence. I would have had to seduce the entire Curia, a feat which was frankly beyond my skill. I did not ask, though, for it was not worth open hostility between us, and I found I did not care if Mavortian thought ill of me.

Cade-Cholera's card turned up with depressing frequency. It might mean change as well as death, and it might mean Malkar's death rather than mine or Mildmay's or any of my allies', but it was not a card of good omen, no matter how hopefully one tried to interpret it.

The Sibyl of Swords showed up repeatedly, as did the Knight of Swords. Mavortian told me how the Knight of Swords had brought Mildmay to him; I bit my tongue against any clever remarks about heresy and agreed that probably the Sibyl of Swords represented me.

"You and he are at the heart of the matter, as you have been all along," Mavortian said, eyeing me thoughtfully as he shuffled the cards again. That was one thing I could not do as well as he, even with practice; the stiffness in my badly healed fingers made it impossible for me to manage even a box shuffle with grace.

I pushed away the memory of cards moving like water through Mildmay's hands and said, "Does it hurt your pride?"

"It is disconcerting," he said after a moment. "But I don't lose sleep over it." And he laid the cards out again.

Mehitabel returned near sundown, bad-tempered but successful. "I'm told this is the first time anyone has paid to get *into* the Bastion," she said. "They all think I'm completely insane."

"Will they talk?" Mavortian asked.

"No. They'd be arrested right along with us, and they know it. But if we are caught in the tunnels, we will be destroying those two old ladies along with ourselves."

"We won't be caught," Mavortian said, and seeing the spark kindle in Mehitabel's eyes, I said hastily, "Tunnels?"

"The last remains of Old Lamia," Mehitabel said, with a raised eyebrow at me that told me she knew what I was doing and was allowing herself to be distracted. "Irene's grandfather dug it out over a century ago—found it by accident, Irene says. And now she and Barbara make at least as much money off looking the other way when people come out of their cellars as they do from the tearoom itself."

"Barbara?"

"Her widowed daughter-in-law." She smiled, a little sharply. "They're expecting us for the dinner service at eight o'clock."

Mildmay

Guards got a routine. They make their rounds after dinner, make sure everybody's tucked in and ain't trying to dig their way out with a spoon or something. And then they don't come round again for a solid four hours.

You learn a lot when you can't sleep.

"Do you think he's mad?" Simon says to Rinaldo.

"Indubitably," Rinaldo says to Simon. "But I also think he's perfectly lucid. I don't know why he wants that lamp, but I'm sure he has a reason."

"Probably to set us all on fire."

"Simon." Rinaldo sounds kind of pained. "He has shown not the slightest inclination to harm either of us once he realized we were not the people who had harmed him."

"Easy for you to say. You're not the one with bruises on your throat."

"I feel quite confident that if he wanted us dead, we would be dead already. We've proved we aren't equipped to defend ourselves against him."

"*Thank* you, Rinaldo." Simon sighs. "I just wish he'd say something. Or that we knew his name. Or *anything*."

"We know who brought him here. Is that not enough?"

Simon's hands flinch back into his pockets. He's had his own run-ins with Strych. "I'd just like to help," he says, kind of sad.

"Until he *lets* us help him, we've done all we can."

They sit and watch like stuffed owls.

The lamp finally comes loose. Rinaldo can hold it. Wire's more useful.

"Is he doing what I think he's doing?" Simon whispers to Rinaldo.

"He seems to be attempting to pick the lock. I wonder if he has the least idea how to—"

Old lock. Not a real good one. The tumblers groan and roll over. A push, and the door swings open. Come on, you stupid hocuses. Come on, move!

"He wants . . ."

"He seems to want us to escape."

"We can't escape from the Bastion!"

Drag 'em, push 'em, just get them on the other side of that fucking door where their magic will work. Don't have to worry about 'em if their magic's working. They're like fucking sheep. Been penned up too long, forgotten how to run. Kick the door closed again with them on the right side of it. Catch the skinny one. Ugly voice, hoarse and muddy, not like a person at all: "Gonna give you one fuck of a distraction. Gonna murder Brinvillier Strych."

Felix

Suddenly, I felt him. It was like the moment when, after searching for something for three days, one finally *sees* it, and it made me spill my tea.

Mavortian, Bernard, and Mehitabel all stared at me, and I felt my face flush crimson. But I remembered to keep my voice low when I said, "I can feel him."

"Feel him?" Mehitabel repeated doubtfully.

"I couldn't before—I don't know why. But now I can. I could walk straight to him."

"Could it be some sort of trap?" Bernard asked. A reasonable question.

"I don't think so." I knew more about binding spells than Malkar did, for all that he'd been the one to teach me about them. He had never figured out how I'd broken the obligation de sang, and if he didn't know that, I did not think he would be able to influence the obligation d'âme so subtly.

"Do you think it's likely to prove temporary?" Mavortian said.

"I don't know."

"Then perhaps, Maselle Parr, our amiable hostesses might be persuaded to show us the way into the cellar now, rather than later?"

"Yes. Wait here a moment." She got up, crossed the room to the elderly lady who sat knitting beside the giant gold-and-red-enameled tea urn. A quick exchange of words, and Mehitabel came back. "Irene says she will not be sorry to have wizards gone from her tearoom." Another sharp smile. "You bring bad luck."

"Is that bad luck the literal or metaphorical kind?" Mavortian asked as he began struggling to his feet.

"In Lamia, it's Imperial dragoons. Come on."

The tunnels beneath Lamia looked like the corridors of the Warren, the same narrow, ruinously old, uneven courses of stonework, smoke-darkened and hostile. Mehitabel carried a lantern the old woman had given her; neither Mavortian nor I felt witchlights were worth the varied risks they would bring with them. If we were spotted, the longer we could keep from being identified as wizards, the better.

"Is the way marked?" I heard Bernard murmur to Mehitabel.

"Yes, if you know what to look for."

"And you know?"

"Better than I'd like." Something bitter in her voice, something old.

But she did not lead us wrong; every turn she took brought me closer to Mildmay. I felt as if I was beginning to be able to breathe again for the first time in three weeks or more. And I could feel Juggernaut ticking.

We climbed a narrow staircase—almost more like a ladder—Bernard carrying Mavortian. At the top, Mehitabel whispered, "This door takes us into the Bastion's cellars. From here, I guess Felix is going to have to lead."

"Unless we go after Messire Gennadion first."

"We discussed this," I said, feeling anger like sparks from a fire float upward in my chest. And I had wondered why he was being so complaisant. He had merely been biding his time. "Since we cannot be sure of killing, or even incapacitating, Malkar, we—"

"Why 'incapacitate'?"

"I beg your pardon?"

Mavortian's eyes had an unpleasant shine in the lanternlight. "Are you not so sure you want Messire Gennadion dead after all? Perhaps you would rather your teacher was left alive?"

"You don't have any idea what you're talking about," I said, stiff with the effort of not letting my temper overwhelm me. "Of course I want him dead. I just don't want him dead more than I want Mildmay alive."

"What if you cannot have both?"

"Then I will save my brother's life. You can do what you want. Mehitabel?"

"I'm with you, Felix."

"You can't let him get away," Mavortian said, a hiss like a snake's.

"It's not like he's running."

"Fine. Suit yourself." The savagery in his voice far outstripped the words themselves. "Bernard and I will do what's necessary."

"It depends on how you define 'necessary,'" I said, and nodded to Mehitabel to open the door.

Mildmay

Fucking hocuses won't go away.

Sheep.

Not a sheepdog. Clear the fuck out already.

Got to find Strych. They ain't a part of it. Need to *go away*.

But they say they don't know where to go. Say they're lost. Keep following. Can't ditch them. They'll get caught, get hurt. Don't know where to take them. Don't know where to find Strych.

No fucking good at thinking anyway.

Footsteps. Lanternlight. No way to hide Rinaldo in the shadows. You could stand in Lyonesse and hear him breathing in Verdigris.

No weapons. Hands will do.

Wave the hocuses back. Useless in a fight. Ain't even got their witchlights lit. Eyes big as bell-wheels, both of 'em. Up to the corner, quick count of seven, swing round and aim hard for the throat.

Fuck. Pull it at the last second, catch at the wall to stay upright.

Mehitabel Parr says, "Are you always this friendly, or did I just get lucky?"

Felix

There was nothing human in his eyes. Truly the eyes of the fox he resembled: cold, flat, filled with fear and savage hatred, a fox brought to bay by monstrous dogs. I was vaguely surprised he did not actually bare his teeth at us in a snarl.

If he recognized us—if he recognized *me*—he gave no sign.

And then a voice said, from around the corner, "Um, has anyone died yet?"

Marathine-speaking, a faint Monspulchran accent. Not a Eusebian, and I managed to take a breath deep enough to get words out. "No, no one has died. Hopefully, no one will."

A small, sharp silence. *"Felix Harrowgate?"*

The lanternlight was abruptly doubled. A tall man, my own height or nearly, long blond hair starting to go gray, wide bright blue eyes behind a pair of terribly battered spectacles. Beside him, a second man, shorter, much fatter, gray-haired, with tiny twinkling eyes like the wise eyes of an infinitely good-natured pig. Both of them with the Mirador's tattoos winding in barbaric beauty around their arms.

Simon Barrister and Rinaldo of Fiora, lost in the Empire years ago, Simon before Thaddeus de Lalage had been sent to Aurelias, Rinaldo so long ago that I barely remembered seeing him, would not have remembered a man of lesser girth. And apparently they had been imprisoned in the Bastion all this time. I would never even have known to look for them.

The corridor was thronged with things we wanted to say, things there was not time for. Simon, with the habitual awkward delicacy of a stork, put his head on one side and said, "Do you know him?" The blue eyes cut sideways at Mildmay.

That's a very good question, I almost said. "He's my brother."

"Oh," said Simon, looking from one to the other of us. "Of course."

"Has he not . . . ?"

Rinaldo said, "The only thing he's said in almost a week is that he's going to murder Brinvillier Strych."

"I'm terribly sorry," Simon said. "We don't know . . . that is, he'd been hurt before we ever saw him, and I'm most awfully afraid it's affected his mind."

Simon was trying to say, politely, that Mildmay was insane. And he was, if he thought he would get anywhere near Malkar like this. But that wasn't what Simon meant.

"Actually," I said, "that part makes perfect sense. You see, Brinvillier Strych is also Malkar Gennadion."

I saw Simon's wince, knew that here was another thing that Malkar had broken in his passage through the world. Rinaldo merely frowned and said, "Can you prove that assertion?"

"Do I need to?"

He thought for a moment, and then his lips quirked in something that was not quite a smile. "No, I suppose you don't. Malkar—"

"This is not," Mehitabel interrupted, "the best place for a convivial chat."

"No. And I need to find Mavortian. If Mildmay's all right."

"I'm not sure Mildmay *is* all right," Mehitabel said.

"He's upright and mobile," I said.

"He got us out of our cell," Simon added.

"Let's call it provisionally all right and get moving," I said.

"Your party, sunshine," Mehitabel said. "What do you want to do?"

"Um." I thought hard. "Will you take Simon and Rinaldo and Mildmay back through the tunnels?"

"How will you and the others get out, then?"

"I'll follow the bond to Mildmay," I said, and did not miss the sharp look Rinaldo gave me. More things that would have to be said later.

"Of course," Mehitabel said. "Silly me. All right. You go play hero. I'll try to get everybody else out alive."

"That's just as heroic as anything else that happens tonight," I said, smiled at her poleaxed expression, and cast into the maze of the Bastion for Malkar.

I only wished it had been harder to find him.

But feeling Malkar was as easy as feeling the poisoned ache of an infected wound. His magic had a flavor to it, a bitter, grinding bite, and he was using magic now, using it—

—using it to kill Mavortian von Heber, one agonized inch at a time.

I took off running.

I knew, even as I ran, that I was already too late, but there was nothing else I could do. I had to try. Even if it was not entirely my fault that

Mavortian had been trapped—and I knew that the blame was truly Malkar's, and to some degree Mavortian's in his own right for choosing to separate from me—part of the responsibility was on my shoulders. I had valued Mildmay over Mavortian, and it seemed that that had not been necessary. Mildmay—and I should have known it—was perfectly capable of rescuing himself. Mavortian was obsessed and reckless with it, and although I had tried to explain, I thought perhaps he had not grasped exactly who and what Brinvillier Strych was, who he was dealing with beyond the man he had hated for so long.

He had not wanted to grasp it, but that did not mean I should have left him to walk into Malkar's jaws alone.

I ran, my witchlights skittering around me, tracing a tangle of corridors and antechambers and half staircases without more than the most passing attention paid to any of it. For once in my life, I was not worried about getting lost.

Stairs down, and more stairs down, and I wondered distractedly what business Malkar had had in the Bastion's subbasements, before I skidded around a corner into a room lit by sulfurous witchlight: chains on the walls, a pentagram inlaid in the floor, a drain gaping like a hungry maw.

Bernard was lying, limp as a rag doll, against one wall, Mavortian's canes broken underneath him; Mavortian was pinned, unnaturally stiff, against another, his eyes bulging from his head, blood already beginning to drip from nose and mouth and ears. Malkar stood in one point of the pentagram, his hands raised, the witchlight reflecting evilly from the rubies in his rings. And then I knew. Somehow, Malkar had felt us coming; I did not know which of us had betrayed himself, Mavortian or I, and it did not matter. Something had alerted Malkar. And being Malkar, he had done what he did best: he had set a trap.

He didn't bother to turn around; he had no need. And all the rich, purring cruelty in the world was in his voice when he said, "There you are, darling. Come to watch the show?"

Mildmay

He's going to find Strych. Mehitabel can look after the hocuses. They'll be fine. *He*'s the one to follow.

No problem getting away from them. They ain't gonna go wandering around in the Bastion. Got a new sheepdog to keep 'em safe, and she's no dummy. Easy to follow him and his little green witchlights. Just keep back, keep out of the way.

Harder to keep up. Long legs, and he's moving fast. Follow. All or nothing.

Down and down. Sim don't run under the Bastion. Small favors. Down, and there's the smell of Strych. You don't forget it once you've learned it.

He turns a corner and stops dead. Hang back, don't get cocky. Strych's voice. Words don't matter. Nothing matters but the smell of death.

A scream. Don't have to look to know somebody's dead. That ain't the sort of scream you live through. *He* says something, like it hurts him. Angle past him, and there's Strych.

Now it's just down to waiting.

Good.

Felix

Mavortian was dead, terribly, a heap of splintered bones in a pool of blood.

"Are you really Brinvillier Strych?" I said into the silence.

"Yes." Malkar's smile was mocking. "I would have told you before if you had asked." He took a step forward.

My back was against the wall before I even realized I was going to move, instincts ingrained by years of pain and fear telling me that when he was like this, I had to keep out of his reach.

Not that it had ever done me any good.

He took another step, his smile widening.

Oh you useless sniveling vermin! Aren't you even going to *fight*? Can't you for once in your damned worthless existence stand up for yourself? But I'd never been able to fight Malkar, not since his gorgons dropped into Lorenzo's palm, and he turned to me with that little smile and said, *Let us find out if you are worth the price.* I could hate him; I could cherish my fury and hoard it like a miser. But face-to-face with him, and all there was left was fear.

Once it was clear I was not going to speak, Malkar said, "It really is amazing, how much you and your brother look alike. I had thought my memory was playing tricks on me."

It was a mistake. He never made mistakes, and I didn't know what had prompted this one—what cue he had misread. It occurred to me, in a moment of sickening shame, that if he'd made Mildmay describe the way I behaved toward him, the picture he would have gotten would have justified a belief that I cared no more for Mildmay than a bear-baiter did for his dogs. But Malkar's words did to me what I had been unable to do to myself: jarred me out of the rut of fear and memory his voice had trapped me in. I saw Mildmay as he had been in my dream, beaten and scared but still fighting, using Malkar's own games against him.

My hands came up, and they were full of fire.

Malkar swatted my lightning aside. "You aren't thinking. You know you can't win—you could never beat me before."

"This isn't before," I said.

Malkar laughed. "And you think you can escape your past, my poor deluded child? Trust me, my darling, it can't be done."

And that was when the shadows behind me, on my bad side, exploded in a snarling howl, the scream of an animal goaded finally beyond endurance; I shied sideways, hard enough that I lost my balance and fell, and it took me a moment to realize it was Mildmay, and he was leaping for Malkar's throat.

Mildmay

Only chance. Only shot. Can't kill a hocus if they see you coming.

Strych laughs, and that's it.

Now.

Now now now.

Aim for the throat. Vulnerable. Windpipe and choke vein and all kinds of good shit. Shove his voice box out through his spine. Both hands, grip hard, bear down. Don't matter that it's him, don't matter how much he hurt you. Just kill the son of a bitch and it'll be over.

He's surprised. Like it on him. Clamp down, hard. It's going to work. It's *gotta* work. Come on, you fucker, die already!

But one big hand's moving. Too late to dodge.

—oh fuck—

Pain. Like before. Raw screaming. On the floor, Strych's foot pressing down. Hard to breathe. Hard to hear. Can't scream anymore, though, and that's good. Strych's voice like thunder. *His* voice answering. Don't do anything stupid, please. Please. Please don't let him hurt you, too.

Please.

Felix

Mildmay was on the floor, Malkar's boot resting across his throat.

"A cunning animal," he said, one hand rubbing his own throat.

I was on my feet again, lightning dancing from finger to finger, but I could not attack, not when all he had to do was redirect my lightning to my brother's helpless body.

"But I can't imagine why you had to cast the obligation d'âme on him, my darling. Surely a creature like this would never dare to be disloyal."

"Your example has taught me never to be overconfident about such things," I said—and regretted it the next moment, as his foot bore down harder, and I heard Mildmay choke.

"Flippancy does not become you, dearest. I suggest instead of being clever, you devote your attention to deciding what you're going to do now. It isn't as if you have many choices."

No, I didn't. I couldn't let him hurt Mildmay, but I could not see how to defeat him otherwise.

You know you can't win—you could never beat me before.

And that was true. I had never been able to defeat Malkar. Never once.

And then the thought turned itself around in my head, and I had to fight to keep sudden enlightenment from showing on my face. I could not defeat Malkar any more than I could have defeated the Sim, but I could—I had always been able to—give in to him.

I did. I lowered my hands, let the lightning fade.

Malkar cocked his head at me, his smile resurfacing. "Surrender, my dear?"

I stepped forward, hoping that he would take my trembling for exhaustion and despair. "I can't . . ." I said, letting my voice trail away. He knew I wasn't articulate at moments like this—he, better than anyone, knew that. It didn't bother him that I didn't say what it was I couldn't do.

"So sudden," he said, "and yet so expected. If you are very good to me, my darling, I may not make you watch me eviscerate your little brother."

He stepped forward himself, meeting me, his foot finally off Mildmay's neck, and said, "Kiss me, sweet. Remind me of what you're good at."

"Yes, Malkar," I said and kissed him.

And with the kiss, I flung my magic around him, locking us together, letting the weight of his attack—which I'd known was coming, as surely as I knew I breathed—carry us both down, not physically, but down into the dark underlayer of dreams, of divination, into my construct-Mélusine. He had been expecting resistance, expecting my strength arrayed against him, so he could not check our fall. But my advantage lasted only the barest moment; as soon as he realized his miscalculation, he was fighting me, his magic twisting against mine, struggling for dominance.

Not for flight. Never for flight.

My raw power was greater than his. He had known that from the moment he found me in the Shining Tiger, had moved quickly, brutally to ensure that I would never be capable of using that strength against him. Even now, it was all I could do simply to withstand him, to keep from rolling over and showing him my belly like a dog.

I held on, thinking of the fear in Mildmay's eyes. Malkar bludgeoned me savagely, but I could feel his confusion; he didn't know what I was trying to do, and that wrong-footed him. He was used to being able to predict my actions, my thoughts. I was his creature, as he had liked to remind me, and as transparent to him as a pane of glass.

But not now. He had always disdained thaumaturgic architecture, sneered at the magic of dreams and divination, and so he could not understand what I had learned from Gideon and Thamuris, from Iosephinus long ago. He was as blind to the world of the spirit, Sand's *manar*, as he was to the idea of compassion, of love, of loyalty that was not anchored and founded in fear. And so he was uncertain, a feeling that had to be an unwelcome novelty to a monster as old and clever as Brinvillier Strych, and he did not strike with quite his full force, did not, even now, try to disengage. And it baffled and enraged him that I would not fight back; he fought harder, his own power now holding him as much as I was, for the more he grappled with my construct-self—rather than drawing back to engage my physical body as he could have done, at least at first—the more he accepted the symbolism of this construct-Mélusine, the more the symbolism accepted him and worked upon him.

And since I was not fighting him, and I was not fighting it, the construct acted as it always wanted to, dragging us both down, back, south, through its jagged mockery of the Seventh Gate and into the dark, mirish madness of the swamps beyond. I dragged Malkar down with me, exerting myself only to hold him. Now he was struggling, now he was trying to free himself from me, but he could not. He himself had let me close—had told me to kiss him. His own symbolism chained him to me, left him vulnerable to my symbols, and as the mire closed over our heads, still locked together in that grotesque, nauseating kiss, I called on the symbols I had been immersed in for the past several days, the stations of the Sibylline: the River, the Drowned Man, the Two-Handed Engine, finally, with every scrap of power and self I possessed, the Heart of Light.

And Malkar screamed.

Screamed and burst into flames.

Our physical bodies jolted apart, so violently that I wasn't even burned. I was screaming, too, I realized distantly, but my attention was focused on holding my spells on him, on keeping him under the knotted web of magic and madness that was killing him.

Later, I came to realize that he probably couldn't have saved himself in any event. Brinvillier Strych or not, greatest living blood-wizard or not, he was burning from within, as if my touch had ignited his bones. Even burning, his eyes were aware, and the look in them, fixed on me, was a searing compound of shock and rage. He hadn't thought I could do it—he hadn't thought *anyone* could. Even then I wondered how long it had been since anyone had hurt him, since anyone had dared to try.

The fire, unnatural as it was, consumed him quickly, but to me it was a ghastly, crawling eternity before something in him—his heart, I thought, for that was where the fire had begun—exploded. I ducked away, cowering against the wall, and felt hot shreds of him fall on my hair and left shoulder and back. It was only partly the pain that had me in a panic to shake them off and beat out the sparks.

When I could look again, Malkar Gennadion was a pile of coals settling slowly into ash. He was dead; he could be nothing but dead. There could be no miraculous resurrection from this for him.

I drew a deep, shuddering, painful breath. I stepped around the remains of my former master, torturer, lover, teacher. Knelt down by my brother.

His eyes blinked open, dazed and hurt, but maybe . . . maybe they were not quite so cold? Maybe I was deluding myself.

"Dead?" His voice was a harsh, slurry rasp, worse than I had ever heard it.

"Yes."

"Need . . ." He reached for me, and I understood. I helped him sit up, edged myself awkwardly around so that he could see.

He looked, unblinking, for a long time. It was only very slowly that I realized he was crying, even more slowly that I realized I was crying, too. I put my arms around him; he hugged me back with surprising strength. We crouched there for some time in the darkness, weeping while the ashes of our nemesis settled and smoldered in the middle of the room.

Chapter 16

Felix

On our own, we might well have stayed there, unmoving, unthinking, until the Eusebians or their soldiers found us. But Bernard stirred, moaned. Then his breath hissed in, and he said, "Ah powers, that poor stupid son of a bitch," in a tone so mixed of bitterness and sympathy, contempt and grief, that I could not begin to categorize it. "He never stood a chance, did he?"

"Not really," I said, straightening cramped limbs, encouraging Mildmay to do the same. He obeyed me, but his eyes seemed as empty as glass.

"What about the other one, whatever his real name was?"

"Dead." There was no pleasure in saying it.

"Well, that's something. You, um . . ." His gaze had found Malkar's pathetic, smoldering remains.

"Yes. I burned him alive. It's what he did to Jane Teveria, you know."

"I wasn't going to criticize."

"Well, that's a first," I said, and he snorted. Almost laughter, almost friendship. But not quite one, and not quite the other. He stood up, slowly, clearly in pain, and hobbled over to Mavortian's body, where he went down, slowly, onto his knees again.

"We can't carry him out." It wasn't really a question.

"We have no way to explain a dead body. Especially one that died like that."

"Powers." I thought Bernard shuddered, although it was hard to tell in frail witchlight. "Yeah. Not an accident."

"But we don't have to leave him here," I said. "If it matters to you, we can find somewhere in the tunnels, somewhere he won't be found."

"Yeah. Stupid of me, isn't it? We didn't like each other, and I know if it was me, he'd just walk over my body and keep going. But . . . yeah. Let's."

And it was at that moment that I realized I had no idea how to find the door to the tunnels again.

Mildmay

Felix was kneeling in front of me, looking worried. He said my name again, kind of sharp, but not angry or nothing, and I realized he wanted something from me, so I nodded to show I'd heard him.

He looked terrible, like he hadn't slept for a month, and his voice was even more breathless than usual, almost not there at all, when he said, "Mildmay, can you find your way back to where you left Mehitabel and the others?"

"Others?" Bernard said, but Felix wasn't paying attention. He was fixed on me.

I nodded, and Felix gave a long sigh of relief. "Good, for I truly do not want the Eusebians to capture us now. Bernard, can you manage?"

"Yeah, I'm fine." Bernard had wrapped up Mavortian's body and broken canes in his long coat, and was holding it slung over one shoulder, like a carpet or something. "You want to tell me why the Eusebians haven't captured us already?"

"Beg pardon?"

"The way I understood you and Mavortian, the wizards here can feel your magic. Or was I wrong?"

"I would bet my rings—as I have in fact bet my life, and yours, and his—that Malkar told the Eusebians not to disturb him tonight, no matter what they felt or thought they felt."

"I wish that didn't make sense," Bernard said. "He led us down here, you know. Mavortian couldn't figure out what he was doing."

"Malkar loved setting traps," Felix said. Then he turned back to me. "Are you ready to go?"

I nodded and got up. It was hard. Everything ached, although the worst pain was in my throat. Felix steadied me, and I let him. "You all right?" he said, and I nodded again.

"Good." And he let me go, kicked the pile of Strych's ashes apart, and knelt down to sift through it.

"Powers, *must* you?" Bernard said.

Felix said, more or less to both of us, "We're going to have to keep going. Leave Lamia tonight."

"We won't get far enough," Bernard said.

"Oh, but we will. Because Malkar's disappeared as well. And without these—" He stood up and held out a handful of dark lumps. Strych's rubies. "There's going to be nothing to say that he didn't take the prisoners somewhere himself."

"Oh," Bernard said and signed himself, looking sick.

"I don't imagine they'll be in any hurry to find him, especially if they think he doesn't want to be found." He shivered hard. Then he kicked through the pile of ashes again, until there wasn't a pile no more. He stuck the rubies in his pocket, although he didn't look happy about it, and said, "Let's go. Please."

It wasn't hard, getting back through the Bastion. There was nobody around, and it looked to me like Felix had guessed right about what Strych had done. After a while, when we were getting near the point that I'd have to lead us back to Simon and Rinaldo's cell because it was the only thing I knew, Bernard grunted and said, "I know where we are now. It's not far." I was happy enough to let him lead. Powers, let somebody else do the work.

Felix

Mehitabel was waiting for us at the foot of that first narrow staircase.

"What are you doing here?" I said, somewhere between fury and overwhelming relief.

But her eyes were focused past my shoulder. "Oh, good. He did run off to find you, then."

I wanted to slap her for her flippancy, but then I saw the naked worry in her face and realized she had not meant it the way it had sounded.

She looked at me and smiled, an impressive effort. "I came back to find you, sunshine. Since you weren't very well going to be able to do your homing pigeon trick if he wasn't where he was supposed to be."

"I would have . . ." But I was too tired to keep up the pretense. "Thank you."

Her smile got a little more real. "You're welcome. Come on. I left the two other wizards just short of Irene's cellar." Bernard came into the pool of mingled lantern- and witchlight, and Mehitabel's eyes widened. "Oh. Is he . . ."

"Very dead," Bernard said. "I didn't want to leave him there."

"No, of course not." She bit her lip. "We can't bring a dead body into the tearoom."

"Felix said we could put him down here somewhere. Where he wouldn't be found."

"Yes," Mehitabel said slowly, thinking. "Yes. We won't have to go far from the marked route." Her mouth twisted. "And I doubt anyone will be coming down here for quite some time."

I explained Malkar's "disappearance" to her as we walked, and her face lightened. "That's good, then. Good that he's dead—and good that perhaps Irene and Barbara won't suffer for this."

"We paid them extremely well."

"And they earn that money, every day they sit up there and don't have the cellars bricked up." She said over her shoulder to Bernard, "Here. Down this corridor."

"How do you know these tunnels so well?" I asked her as we turned aside, a strange parody of a funeral cortège. "Is this how you left the Bastion?"

She hesitated just a split second too long, and I knew she lied when she said, "Yes."

🕮

We could not give Mavortian much of a funeral, but at least, as Bernard said, he would be left alone. Then back through the tunnels, collecting Simon and Rinaldo, up into the tearoom, deserted now except for the elderly lady by the tea urn, who clucked and fussed in a completely impenetrable Midlander dialect, and would not let us leave without washing our hands and faces. She insisted on giving Mildmay a coat, made for a much larger man; he blinked at her, green eyes still distant, still dazed, and nodded his thanks. If the elderly lady noticed the tattoos on Simon's hands, on Rinaldo's, on mine—I remembered, and fetched out my gloves, wincing as my fingers brushed the dull, slightly greasy lumps of Malkar's rubies—she gave no sign.

Out into Lamia. I stayed outside the hotel with the two wizards and my brother while Mehitabel and Bernard went in to collect our belongings and settle the bill. I wondered how many people in this city made their careers out of not asking questions.

Not much of my "traveling expenses" remained, but enough to buy tickets on the diligence to Medeia. Tickets for five, not six: Bernard caught my arm in the yard of the posting house and said, "There's no reason for me to travel farther with you. And I think we'll both be happier if I don't."

I didn't have the strength to pretend to disagree with him, but I was worried. "Are you sure? I mean—"

"Don't take this the wrong way, but I think I'll be safer on my own."

I grimaced at the truth of what he said. Mehitabel and I had done our best—and Bernard had given us permission to ransack Mavortian's effects—but there was no denying we were an eccentric lot, nor that we were safe only so long as no one was looking for us.

"If we're very lucky," Bernard said, "we'll never see each other again. But I think you should have this."

I looked at what he was holding out to me, and for a moment didn't recognize it. A box, inlaid with vines. Moonflowers. "The Sibylline? You—"

"I don't know if he'd want you to have it, or if he would have wanted me to leave it to rot with his corpse. But I know they're not *his* cards." He looked me dead in the eye, daring me to say anything.

I looked down, watched my hands take the box from him. Forced myself to say, "Thank you," because I knew I would regret it if I did not.

"Like I said, if we're lucky, we'll never see each other again. And I wish you the very best of luck."

"Luck," I said, but I didn't know if he heard me. He'd already turned and was disappearing into the maze of canvas.

I shook myself, put the box in my inner coat pocket, and went to join the others.

We bought our tickets and boarded the diligence in two groups: Mildmay and I together, since our blood-kinship was too obvious to be denied; Mehitabel and Simon and Rinaldo as a group of father, son, and daughter-in-law. Mehitabel was effortlessly convincing, and Rinaldo played up to better effect than I would have expected. Simon was rather stiff, but since Mehitabel and Rinaldo bickered like a pair of spoiled children around him, it was not to be wondered at.

Mildmay said nothing. He slept for much of the two-day journey to Medeia, but even when he was awake, he was silent. I reminded myself that he had spoken, both to me and to Simon, and that there was nothing I could do but wait. There was at least awareness in his eyes, although it was that feral watchfulness rather than the deep, accepting observation I had grown accustomed to and now missed terribly.

In Medeia, Mehitabel took charge again, choosing a small and inexpensive hotel, and at once set about discovering which acting troupes were in the city and whether any of them could help us. "You're lucky I'm with you, sunshine," she growled more than once, and I could only agree with her.

Mildmay sat silently by the window in the room we shared; I took to spending my time in the adjacent room, where Mehitabel and Simon and Rinaldo were staying. Since none of us wanted to chance going out, we occupied ourselves with cards, using the Sibylline until Mehitabel, ever resourceful, found us an ordinary deck.

We played a western variant of Long Tiffany called Dragon's Clutch. I lost, hand after hand. But the game wasn't what was important, and I thought all three of us knew it. Simon and Rinaldo had not been starved or mistreated or tortured, except for the one frightful incident with Malkar that Simon would not discuss—though after the first few rounds of Dragon's Clutch, he seemed to lose most of his self-consciousness about his mutilated hands. But they had been prisoners for a long time. They were uneasy still, jumpy, agoraphobic. The endless game of Dragon's Clutch was a way to soften the edges of the transition.

We talked about the Mirador, as Cabaline wizards inevitably do. They knew of the breaking of the Virtu, could tell me of General Mercator's suspicion, his caution. "He wouldn't move. He wanted to believe Malkar, but when it came right down to it, he never *trusted* him. To be fair, *no one* could believe he'd succeeded in breaking the Virtu, and then later, when he said he'd gone in through a dream, and the Mirador was burning . . . the

General waited for confirmation. And by the time it came, the Coeurterre had moved in."

"Malkar was livid," Rinaldo said quietly, almost gently. I took the hint and changed the subject.

They also told me what they could about what had happened to Mildmay, although that was painfully little. "He almost killed me when he first regained consciousness," Simon said, touching the faint yellow bruises on his neck. "It was amazing—although difficult to appreciate properly at the time. One second he was, for all intents and purposes, out cold; the next he had me flat on the floor and my vision was going excitingly black, just the way they tell you it will in books. But as soon as he saw me clearly, he let me go."

"He never made a sound," Rinaldo said. "Not a word, not a whimper. We really thought he might be a mute."

"They'd cleaned him up before they dumped him in with us." Simon again, and I'd noticed before the way that the two of them would hand a single line of thought back and forth. "And we didn't want to abrogate his privacy—there's so little of it, you understand. He and I already had to share a bed. Not that it mattered, since I don't believe he slept."

"No wonder he's been sleeping so much," I said; I hoped the unsteadiness in my voice wasn't audible to them.

"What we wondered," Rinaldo said, "and he didn't tell us, of course, is how he came to be in Malkar's hands to begin with." He raised his eyebrows at me, both an invitation and a warning that he was already beginning to guess.

I told them the truth. I did not try to make excuses for myself, or hide what I had done. If I did not tell them the full truth about my relationship with Malkar, that mattered less. All that mattered was that I had let my hatred of him control me.

They listened quietly, attentively; when I was done, I waited, eyes down, watching my stiff fingers shuffle the cards over and over again.

"That's quite a confession," Rinaldo said.

"I would tell you to ask Mildmay, if I thought he would answer you. But Mehitabel can confirm it's the truth."

"I wasn't suggesting I doubt your veracity. I meant that it must be a very painful story to relate."

"I brought it on myself."

"Also not what I said."

And then Simon burst out with: "But how on earth did you know how to cast the obligation d'âme in the first place?"

"Malkar taught me. Malkar taught me almost everything I wish I didn't know. He . . ." And then the words simply bolted out: "He cast the obligation de sang on me when I was sixteen."

"The binding-by-blood," Rinaldo said thoughtfully; he didn't sound surprised. "He would have been burned at the stake if you'd told anyone."

"He told me I'd be burned with him."

"But that's—"

"No. He didn't say the Mirador would burn me. He said that if he burned, I would burn along with him. Even if I jumped into the Sim." And he had known perfectly well that there was nothing I was less likely to do.

"Was that true?" Rinaldo asked.

"I don't know. I, um, I broke the obligation de sang when I was twenty, so—"

"How?"

"Nothing you want to know about. I don't think, in any event, that it was entirely successful."

"I am going to guess," Rinaldo said, "that your reasons for hating Malkar Gennadion run rather deeper than what you have told us."

"It doesn't—" I began, when Simon interrupted me.

"Was it your dream?"

"I beg your pardon?"

"Malkar said he broached the Mirador's defenses through a dream. It was your dream, wasn't it? And you were his cat's-paw—his word, not one I would choose—when he broke the Virtu."

"I don't know what you're talking about."

Rinaldo said sharply, "Simon, let him be," and Simon subsided.

I said, "Someone else should deal," and shoved the cards into the middle of the table. After a moment, Rinaldo picked them up, and the game went on, until Mehitabel came in, her step light and her eyes shining, to say she'd gotten the details worked out, and in the morning we could leave for home.

Mildmay

We'd be leaving Medeia in the morning. Mehitabel had come in to tell me, and now she was standing by the door like she was waiting for something.

I couldn't think what it could be, and I didn't figure it was on my account anyway. I was watching people go by, people with real lives. People who weren't monsters and never had been. A lamplighter, doing his job, kindling lights one by one.

She said suddenly, "Have you taken a vow of silence or something?"

I thought it over. "Nothing to say."

"No?" I heard her come closer, but I didn't turn. "Not even things like, 'Good morning,' or 'Please pass the salt,' or 'Thank you for saving my life'?"

I said in a mumble, "Shouldn't've bothered."

"*What?* Goddammit, would you at least *look* at me while we're having this stupid not-conversation?"

She sounded really upset. So I turned. Looked up at her.

"Better. Now, what was it you said?"

"Don't matter."

"*Yes, it does.*"

Too much, too loud. I hunched one shoulder and turned back to the window.

"Mildmay, *please.*" I startled at her hand on my arm, realized she'd gone down on her knees beside the chair. "Tell me why you're doing this. Is it just that you're mad at Felix? Because I can understand that."

"Not doing nothing."

"Yes, I know. That's my point. It's like you're just sitting here waiting to die. Please tell me you're not."

I shrugged.

"You're going to let Messire Gennadion win?"

"Cut that the fuck out."

"What?"

"Ain't about winning," I said. Powers, my voice was ugly. Just fucking *ugly*.

"Then what is it about?"

I shook my head, looked at a gal on the sidewalk carrying a pair of white ducks, one under each arm.

Mehitabel's hand caught my jaw, dragged me back around to face her. I could have broken her wrist, but I didn't. "What is this about?"

"You don't care."

"Yes, I do. I care very much."

"You got no reason."

"Do I need a reason?"

She'd kissed me, I remembered. Before I went off to kill Vey Coruscant. She'd kissed me on the mouth. I said, "I don't understand what you want."

"Tell me why you're not talking to anyone. Tell me what Malkar did to you."

"Don't remember."

"You don't remember?"

" 'S what I said. I mean, I remember he hurt me. But that's all."

"You don't remember, or you don't *want* to remember?"

"I don't remember." Didn't want to remember, neither, but I wasn't stupid enough to think that mattered. I just knew I'd woken up in Simon and Rinaldo's cell, and everything had hurt. *Everything.*

"And that's why you're not talking?"

"I told you. Nothing to say."

"Oh, I don't think so. I think you've got a lot to say. You're just not letting yourself say it."

"Powers, would you at least pretend you don't think I'm that stupid?"

"Sorry?"

"I ain't that stupid," I said slowly, carefully.

"I didn't say you were stupid."

"You think I am, though."

"I don't. I think you're extremely intelligent. And I think you're in a lot of pain."

"I'm fine."

"You are *not* fine, and we all know it. If you're not stupid, then quit lying!"

"If you don't want me lying, leave me the fuck alone."

"No."

I stared at her.

She went red, but she didn't move. "Felix is so knotted up in his own guilt that he'd probably let you go ahead and kill yourself because he wouldn't think he had the right to interfere. And Simon and Rinaldo can't really understand what's wrong. They didn't know you before. That leaves me."

"Why the *fuck* do you care?"

"Because I like you. I don't want you to disappear into yourself the way you're trying to do." She squeezed my forearm very gently. "I want you to tell me what it is you're punishing yourself for."

I sighed and said it, flat out. "I thought I was done being a monster."

"You mean the way you tried to kill Messire Gennadion?"

"The way it was just like all the other people I killed. Him and Vey and that goon in Klepsydra. I quit, you know. It was supposed to be *done*."

She thought about it for a minute, but she didn't try and make like she didn't understand what I meant. "Dealing with the past is never that simple. I don't think anything is ever really 'done.' Part of me is still fifteen and scared and shamed and furious, crawling out of a second-story window in the middle of the night because I know by the next day my uncle will have worked himself up to rape. Part of me is still sitting in the Bastion, ripping a sheet to pieces instead of mending it because I hate where I am and I hate what I do and I hate myself, but I'm trapped. And part of me will always be the Gauthys' governess, sleeping with a man I don't love because it's the best option open to me. But that doesn't mean I have to stay within those boundaries. Mildmay . . . Look. Nobody's blaming you for wanting him dead. Nobody's blaming you for having been a little distraught—"

"Batfuck crazy."

"Whatever you want to call it. Think about it this way: Felix was worse. You didn't hurt anybody else. You rescued Simon and Rinaldo. On that showing, you're not a monster at all." And she leaned up and kissed me.

"What was that for?" I said, the same way I had back in the Mirador.

But this time, she didn't answer. She just kissed me again, hot and knowing—and I got my hands up between us. "Mehitabel, what're you doing?"

"I must be slipping. I wouldn't have thought you'd need to ask."

"But you can't want—"

She kissed me again.

"Wait. Stop. *Why?*"

She shrugged. "Because I think it would be better for you than sulking? Because it seems like fun? Because I've wanted to ever since that kiss in Aiaia?"

"You have?"

"Oh, *God*, yes." She grinned at me. "Been dreaming about it, if you really want to know."

"Oh," I said. If it would make her happy, I was willing to do it. "Okay."

"Then lock the door and come to bed."

"Felix—"

"Fuck Felix."

"No thanks," I said, and she was laughing as she dragged me to my feet.

I locked the door. When I turned, she was standing by the bed, starting to take down her hair.

"Lemme do that," I said. Keeper and Ginevra had both liked having me take the pins out of their hair.

"All right," Mehitabel said. She lowered her head as I came over, and I found her hairpins one by one, putting them on the windowsill. For a moment, her hair stayed just like it was, and then I dug my fingers in and it uncoiled down her back like a flood.

"You're pandering to my vanity," she said.

"So?" I said, and made her laugh.

She straightened up—just a little taller than me, so when she leaned in to kiss me, neither of us had to crane our necks. It was quite a bit later and we were both breathless when she pulled back, tugging the ribbon out of my braid. I shook my head and my hair fell forward.

"Should cut it."

"Don't. It's beautiful."

I snorted.

"Some people like foxes, you know. I always have."

"Some people are crazy."

She laughed and said, "Oh, shut up and help me with these damnable buttons."

I undid the buttons down her back while she held her hair out of the way, and then she undid my buttons, and we got ourselves out of our clothes. She wasn't built generous, not like Ginevra—little tits, and narrow hips for a gal. She gave me a once-over and said in this low, throaty voice, "Well, I certainly like what I see." Made me blush, too, and I was already hard.

"It's nice to be appreciated," she said, coming closer, and I yelped when she touched me. Her fingers were just as knowing as her mouth.

"What? You're not a virgin, are you?"

"No. It's just . . . well, it's been a while, is all."

"How long?"

"Oh, powers, I don't know. A while."

"I hope you haven't forgotten what to do," she said, nudging me backward toward the bed. "But if you have, I'm sure I can remind you."

"Think I can figure it out," I said and sat down.

She followed me, pushing me flat on my back and climbing over me to straddle my chest. "Good." I ran my hands up her thighs, found her clit with my thumb. "*Very* good," she said and smiled down at me. "I like a man who can find his way around."

"I don't get lost," I said, and she laughed and leaned down to kiss me, and let me roll her over to where I could get at her tits and the soft skin of her belly and her cunt.

I brought her off once with my hands and my mouth, and then she dragged me back up the bed to where she could kiss me. "I've never had a man do that without being asked before. Thank you."

"It's no big deal," I said and ducked my head to kiss her collarbone so she couldn't see my face.

"I would've thought this would make it uncomfortable," she said, and I half felt a finger tracing my scar.

"Don't," I said, jerking my head away before I could stop myself.

"Sorry. Did I hurt you?"

"Nah. Hardly any feeling there. I just don't like—"

"Having it touched. I *am* sorry."

"It's okay." I cupped one of her little tits. "You up for more?"

"I hate to break this to you, but *I'm* not the one who needs to be up."

Powers and saints, I blushed like a bonfire, and she laughed. Her real laugh, not the sexy one, and that made it okay. "To answer your question," she said, "yes, I'd love another round. But let's do something for you this time."

"You don't gotta—"

"No? What's your plan then? Kill me with delight, then skulk off to the water closet to masturbate?"

"Mehitabel!"

And she was laughing again, even as she shoved me flat and knelt over me. "Do you mind?"

"Whatever you want . . . 's fine with me," I said, going breathless in the middle as she brought herself down.

"You really are almost frighteningly agreeable." She shifted her hips and flexed something, grinning when I couldn't bite back a moan. "My mother was a sideshow dancer. I think she'd be quite pleased by the uses to which I've put her lessons."

She flexed again, tightening herself around me, and Kethe I tried not to, but I couldn't help my hips bucking up, and Mehitabel said, "Yes, come on, Mildmay. A little less of the gentleman, if you please."

"Don't wanna hurt . . ."

"You won't hurt me. I'm not a porcelain doll." She arched her back, and things flexed a whole different way, making my hips buck again, and she said, "Oh, God, yes! Right like that! Like *that*!"

And we were moving together, her making breathless little coyote yelps, me with my teeth gritted not to make any noise at all. It didn't take long before I felt her come, her fingers digging into my shoulders. Slid my hand between her legs, found her clit again, and she bucked and shuddered and snarled, "Take something for *yourself*, damn you!" And I could feel it building, white heat in my balls and cock and the pit of my belly, white shrieking yowling heat, and my other hand clamped around her hip, and I thrust up into her just as hard as she brought herself down, once, twice, and then, Kethe, I came like I was turning inside out, came like I was trying to break something.

And for a second, a single blessed second, I wasn't nothing at all.

෪ᶴ

Afterward, she said, "We'll have to do this again sometime."

"If you want."

"You don't?"

"Sure. I mean—"

She laughed, kissed me again. "You're not a monster, Mildmay. Not even close. Anytime you need someone to remind you of that, you come find me."

"It was okay, then?"

"Good God, man, you need to ask?"

She made me laugh with that, and I felt better. Felt like maybe it'd been worth her while.

"I do need to go," she said and made a face. "Appearances to keep up."

"Yeah." I watched her get dressed, pin her hair back up. Made myself say, "Thanks."

"You're more than welcome. Just stay with us, all right?"

"Okay," I said, and she gave me a smile that left me breathless and swept out.

When Felix came in, he looked at me, and I looked at him, and I saw him deciding not to say whatever it was he wanted to say. I laid down again, rolled to face the wall. Thought, oh fuck this, and said, "Good night, Felix."

Silence. A long silence, long enough that even though I was waiting, I was half-asleep when he said, real quiet, "Good night."

Felix

Somewhere between Medeia and Mélusine, I dreamed.

My construct-Mélusine was clean and light; for once, even the brooding presence of the Sim did not distort things. Horn Gate was open, and through it, I could see the perseïdes beckoning.

I had not been able to reach the Khloïdanikos for weeks, first because the mending of the Virtu left me no energy, and then because my sick guilt destroyed my concentration, making it impossible even to form the construct, much less use it. I went through Horn Gate gladly, gratefully. The Khloïdanikos noticed me as little as ever, but I did not care; part of its peace was its sublime indifference, that sense that whatever its builders had intended, it was continuing serenely, creating its own pattern as it saw fit.

I wandered for a while, basking in the silence and the warmth, but when I felt Thamuris enter the dream, I made my way to our usual meeting place.

We reached it at the same time. He looked better than he had the last time I had seen him, the hectic color no longer flaming in his cheeks, his real self no longer bleeding through his dream image. "It has been a long time."

"I know," I said. "Things got . . . complicated. But they're better now." I didn't want to discuss Malkar with Thamuris, or what I had done to Mildmay. Any of it. I had confessed to Simon and Rinaldo; surely that was penance enough.

"I was worried," he said mildly. "I couldn't find you, and your gate was never here."

"You can see it?" I twisted around, seeing its dark bulk over the trees.

"Well, of course," he said. "But it's not here if you aren't, although sometimes I see . . . a shadow? a ghost?"

I shivered. "If I keep coming here, do you think it will become permanent?"

"I don't know. I don't know how the Khloïdanikos changes. *If* it changes. Which reminds me, I should go see if the dead tree is still here and still dead."

I got up to follow him. "The what?"

"When you were gone," he said. "I found a dead perseïd tree. I don't think it was here before, and I've been going back to see what happens to it."

"A dead tree—here?"

"That is what I said." He was eyeing me with some amusement, but he frowned suddenly, stopping in front of me so that I was forced to stop, too. "What on earth is the matter?"

"Matter?"

"You look distressed."

Damn the Khloïdanikos and the things it would not allow me to hide. "It's just that a dead tree is a symbol in a system I've been learning recently, and—"

"Something happened to Mildmay," Thamuris said, and his voice was hard with that sickening intuitive leap. "*The dead tree will not shelter you. Is he all right?*"

I stared at him, wide-eyed, voiceless. I had forgotten about the huphantike he had told me: *Love and betrayal, the gorgon and the wheel. The dead tree will not shelter you, and the dead will not stay dead. Though you do not seek revenge, it will seek you all the same.* Forgotten it and enacted it, like a puppet willfully blind to the strings that pulled its limbs.

"Felix! Is he all right?"

"Yes," I said, my voice a choked whisper. "Love and betrayal, two sides of the same coin. He loved me and I betrayed him. The dead tree—the Mirador. Or the obligation d'âme. Or maybe his friends, the monster, the little cade-skiff. They couldn't help him, either. And the dead will not stay dead." I bit my lower lip, hard, to kill a fit of hysterical giggles. "Brinvillier Strych certainly did not. And revenge. He didn't want revenge. He knew it wouldn't do anyone any good. And I didn't listen."

"Come sit down," Thamuris said, shepherding me onto the grass.

"I didn't listen," I said to him, folding down onto my knees. "I didn't listen to him, and I didn't listen to you, and I made it happen."

"It would have happened regardless." I turned away, and he caught my wrist. "No. Listen to me. *It would have happened regardless.* That pattern.

The huphantike that I made true. It might not have been those events, but it would still have happened."

"Yes," I agreed desolately. "But it might not have been my fault."

Thamuris blinked wise, dreamy golden eyes at me and said, "Who else could it have been? Who else does he love?"

Cruel truth, and it burned like acid. I held myself still before it for ten deep, slow breaths, and then said, "Let's go see about your dead tree, shall we?" I scrambled up, hauled Thamuris to his feet.

The perseïd tree was a black, shattered huddle of branches against a tumbledown stone wall. Dead indeed. I knelt, reached out to touch the knotted bark, gently, as if I thought I had the right to apologize. The wood was cold and wet beneath my fingers.

I let my hand drop, looked at the small shining pebbles among the roots of the tree while I tried to regain my composure, put myself back together again around my guilt and my failure. Then Thamuris said, "Look!" his hand gripping my shoulder, and I looked up and saw at the end of an out-flung twig the first tender unfurling of green.

✂

No fanfare accompanied our return to the Mirador. But, on the other hand, I wasn't arrested and thrown on a pyre the instant I walked through the Harriers' Gate, either. Mehitabel separated from us at the second major branching past the gate—the Tree of Ash, it was called on the older maps— kissing Mildmay on the cheek and whispering something in his ear that made him blush. I did not ask. Although he was speaking again, even having something approaching conversations with Mehitabel and Simon, to me he had said nothing more than "good morning" and "good night." It was his choice; I had no right to make him talk to me. I was leaning away from the obligation d'âme as hard as I could, trying to pretend it wasn't there, trying to pretend there was no obligation, in the wider sense, between us.

Of course, there was. Otherwise, he would not be here, padding silently at my heels as we wound our way into the Mirador to find Master Archi-trave and tell him rooms were needed for Simon Barrister and Rinaldo of Fiora. But all I could do was pretend.

Master Architrave was delighted and flummoxed; we left Rinaldo and Simon in his more than capable hands, and I led the way to my rooms, where the door opened on firelight and warmth, and Gideon looking up from his book, first blankly, and then with a look of such transparent joy that I nearly stumbled. Then he looked past me, saw Mildmay, and came to his feet.

" 'M all right," Mildmay said, forestalling the need for Gideon to relay the question through me. "Going to bed." Slurred into one mumbled word: *gontabed.*

Gideon raised his eyebrows at me. I shrugged helplessly and said, "Good night. Sleep well."

" 'Night," Mildmay said, without turning, and the door of his small room shut decisively behind him, leaving Gideon and me in a silence that stretched from awkward to uncomfortable to excruciating, until finally, desperately, I said, "Did Thaddeus leave you alone?"

:Thank you, yes. Your suite is very peaceful, and the servants most polite. I believe they lied to Thaddeus on my behalf more than once.:

The gossip in the Mirador could be trusted to be up-to-date and accurate; I was not surprised that the soft-footed young men who tended the rooms on this hall had known who Gideon was and why he was in my suite. I had told them only that a guest would be staying, and they had not asked me questions.

"You're, ah, welcome to stay. If you'd like."

One eyebrow rose sardonically; I turned away, my face heating, and went to poke up the fire.

:How is Mildmay?:

"I don't know. He didn't talk to anyone for five days. He still isn't talking to me, particularly. Mehitabel told me he told her he doesn't remember what Malkar did to him."

:It would not be surprising,: Gideon said and added pointedly, :It is a common defensive reaction to severe trauma.:

"Thank you so very much."

:Give him time.:

"There's nothing else I *can* give him." I sighed, setting the poker down; Gideon came up beside me and gently laid a hand on my shoulder.

:If I were to stay . . .:

"Yes?"

:You will treat him—:

"Like he was my brother, yes." I felt Gideon's flinch at my bitterness.

:And how will you treat me?:

I turned to look down at him, to meet those grave, dark eyes. He did not ask the question idly or rhetorically.

And I had been thinking about this, too, in the long silent hours between Medeia and Mélusine. "You said you didn't expect me to be other than what I am. But I don't want to make you be other than yourself, either. And I don't know how . . ."

:Negotiation is supposed to be good for treaty-making.:

I stared at him for a moment, until he lost the battle to keep his face impassive; he was smiling again, beaming, an expression of such simple happiness that it made my heart turn over.

I smiled back at him, and then took his face gently between my hands and kissed him. And I promised myself, as the kiss deepened, as our bodies began to press together, that I would make this treaty work.

ᔥᔨ

No one remarked on either my absence or my return when I appeared in the Hall of the Chimeras the next morning. Nor did anyone appear to notice Mildmay at all. A great fuss was being made of Simon and Rinaldo, and I was glad of it, glad that for once the Mirador was recognizing those who deserved her praise, those who had suffered in her service. I dared to hope I would escape unscathed—until, as Stephen was standing to dismiss the court, he said, "Lord Felix, a word with you please."

He'd planned it. I knew that, even as I controlled a wince, even as I murmured, "Of course, my lord," and nodded at Mildmay to follow me. Stephen didn't normally indulge in that sort of game, but it wasn't as if I could deny I deserved it.

It occurred to me to wish that I had not taken Malkar quite so slavishly as my model.

"Let us retire to the Attercop," Stephen said. "I don't think you want to have this discussion in public."

"As you wish, my lord," I said, while my heart sank.

But as we followed Stephen, Mildmay bumped my shoulder gently—so gently it might almost have been an accident, except that I knew better. I glanced over; he met my eyes, and although there was no expression on his face, I suddenly felt better.

Giancarlo was waiting in the Attercop, and my heart sank again. Stephen sat down in the room's only chair; I swallowed hard and straightened my shoulders.

"Lord Felix," Stephen said, "I really would like an explanation."

"An explanation, my lord? Of wh—?"

The look he gave me killed my voice in my throat. "I have a list," he said. "Starting with necromancy and ending with Simon Barrister and Rinaldo of Fiora."

"Lord Simon and Lord Rinaldo can surely speak for themselves."

"If that's how you prefer it." Stephen's smile was not pleasant. "But before Court and Curia, I ask you, kindly explain what you were doing on the night of Eré thirty-first that has every necromancer in the Lower City on the verge of a nervous breakdown."

The formal phrasing was a bad sign, although I reminded myself to be grateful that Stephen had interpreted "Court and Curia" in this instance to mean one representative of each. Mildmay had warned me that Stephen would find out, and Stephen had.

I took a deep breath, forced my fingers straight, and told Stephen and Giancarlo the truth. The truth of what the Cabal had done, the truth of what I had done in answer. They heard me out in silence, aside from the occasional strangled exclamation, and when I was done, Stephen said, "It feels very odd to say this, but I actually appreciate your tact in not wanting this to become common knowledge."

"It does no one any good," I said.

"You realize you didn't at all have the right to make that decision on your own," Giancarlo said.

"Yes. But I won't say I wouldn't do it again."

"Felix . . ." Giancarlo sighed.

"I can't very well have you burned for heresy," Stephen said, "since I'd have to have every wizard since the Cabal burned right along with you." His look was not gracious. "I'll want to talk to you again, after I've spoken to Lord Rinaldo and Lord Simon, but since you're going to lie to me anyway, I might as well give you a chance to get your story straight. But tell me this, at least. *Is* Malkar Gennadion dead?"

"Yes, my lord."

"And if I asked you how you accomplished it?"

I met his eyes. "I would tell you Mildmay killed him." It wasn't heresy for an annemer to kill a wizard, and we'd already established that my protection of Mildmay made other matters moot—including the possibility that the Bastion might come baying for his blood.

Neither Stephen nor Giancarlo believed me, but I didn't need them to. After a moment, Stephen snorted and said, "All right. Go on then. Clear out."

Mildmay and I didn't wait to be told twice. We cleared.

I hesitated in the hall outside the Attercop, wondering whether to go to my workroom, back to my suite, or to the Fevrier Archive, where my research was still unfinished. And then, almost defiantly, I did something completely different. I climbed up to the Crown of Nails, Mildmay following loyally behind.

The day was bright, cold. I went to the battlements and looked at Mélusine spread out below us like a wanton lover. Mildmay stood beside me, and I noticed that he was not looking at the city, but up at the deep blue of the sky, as an angel might, its wings broken, knowing that it would never reach its home again.

We stood together silently for a long time. The words gathered in my throat, pushed against my chest. My heart was beating too hard, and I could feel the scalding blood in my cheeks. It was so inadequate, so stupid. And yet it was the only thing I had that I could say.

"I'm sorry."

"Nice to hear."

"I hate saying it."

"I know."

"Can you . . ." I looked down at my hands and hated the way my voice got small. "Do you think you'll ever be able to forgive me?"

Another silence. I glanced at him sidelong, afraid to risk meeting his eyes. His face was as unreadable as ever, but I knew that he was genuinely thinking about my question. It was the hardest thing in the world, but I waited.

And after a while, he said slowly, "I don't know." What he always said when faced with a question he didn't want to answer. But he was struggling with it still, and I wished fiercely, uselessly, that words were not so difficult for him.

He bent his head, staring down at his hands where they gripped the parapet, the long fingers, lumped knuckles, the scars and discolorations of injuries that had healed but could never quite be forgotten about. Then he said, "You and Strych . . . I mean . . . it ain't like . . ." He fell silent again. I continued waiting, feeling as if the entire city held its breath with me. Finally, he said, "I understand."

And those two words said a great deal. The things we couldn't say now, the things that we would have to say to each other in the days and weeks and months to come, they were there, but those two simple words from him made it seem possible to me, for the first time, that we could find a way to say them.

" 'Isn't,' " I said. " 'Isn't as if.' Not 'ain't like.' "

For a minute I thought I'd jumped the wrong way, that even though I knew he wouldn't want his wounds touched, I'd said the wrong thing, but then he burst out laughing.

"Pax?" I said.

It was an old piece of street slang; I didn't know why it had surfaced then, but he turned to look at me, and his face lit up in that unsmiling way I had missed so very badly.

"Pax," he said.